Fury and *Black River* are the first two novels
in the highly acclaimed Frank Corso series.
G. M. Ford lives in Seattle.

By G.M. Ford

FURY

BLACK RIVER

A BLIND EYE

RED TIDE

G. M. FORD

FURY
&
BLACK
RIVER

PAN BOOKS

Fury first published 2001 by William Morrow,
an imprint of HarperCollins Publishers, New York.
Black River first published 2002 by HarperCollins Publishers, New York.
First published in Great Britain in paperback 2004 by Pan Books.

This omnibus first published 2006 by Pan Books
an imprint of Pan Macmillan Ltd
Pan Macmillan, 20 New Wharf Road, London N1 9RR
Basingstoke and Oxford
Associated companies throughout the world
www.panmacmillan.com

ISBN-13: 978-0-330-44685-3
ISBN-10: 0-330-44685-1

1 3 5 7 9 8 6 4 2

A CIP catalogue record for this book is available from
the British Library.

Printed and bound in Great Britain by
Mackays of Chatham plc, Chatham, Kent

FURY

In this dreary and comfortless region, it was no inconsiderable piece of good fortune to find a little cove in which we could take shelter, and a small spot of level ground on which we could erect our tent . . .

– From the journals of Captain George Vancouver

A POUND
OF FLESH

God only knows where he found an orange-plaid suit. Probably some retro consignment joint up on Broadway. Jacket two sizes too small, with the shoulders sticking up like epaulets. Trousers six inches too short, like he was expecting a flood or something. Big cuffs . . . brogans . . . no socks.

His lawyer, Myron Mendenhal, on the other hand, was the very soul of sartorial elegance. Natty in a charcoal-gray three-piece. Pinky ring, with a diamond as big as the Ritz. A habitual cuff shooter who kept the Rolex double diamond tastefully in view at all times. After all, when one tilled the personal injury end of the legal field, it was merely good business to look as prosperous as possible.

Mendenhal had already stated his case. Two or three times, in fact. On behalf of his client, he was filing a lawsuit against both the city of Seattle and the state of Washington. Wrongful and malicious prosecution. Three million in compensatory damages. Ten million in punitive damages. Each. Individual civil actions to follow.

Only reason he was still talking was so his client wouldn't. Last time Bozo'd opened his trap, all hell had broken loose. A guy in the front row had lost his composure and tried to crawl over the table at them. He'd clawed halfway through the forest of microphones before the female cop grabbed him by the belt and jerked him to the floor. Took four officers to get him out of the room and ten minutes to get the electronics back in order. The echo of the man's anguished cries still ruffled the drapes, and a scent of spent hormones hovered in the air like gunsmoke. No doubt about it; Myron Mendenhal was prepared to run his mouth for as long as it took.

"How do you compensate a man for three years of his life?" he asked. "Is there some dollar figure that can repair the heart of a man who has lived for years under the specter of his own imminent death? Who has lain upon the table of death? I think not. Can we—"

The client leaned toward the mikes. "If it ain't me or him, just gonna be somebody else, you know."

"Excuse me?" one of the reporters lining the wall said.

Mendenhal covered the nearest mikes with his arm and whispered something to his client. First, imploring. Then, insisting. The audience caught its collective breath when the client reached over and clamped his big hand over Mendenhal's nose and mouth. With the bug-eyed lawyer still squirming behind his half-acre palm, the client curled his rubbery lips and scooted his chair closer to the alphabet-soup collection of microphones.

"Said there's always gonna be somebody out there killin' bitches. Bitches and mo' bitches is gonna be dyin' all over the damn place, till you-all up to your damn ass in dead bitches."

Seven separate cameras recorded the onset of what happened next. The man sitting front-row center slowly got to his feet. He ran both hands over his face, like he was wiping away spiderwebs. He turned his back on Mendenhal and his client. Leaned over and appeared to whisper in the ear of the woman seated in the chair beside him. By then, the half dozen rent-a-cops stationed around the hotel ballroom were all moving his way, but it was too late.

When the man straightened up, he was holding a WWII-vintage Colt forty-five automatic in both hands. With tears in his eyes, he looked out over the crowded ballroom and uttered a single syllable. And then he turned toward the front of the room, raised the gun, and began pulling the trigger.

Run the NBC tape and you can see the client take four direct hits in the chest. Each time the force rocks his chair up onto two legs, only to have his weight slam it back to earth. Slow it down and you can see the impact of the bullets as they tear through the garish fabric of his suit. Watch the second slug go high left, taking off part of the shoulder, painting the side of Myron Mendenhal's face with a high-pressure spray of blood and bone. Stop it right after the third impact dents the suit; run a couple more frames. Then, right before your eyes, seems like all at once, the plaid fades to red and the client falls slowly from his chair with that odd, enigmatic smile still frozen on his lips.

By that time, the ballroom is in complete panic. When the man with the gun turns back toward the crowd, only the brass-balls NBC cameraman keeps it rolling. Everybody else hits the deck. The rest of the network footage looks like *The Blair Witch Project*.

People who were there—and God knows half the city claims to have been present at the time—say the air was instantly sucked from the room, leaving the lungs scratched and dry, in that awful silent moment when the guy put the gun in his mouth and pulled the trigger.

I n the year when summer never came, the spring rains lasted through July and then into August and September, until finally, with the leaves still green on the trees, people bowed to the inevitable and abandoned their memories of the sun.

More out of habit than duty, Bill Post flicked his eyes toward the street. Just in time to see her dismount the number 30 bus and step awkwardly out into a gray, driving rain. He watched as she pulled the hood low on her head and sloshed her big brown shoes across the sidewalk toward the front doors. Once inside, she removed her green raincoat and shook it out over the black rubber runner. He couldn't remember ever seeing anyone go to that much trouble to keep water off the floor. Like somebody was going to make her clean it up or something.

In other years, he might have mentioned the rain, and they would have nurtured the bond that forms among those who suffer together. Not this year, though. This year, spring and summer had come and gone like wishes, washing any expectation of relief so far downstream that the state of the weather was no longer considered polite conversation.

From behind the security desk he asked, "Something I can help you with?"

She seemed startled by the sound of his voice. "I hope so," she said. "I need to see a Mr. Frank Corso. He's a writer . . . a reporter here." She draped the dripping coat over her arm and approached the desk.

"Is Mr. Corso in?"

"Not that I ever seen," the guard said with a chuckle. "The guy I replaced said he used to see him once in a while, but I been here just under two years and he ain't never been in during my shift. Night crew says he comes in sometimes to see Mrs. Van Der Hoven, but I personally ain't never seen him myself." He leaned back in his chair.

When he tilted his head forward and looked at her through the upper half of his bifocals, he instantly realized he was supposed to know who she was. He sat up straight. Closed the travel brochures he'd been reading and stuffed them in the top drawer. Tried to let it come to him, but wasn't surprised when he couldn't put a name to the face. In recent months, he seldom could. Hell, if he didn't hang his car keys on the same hook in the kitchen every night, he couldn't find the damn things in the morning.

"Maybe somebody else could help you, Miss . . . ?" He left it a question.

She looked like she was going to cry. "Mr. Corso *has* to see me." She said it like daytime TV. "You tell him Leanne Samples is downstairs and needs to talk with him on a matter of life and death."

The name did it. It was her all right. The girl from the TV. He kicked himself for not recognizing her right away and wondered again if he shouldn't discuss his failing memory with his doctor. He picked up the phone. Who? Mr. Hawes? He was the honcho. The managing editor and all that jazz. Yeah. Last button on the right.

* * *

Natalie Van Der Hoven pulled her head back and looked down her nose at Bennett Hawes, her managing editor. She was in her mid-sixties, with a face from an ancient coin. Pointed and haughty like a hawk, with a "fear of God" gaze to match. Wrought-iron hair and shoulders wider than most men's. Machete murderers jumped to their feet and doffed their caps when she entered a room. She had that kind of style.

"You can't be serious," she said.

"That's all she'll say. She lied at the trial. That and how she won't cooperate with us unless Corso writes the story."

Always impeccable, in a Nordstrom three-piece suit, Hawes claimed to be five-nine, but in reality stood about five foot seven. He wore what remained of his sandy hair combed completely across his scalp and sprayed in place. Worked out five days a week at the gym up the street. Everything he did, he did quickly.

She raised an eyebrow. "Surely she can be persuaded."

He scratched the back of his neck. "I don't think so," he said.

"You explained that Mr. Corso no longer works directly for the paper?"

"The distinction between direct and indirect employees seems to be lost on Miss Samples. As far as she's concerned, she reads his column in the paper twice a month, so he works here."

"Did you explain Mr. Corso's aversion to the limelight? That he hasn't been seen in public since he hit the bestseller list?"

Hawes nodded disgustedly. "She doesn't care. We either produce Corso today or she takes her story up the road." He turned his palms toward the ceiling. "Why she wants Corso is beyond me."

"Did you ask?"

Hawes made a sour face. "She said it was because he was"—he used his fingers to make quotation marks in the air—"*nice* to her back then." Jamming his hands in his pockets, he paced across the room.

"Do we have a number for Mr. Corso?"

"I was hoping you had one," he said.

She shook her head. "When Mr. Corso wants to chat, he calls me."

"What about his agent?"

"Some woman in New York named Vance."

"She'll have a number."

"Not that she'll share with us," Mrs. V. said. "I've tried before."

"I went down to accounting. We send his checks to a P.O. box in the U District." Hawes's normal pacing suddenly took on the air of a strut. She searched him with her eyes. "You think you know something, don't you?" she said.

He kept his face as bland as a cabbage. "I might," he admitted.

"Come on now, Bennett," she prompted. "Out with it."

A smile escaped his thin lips. "While I was down in accounting, I went through his expense file. Gave me an idea how we might be able to find him quickly," he said.

"Oh?" she said. "At one time, people made careers of trying to find our Mr. Corso. What makes you think you can run him to ground?"

"They never had to pay his expenses."

"Such as?"

"Such as Corso hired a local private eye a couple of times. I know because we paid the guy's bill. I think the guy probably knows where to find Corso."

"Who would that be?"

"Guy named Leo Waterman."

"Bill Waterman's boy?"

"Yeah."

She managed a small smile. "I haven't seen Leo since he was in short pants," she said. "As you know, his father and my late husband, Edmund, were quite close. What makes you think Leo could find Mr. Corso?"

"I saw the two of them having a beer together one time, when I stopped for cigarettes. Over on Eastlake, a neighborhood dive called the Zoo."

"That's all?"

"You know how Corso is. He hates everybody. For him, having a beer with somebody is like a long-term relationship."

"He's not *that* bad, Bennett," she scoffed. "That's just his act."

Hawes made a noise with his lips. "If that arrogance of his is an act, he ought to get an Academy Award."

"It's just his way of protecting himself."

Hawes snorted. "By this time, if anybody out there still wanted him dead, he'd be dead."

"Not *physically*. Emotionally."

Hawes scowled. "Christ, I feel like I'm on *Oprah*." He crossed the room. "So, what do you want to do?"

"I don't see how we have a choice here," she said after a moment. "The Himes execution is six days off. Not only do we have a moral obligation to the public, but I don't have to tell you what a story such as this could mean to the paper."

No . . . she didn't. An exclusive like this could go a long way toward rescuing the *Sun*. If not financially, then at least in terms of restoring some measure of credibility.

"Problem is, even if we do find him, he won't do it," Hawes said. "Why should he?" He kept pacing the room, slowly shaking his head. "Last time I looked, that new book of his was number seven on the *New York Times* bestseller list. He doesn't do interviews of any kind. He doesn't sign books. He sure as hell doesn't need the money anymore. Why in God's name would he open himself up to all that abuse? Quite frankly, I'm amazed he still sends in his columns."

Mrs. V. smiled. "Mr. Corso and I have an agreement," she said. "And Mr. Corso is an unusually honorable man."

"Lotta people don't think so."

"Lots of people like professional wrestling," she said.

Hawes snorted and shook his head. "He'd have to be crazy to get involved in something like this. The whole *New York Times* libel thing is going to end up right back on the front page. No way he's going to let that happen."

"Ironic, isn't it?" Mrs. V. said.

"What's that?"

"That the same mighty newspaper that so publicly fired Mr. Corso for fabricating a story now gives him free publicity for his fictionalized reporting efforts."

Bennett Hawes was beyond wistful irony. He paced the room at breakneck speed. "Even if I do find him, he's just going to tell me to kiss his ass," he blurted out. "Excuse my French, but you know he and I aren't exactly . . . ," he said.

Bennett Hawes had been managing editor for twenty-one years prior to Corso's arrival. He'd lobbied long and hard for Corso not to be hired. First time they met, he'd asked Corso for an explanation of New York. Corso told him he didn't have one. "Then I'll never be sure I can trust you," Hawes had said. Corso said he didn't blame him. Said he wouldn't hire himself either. Fortunately or unfortunately, depending on your outlook, Mrs. V. had insisted.

"I know," Mrs. V. said.

She opened the top drawer of her desk, pulled out a piece of pale blue notepaper and a matching envelope. He couldn't see what she wrote, but whatever it was fit on a single line. She then reached down into her bottom drawer and fingered her way to what she was looking for. Found it. A scrap of white paper folded in thirds. She signed her name to the note, folded the page in half, slipped the white scrap inside, and sealed the envelope. "If he can find him, have Leo give this to Mr. Corso."

The hunted develop an eye for detail. An inner lens for imprinting the lay of familiar land or the fall of shadows at a certain time of day. He spotted the silhouette as soon as he turned the corner. A guy waiting by the women's showers. He stopped the car. Shifted into reverse and then backed to the far end of the lot.

As he got out and walked to the back of the car, he flicked his eyes in the guy's direction. Big son of a bitch . . . whoever he was. He opened the hatchback and bent down as if to remove something from the car. Then quickly duck-walked between parked cars until he reached the opposite side of the shower building.

He slipped off his boat shoes and pulled a steel ballpoint pen from the pocket of his raincoat. With his shoes stuffed into his coat pockets, he peeked around the short side of the building. Empty. He covered the distance and then peeked again. The guy still stood in the eaves, peering out at the Datsun through the beaded curtain of rain that ran headlong from the gutterless roof.

He took two silent steps forward, grabbed the guy by the back of his hair, and jammed the point of the pen into the hollow behind the big guy's ear. The guy made a surprisingly fast move to duck and turn, but Corso moved with him, increasing the pressure on the pen until it threatened to burst his eardrum, lifting him up onto his tiptoes, as if he were climbing a ladder.

"Easy now . . . easy now," the big guy chanted in a strained tenor.

Corso recognized the voice. Pulled the pen back and spun the guy around. The guy rubbed behind his ear. Scowled. "What the hell's with the Apache routine, Frank?" he asked. "You could seriously piss a guy off with that kind of shit."

"Apache, my ass. I should be asking you what's with the lurking routine?"

The big guy patted the hair at the back of his head. His face was red. "I'm a professional lurker, Frank. Remember? I'm a detective. Lurkers Are Us."

Corso slipped his shoes onto his feet, shouldered his way past the guy, and headed back to the car. The guy followed Corso into the rain.

"You don't generate much paperwork, Frank," he said to Corso's back. "You don't exactly leave a guy a lot of choices when it comes to finding you."

"Might lead some guys to figure I don't want to be found," Corso said. He stuck his head inside the car.

"Took me damn near two hours yammering on the phone," the guy complained as he ambled through the downpour.

"Come over here and make your big ass useful," Corso said.

The big man crossed the parking lot to Corso's side. Both men stood six-four, but that was where the similarities ended. Corso had a loose-jointed, raw-boned quality about him. Leo Waterman was big all over. Fingers twice the size of Corso's. One of those guys you could hit with a shovel, only to have him rise from the ground, smiling at you, with blood on his teeth. That was Leo's edge, what made him a good private investigator. By the time you figured out he was about three times as smart as you'd imagined, it was too late. You were screwed. Worse yet, if you had a problem with it, Leo doubled as his own complaint department.

Corso straightened up. Heaved a sigh. Looked the big man in the eye.

"How you been, Leo?" Corso asked.

"Hangin' in there, Frank."

Corso clapped him on the shoulder. "Good to see you again. How's Rebecca?"

"Dating a gynecologist."

"Sorry to hear that, Leo. You guys were together a long time."

Leo looked off into the distance. "Yeah," he said. "Almost twenty years. She says I'm not 'emotionally available.' "

"What's that mean?"

"Damned if I know," Leo said. "I've been trying to work up a picture of it for the past four months so's I could fake it."

"Sorry to hear it," Corso said again.

Leo made a face. "Not only am I back to eating my own cooking, but I'm so horny the crack of dawn better be careful around me," he said.

"A gynecologist, huh?"

"He's thirty," Leo said. "Named Brendan."

"I remember when thirty sounded so old," Corso mused.

"Yeah, me too," Leo said miserably.

They stood for a moment, sharing a silent grimace with the rain.

"Grab ahold here," Corso said.

Leo stepped around the corner of the car. A Rolls marine battery. Two hundred or so pounds of lead and acid with a plastic handle at each end.

Together the two men carried the battery down the ramp to the dock. Set it down while Corso unlocked the chain-link gate to C dock and then lugged it all the way out to the end. By the time they set the load down, Corso was heeled so far over on one side his knuckles threatened to drag on the dock and his hand felt as if it was being cut in two. Leo didn't seem to notice either Corso's discomfort or the weight of the load. Corso reckoned how if he were Brendan the gynecologist, he'd make it a point to stay a long way from Leo.

Leo looked the boat over. Whistled. "Yours, huh?" he asked.

Corso allowed how it surely was.

"This true-crime writing shit must really pay," Leo said. "Maybe I oughta pen my memoirs." He walked along the slip, taking the boat in. "How big?"

"Fifty-one feet," Corso said. "A Monk design."

"A beauty."

"Think of it as my house and it won't seem so extravagant," Corso said. "I live aboard." Corso stepped up onto his combination dock box and boarding stairs. "Come on," he said, stepping over the rail onto the deck.

Leo reached down, grabbed both of the handles, and, without so much as a grunt, set the battery on the rail. Corso thought he might have detected the hint of a smile forming on Leo's lips. Corso spread his feet wide, grabbed the handles, and pulled upward. Nothing. Corso looked down at Leo, who was openly grinning now.

"Awkward angle," Corso said.

Leo just kept smiling. Annoyed now, Corso yanked the battery for all he was worth, getting just enough clearance to allow the load to bang down onto the deck between his feet. The big boat rocked from the impact, but he still had his toes. Thank God for inch-and-a-half-thick teak decks.

Corso slid the door open and stepped into the boat. Leo climbed aboard. Still smiling. "Ya didn't hurt yourself, did ya, Frank?"

"Stop grinning at me, goddamn it," Corso snapped.

Leo used a massive hand to wipe the smile from his face, then nodded at the battery. "Where's this baby go?" he asked.

Corso pointed to the floor beneath his feet. "Down in the engine room," he said.

"Why don't we put it down there? Wouldn't want you to sink the damn boat. It's way too pretty for that."

Corso had spent just enough time around Leo to know this was the only chance he was going to get. With Leo, it wasn't a good idea to go all demure at a time like this. You made any noise about how you could handle it on your own and Leo was just the guy to give you a wink and allow how he knew all along you could.

Corso grabbed a D-ring in the teak-planked floor and pulled up a four-by-four-foot section of floor. Before he could set the hatch aside and lend a hand, Leo swung the battery over to the edge of the opening. He dropped to his knees, then down onto his belly, grabbed the handles, and managed to set the battery down gently in the engine compartment. As he worked the hatch back into place, Corso thought, once again, that if he were Dr. Stirrups he'd make it a point to give Leo a wide berth.

"So," Leo said. "You want to know who's looking for you?"

"Nope," Corso said. "Couldn't give less of a shit. As soon as I get that battery installed, I'm firing up and heading to the islands for a couple of weeks. A little cruising. A little fishing. Maybe some writing."

"Not even curious?"

"Just tell 'em that you told me whatever you were supposed to tell me."

"Actually, I wasn't supposed to tell you anything."

Leo reached into the pocket of his coat and produced a pale blue envelope. "I was just asked to give you this. You don't want to read it, don't."

Corso knew the stationery right away. "Shit," he said and snatched the envelope.

"Mind if I look around?" Leo asked.

Distracted, Corso told him to go for it. He held the envelope but didn't open it.

He vividly recalled the day her first note had arrived in the mail. He'd been sitting on a trunk in the East Village apartment, eating cornflakes out of an empty margarine tub. Waiting for the lease to expire at the end of the month and wondering what in hell he was going to do with the rest of his life. It was two weeks after the front-page saga of his disgrace and firing, and about ten days after Cynthia had packed in their lives and fled, leaving only the trunk, a brass end table, and a pile of partially addressed wedding invitations adrift on the mantel.

Bent in half and stuffed into the top of his mailbox. A plain manila envelope with a baby blue note that read:

> Dear Mr. Corso,
> If you would be interested in discussing a position with the Seattle Sun, please use the attached ticket to fly to Seattle on July 9, 1998. A room has been booked for you at the Sorrento Hotel. Confirmation #032011134. I look forward to seeing you at 9 A.M. on July 10, 1998, at the Seattle Sun Building, 2376 Western Avenue, Seattle, WA.
>
> Natalie Van Der Hoven
> Owner-Publisher
> Seattle Sun

A bit odd, to be sure, but . . . I mean, why not? Wasn't like he'd had other offers. The way Corso saw it, for the next thirty years or so, he'd be lucky to land a job writing copy for a union newsletter. Why not, indeed?

She never asked him for an explanation of the New York fiasco. Just said she was a longtime fan. She also had a rather audacious plan. The kind of leap of faith only attempted by the desperate. She was willing to bet that Corso's syndication readers would follow him, regardless of what had happened in the past. She offered to give him back his press credentials. Said she'd make him the *Seattle Sun*'s roving reporter. He could call his own shots. Thousand bucks a column. Expenses agreed upon in advance. No bennies.

What she wanted in return was all of his syndication revenues. After New York? Hell, it was a no-brainer. Like that old Billy Preston song: "Nothin' from nothin' leaves nothin'." So Corso had agreed. The deal had worked out for both of them. Over the past three years, she'd built Corso's syndication numbers nearly back to where they had been before his firing. The extra revenue was a major factor in keeping the *Seattle Sun* afloat. As for Corso, he'd rebuilt some measure of confidence in his own sanity and had finally finished the book he'd started ten years earlier. When *Those Who Favor Fire* had gone to the top of the bestseller lists last year, they'd negotiated the weekly column back to twice a month. Two grand a pop.

He used his thumb to rip open the flap of the envelope. Written in her crisp schoolteacher hand it read: *Same story. This time the marker is mine*. Signed *Natalie Van Der Hoven*. A scrap of white paper waffled to the floor. Corso heaved a heavy sigh and dropped the note on the chart table. Left the paper on the floor. He knew what it said. Read the note again. Same story? Walter Leroy Himes?

Leo was out on the stern checking out the view of Lake Union and foggy Queen Anne Hill beyond. A floatplane roared north, bouncing across the choppy green water until it lurched into the sky and disappeared over Gasworks Park.

"Hey," Corso yelled. Leo stepped over and poked his head into the cabin.

"Himes is scheduled for execution on Saturday, right?" Corso asked.

Leo made a move like he was giving himself an injection. "Yeah," he said. "Midnight. Walter Leroy boots up the cosmic Kool-Aid over in Walla Walla."

For over eleven weeks in 1998, a serial killer had shaken Seattle like a maraca. Eight bodies in eighty days. Eight girls strangled, raped, and thrown into Dumpsters like urban litter. Taken from crowded places, where the volume of traffic alone should have made abductions impossible. As the weeks passed and the bodies became more frequent, the killer began to take on almost mythic properties. The media started calling him the Trashman. By the end, the streets were deserted after dark, and the pressure on the Seattle Police Department to find the killer was unrelenting.

SPD had no called in the county, the state, and the FBI. They hunted and harangued and profiled and pontificated, until, like clockwork, the sixth girl was found dead in an alley below the Pike Street Market. And then the seventh girl turned up. Hysteria reigned. A chorus called for the ouster of the chief of police. Others wanted the National Guard to safeguard the streets. Then, just when they feared another body was due to be found, they finally got lucky.

Two uniformed officers in a patrol car came upon an eighteen-year-old girl, Leanne Samples, staggering down a snow-covered service road in Volunteer Park, her panties missing in action, her face scratched and bleeding, her blouse torn to shreds and hanging at her wrists. When finally calm enough to talk, she told the officers that she'd been dragged into the bushes and had been in the process of being raped when the sound of the squad car caused her attacker to flee. The officers called for an aide car and all the backup in the world.

About the time Leanne Samples arrived at Harborview Medical Center, nearly a hundred cops and FBI agents swept through the park like fire ants. They found her white cotton panties beneath a dormant azalea; they also found the owner of a local auto-body shop getting a blow job from a fifteen-year-old runaway boy from Saginaw, Michigan. Most significant, however, they found a homeless transient by the name of Walter Leroy Himes playing with himself in the men's room behind the bandshell.

By the time detectives arrived at Harborview Medical Center, Leanne's parents, who were members of a Christian fundamentalist congregation, had put a stop to her medical treatment. Seems they and their brethren didn't hold with any of that scientific hocus-pocus. No fluid workups, no DNA testing. No nothing. The Devil's handiwork and all that, you know.

Faced with the total loss of forensic evidence, the desperate detectives showed Leanne a five-year-old mug shot of Walter Leroy Himes. After some prodding, she said yes, that was the man who'd tried to rape her. Two days later, Leanne picked Walter Leroy Himes out of a six-man lineup. The rest, as they say, was history. Hell, Himes made it easy for them.

Walter Leroy Himes was, after all, everything a murdering scumbag was supposed to be. For starters, he was every bit as ugly as he was big. A mouth-breather with big red lips and truly lamentable personal hygiene. Not only was he uneducated, but he was stupid besides. Refusing a lawyer until the last moment, when Judge Spearbeck stuck him with a wet-behind-the-ears public defender who had no idea how to deal with a client who wouldn't shut up in court, who wound up duct-taped to his chair, wearing a bright orange ball gag the judge ordered from the sex shop up the street from the courthouse. The capper was that Himes turned out to have an extensive record of sex offenses. Three county convictions for public nudity back in his native North Carolina. Seems he liked to wave his winkie at schoolkids. Worse yet, he'd recently done nineteen months at the Twin Rivers Correctional Facility for fondling an eleven-year-old girl in a downtown mini-mart. He had been released from prison a scant three weeks before the killings began. If ever a man was a natural to catch a rap, it was Walter Leroy Himes. And catch it he did. Big time. Eight counts of aggravated murder. Eight death sentences.

Leo stepped into the salon, sliding the teak door closed behind him. "What do you think?" he asked. "Now that Judgment Day is close at hand, you figure old Walter Leroy wishes he hadn't kept referring to the governor as 'the chink'?"

Corso thought it over. "If Himes was wired for regret, he wouldn't be on death row at all," he said finally. Leo nodded in silent agreement.

The state of Washington has never been particularly anxious to enforce its death penalty. Had Himes had sense enough to keep his mouth shut, they would have locked him up and let him appeal until he rotted. Not Himes though. No . . . Himes immediately tried to waive his right to appeal and demanded his death sentence be carried out posthaste. Claimed his maker knew he hadn't killed those girls. Figured when he got to wherever he was going, first thing he'd do was he'd rape those eight, what he called "stuck-up bitches," good and proper. Give 'em an eternity of what he figured they'd been asking for anyway. Way Himes saw it, since he was an innocent man, they owed it to him. Needless to say, such pronouncements did little to enhance Walter Leroy's popularity.

Such quantum stupidity quite naturally attracted the attention of the ACLU, which then had spent the last three years and the better part of four million dollars exhausting every legal avenue in an ill-fated effort to save Walter Leroy Himes from both the state of Washington and himself.

Leo ambled back through the boat to Corso's side. "Just for my peace of mind, Frank, who owns the Datsun?"

"Why?"

" 'Cause you don't. You don't even have a Washington driver's license. If you owned a car or had a license, I'd have been here two hours ago."

"It's a dock car. Parking got to be so damn bad a bunch of us chipped in and bought it. You just sign up to use it whenever you need it. I need a car for anything serious, I rent one."

"No phone number, listed or not. No utility bills under your own name. No library card. No traffic tickets. No tax bills. You don't take any of the papers. No magazine subscriptions. No cable TV. You're not on-line with any of the local Internet providers. You're a regular Ted Kaczynski, you know that, Corso?"

Corso grinned. "So . . . just for *my* peace of mind, how *did* you find me?"

"Pizza," Leo said. "Pagliacci's has everybody in town who's ever ordered a pizza in their database." He eyed Corso. "Anchovy . . . Jesus, man."

Corso washed his hands in the sink and then dried them with a paper towel.

"Since you just fucked up my fishing plans and quite possibly my life, how about you giving me a ride down to the *Sun*? Somebody else is signed up for the car this afternoon." His tone had a resigned quality Leo had never heard before.

Leo held up a moderating hand. "I don't know what this is about, Frank, and quite honestly, I don't give a shit, but whatever it is—if you don't want to do it, then don't."

"Easier said than done."

"I gave up guilt for Lent," Leo said. "Maybe you ought to do the same."

"What if you're actually guilty?" Corso asked.

"There's always denial."

"Let's go," Corso said.

They were halfway back to the gate when Leo said, "Whaddya think, Frank? You figure gynecologists—you know—know stuff that the rest of us don't?"

Corso pulled open the gate. "What kind of stuff?"

Leo waved a big hand. "You know . . . techniques . . ." He shot Corso a quick glance. "You know . . . like in bed."

"How long did you say it took you to find me?"

"Couple hours. Why?"

"How long do you think it would have taken Brendan the gynecologist?"

Leo gave the question serious consideration.

"Sorry I asked," the big guy said.

Monday, September 17
2:58 P.M. Day 1 of 6

Looked kinda like an older version of that karate movie guy. Steven Somethingorother. The guy with the long black ponytail. Bill Post tried to recall the actor's name. Yeah . . . Steven Something. The guy pulled the door open and strode into the lobby. Without so much as a by-your-leave, he took a hard left and headed for the elevator. What the hell . . .

Post scrambled out from behind the desk. "Hey . . . hey . . . there," he said. "This is a full security area, you can't just . . ." Bill Post reached out and grabbed the guy by the shoulder. Next thing he knew, ponytail had ahold of his hand. With his thumb, the guy found some pressure point in the soft meat between Post's thumb and forefinger, sending an electric shock up the length of the old man's arm. The arm dropped uselessly to Post's side. "Damn." Post flapped his wing like an injured bird.

"Now there's no cause to be . . . ," the old man sputtered. Rubbing his hand and trying to shake some feeling back into his palsied arm. "I can get the cops down here, if you want. You think you're Mr.—"

Ponytail pulled something out of the pocket of his black overcoat with one hand and pushed the elevator button with the other. A press credential. With his working arm, Post reached for the laminated card but the guy pulled it back, out of reach. A muted ding announced the elevator's arrival. He tilted his head back, squinted at the card: THE SEATTLE SUN. Frank Corso. The picture had short hair, but it was him all right.

Post began to stammer. "Oh . . . well, then . . . yes . . . sorry, Mr. Corso."

Corso stepped into the elevator.

"I'm supposed to send you to the second-floor lunchroom," Post said.

The door slid shut.

Post turned and headed back to his desk. The elevator bell sounded again.

"Hey," a voice called.

Post turned back. Corso again.

"Sorry about the hand," he said. "You okay?"

Post stopped trying to shake the feeling back into his arm.

"It's nothin'," he said. "I'll be fine."

"I'm a little jumpy sometimes," Corso explained. "I think maybe I spend a little too much time alone."

Post said he understood. Watched as Corso got back in the elevator and the steel door again slid closed. Post went back to massaging his arm as he stood and stared at the door for a moment. "Seagal. That's it, damnit. He looks like Steven Seagal."

He smiled as he started back toward his desk. "Nothin' wrong with my memory. No, sir. Nothin' at all."

* * *

The minute he pulled open the door, Corso knew what was going on. Six days before Walter Leroy Himes's scheduled execution and she'd changed her tune. What he couldn't fathom, however, was what it had to do with him. Sure, he'd covered the trial for the *Sun*. His first big story in Seattle and damn near his last. He'd spoken to Leanne a couple of times. Interviewed her once. So what?

Fresh from the debacle in New York, Corso had found himself the only person in the Pacific Northwest who thought Himes had gotten the shaft and had insisted on writing a dissent. It started: "If Walter Leroy Himes hadn't existed, local law enforcement surely would have invented him." Hawes, on the other hand, quite rightly saw any dissent whatsoever as a public relations nightmare and had refused the piece. Corso went upstairs. Reminded Mrs. V. of their agreement. Mrs. V. said, "Run it," and the most unpopular piece of journalism in the city's history had appeared on page one the next morning.

Public furor had been costly. From Corso's end, the piece had motivated a couple of outraged rednecks from Kent to damn near beat him to death with tire irons. As for the paper, the *Seattle Sun* lost four thousand subscribers, 8 percent of its advertising revenue, and thus was forced to abandon its century-old broadsheet format. If Hawes had had his way, it would have cost Corso his job. Maybe his life. Corso was amazed when Mrs. V. chalked it off to experience. He'd gone to her office and handed her his handwritten IOU. "I owe you another one," he'd said. She'd agreed and tucked the slip of paper away for a rainy day. Like today.

Hawes read the girl's startled expression. Looked back over his shoulder and then got to his feet. He said something to Leanne.

She nodded. Hawes crossed the room to Corso's side. He gestured with his head and then led Corso over to an uninhabited corner of the room.

"She says she lied at the Himes trial."

"So what?"

"That's all she'll say. She insists on talking to you."

"Why me?"

Hawes sneered at him. "Funny, but I've been asking myself that very question."

"I don't need this shit," Corso said.

Hawes had his jaw clamped so hard he looked like a large-mouth bass.

Corso removed his coat and folded it over his left arm. "Tell Mrs. V. I'll be up when I get through chatting with Leanne." Hawes nodded. Corso excused himself and walked across the room. Leanne squirmed in her seat. From six feet away, Corso could see that the rim of the paper Pepsi cup in front of her had been picked to shreds. Two other similarly shredded cups leaned against the wall. Bits of waxed paper littered the table.

Instead of taking Hawes's seat across the table from Leanne, Corso slid onto the bench next to her. Eyes wide, she scooted over by the wall. "Long time no see, Miss Samples," he said. She nodded. "It is still *Miss* Samples, isn't it?"

Leanne managed an uncertain smile and said why of course it was still Miss.

"I thought maybe some young man might have spirited you away by now," he said. "Off to the Casbah or something."

The young woman reddened and hid her face with her hands.

"Stop it," she said with a giggle.

She hadn't changed a great deal. Same wide-open face and deep-set eyes. Her brown hair was, if anything, thicker, and she might have lost a little weight. She was, what? Twenty-one or so now. She'd been something like eighteen at the time. Probably not the PC nomenclature anymore, but, back then, Corso had decided that "slow" was the proper term for Leanne Samples. Eventually, Leanne got to the right answer. It just took her a bit longer than it did most folks.

"Leanne . . . ," Corso began. "I hope you won't mind if we get right down to business here." She nodded. "Did you tell Mr. Hawes that Mr. Himes did not attempt to rape you? Is that what you told him?" Before she could answer, Corso waved a finger in her face. "Because . . . if you are . . . I mean, girl, I've got to tell you right up front what a serious matter you're getting yourself into here."

She was chewing her thumb. Moving her head up and down.

"I did," she said softly.

The bench squeaked as Corso leaned back against the wall. His scalp tingled.

"Now why would a nice girl like you want to do a thing like that, Leanne? Why would you want to go and tell a lie about something so important?"

She thought it over. "I was scared," she said finally.

"Scared of what?"

"Of my parents."

"Why would you be afraid of your parents?"

"I thought I was pregnant."

"Pregnant by whom?"

She shrugged. "Some boy from school." She pulled her hand from her mouth and waved it as if she were shooing a fly. "You remember my parents . . ." She looked pleadingly at Corso. He nodded. "They'd go crazy," she said. "They'd . . ."

"So you . . ."

"So I went to the park. I tore up my clothes . . . scratched myself . . ." Unconsciously, she brought her fingertips to her cheek. "You know, to make it look like I was attacked. So . . . you know . . . in case I turned out to be pregnant . . . I could say I'd been . . ."

"What did you think the cops would do?" he pressed.

"There weren't supposed to be any police," she blurted out.

The lunchroom fell silent around them. She looked around. She started her thumb to her mouth, caught herself, jammed it back in her lap.

"I was just going to go home and tell my parents. That was all," she whispered. "They'd keep the shame in the family. It's their way." She waved her hand again. "The policemen just drove up. I didn't—"

"You identified a picture of Mr. Himes."

"They kept asking me to look again and look again and look again. I didn't know what else to do," she whined.

"You picked him out of a lineup."

"He was the man in the picture," she said. "I thought—"

"You testified in court," Corso interrupted.

She began to cry. "They're going to kill him. I never thought . . . I thought—"

"You thought what?" Corso pushed.

Her shoulders shook as she began to sob. "I thought he was a bad man and that they would put him away where he could get better and not hurt anybody."

Over the top of her head, he could see that the room had nearly stopped again as people realized who they were. The air was still and electrically charged, like in the seconds before a cloudburst.

"Have you been to the authorities?"

Her eyes again filled with tears. When she nodded, droplets rolled down her cheeks. "They didn't believe me. They said I'd have to go to jail."

Corso wasn't surprised. Recanting testimony was nearly impossible. Careers were at stake even in low-profile cases. In a case as emotionally charged as Walter Leroy Himes's, God only knew how far they'd go to cover their collective asses.

"Who did you talk to?" he asked.

She picked her purse up from the floor. Her hand came out with a business card. County seal. Assistant District Attorney. Timothy Beal.

"And then they brought some other men in. They said I was a liar."

She began to cry in earnest now. Corso waited as she found a twisted Kleenex in her coat pocket and applied it to her dripping nose. With the other hand, she fumbled in her purse and produced a yellowed and much-fingered piece of newsprint. "I showed them your article about how Mr. Himes was innocent. And you know what?" She didn't wait for an answer. "They said you were a liar too. That you got fired for printing lies. And that was why you were working here instead of wherever you used to work."

Corso kept his mouth shut.

"Did you?" she insisted.

"Did I what? Get fired for fabricating a story? Yes, I did."

"Not that," she whined. "Did you lie?"

"Not on purpose," he said.

"You made a mistake?"

He grudgingly nodded. "In some way I still don't understand, I must have gotten sloppy. Overconfident, maybe . . . something like that."

Corso recalled Cynthia's face, watching it melt like a cake in the rain as he told her the real story of what he thought had happened. And then the silence and the look of pity as she asked, "You don't really think anyone is going to believe that, do you?" After that she began to rave about how if he'd just admit to making a mistake, maybe he could salvage what was left of his career.

About how telling the story he'd just told her would accomplish nothing except to get him branded as not only a liar but as a paranoid schizophrenic as well. Corso had never told the story again. Not to Ben Gardner, his editor at the *New York Times* who fired him, and not to Mrs. V. here at the *Seattle Sun* when she hired him. So why, he wondered, did he feel compelled to tell Leanne Samples?

"Leanne," he said, "what happened to me back in New York is a very complicated story." He looked into her eyes. They were nearly black. "I say that not because I think you'll have any trouble understanding it. I say it because I don't understand the details of it myself. All I know for sure is that it happened."

She sat up straight, as if she were at school. Said she understood.

"I was writing a series about a very rich and powerful man." Corso paused. Took a deep breath. "He invited me to his office one day. Real polite and everything. Had a catered lunch there for us." Corso gathered himself. "After lunch—over coffee—he told me to stop. No more writing about him, he said." Corso snapped his fingers. "Just like that. 'Stop,' he told me. He said he'd squash me like a bug if I didn't." Corso ground his thumb on the table for emphasis.

Leanne cringed. "But you didn't stop, did you?" she said hopefully.

"No," Corso said. "I didn't. I kept picking at it."

She looked at her own thumb. "And he—"

"Like a bug." Corso sighed. "People got fired," he said. "Some of them held me responsible for ruining their lives."

"How?" she asked.

Yeah . . . that was the double jeopardy question, wasn't it? How could such a thing have happened? To a raw rookie, maybe. But to a seasoned investigative reporter? He wakes up one day and a whole raft of otherwise respectable people are suddenly conspiring against him. Spare us. We wanna hear that crap, we'll watch *The X-Files.*

"Money and pride," Corso said after a moment. "He had enough money to be truly dangerous, and I had enough pride to be truly stupid."

"Mama says money won't buy happiness," Leanne said.

"What's your mama have to say about pride?" he asked.

"Mama always says that 'pride goeth before a fall.' "

"I'm living proof your mama is right," Corso said.

"I knew you wouldn't lie on purpose."

"Thanks," Corso said with a chuckle. "You're now executive vice president of the Frank Corso Fan Club."

"Do you really have a fan club?" He'd forgotten how earnest she could be. Made a mental note to be careful about joking with her.

"Here we are," Corso said. "All of us."

She laughed again and used the Kleenex to dab at her eyes.

"If you don't mind me asking, Leanne, why me?"

She shrugged but didn't answer. She had an odd way of stepping back inside herself. Almost like she had a closet back there somewhere where she could go to hide.

"Well, then, I'll have to assume it's my boyish charm and rugged good looks," Corso said. "You probably didn't know this, Leanne, but women regularly swoon at the very sight of me. As a matter of fact, it's pretty amazing that you're still conscious."

Leanne laughed behind her hand. Told him again to stop it. Then suddenly got serious. "You always treated me nice like this. Like I mattered. Always listened to me like I was somebody important. Not like I was a spaz, like the others do. So . . . will you, please?" she pleaded.

"Will I what?"

"Will you make them listen to me?"

Corso thought about it. With the exception of Himes's ACLU

lawyer, nobody but nobody was going to want any part of this story. In six days, dozens of heartbroken souls were finally scheduled to be granted some small measure of relief. A flawed but final resolution to a three-year-old nightmare and . . . what? Somebody was going to come along and say, Oops . . . waita-minute . . . there's been a minor glitch here. Back to square one. Feel free to return to your grieving.

Corso's insides suddenly had that sheet-metal feel. The feeling he'd first experienced in New York and had carried with him, on and off, ever since. A cold, dull ache in the pit of his stomach, as if he'd swallowed ball bearings. A pain that only subsided when he was floating alone on deep, green water.

He got to his feet and looked to the windows on the far side of the room. Outside, the steel-wool sky engulfed on Queen Anne Hill. A steady rain coated the streets, leaving the cars to hiss along inside silver canopies of mist.

"Come on," he said.

Halfway down the hall to the elevator, Blaine Newton came across the red-tile floor toward Corso and Leanne, holding his oversize lunch bag by his side. Newton was about thirty and already lapping over his belt. Blaine Newton had been, for the past few years, Hawes's pet-reporter project. Another fancy dresser from the University of Washington journalism department, where Hawes moonlighted as an assistant professor. He was a better writer than a reporter. Next in line for the metro-crime beat, whenever Nathan Hopkins could be persuaded to retire. Corso disliked him on principle. When he recognized Corso, his big pink cheeks very nearly squeezed his eyes shut.

"Finally find yourself a date, Corso?"

"I'm saving it for Judith. She's all I can handle."

"Har-har," Newton barked. "Very funny."

"Give us a chorus of 'Danke Schoen,'" Corso said as they passed. Newton stopped in his tracks. "What the hell is that supposed to mean? You always say that like it's supposed to be a big joke or something."

Corso kept walking. "Ask Judith," he said.

"You're so funny," Newton said to his back.

Leanne leaned in and whispered, "Who's Judith?"

"His wife," Corso said in a loud voice. "She's very demanding."

Leanne giggled and squeezed his arm. When the elevator opened, Corso stepped aside and allowed her to enter first.

4

The pictures on her desk made the facts of her life clear. Sons in college? Two. Husbands in residence? None. Violet Rogers was a sturdily built, no-nonsense woman of forty-five. Motherly, she wore her long hair braided and wound around her head like shiny black ropes.

The sound of the elevator pulled her eyes from the computer screen to the sliding door. "Why, Mr. Corso," she said with a smile. "It's been far too long."

She removed an earpiece from the side of her head and got to her feet. They shook hands. "Violet," Corso said, "this is Leanne Samples."

"I know . . . I know. It's not often we have such a celebrity up here."

Leanne blushed and began to stammer, "Oh . . . I'm not a celebrity . . . no, please . . ."

Corso inclined his head toward Mrs. V.'s office and raised his eyebrow. Violet instantly picked up on his drift. She took Leanne by the hand.

"What can I get you, honey?" she asked. "Coffee? Tea?"

Leanne swiveled her head around the room. "Is there a . . . a facilities on this floor?"

Violet emitted a deep, booming laugh. "Honey, this is the executive floor. We've got a facilities you won't believe. You just come along with me."

Corso watched the women wade through the ankle-deep carpet and disappear around the corner. Without knocking, he pulled open the door and stepped into Natalie Van Der Hoven's office. Bennett Hawes was pacing the center of the room with his hands jammed in his pants. Mrs. V. was seated behind her ornate mahogany desk opening mail with a silver letter opener.

"Thank you for coming, Mr. Corso," she said.

Corso crossed the room and shook the woman's hand. "Nice to see you again, Mrs. V.," he said. "You're the only thing about this business I miss."

"You flatter me, Mr. Corso."

"It's true," Corso insisted.

"I'm enchanted that you think so."

"You wanna tell us what she said, or what?" Hawes huffed.

Corso gave them the short version of what Leanne had told him. As always, Hawes refused to tilt his head back far enough to maintain eye contact with Corso and listened while staring at Corso's shirtfront.

From a newspaperman's point of view, one question now begged an answer. Mrs. V. was all over it. "Who else has she told?"

Corso handed her the ADA's business card.

"And how was her information received?" she asked.

"Just as you'd imagine. They threatened her and threw her out."

"You think they'll go public?" Hawes asked.

"No way. They'll stonewall for as long as they can."

"And she told nobody else?" Hawes pressed.

"She says the Beal guy called in a couple of suits. I'm guessing cops."

"So we print what? 'Himes Innocent'?" Hawes asked sarcastically.

"We print 'State's Witness Says She Lied' " Mrs. V. said.

Before Hawes could open his mouth, Corso said, "She's all the case they had."

Natalie Van Der Hoven sighed and rocked back in her chair. She knew where this was going. May as well let them work it out of their systems, she thought.

"He confessed," Hawes insisted.

According to the arresting officer, as he and Himes stood together in the corridor outside central booking, Himes had admitted to killing the girls.

"Himes always claimed the cop was lying."

"The killings stopped, goddamn it," Hawes spat out. "Let's not waste our time arguing about all this crap again. From the day they picked that slimeball up, there's never been another Trashman killing, period." He dotted the air with his index finger.

"No period," Corso said. "As I recall, they found the eighth victim several days after Himes was arrested."

"She was killed beforehand," Hawes said. "Took that long to find her."

"That's not how I remember it," Corso said quickly. "I seem to recall there was some reason or other why the time of death couldn't be established for the last girl."

"They had other forensic material," Hawes insisted.

"If they had a match, they'd have used it."

The official word on the forensics had been that although they had collected a great deal of forensic material, the fact that the victims had been found in Dumpsters raised the unfortunate specter of outside contamination to such a level that any competent defense attorney could easily get the forensics excluded. As far as Corso was concerned, in the end, Leanne Samples was the state's case.

"They had Himes dead to rights," Hawes persisted.

"The FBI sure as hell didn't think so," Corso countered.

Hawes made a disgusted face. "Oh, don't start that crap again."

"I'll tell you again—same thing I told you back then—the Bureau doesn't miss photo opportunities. I've worked around them a lot."

Hawes got theatrical now. Parading around with his hands on his hips. "Back before you were a famous true-crime writer. Back when you were the golden boy of the *New Yaaaawk Times*," he mocked. "Haaaaaavard scholar. Nieeeeeeman Fellow."

Corso swallowed his anger, took a deep breath. "Yeah, Bennett, way back then . . . And you know as well as I do, that's why local law enforcement hates working with them. No matter who breaks the case, they take the credit. Hell, it was a couple of Oklahoma troopers who pulled Timothy McVeigh over and made the collar. You remember seeing those good old boys up at the podium when they announced the arrest?" Before the older man could open his mouth, Corso said, "Yeah . . . me neither."

Bennett Hawes sighed and turned his back to Corso. He walked to the right side of the desk and sat heavily in the matching red leather chair. His face was sour. "And that tells you Himes was innocent?"

"No," Corso said. "What it tells me is that the FBI wanted nothing to do with the case against Walter Leroy Himes. That they wanted to distance themselves from the whole thing. I'm telling you, if Miss Samples out there keeps telling her present tale, we're about to see the biggest public ass covering since Pontius Pilate."

Mrs. V. slapped a palm on her desktop. The resounding silenced the men. "Enough," she said. "I've heard it all before. Ad nauseam," she added.

"And you remember what happened," Hawes snapped. "We're less than a week from a final resolution and I'm telling you"—he waved his arm at the skyline of the city—"these people want their pound of flesh. If they don't get Himes, they're gonna settle for whoever brings them the bad news."

No doubt about it. The execution frenzy was building to a peak. Just inside the prison gates, a herd of mobile television units aimed their concave eyes at the sky. Outside the gates of the prison, a tent city was growing. UPI estimated that by the time Himes was administered the lethal injection, three to four thousand souls would be gathered outside the gates to speed him on his way to eternity.

Corso knew the execution crowds. The foam baseball caps and the battered motor homes. He'd rubbed elbows with the soapbox preachers and the legions of lonely women. He'd personally witnessed two electrocutions and a hanging. All part of being in a business where a phone call could drag you from the sanctity of your bed and send you kicking amid the rubble of a bombed-out building, watching your tasseled feet slide amid the blood and the baby shoes and the broken bricks of other people's lives. The way Corso saw it, if you had the nerve to insert yourself into such moments of personal tragedy, the least you could do was not watch from the bleachers. You had to get down on the field and play. You owed it to both the living and the dead.

"Where is Miss Samples?" Mrs. V. demanded.

"Outside with Violet," Corso said.

She pushed a button on her phone. "Violet, would you please

send in Miss Samples?" Violet said it would be her pleasure. A few seconds later, the door eased open.

Leanne Samples stopped in the doorway, one hand gripping each side of the opening, like Samson about to pull down the temple. Her eyes darted around the room, taking in the gallery of mutton-chopped forebears whose portraits lined the walls. Her gaze finally came to rest on the portrait of Natalie Van Der Hoven that hung behind her desk. Mrs. V. got to her feet. "Please come in," Mrs. V. prompted. Leanne stayed put, staring at the portraits. "The paper has been in my family for over a hundred years," Mrs. V. tried.

Leanne let go of the doorway and took several tentative steps into the room. Hawes slipped behind her, closed the door, gently placed a hand on her shoulder, and began to aim her to one of the chairs to the right of Mrs. V.'s desk. Leanne, however, was having none of it. She shook off his hand and made a beeline for Corso, who, in the manner of a matador, eased the young woman past the edge of the desk and into the guest chair. She sat, halfway into the seat, leaning forward, her hands clasped in her lap.

"Can I get you something?" Mrs. V. inquired. "Coffee? A soft drink? A bottled water?" Leanne shook her head.

"A hundred years is a long time," she said after a moment.

"And quite a responsibility," Mrs. V. added. "The portraits make me feel as if they're all watching over me. Making sure I do the right thing."

"That's why I came here today," Leanne said.

Mrs. V. settled back into her seat. "To do the right thing?"

Leanne nodded. "I had to. I couldn't let somebody—Mr. Himes—be dead on account of me."

"I owe it to all of my readers to make sure that what I print in this paper is accurate." Mrs. V. locked Leanne with her gaze. The young woman seemed to steel herself, sitting up straight. Stilling her hands.

"What I told Mr. Corso is true." She looked back over her shoulder at Corso. He gave her a nod. "I lied about Mr. Himes, and now I have to fix it."

"That won't be easy," Mrs. V. said.

"I know," Leanne said softly.

"This is a very serious matter," Hawes added.

"I know," she said again, softer this time.

"Then I'm certain you will want to—" Mrs. V. began.

Leanne exploded like a cherry bomb. "No," she shouted. "Don't you dare start telling me what I want. I *know* what I want." She looked over at Hawes. "My whole life people have been telling me what I really want or what I really mean—like I'm such a retard I don't even know what's going on inside of me."

She turned finally to Corso. "Mr. Corso . . . he just listens to me like he listens to everybody else."

Natalie Van Der Hoven looked to Corso for an explanation.

"She means I treat everybody like they're retarded," he said.

Leanne covered her mouth and laughed. Mrs. V. returned to her seat behind the desk, leaned forward, pushed the red button on her phone. "Violet, could you come in here, please?"

"Yes, Mrs. Van Der Hoven," crackled the voice.

Mrs. V. looked over at Leanne. "Do you still live with your parents?"

Leanne shook her head. Said she was living in a group home on Harvard Avenue. Transitioning into the workplace, as it were. Place was called Pathways.

The office door opened. Violet stepped in. "Are either of the boys home from college, Violet?" Mrs. V. asked.

"No, Mrs. Van Der Hoven. Not for a couple more weeks."

"How would you feel about spending the next few days in a fancy hotel ordering room service?"

Her face lit up. "I don't believe I understand—" she began.

"Miss Samples is going to be a guest of the paper for a few

days. I was wondering if it would be too much of an imposition to ask you to act as her chaperone."

It took a bit of talking, but they worked it out. Leanne suddenly found herself beyond where she'd thought things through and took a little convincing. Violet wouldn't hear of Mrs. V. fielding her own calls and insisted on arranging a suitable temp for herself. They settled on the Carlisle Hotel where the *Sun* had an account they used for out-of-town visitors. They were to get a couple of rooms. Not use their own names. Violet was going to stop at home and gather whatever personal things she might need for an overnight stay. Anything Leanne needed would come out of petty cash. Mrs. V. gave Violet her personal cell phone number and told her to call Pathways as soon as they were settled. Wouldn't want them sending out a search party. Violet was explaining the concept of room service to Leanne as they walked out the door. "Honey, you can order anything!" she said. "You ever had a surf and turf?"

Leanne kept her eyes locked on Corso. He waved. She mustered a tight smile she didn't mean and backed out the door.

Mrs. V. turned to Hawes. "Call Mr. Robbins at the plant. Have him up tonight's street run by fifty percent."

Hawes sighed. "He's gonna say it can't be done."

"He always says it can't be done. Just tell him I said to do it. And tell him I want the first papers in the machines by four-thirty."

They watched as Bennett Hawes hurried out the door.

5

Monday, September 17
4:21 P.M. Day 1 of 6

Corso sat in the red leather chair and watched the rain close over Elliott Bay like a steel curtain. In the distance, the outline of the westbound Bainbridge Island ferry was little more than a half-erased pencil drawing.

"I don't need this right now," Corso said.

"I know."

"My fifteen minutes of fame are over. I'm no longer the Typhoid Mary of the newspaper business. I can walk up the street for a latte without anybody pointing a camera at me. Hell, I can't even remember the last time anybody threatened to kill me. I like things the way they are. If I've got something that pisses me off, I write a column about it. If it really pisses me off, I write a book. For this, people throw money at me. How bad can things be?"

When she didn't reply, he got to his feet and walked over to the window. Six stories below, in Myrtle Edwards Park, skeletal trees shivered in the wind. Rain skittered across the black asphalt walkways in sweeping silver lines. Beyond the park, Puget Sound hurled itself upon the black boulders of shore, sending plumes of spray high into the dark sky. Corso tried to remember who it was who said that living in Seattle was like being married to a beautiful woman who was sick all the time. Leo, maybe.

"You're going to make me be the one to say it out loud, aren't you?" he asked after a moment. "Not even going to cut me the slack of saying it first."

Natalie Van Der Hoven used class the way Leo used big. As a shield. Corso knew better than to underestimate her. She was a shrewd executive and a practiced negotiator. If you weren't careful, you found yourself nodding at everything she said, not because you agreed but because any sort of disagreement seemed positively rude.

She brought a hand to her throat and did her best Scarlett O'Hara. "Whatever do you mean?"

"That I owe you. That you gave me a job when I was a national leper. After my last employer lost a ten-million-dollar libel judgment on my account. And you take me in and give me a job and what do I do? I screw up again. You damn near lose a newspaper that's been in your family for a hundred years and guess what? You don't fire me, you let me keep my job."

"I'd like to think our relationship has grown beyond a simple case of mutual obligation," she said.

"Don't start with me," Corso scoffed. "You know damn well we're friends, and you know damn well that's not the point."

Corso leaned his forehead against the cool glass. Overhead, a clap of thunder rolled like cannon fire. The tick of rain on the windows rose to a sustained hiss, and then, just as suddenly, abated. Mrs. V. broke the spell.

"I don't suppose I have to tell you what a precarious position the *Sun* finds itself in," she began. "We've reached that unfortunate position on the newspaper food chain where our finances force us to consider our editorial policy." She took a deep breath. "And allowing finances to dictate news is, as we all know, the first step in a slide toward journalistic hell." She looked out, over Corso's head. "A journey, which I say, quite frankly, I have no intention of making. I'll close the doors first."

Something in Corso's reflected face betrayed him. Mrs. V. seemed to read his thoughts. "You're thinking that I already made that mistake, aren't you? You're thinking the Himes case was the first time." Before Corso could lie, she continued, "I quashed the follow-up to your Himes story, quite simply because I thought you were wrong. The public hysteria had nothing to do with my decision. You were new to us. I thought you were overreacting to what had happened to you in New York. It seemed plain to me that you were merely trying a bit too hard to make a new name for yourself." She shrugged. "Human nature, I supposed."

"The screwup was mine," Corso said. "The piece was self-indulgent. Part of the job is knowing which way the wind blows and then tailoring your approach to the weather. I didn't do my job."

"You're too hard on yourself, Mr. Corso," she said.

Down in the park, an elderly Asian woman walked a little brown-and-white dog whose swinging belly nearly dragged on the pavement. With one hand she jerked the leash, as if teaching the dog to heel; with the other she fought to keep her red umbrella from turning inside out in the gale.

"I'm pained to have been forced to prevail upon you in this manner, Mr. Corso. I know what you've been through."

"Pained enough to tell me to forget about it and go fishing?"

"No."

A sudden swirling gust tore the red umbrella from the old woman's hand. She lunged for it, missed, slipped on the wet grass, and went down heavily on her side, dropping the leash as she fell. The dog took off, running after the tumbling umbrella on four-inch legs. The woman struggled to her feet and started after the dog in an arthritic, splay-footed shuffle, waving an arm, shouting.

"I don't want any part of this," Corso said.

"I don't blame you."

The umbrella lodged halfway up the fence on the east side of the park. The little dog hopped on its hind legs in a single-minded frenzy to pull it back to earth. By the time the old woman arrived, her hair was plastered to her head and the umbrella was history. The wind had torn the red fabric free, dropping the metal frame at the base of the fence. She grabbed the leash and nearly fell again as she dragged the dog back onto the pavement. In the deepening gloom, the red nylon waved like a signal flag.

Corso folded his arms across his chest and turned back toward the room. His face was grim and the look in his eyes suggested he might be capable of casual cruelty.

"If I do this . . . this will clear our slate," he said. "Once and for all."

She tapped her manicured fingertips together. "The column too?" she asked.

He thought it over. "Way I see it, the column works out for both of us. The syndication keeps you afloat and the press credentials get me into places I couldn't otherwise get into. I can't see any reason to change that. Unless you want to quit."

"Of course not."

"Well?"

"I suppose I deserve this," she said.

"You suppose correctly."

She fixed him with a steely gaze as she thought over his proposition. "All you have to say is no," she said.

"But we both know I won't, don't we?"

Annoyed now, she arched an eyebrow. "What we both know, Mr. Corso, is that above and beyond either our friendship or our mutual indebtedness"—she waggled a finger at him—"you harbor a certain quixotic spark. . . ."

Corso opened his mouth to protest, but she waved him off. "You say what you want," she said quickly. "It comes out in your columns, in your books. There's a messianic tendency at the very center of you, Mr. Corso. You know it and I know it. You write as if there's a single path to the truth, and you're the only one with a map." She shrugged. "Trust me. It doesn't go unnoticed. I read your hate mail."

"I've always inspired damn little ambivalence," Corso said.

"No doubt."

Corso smiled. "My mama used to say I had enough moral indignation for half a dozen preachers."

Beneath the words, she thought she heard the lazy trace of a drawl. She'd noticed it before. Sometimes when they talked late at night. When he was tired and his guard was down, you could almost hear another voice.

"Your mama had a point," she said.

She watched as his eyes turned inward. "I remember the first time anybody ever told me life wasn't fair," Corso said. "I was three or four . . . something like that. I was pissing and moaning about something not being fair and my aunt Jean leaned over the dinner table and told me how I might as well shut up and get used to the idea."

"And?"

He made eye contact. "I didn't believe it then and I don't believe it now," he said. "If I thought for a minute the world was that arbitrary. I'd go down to my boat and blow my brains out."

A sudden gust of wind rattled the windows. Corso heaved a sigh, cursing silently.

"And you want me to do what?" he asked.

She held up two fingers. "Two things. If Walter Himes didn't kill those young women, then I want to know who did."

"Good thing you don't want much."

"Second, while you're looking into this, I want you to write the stories."

"Hawes is right, you know. Getting between the people and their pound of flesh is going to generate a lot of heat, and having my name on the byline is gonna be like throwing gasoline on the fire."

"I'm aware of that," she said. "The situation, however, is desperate. We've reached the point where we at the *Sun* can no longer concern ourselves with what people may be saying about us as long as they're saying something."

"It's going to get ugly."

"I can handle the heat. Can you?"

"We're gonna find out, aren't we?"

She pulled a small leather-bound pad toward her.

"How much space are you going to need?"

"For the 'Leanne Samples Changes Her Story' story?"

"Yes."

"With a recap . . . probably sixteen hundred words."

"If we're upping the street run, I'm going to need it by nine."

"I'll have it ready," Corso assured her.

"Anything else?"

"Have somebody call Himes's attorney of record and ask if Himes will agree to see me. Tomorrow. As soon as possible."

"He hasn't spoken to the press in nearly two years. What makes you think he'll talk to you?"

"Have whoever calls tell the attorney about the story we're running tomorrow morning. Tell him who wrote it. Remind him of the 'rush to judgment' piece. Run my famous-author status by him. See if maybe that doesn't loosen things up."

"Excellent idea," Mrs. V. said. "As I recall, he wanted to see you rather badly way back when . . ." She let it hang.

"Ask if we can bring a photographer. Somebody other than Harry Dent," he said, naming the *Sun's* ancient photo editor whose outdated noir style of photography regularly made baby showers look lurid.

"Mr. Dent is the only photographer we have left on staff," she said. She read Corso's pained expression. "He had seniority."

"Who took the shots of the bus accident on Aurora a couple of weeks ago?"

"A freelancer," Mrs. V. said. "A woman named Dougherty, I believe."

Corso recalled the battered metro bus lying on its side. The anguished looks on the faces of the citizens who risked their lives to rescue passengers from the smoldering ruins. Pictures that seemed to jump off the page at the reader.

"Can you get her?"

"Miss Dougherty is . . . as I understand it . . . how shall I put this? I've been led to believe she's somewhat exotic and perhaps a bit . . . forward." She seemed pleased by her choice of words.

Corso chuckled. "We ought to make an interesting pair," he said.

"I'll see what I can do. Anything else?"

Corso gave it some thought. "That's it for right now," he said.

"And you?" Mrs. V. asked of Corso.

"I guess I'm headed downtown. See if I can't scratch up a denial." She looked at him as if he'd broken wind.

"At the *Sun*, we don't generally preview stories," she intoned.

"Neither do I," said Corso, "but, as much as I hate to agree with Hawes twice in the same day, I want to make sure our asses are covered on this one."

She thought it over. "As much as the precedent pains me,

you're no doubt right. After all, exclusives like this don't drop on one's doorstep every day."

"Nice touch, by the way, the room at the Carlisle. The watch-dog and all," Corso offered with a grin.

She looked offended. "It was my Christian duty. Could we, after all, have the young woman's group home inundated with the press?"

"As long as we have her to ourselves, we have the story to our-selves."

She gave Corso a wicked smile. "At best, we'll get a day out of the Carlisle," she said. "By this time tomorrow, the hounds will have found her."

"There's lots of hotels."

"My thinking exactly."

She got to her feet, stretched, and then checked her watch.

"You haven't done anything like this in a while."

"I remember how."

"Are you sure you have the stomach for it? It's going to be New York all over again. Whatever personal space you've cut out for yourself in the past couple of years is going to be gone."

"Did I miss the part where you left me a choice?"

She raised an eyebrow. "As you just so poignantly pointed out to me, Mr. Corso, choices come in all sizes and shapes."

"Yeah, but some of them are easier to live with than others."

She smiled that wicked smile again.

"Every form of refuge has its price, Mr. Corso."

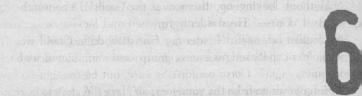

6

Monday, September 17
5:05 P.M.   Day 1 of 6

Corner of Fifth and James. The Public Safety Building is notched hard into the side of the hill, sentencing an entire city block to perpetual shade. Connected by a seventh-floor covered walkway to the King County jail, the complex is a remnant of an age when signs on the freeway implored the last person leaving town to please turn out the lights. A pair of ten-story poured-concrete monuments to fiscal restraint, they looked remarkably like waffles standing on end and were quite easily the ugliest buildings in the city's gleaming downtown core.

Two officers at the front desk. Blue shirts, sitting way up high in the power position. Typical city cops. If your aorta wasn't severed, they were going to finish what they were doing before they bothered with you. Corso reached up and dropped a business card faceup in front of the older of the two. When neither of them so much as glanced at the card, Corso asked, "Either of you remember the officers of record in the Trashman killings?"

Without looking up, the young cop said, "Densmore's the three. I don't—" He suddenly frowned and looked desperately toward his lap, as if the older cop had grabbed him by the balls. The older cop locked his eyes on Corso and said, "You mean back in ninety-eight?" Corso couldn't be sure, but he thought he saw some color drain from the younger man's face. "Yeah," said Corso.

"Chucky Donald was one of them. He's a lieutenant in the East Precinct. Him and whoever was his partner at the time. I think the guy pulled the pin a couple years back." Corso thanked him and wrote Donald's name in his notebook.

"Help you with something?" the older one asked. He now held Corso's card with his fingertips, as if it were radioactive.

"I need to see whoever's in charge of public affairs."

"Dorothy Sheridan," the older cop said. "She's in a meeting."

"Does she have an assistant?"

"Bunches," he said with a sneer. "They're all in the meeting."

Corso searched the cop's face for some indication as to whether the guy was busting his balls for fun. Officer John McCarty, according to the name tag, wasn't, however, offering any hints. When in doubt, keep talking, asking questions— anything to keep a dialogue going. "Do you have a direct number where I could reach Lieutenant Donald at the East Precinct?"

The cop shifted to his left and touched the keyboard. His pockmarked face was bathed in blue light. He pushed a couple of more buttons. "Three, two, nine, three, nine, four, five, extension eleven twenty-nine." The screen went black. For the first time, the younger officer was looking at Corso, who thought he detected a hint of amusement in the guy's eyes. "Was it something I said, fellas?" Corso asked. He pulled open his coat and sniffed at his right armpit. "Deodorant failure?"

Officer McCarty looked only slightly amused when he said, "Happens Lieutenant Donald's in the same meeting."

Corso smiled. He now knew the meeting must be here in the Public Safety Building, otherwise a couple of desk cops wouldn't be privy to it. He took a chance. "Wouldn't be that an ADA name of Timothy Beal is in there with them, would it?" He hunched his shoulders, spread his hands. "Just a guess."

The younger cop checked the screen in front of his face, tapped the keyboard twice, and then looked to McCarty, who leaned over in front of the younger man's video display.

"You read palms on the side?" the older cop asked.

"The bumps on your head," Corso said. "Phrenology."

The cop looked like he was considering adding a few bumps to Corso's head.

"I think you better let me see this Ms. Sheridan."

McCarty weighed his options. "I drag her out of a meeting and this turns out to be crap, there's going to be a problem."

"I understand."

McCarty finally read his way through Corso's card. "Hopkins covers crime for the *Sun*. Says here you write features."

"That's right."

"How long you been with the paper?"

"Three years or so."

"So how come I've never seen you before?"

"Just lucky, I guess," Corso joked. McCarty was not amused.

"Hopkins under the weather?" he asked.

"Not that I know of," Corso said.

McCarty waited for an explanation.

"I need to run a story by someone in authority. To give 'em a chance to confirm or deny." The cop wasn't impressed. "I'm guessing it's the same story they're sitting in there talking about," Corso added.

McCarty got to his feet. Took Corso in from head to toe. Pointed across the room to the built-in bench running along the north wall. "Take a seat over there."

McCarty disappeared through a door behind the desk. Corso planted himself on the blue Naugahyde. The sticky plastic groaned as he slid back. No magazines. No cigarette butts. Just an overgrown jade plant, its thick leaves covered with dust, meandering its way around the dirty window. Corso took his notebook from his coat pocket and had begun to leaf through it when the front doors were pulled open wide.

Deep voices filled the room. SWAT. The storm troopers of the status quo. A full tactical unit, fresh from an operation. Still coming down from the adrenaline rush. Eight jackbooted, armored urban warriors. All in black. Darth Vader helmets. Huge men. Three white, four black, one other. Olympic weight lifters with twenty-inch biceps carrying bulging equipment bags full of body armor. A four-foot steel battering ram swung from the arm of an immense black man who carried what appeared to be an M16 in his other hand. The noise of their walking toward the elevator drowned the rush of the wind and the wet hissing of tires. When the elevator came, only four could fit in the car. Four went. Four waited.

McCarty came out from behind the desk. Clipped a visitor's badge on Corso's collar. "Follow me," he said. Together they crossed to the elevator. The door slid open.

"Hold it, fellas," McCarty said. "Got a priority here."

The SWAT team stopped talking. Didn't move an inch. Made McCarty and Corso squeeze around them and into the elevator. They reminded Corso of those space droids you see on TV. The ones with the tubes coming out of the sides of their heads. Steroid suicide squads, protecting truth, justice, and the American way. Mercifully, the door slid shut. McCarty pushed the button for the eighth floor. "I don't know how the criminals feel about guys like that," Corso said, "but they scare the hell out of me."

"They're supposed to," McCarty said.

She was waiting just outside the elevator. She was pushing forty. Still winning the battle of the bulge. Short blond hair and a bad color sense. She wore a yellow-and-green-plaid sweater and a bright yellow skirt. The yellows didn't quite match and the gold glow lent her complexion a sallow, almost jaundiced tinge.

McCarty held the door open with his arm, handed her Corso's business card.

"And this is about what?" she asked.

"Leanne Samples," Corso said.

She raked her free hand through her hair, thought about running a "Leanne who?" number on Corso and then decided against it. She gestured with her fingers for Corso to get off the elevator. Corso stepped off. The door slid shut.

Corso held out his hand. "Frank Corso."

She made no move to shake. "So it says."

Corso put on a smile. "And your name is?"

Her facial expression said "worst-case scenario." She sighed.

"Dorothy Sheridan. What is it you need, Mr. Corso?"

He pulled out his notepad. "We're running a story in tomorrow morning's edition to the effect that Leanne Samples, who, if you'll recall, was the state's star witness in the Walter Leroy Himes case, that Miss Samples has told both the DA and the SPD that she lied three years ago when she testified that Mr. Himes had sexually assaulted her."

"And?"

"And we wanted to give the department the opportunity to comment on the story beforehand. Just as a professional courtesy."

"Anything that may or may not have been said between Miss

Samples and any member of the law-enforcement community would certainly be—"

"I've got her on tape," Corso said, "I've also got a deadline, so I don't have time to dance, Ms. Sheridan. Lead, follow, or get out of the way. Confirm, deny, or tell me 'no comment.' "

Her cheeks reddened. "Are you threatening me?"

"No, ma'am," Corso assured her. "If I were threatening you, my position would be that you either talk to me or I'll go to print. That would be unethical. This isn't like that. We're going to print with the story. That's a given. I'm merely providing the subjects of the story with an opportunity to comment prior to publication. In the interest of both accuracy and balanced reporting."

She folded her arms so tightly across her chest that her sweater rode up over the waistband of her skirt, revealing a patch of stark-white skin. "Weeeell . . . aren't you just Mr. Smooth. How is it that we haven't crossed swords before?"

"I'm a little out of my beat."

"Which is?"

"Features."

And then she got it. She looked down at the card in her hand and then back at Corso. Inhaled the smile. She knew who he was.

"Stay here," she said. "I'll be right back."

When she looked over her shoulder, Corso was leaning back against the wall. She turned to the right and started down the short hall, turned left at the end.

Corso listened to the clicking of her sensible heels until he thought he detected a change in the sound, then hustled over and peeked around the corner just in time to see the woman disappear down a hall to the left. He tiptoed up to the next corner. Peeked around. Watched as she walked to the center of the corridor, grabbed a door handle on the right side of the hall. The lettering on the door read CONFERENCE ROOM A. She disappeared inside.

Corso checked his watch. Waited a full minute. Started down the hall.

On the left, two rooms. Corso could hear voices. Speaking Spanish. He straightened his jacket and put on his best confident stride. First room held three copy machines. The second, vending machines. Two janitors, both Hispanic. One male, one female; according to the patches on their blue uniform shirts, Luis and Carlotta. Corso nodded as he walked past. They nodded back.

He stopped at the door to Conference Room A. The voices were muffled, the words unintelligible. Corso checked the hall in both directions. To the left, two more small rooms and then a dead end. To the right, he could hear Luis and Carlotta laughing.

Corso leaned his ear against the glass. A familiar voice said, "I don't give a rat's ass about Walter Leroy Himes. What I care about is that nothing we do compromises the ongoing investigation of these . . ."

Corso didn't catch the rest of it. Two uniformed cops turned the corner in front of him. The one on the right pointed at Corso and hollered, "Hey . . . you . . ."

Corso smiled at the cop, waved, and then grabbed the handle and stepped into Conference Room A.

7

The mayor stopped in mid-sentence when Dorothy Sheridan reentered the room. She looked around the table and sighed. A tough crowd. One of those crowds you didn't want to be telling anything they didn't want to hear, which was, of course, precisely what she did for a living. She told eager reporters that the SPD wouldn't be releasing information anytime soon. She told shocked survivors that the remains of their loved ones couldn't be released until the lab guys were finished. She peered straight-faced into banks of cameras and claimed the department was developing leads when she knew damn well they weren't. Still, this was a rough crowd. Messenger murderers all. Another sigh. "I've got a live one out there, folks. Guy named Corso from the *Sun*."

"Where's Hopkins?" Chief of Police Ben Kesey demanded. Kesey was fifty-three, with a great shock of white hair combed straight back. A master politician, given to wearing his dress blues as a way of maintaining contact with his officers in the streets, who whispered that he looked like a rear admiral and were so moved by his humility they'd given him a vote of no confidence at the last two union meetings.

"Looks to me like they've sent in the first team," Sheridan said. "This guy Corso is that famous reporter Natalie Van Der Hoven hired after he got canned from the *New York Times* for fabricating a story. He writes books these days."

"A reporter who writes fiction," the mayor mused. "How redundant."

Mayor Stanley Seifort had a scholarly look. Wide, expansive face and enough bare forehead to post bills on. Like his most recent predecessors in the mayor's office, Seifort was, other than possessing a zealous desire to make Seattle into Perfect City, USA, totally devoid of politics.

Sheridan continued to stand behind her chair. "With all due respect, Your Honor, please take my word for it, fact or fiction, credibility or no credibility, this guy is going to be a pain in the butt."

"Why's that?" Seifort asked.

"Because he's not housebroken. We could have asked Nathan Hopkins to hold off on the story and he would have kept it to himself for a day or two. Not this Corso character. He's the type who's never going to be paper-trained. I can tell."

"Why do we have to tell him anything?" Chief Kesey asked. "Tell him to get the hell out of the building."

Dorothy Sheridan worked to keep the impatience out of her voice. Although she was a civilian employee of the SPD, technically Kesey was still her boss. She pictured her daughter Brandy in her new braces. She'd had a migraine for a day and a half after finding out that eighty percent of the braces was going to come out of her own pocket. Had to lie on her bed with a cold rag pressed to her forehead, thinking positive thoughts, picturing her retirement, chanting "twelve down . . . eight to go." She chose her words carefully. "Because the *Sun* is going to press in the morning with Leanne Samples's new story. We have to tell him something. Either that or he prints that we had no comment."

"So . . . tell him no goddamn comment," the chief snapped.

"I'm not sure we want to do that," Dorothy said.

"Why in hell not?" the chief demanded. "Has it gotten to the point where we can't even issue a simple 'No comment'?"

Dorothy was still trying to compose a sentence that did not contain the words "Walter Leroy Himes" when the cute little ADA started waving his arm. Thank God.

Sitting at the center of the long table, Timothy Beal raised his hand like he was in grammar school. "May I say something?" he asked.

Sheridan thought, Go for it, mullet head.

When nobody objected, Beal spoke. "We've been talking about this for an hour and I haven't heard so much as a whisper of the name Walter Leroy Himes. The guy who's scheduled to die by lethal injection less than a week from now. Why is that?"

Sheridan watched as Chucky Donald, who sat directly across from the ADA, winced, as if to say, "Wrong question, dweebus. Bite your tongue." Donald was Kesey's boy. Said to be in line to make captain. Maybe the youngest in history.

Thirty-eight hundred bucks for braces. She'd called her rotten ex. Asked him to pony up some of the cash, reminded him that Brandy was, after all, his kid too. . . . But, you know, the demands of a new family, two kids under three . . . besides which, his paying for braces wasn't in the divorce contract— you're the one who wanted sole custody—he'd have to discuss it with Sheila and you know how Sheila feels about . . . what was a guy gonna do? You understand.

The chief leaned forward, looked down the table at the young ADA. "Listen, Mr. Beal, I don't give a rat's ass about Walter Leroy Himes. What I care about is maintaining the credibility of my department and making damn sure that a highly sensitive, ongoing investigation is not going to be compromised by—"

A shout from the hall broke his train of thought. The conference room door opened. A tall man with a black ponytail stepped into the room, closing the door before turning to the assembled multitude. He showed his perfect teeth and spoke. "Oh, excuse me. I was looking for the men's room," he said.

* * *

Bennett Hawes had his notepad out. "Gimme those names again."

Corso counted off on his fingers. "Hizhonor the mayor. Chief Kesey. Dorothy Sheridan and a couple of her assistants in public affairs. I don't know their names. ADA Beal, who's the one Leanne originally told her story to. A nasty cop named Densmore. Another cop named Donald. Charles Donald. A lieutenant from the East Precinct who just happens to be not only one of the arresting officers in the Himes case, but is also the officer to whom Himes supposedly confessed."

"Spelled like the duck?" Hawes asked.

"Yeah."

"Who else?"

"That bald guy who's always standing behind the mayor in photographs."

"Marvin Hale. He's the district attorney," Mrs. V. said.

"That it?" Hawes asked.

"That's all of them," Corso said.

"And you're sure that Miss Samples was the subject of the conversation?"

"Positive."

Hawes looked to Mrs. V. "We'll run the meeting and the refusal to comment as a sidebar to the Samples story."

"I like it," she said.

Hawes snapped his notebook shut. He almost smiled. "So what happened after you claimed you were looking for the john?"

* * *

Dorothy Sheridan gestured toward Corso. "The aforementioned Mr. Corso," she said. "Making the aforementioned pain in the butt of himself."

The mayor rubbed his chin and whispered over his shoulder to the district attorney. A skinny guy in a blue suit jumped to his feet, sending his chair sliding back into the wall. He glared at Dorothy Sheridan. "What the hell is he doing here?"

She stammered. "He . . . I told him to wait . . ."

"It's not her fault," Corso said quickly. "She told me to wait by the elevators. I have a very limited attention span."

Blue Suit blustered his way around the table until he was nose to nose with Corso. His skin was oily. His mean little eyes crawled over Corso like ants. "Turn around," he bellowed. Corso stood still. "You're under arrest for criminal trespass," he said. "Now turn around, you son of a bitch."

"Andy," Kesey said. "Lighten up."

"It's not trespass," Corso said. "I checked in downstairs." He flicked the plastic badge clipped on his collar. "See—I've got a handy-dandy badge."

The guy swung his hand, knocking the badge to the floor. Then poked Corso hard in the chest with his finger. "Didn't I tell you to turn around?" He poked Corso again. Harder. "Densmore," the chief said.

Corso kept his smile locked in place. "You poke me again, Andy, and you're gonna need to wipe your ass with your other hand," he said evenly.

Sharp intake of collective breath. Dead silence. Blue Suit fixed Corso with what he imagined to be his most baleful stare. Bobbed his narrow head up and down. Agreeing with himself. "I'll remember you—you son of a bitch. Don't you think I won't."

"It's always nice to be remembered," Corso said, still smiling.

Densmore balled one hand and used the other to grab Corso by the shirtfront.

"Andy," cautioned the district attorney.

Reluctantly, he let go of Corso's shirt and pointed to the guy in the gray suit. "Donald," he growled, "get him out of here. I swear to God . . . Get him out of here before I . . ." He started back around the table, toward his chair.

Gray Suit got to his feet. Corso pulled out his notebook. "Should I take this to be a no comment, Chief?" he asked. Densmore turned on his heel and started back for Corso.

"Andy," the district attorney said again. Louder this time. Dorothy Sheridan stepped between the cop and Corso. Her face was white. "Sergeant Densmore, please," she said. He stopped one pace short of Sheridan. Stood there rocking on the balls of his feet. Donald grabbed Corso by the arm.

"Get him the hell out of here," the chief shouted.

Corso let Donald steer him back out into the hall. "Come on," he said. "Let's go." He had a deep, resonant voice reminiscent of a TV anchorman's, and a first-class tan. Couldn't have been much more than thirty. Young for a lieutenant, with one of those youthful faces that linger well past middle age. Thick, Hugh Grant hair. Very trendy. Hawes would have killed for the suit. Italian. Silk. At least a grand and a half, maybe two. Corso checked his feet. Three hundred bucks' worth of Bally loafers. "Andy's a bit testy today," Corso commented.

"Lotta pressure," the cop said. "Move. Let's go."

"You were the arresting officer on the Himes bust," Corso tried.

"Come on," Donald said, herding Corso down the hall and back toward the elevator. Luis and Carlotta were still yukking it up by the Coke machine.

"It's a matter of public record," Corso said. "What's the big deal?"

Donald pushed the elevator button. "The big deal, Mr. Corso, is that you're messing with something you don't understand here."

"What's not to understand? The prime—the only—witness in the case against Walter Leroy Himes now says she lied. The guy's six days from execution. All I want to know is what you guys are going to do about it."

"She wasn't the only witness," Donald said a bit too quickly. Pushed the button again. Twice. Adjusted his tie. Pushed the button again.

"It was you, wasn't it?" Corso said. "You're the one who supposedly heard Himes confess." Donald didn't answer. Just stood and watched the lighted indicator work its way up to eight. The door slid open. Corso stepped in first. Donald followed. Pushed one. "All you people care about is selling newspapers," he said as the door closed. "You never think about the effects of what you print," he said as the door closed. "You never think about the effects of what you print, as long as you sell papers." Corso kept his mouth shut. He'd heard it a million times before. The truth was that as long as they got a check once a month, most reporters couldn't care less about circulation. Reporters don't write stories to sell papers, they write stories to get their name above the fold on the front page. If the paper has a fold, that is.

"What exactly did Himes say that day?" Corso asked. Donald snorted and shook his head. The elevator door opened. Donald walked him toward the front door. Over his shoulder, Corso caught a glimpse of the two desk cops. McCarty was beet red, whispering some very unsweet nothings in the younger man's ear. Banging his knuckles on the desk to emphasize his point. The young guy was ashen-faced and looked frozen in place. Corso tried to slow down, but it was too late, Donald pushed him out the door into the cold, slanting rain. Corso pulled his 'collar around his ears and looked back through the glass door. McCarty was still red and still talking, except now he was pointing at Corso.

* * *

"What about Himes? Will he see me?"

Bennett Hawes looked like he was passing a kidney stone. "Day after tomorrow. Wednesday. One o'clock," he said.

"A nice call, Mr. Corso," said Mrs. V. "I understand he's turned down everyone else in town."

"Can we bring a photographer?"

"Yeah," Hawes said. "I've got the freelancer you wanted." He crossed the room, punched a button on Mrs. V.'s phone. "Send Miss Dougherty upstairs." He turned back to Corso. "Her name is Meg Dougherty." He said it like he was expecting Corso to recognize the name. "The tattoo girl," he growled. "You remember— couple years back—girl wakes up and finds herself tattooed from head to foot."

Corso remembered the story well. She'd been a successful young photo artist. Already had had a couple of very hot local shows and was beginning to attract national attention. Dating a trendy Seattle tattoo artist. Guy who kinda looked like Billy Idol. You'd see them all the time in the alternative press. Unfortunately, while she's developing photos, he's developing a cocaine habit. She tells him she wants to break it off. He seems to take it well. They agree to have a farewell dinner together. She drinks half a glass of wine and—bam—the lights go out. She wakes up thirty-six hours later in Providence Hospital. In shock. Nearly without vital signs. Tattooed from head to toe with what was rumored to be some pretty weird stuff. A Maori swirl design on her face. The boyfriend nowhere to be found. "They ever find the asshole who did it?" Corso asked.

"Not that I heard," Hawes said.

They stood silently for a moment, as if mourning something lost. Mrs. V. broke the spell. "You'll need to start early, Mr. Corso," she said. "The budget won't manage airplanes for something like this."

"How far is it?" Corso asked.

"Two hundred forty miles," Hawes said.

Mrs. V. said, "I've reserved you a company car."

All heads turned toward the knock at the office door. Hawes started across the office. Didn't get halfway there before she pulled open the door and stepped inside. Twenty-five or so. Six feet with an inch to spare. Pure Seattle Gothic. Black everything. Spider-lady dress down to her ankles and wrists. Doc Martens with soles as thick as bricks. Hair, eyebrows, lipstick. Everything black. She was heavy but nicely shaped. Rubenesque. Full-figured. Whatever you wanted to call it. The facial tattoos Corso remembered from the news photos were either gone or covered up.

Mrs. V. wandered out from behind her desk. Hawes introduced the women to each other first, then turned to Corso. "Frank, this is Meg Dougherty."

She crossed to him. "You write great stuff," she said. "Should be fun working with you."

Up close, the skin on her face had a plastic quality. Shiny and brittle, looking like it had recently been sanded. What Corso had taken to be jewelry was, instead, tattoos. A black barbed-wire bracelet on one wrist and a gold-link bracelet tattooed on the other.

"We're going to drive," Corso said. "So we'll need to leave around seven. It's probably four hours or so each way. That work for you?"

She said it did. "What kinds of shots are we looking at?" she asked.

"A little of everything," Corso said.

"Interiors?"

"Lots of dull metal and dirty linoleum. Overhead fluorescent lights. You'll probably be shooting Himes through two inches of wire-mesh Plexiglas, so you'll want to bring whatever you've got to reduce the glare." She nodded. Corso went on. "Remember that whatever equipment you bring is probably going to get taken apart. Maybe more than once. Maybe even X-rayed. The people I've worked with before don't load the cameras until they're past security."

"Thanks for the tip," she said, "I'd have shown up loaded for bear and wasted forty bucks' worth of film."

"Seven on Wednesday, then," Corso said.

She offered thanks and good-byes all around and was nearly back to the door when Hawes said, "Blaine Newton will be going with you guys."

Unsure whether the remark had been directed at her, Meg Dougherty stopped and turned around. "Excuse me?"

Corso cursed himself. He should have seen it coming. Hawes had his Leanne Samples exclusive. He was willing to take his chances on the rest of it. Clever little bastard knew exactly what Corso would say to the idea of working with Newton. Not only that, but he gets two for the price of one. Gets Corso to renege on his promise to Mrs. V. and then gets to spoon-feed a national story to his personal-reporter project.

"I'm not working with Newton," Corso said.

"You're working with whoever I say you're working with," Hawes said.

"There's a great deal of background work to be done here, Mr. Corso," Mrs. Van Der Hoven said. "Not to mention the day-to-day follow-up. If you're going to be lead man on the story, you're certainly going to require some help."

"No question about it," Corso said. "I'm definitely gonna need some help. But not Blaine Newton. Anybody but Newton."

Hawes's scalp was beginning to glow. "Hey . . . ," he said. "You're not making personnel decisions around here, Corso, I am. You don't like my decisions, feel free to take it up the road. But don't stand here and tell me how to do my job."

Mrs. V. jumped in. "Mr. Hawes believes that Mr. Newton will profit from the experience. That he can learn the rudiments of investigation at your knee . . . so to speak."

Corso kept his gaze on Hawes. Wishing like hell he hadn't let himself get backed into a corner like this but too pissed to keep his mouth shut.

"I'm not working with Newton," Corso said again.

The red glow had worked its way down Hawes's ears. He was smiling like a piranha. Before Corso could open his mouth, another, calmer voice said, "I could do it." Meg Dougherty from the doorway.

"What?" Hawes growled.

"I said, I could help out with the background and follow-up. Right after I got out of college, I did that kind of thing for Barton and Browne," she said, naming the city's largest law firm.

Dead silence.

"Works for me," Corso said in a hurry.

"That's not the goddamn point," Hawes snapped. "We're not

talking about what works for you, Corso; we're talking about who and what works for me."

Hawes stood glaring at Corso. Weighing the value of a personal victory versus the magnitude of the story. Tough call. Super Bowls, both.

"What'll it be, Mr. Hawes?" Mrs. V. asked. She checked her watch. "As I see it, we have very little moral or ethical latitude here. We've got something like a hundred hours to do everything we can to see to it that a miscarriage of justice does not take place under our very noses." She folded her arms across her chest. "The decision is yours, Mr. Hawes. But I think you would have to agree that if indeed Mr. Corso has been correct all along and something is rotten here, our chances of getting to the bottom of the matter in the meager time left to us are considerably better with Mr. Corso's help than without."

She was slick. Made it easy for him. He made a resigned face and forced a strangled "Okay" from between his lips.

No eat?" the waitress asked.

"Just coffee," Corso said. He wrinkled an eyebrow at Meg Dougherty.

"Two," she added.

The waitress scowled at the pair, stuffed the order pad into her apron, and walked away muttering beneath her breath.

The dim overhead light cast a feeble yellow circle over the center of the table, leaving the rest of the booth bathed in shadows. She thought Corso might have smiled.

"Thanks for bailing me out upstairs," he said.

She waved the notion away. "Just saving my own gig, Corso. I don't do lifeguard work. Believe me, I need the money."

The fall of his hair was silhouetted by the windows. Of his face, only the thick black eyebrows were visible in the gloom.

"You were going to push it, weren't you?" she asked.

"I've got a bad temper," he said. "Gets me in trouble some-times."

"He was going to fire your ass."

"No," Corso said. "He can't fire me. He wanted me to quit."

"What's the difference?"

"It's a long story."

"I've got time."

"Hawes and I have quite a history," Corso explained. "You walked in on the culmination of something that's been going on for years. It all just sort of came to a head today."

Outside, daylight was losing ground to the elements. Cars on Elliott Avenue had their headlights on at three-fifteen in the afternoon. A ground fog, brown with exhaust fumes, stretched upward, reaching to join the thick gray clouds hovering above.

"You asked for me by name?"

"What makes you say that?"

"Mr. Hawes wouldn't have called me if you hadn't."

"I saw those shots of the bus accident," Corso said. "Good stuff." The waitress reappeared. Slid two steaming white mugs across the table.

"You sure? No eat?"

Corso said they were sure, sending her muttering back into the kitchen, where she began practicing for the national pot-banging finals.

"What do you do other than string for the *Sun*?"

"Anything I can," she answered. "Do quite a bit of work for the *Post Intelligencer* and the *Times*. The alternative rags, when they've got money to spend. I'm working on a photo essay of the club scene for the local PBS affiliate. In my spare time, I'm trying to get somebody interested in helping me put together a new show."

"You said you worked for Barton and Browne?"

"I started out taking accident pictures. Cracks in sidewalks.

Faulty steps. That kind of thing. After a while, they started letting me do witness interviews and victim depositions. Right before I left, I was doing background checks on prospective clients."

He had an interesting way of mirroring her actions. Every time she leaned forward into the light, he receded farther into the shadows. If she sat back, he moved forward, as if, for some reason, he needed to maintain a specific distance between them.

"What about you?"

"What about me?" he asked.

"What's all this big mystery thing surrounding you?"

"There's no mystery thing," he said.

"Come on," she countered. "I asked around the newsroom. You're some kind of famous true-crime writer these days. They say you just about killed a reporter who snuck up on you one time. Put him in the hospital for months."

"He was stealing from me," Corso said.

"Stealing what?"

"My privacy."

She searched his eyes for irony. Didn't find it. "They say you haven't been in the building for years. Nobody knows anything about you." She hesitated for a moment. Corso read her mind.

"Except for the libel suit," he said with a sneer.

"That just makes it all the more mysterious," she said. She held a finger to her dark lips. "Famous disgraced reporter turned writer. Syndicated in a couple of hundred papers but works for the lowly *Seattle Sun*. Not part of the regular staff. You're supposed to be like this real dangerous dude who works directly for the owner."

"See . . . people know things about me."

"Phooey," she said. "They say that even back before the books you worked all by yourself. Nobody knew what you were working on. All really hush-hush like."

"I'm very shy."

She laughed out loud at him and, for the first time, felt him tighten up.

"You're not going to be like this all the time, are you?" he asked.

"Like what?"

"Like"—he searched for a neutral word—"inquisitive," he said finally.

"And pushy," she added.

"You said that, I didn't," Corso protested.

"It's what you meant, though, wasn't it?"

"I'm renowned for being able to say exactly what I mean," Corso said.

She cast an annoyed gaze his way, and quickly changed the subject.

"I cried when I read that piece of yours on the housing-project shootings."

She could still see the room, as Corso had described it. The rotting plaster and the peeling paint and the young mother, blank behind her eyes, telling him the story of how her little girl had been killed one morning by a stray bullet as she left for school. Of the surprised look on the little girl's face at the moment of impact and of how her red plastic pencil box had fallen to pieces on the cement steps. And the bumps and the shrill cries of the other children as they ran madly through the apartment, because she no longer allowed them to play outside in the battle zone her project courtyard had become.

Instead of responding, Corso leaned back into the deep shadows and closed his eyes.

"You remember Leanne Samples?" he asked after a moment.

"From the TV this week?"

He told her the story of his day.

"No shit," she said when he finished.

"No shit."

"What do you need me to do?"

"I take it you probably know your way around the courthouse."

"It's been a while, but I remember how."

"Okay then, spend tomorrow down there. I want to take a fresh look at everybody involved with Himes's trial. The judge, the prosecutor, the defense. All of it."

She extricated a spiral-bound notebook from her bag. She wiggled a green golf pencil out from among the coils of wire.

"The judge was a guy named Sheldon Spearbeck." Corso spelled it. "He's still around. I see him on the tube once in a while."

"What do you want to know?" she asked.

"First off," Corso said, "find out about his work habits. Some judges come early and stay late. Others waltz in at noon and are on the golf course every day by two. I want to know where this guy falls on the continuum. I want to know what his caseload was like at the time of the trial."

"I'll look up the dates of the trial and then check the docket. Then see what kind of case backlog he's got now."

"I want to know how often his decisions are overturned by appellate courts and what the normal rate of overturn is."

"I'll look him up in *Legal Times*," she said.

She wrote for a while and then looked up.

"I want to know how many contempt citations he issues against lawyers and how that number compares with other judges' citations." More hurried scribbling.

"I want to know about his financial status."

"I'll call the election commission," she said without looking up, "have them fax me a copy of his financial statement; then I'll call the Washington State Bar Association and see if any complaints have been filed against him. If so, I'll get copies."

Finally, she looked up. He'd make a lousy poker player, she

thought. Wore everything right there on his face. Like right now. He was impressed with what she knew about legal research but just couldn't bring himself to say so.

"What else?" she asked in her best bored voice.

"New page," Corso said. "The prosecutor. I don't remember his name."

"Shouldn't be hard to find," she said.

"I want to know where he ranked in his law school class. I want to know about whatever lawyer jobs he may have had prior to public service. Check his caseload at the time of the trial. Check his caseload now. Find out how many of his cases go to trial and how many are plea-bargained and how those figures square with the norm."

"I'll look at the recent docket. See which defense attorneys have jousted with him lately. Maybe call a few. See what they have to say about him."

"Good idea," Corso said.

She crossed her legs, rested the pad on her knee. She had a cramp in her writing hand but wasn't about to shake it out in front of Corso.

"What about the defense attorney?" she asked.

"Where is he now? How much trial experience did he have at the time? How many capital cases? What was his won-loss record at the time? What was his caseload? We're looking to see if he had the time to be thorough." Corso thought for a second. "And get a copy of his bill to the county. Let's see what that looks like."

She leafed back a couple of pages and read the list back to Corso.

"That it?"

"If you have time, see what you can find out about a police lieutenant named Charles Donald. East Precinct. He was one of Himes's arresting officers and the guy Himes supposedly confessed to. Find out who his partner was at the time of the arrest and where he is now."

"What do you want on Donald?"

Corso thought it over. "When I saw Lieutenant Donald earlier today, he was wearing a couple of thousand dollars' worth of duds, which says to me that either he spends his entire salary on his wardrobe and sleeps in the trunk of his car, or that he has some outside source of income."

"Anything else?" she asked.

"Not that I can think of," Corso said.

She leafed back through her notes. "This is going to take more than one day."

"Take your time. I'll do what I can to see to it you get paid a living wage."

She got to her feet. Something about Corso's manner gave her the urge to make damn sure he wasn't sitting around on his ass while she was out working.

"What are you going to be doing while I'm tearing the courthouse down?"

"I've got to have the Leanne Samples story ready by nine. And then first thing tomorrow morning, I've got an idea about how I might be able to dig us up a story for Wednesday. Which I'm then gonna have to write."

"If I need help or have questions?"

He wrote a telephone number on the back of a business card. Gave it to her.

"I could get a pretty penny for this from one of the tabloids," she joked.

"We are one of the tabloids," he said.

Tuesday, September 18
10:25 A.M. Day 2 of 6

Special Agent Edward Lewis pushed the earlybird edition of the *Seattle Sun* across the scarred face of the table. The headline screamed "I LIED." Leanne Samples's story covered pages one through three and then jumped to page thirteen for the finish and the sidebar. The street edition had completely sold out by 9:30 A.M.

"Is this your work?" Lewis asked. He had a way of looking at you over his glasses that seemed to ask you to consider your answers carefully.

They sat together in an interrogation room on the eleventh floor of the Henry M. Jackson Federal Building. The room was a low-ceilinged, lime-green rectangle that smelled of piss and desperation. The table was bolted to the floor. Behind Agent Lewis, the obligatory mirrored wall loomed like a tunnel. They'd been trading snappy repartee for twenty minutes.

"Sure is," Corso said.

"You must be feeling pretty good about yourself."

Corso shook his head. "Way I see it, there's no 'feel good' in this one. Just a lot of prolonged pain for a lot of innocent people."

"That's what you journalists do, isn't it?" Lewis said.

"What's that?"

"Muck around in other people's tragedies."

Corso ignored the barb. "I had a professor once who said that journalists are charged with writing the first draft of history. After that, he claimed, the job fell to editors and historians."

Lewis shrugged. "So then I'm sure you'll understand why the Bureau is going to maintain its distance here."

"Why's that?"

"We'd prefer to wait for the final edition."

"Walter Leroy Himes doesn't have that option."

"You'll excuse me if I seem callous, Mr. Corso, but I just can't work up a great deal of remorse over the idea that Mr. Walter Leroy Himes will soon no longer be among the living."

"Who can?" Corso said quickly. "Walter Himes is a big, fat, ugly, child-molesting chunk of dog meat who's probably committed a barrelful of unchronicled crimes, and who's spent the past three years belittling the victims and taunting the survivors." Corso hesitated, held up a hand. "None of which, however, makes him a mass murderer or a candidate for a lethal injection," he finished.

Lewis curled his lips slightly. "Your capacity for compassion is noteworthy, Mr. Corso. You sound a bit like a man of the cloth. Have you ever thought that perhaps you missed your calling?"

"What I think, Agent Lewis, is that tomorrow morning I'm going to print with a story that says that back in ninety-eight the FBI developed a profile of the Trashman murderer and that Walter Leroy Himes wasn't anywhere near a match."

Lewis took a sip of his coffee, then picked up his spoon and began to stir the mixture. He smiled. "You know, Mr. Corso, with your unfortunate past history, I'd be extra careful about what I put into print." Lewis began to read: "January ninety-eight, fired by the *New York Times* for fabricating an investigative story. Subject of the article sues the paper for ten mil . . . eventually settles for three and change. A month later you end up at the *Seattle Sun*. In April of that same year, you're attacked outside your Capital Hill apartment. Coupla guys who took issue with your sympathy for Walter Himes. Left you with a skull fracture, a broken nose, fractured collarbone, five broken fingers, and a severe concussion." Lewis looked up, as if expecting rebuttal from Corso. Corso checked his cuticles.

"Then July ninety-eight." Lewis flipped a page. "You're no longer in the direct employ of the *Sun*. Indicted for first-degree assault."

"Acquitted."

"August . . . same summer. Charged with destruction of property—a fifty-six-hundred-dollar camera and simple assault on the cameraman."

"Acquitted again."

"June ninety-nine—assault with a dangerous weapon. Namely, a boat."

"Some folks think boats have brakes."

"Judge thought you didn't make much of an effort to avoid. He fined you thirty-five hundred dollars and put you on three years' probation."

Lewis removed his glasses, set them on the papers, and massaged the bridge of his nose. "If you'll permit me a professional courtesy, Mr. Corso. If I were you, I think I'd maintain a considerably lower profile. Seems to me that with your recent past and known associates, you're about fresh out of judicial understanding."

"Which known associates would those be?"

Lewis retrieved his glasses. Turned a page. "You're denying your association with Anitole Kashlikov?"

"I know Mr. Kashlikov."

"In what capacity?"

"I hired Mr. Kashlikov as a security consultant."

"To protect you?"

"To teach me how to protect myself."

Lewis fanned the pages.

"Seems he did his job rather well."

"He came highly recommended."

"Perhaps it would surprise you to know that Mr. Kashlikov is a former KGB operative."

"So he said."

"Did he also say that he was personally responsible for what some members of our intelligence community believe to be nearly a hundred killings?"

"He must have skipped that part."

Before the agent could continue, Corso said, "Agent Lewis, much as I appreciate the little rap-sheet retrospective, as *my* professional courtesy, I'm offering you and the Bureau this opportunity to comment on the story before it appears. If you'd prefer not to . . ." Corso spread his hands.

Lewis pointed the spoon at him. "As much as I'm touched by your consideration, Mr. Corso, I'm afraid I must admit to a bit of personal annoyance."

Corso tried to look surprised. "Oh?"

"I mean, it's not every day that a felon comes waltzing into my office and starts throwing around veiled threats."

Corso pulled his notepad from his back pocket. "Can I quote you on that?" he asked. "We do like to provide balanced coverage."

The two men maintained eye contact for a long moment. Lewis blinked first.

"The Bureau was involved in the Himes case in a purely con-sultational and tangential manner." He said it like that was sup-posed to be the end of it.

"You had two Quantico profilers in town for a month," Corso said. "They must have been doing something other than sampling the salmon."

"Profiling is still a new science," Lewis said. "At best, we can help to narrow down a list of suspects. All we are able to do is to describe the general type of individual we believe most likely to have committed the crime, based on the information we've been given by local law-enforcement authorities." He waved the spoon. "Sometimes the magic works; sometimes it doesn't."

Corso got to his feet. Played his hole card. Hoping like hell that old habits did indeed die hard. "Thanks for your time, Agent Lewis. I appreciate your seeing me on such short notice. I thought maybe you'd prefer being part of the story rather than being forced to recite the company line every day until it becomes untenable." He slapped the side of his head with his palm. "Can't imagine what I was thinking." He started for the door. Got all the way across the room, grabbed the handle.

"You're one arrogant prick, you know that, Corso?" Lewis said.

It took all of Corso's resolve not to grin. As much as the Fed-eral Bureau of Investigation loved to hog the limelight, they hated any hint of blame even more. Latent J. Edgar Hooverism: Rule one: *When you secretly wear a tutu, there's no such thing as paranoia.*

Corso threw his final card. " 'Cause you know, Agent Lewis, when the Bureau has to come back later on and admit their ear-lier denials were a crock of shit, it'll be your ass up there in front of the microphones explaining away the fertilizer."

Lewis started to speak. Corso raised his voice. ". . . and then it's gonna be your ass transferred to some godforsaken outpost where you won't be holding any further press conferences. That's how they work. You know the drill better than I do."

Lewis's jaw was set. Corso forced himself to stand still and shut up.

"I'll have to make some calls," Lewis said finally.

"I'm not waiting in here," Corso said.

The agent's lips curled in a thin smile. "You don't like the decor?"

"The boogers on the walls are a nice touch," Corso said.

"We strive for authenticity."

* * *

"No attribution. *An unnamed source* . . . That's all."

"Agreed."

"For the time being, the Bureau is neither going to confirm nor deny."

"Understood."

"And"—he waved two fingers at Corso—"should we deem it necessary, you will publicly acknowledge that the Bureau has cooperated from the very outset of your investigation."

"Done."

Lewis opened a red spiral-bound case file. "What do you know about profiling?"

"I covered the Wayne Williams trial in Atlanta," Corso said. 1981. His first big story for the *Atlanta Constitution*. The FBI's first big profiling victory. Conventional wisdom insisted the murder of so many black children surely must be a crime with overt racial overtones, perhaps even intended as the prelude to a race war. Despite heavy criticism, the Bureau's newly appointed behavioral specialists steadfastly insisted the perp would turn out to be a soft-spoken black man, who, in all likelihood, lived at home with his parents and who would at some point in the investigation likely offer his services to the investigating officers.

About the time Wayne Williams walked up and offered to act as a crime-scene photographer, profiling took a major leap forward. Corso could still see the soft mama's boy with the "I wouldn't hurt a fly" face. And still smell the brown, roiling waters of the Chattahoochee River where Williams threw nearly thirty children after he'd finished mutilating and sexually abusing them.

"Then you know the basics. What we're talking about here is educated guesswork and extensive crime-scene analysis." Lewis leafed to the back of the document. "We postulated a white male between twenty-five and thirty-five." Lewis looked up. So far so good: Himes had been thirty-four at the time of his arrest.

"Employed in some menial capacity," Lewis continued.

"Why employed?" Corso asked. Himes had been long-term homeless, with virtually no work history at all.

Lewis flattened the report with his palm and turned the page toward Corso. A greater Seattle map with bright green dots marking the crime scenes.

"The distance between the crime scenes. Seven miles, north to south. Too far to walk. Had to have a car. A van, we figured."

"Why a van?"

Lewis took off his glasses and massaged the bridge of his nose. "Because of the way he took his time with the victims. He had to have someplace secure where he could have his way with them at his leisure."

"Leisure?"

"That was one of the holdbacks," Lewis said. Holdbacks are significant pieces of signature evidence that investigators "hold back" from the media. Sometimes as a means of weeding out copycat killers and false confessors. Sometimes merely to spare the survivors particularly gruesome details. Lewis went on. "The killer took his time with them. Strangled them some, then sexually assaulted them, then strangled them some more. Then another assault. Got longer and longer as the spree went on.

There's evidence to suggest he kept the last three alive overnight." Lewis read Corso's mind. "Ligature shows up as hemorrhages on the victims' eyeballs. The more hemorrhages, the more repetitions of ligature."

Corso felt his breakfast shift. "So he had a car, probably a van. Which means he probably had a driver's license and on some level was getting by in society."

"Most likely," Lewis agreed.

Didn't sound a bit like Walter Leroy. "Why a menial job?" Corso asked.

"Experience suggests that most often this kind of suspect lacks normal interpersonal skills. Probably has a spotty employment history. Has trouble getting along with other people. Has problems with authority. He's usually the guy who eats lunch by himself because he'd rather be alone."

"What else?"

"Probably lives in a dependent relationship with someone from whom he derives monetary support. Most likely a woman. A sister . . . a mother. Probably not a wife. A conflict with the female is most likely what triggered the first murder." Lewis looked up at Corso. "Which, unfortunately, we were not onboard for. They didn't call us in until the third girl was found. That made things a lot harder."

"Why's that?"

"Because abducting women from public places is so high-risk, we would assume that the perp knew the early crime scenes well. Violent offenders usually start off in places where they feel most comfortable and at home. That's why the first crime in a series is so important. Back in eighty-nine, the Quantico boys turned a guy in Alabama who'd killed four women. Found a couple of neighborhood hookers who told them about a customer who couldn't get his rocks off unless they played dead. Bingo."

"Remind me—where was the first body found?"

Lewis rifled through the report. "Susanne Tovar. Twenty-two. Found in a Dumpster behind Julia's Bakery on Eastlake Avenue. January seventh, nineteen ninety-eight." He turned back to the first page. "We didn't come onboard until the twenty-ninth of the month."

"So they missed their best chance."

"Don't get me wrong, we worked the area like a big dog. It stood to reason that he might have been a neighborhood problem for years. Burglaries . . . assaults . . . maybe fires. Killers don't go from shoplifting to serial murders. They generally work their way up to it with a series of increasingly violent crimes, until some stressor in their lives finally pushes them over the top. After that, they're like junkies. It takes more and more to get them off."

"So you would expect the suspect to have a record that reflected a history of escalating violence? Not a kiddie pervert like Himes."

"Exactly," Lewis said. "Crimes against kids exhibit a completely different psychology than crimes against adults."

Walter Leroy Himes had neither a history of violence nor of sex crimes involving other adults. "So," Corso began, "what we would expect to see is a single white man between the ages of twenty-five and thirty-five. A loner, working at some menial job. Nominally, at least, getting along in society. Capable of getting from point A to point B on his own. Probably drives a van of some sort. Most likely lives with his mother or sister. History of increasingly violent acts against adults. Did I leave anything out?"

"A possible religious element."

"Oh?"

"The team felt that the Dumpster angle might have had symbolic overtones. The perp went to a lot of trouble in the way the girls were arranged. In several cases, he rearranged the contents of the Dumpsters so he could lay the girls out the way he wanted.

As if he were trying to say something. They had the feeling that the ceremonial nature of the arrangement was his way of justifying his actions. Almost as if by placing his victims just so, the perp was saying that he had a right to do what he was doing."

"That's pretty goddamn crazy," Corso said.

"A lot crazier than Himes has ever been."

"And you shared all this with the Seattle Police Department?"

Lewis leafed back to the front of the report. "SPD received the report on April fifth, nineteen ninety-eight. Three weeks after the arrest. Two months before trial."

Corso flipped through his notes. "A while back you said that the way the Trashman dallied with his victims was 'one of the holdbacks.' Were there others?"

Lewis nodded but didn't speak. "The tags," he said after a moment. Corso waited. "Ovine ear tags," Lewis said. "In the left ear of each victim."

"Ovine?"

"Sheep," Lewis said. "Postmortem, he punched a hole in the earlobe and tagged each of them like livestock. Drew a heart on the tag with Magic Marker." Lewis slid over a glossy photograph from the report. Mercifully, it was an extreme close-up. Dark hair obscuring the eye. The nape of a thin neck dotted by bits of eggshell. A white plastic band, doubled and connected to the left ear by a rivet.

Crooked little heart drawn on the white plastic.

Corso raised his eyes to meet Lewis's. The agent shrugged. Retrieved the photo. Closed the report. Got to his feet. He started for the door.

"Off the record," Corso said to his back.

Lewis stopped and turned. "Yes?"

"Just between you and me and the wall. You think SPD got the right guy? You think Himes is the Trashman?"

"No way," Lewis said. "I didn't think so then, and I don't think so now."

"The killings stopped."

"Most likely he's in jail for something else. Maybe he moved. Maybe he died." His lips formed a crooked smile. "Look on the bright side, Corso. You've got a whole four days to figure it out."

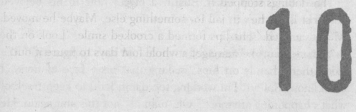

Robert." That voice from downstairs. Sounded like a machine needed oil. He was glad for the sound of the damn radio. Even some lame-ass Doobie Brothers shit about Jesus bein' all right was better than the voice.

"Robert" again. He rolled over and faced the wall. And what the hell was with the Robert shit anyway? How many times he have to tell her? Nobody but her call him Robert. Name be Fury. You ask anybody. They'll tell you that man Fury is a taggin' fool. Look around, man. Fury's name is everywhere.

"Robert." Oh crap, she was coming up the stairs. Maybe she'd forget about the missing tread. Serve her right to bust her ass. He heard her grunt as she stepped over the hole. Shit! He rolled over, swung his legs upward, and put his feet on the floor. Rubbed his eyes with his knuckles. Eyeballs felt like they were full of sand. He cracked his eyes open, glanced at the digital clock on his nightstand: 11:25. On her way to work. Get through the next five minutes and her sorry ass be gone till late.

The door banged open. Bustin' a bigger hole in his beloved Tony Hawk poster.

"Let's go," she said.

"Hey . . . hey," he managed to croak. "What's happening?" She stood there, hands on hips, making that pissy face of hers. "I doan know, Robert. I'm working too damn hard to keep track of what's happening anymore." Oh, man . . . not this shit again. He bent his head and began picking the lint from between his toes. "I'll tell you one thing, though, whatever is happening, happened about three hours ago. Ain't nothing much going to happen, you doan get yourself out of bed in the morning, boy." He tried not to groan. Jesus, ain't got no respect for me at all.

"So where you lookin' for a job today?"

He checked the window. More rain. Can't look for work in the rain.

"Doan gimme that look!" she hollered.

"I din' say nothin'."

"What kind of look is that? Getting a job is what folks do when they ain't going to school no more. No cause to be lookin' at me like that. I'm not the one got myself expelled from Garfield High School. So now you get your butt out there and find yourself a job. You think I'm spending the rest of my life supportin' yourself, you gotta nother think comin'. You hear me, young man? Anotha think comin'."

"I been lookin'," he protested.

"Maybe do something profitable wid your time, insteada hangin' out wid losers like that Tommy Hutton and that other one wid the thing in his tongue, wid them damn spray cans of you-alls, vandalizin' other people's walls and everything."

"I'm lookin', Mom," he said. He unwound himself from the

covers and got to his feet, stretched his arms over his head hoping his morning hard-on would drive her out of the room.

"Gonna be late tonight. You be here when I get home. You hear me?"

He wanted to tell her to page him. Call whenever she got through screwin' that fat Korean grocer she work for. Instead, said, "Yeah . . . sure."

She gave him another long dose of the pissy look and said, "This here is serious shit. Robert. Ain't about no job pushin' burgers . . . the question is about what in hell you gonna do wid the rest of your life. And believe me, baby, you listen to your momma here—the rest of your life is a hell of a long time."

No, Robert thought, the question is . . . where in hell am I gonna get eighteen bucks for paint? This kinda shitty weather, nothin' but the best will stick. Cheap shit just roll down, make a puddle on the ground.

She turned and left the room. Left the damn door open. No respect at all.

11

S he brought the morning paper. Dropped it on the seat between them. "FBI—No Way!" A cup of Starbucks coffee steamed softly between her hands.

"Morning," she said. Her eyes were puffy around the edges, and a faint pillow mark dented her right cheek. "You want to hear what I got yesterday?"

"Too early," Corso growled. "You'd just have to tell me again."

"Good," she said, sipping the coffee, rolling the cup in her hands. She snuggled the cup against her chest, pointed at the paper. "Quarter to seven in the morning and that was the last paper left in the machine," she said.

"Hawes said the plant's got orders to keep printing today's street edition until somebody tells them to stop," Corso said. "CNN was quoting us this morning."

She leaned her head against the window and closed her eyes.

"You want to drive?" he asked, hoping like hell she didn't.

"No" was the last word she said until Corso stopped for gas on the outskirts of Yakima, two hours later. He was pumping gas when she buzzed the window down and poured out the leftover coffee. "Where are we?" She yawned. Corso told her.

"Halfway?" she growled as she stretched in the seat.

"More or less."

She headed for the ladies' room while Corso pumped gas. She was standing by the passenger door when Corso emerged from the station. Her breath rose in front of her face.

"Cold over here."

"At least it's not raining."

Overhead, a mouse-gray sky moved at warp speed. Sliding east as a single sheet of slate, rolling toward the horizon and the upper Midwest beyond.

"Really different from Seattle."

Two totally different ecosystems. West of the Cascades, along the I-5 corridor, was what most people thought of as the Pacific Northwest. The evergreen rain belt running the length of Oregon, Washington, and British Columbia. Puget Sound, Vancouver Island, rain forests, rocky coasts, software geeks, and the omnipresent latte stands. East of the Cascades was another world. High desert. Scrub pine and manzanita. Creosote bushes and delicate wildflowers. Hot as hell in the summer, cold as hell in the winter. Grapes, fruit trees, pickers, and cowboys.

"You ever been this side of the mountains before?"

"First time," she said.

She watched with amusement as Corso closed his eyes and stretched his back one last time. Held his arms out horizontally and did some twists, then got back in the car. She followed suit. Buckled up. Looked over at Corso. Shook her head. "You're a weird dude, you know that, Corso?"

He started the car. Sort of smiled, but didn't answer, so she

dropped her voice an octave and did a bad Corso impression.
" 'Why do you say that?' "

"It's the way you never seem to pick up your end of the conversation." She saw his eyebrow move and figured he must be listening. "I tell you I was moved to tears by a piece of your work
and your response is to go into a coma and then ask me if I
remember Leanne Samples, which—if you don't mind me saying, Corso—wasn't exactly the response I was looking for."

He pushed the accelerator several times, racing the engine in
neutral. "If there's a script, maybe you oughta give me a copy,"
Corso said with a grin.

"Of course there's a script. It's how people get to know one
another."

She reached over and turned up the heat. "Today—you know—
two minutes ago when I just told you this was the first time I've
been over here."

"Yeah? What about it?" he asked.

He pulled the shift lever down into drive and checked back
over his shoulder. A tandem livestock carrier roared by, leaving
the air full of straw. And then another screaming along in the
blurred air of the wake.

"Ninety-nine guys out of a hundred would have taken that as
an opportunity to ask me how long I've lived in Washington.
Where I came from . . . yadda yadda. Most guys would give me
some sort of little geography lesson to show me how much they
know. How smart they are. You know, like showing off. That sort
of stuff is just what comes next in the conversation."

"I'm not good at small talk," Corso said.

"Of course you are!" She slapped the paper on the seat. "Anybody who can beat an exclusive story like this out of the FBI is
the Picasso of small talk."

Corso grunted.

"Hell, you haven't even asked about the goddamn tattoos. I know damn well you must know the story. Everybody knows the goddamn story. All the weird shit I'm supposed to have all over me. By now most guys are tripping all over themselves wondering if all the shit they heard is true."

"Well, is it?"

"What?"

"True that you have some pretty weird shit on you."

"Wouldn't you like to know."

"I'm not saying it never crossed my mind," Corso admitted.

"So why haven't you asked?"

"I didn't want to pry."

"You pry for a living."

"The cops ever find—"

"Brian," she said, shaking her head in the darkness. "Brian Bohannon. They think maybe he's in southern France some-where. His parents are very wealthy. I'm sure they're supporting him. They see the whole thing as some sort of boyish prank. Can't understand what all the fuss is about. They offered me money not to press charges against him."

"How'd they get them off your face?"

"Lasers," she said. "Dermabrasion."

"What's that?"

"That's where they freeze a section of your face and then sand it."

"Sounds like fun."

"And of course the always exciting chemical peel."

"What's that do?"

"That makes the rest of your face look like a burn victim's, so you can't see where the designs were."

In the darkness, Corso winced. "Hurt?"

She shrugged. "The pain I can handle. It's the money that's

killing me," she said. "I've had over twenty treatments so far for my face." She brought her fingertips to her cheek. "They say, in another year or so, I'll just look like I had bad skin as a teenager."

She laughed bitterly.

"Of course, my HMO says the removal procedures are elective and won't pay for it."

"No parents or anybody to help you out?"

He couldn't be sure, but he thought perhaps she laughed. "My parents had other plans for me. They're from a little town in Iowa. Robbinsville, Iowa. Two *b*'s. They didn't approve of my moving to Seattle. They didn't approve of photography as a career for me. They didn't approve of my lifestyle, and they particularly didn't approve of Brian. The way they see it, what happened to me was some kind of divine retribution."

They rode in silence for a moment.

"What the hell was this guy thinking?" Corso asked.

"He was thinking that if he couldn't have me, he was going to make damn sure nobody else was going to have me either. 'Nobody leaves Brian.' That's what he said just as I was passing out. 'Nobody leaves Brian.' Like he was in the third person or something. He left a note in his shop. Said I would remain for all eternity . . . his palette, his personal work of art."

She pulled her jacket over her chest and settled back against the door with her eyes closed. He mashed the accelerator and sent the white Chevy Citation lumbering out onto I-85, rolling south toward the tri-cities and the Columbia River. The eastern Cascades were capped in snow. The low hills were swathed in orchards. Rows of gray, skeletal trees filled the valleys and wound like a bezel around the cut, brown contours of the hills. Apple and pear and peach and cherry. Amputated for winter and huddled together for warmth. The kind of dead, lifeless country that comes alive and green only around the rivers and creeks, and even then after lifetimes of toil. The kind of artificial Eden that, for reasons too many to enumerate, would forever elude the likes of Walter Leroy Himes and his kin.

No . . . Walter Leroy and his ilk were remnants of those folks whose sole contribution to modern society has been an uncanny ability to make sagging front porches look comfortable. Walter was a direct descendant of those untimely souls who, by indolence or ignorance or both, always managed to arrive places a day late and a dollar short, always to find the rich bottomland already under the plow, and themselves relegated to the hardpan at the edge of town, to the steep, deep "gullies and hollers" between hills or to these "touch and go" arid, barren acres where the irrigated prairie suddenly becomes desert and blows away.

His parents came from North Carolina for the trial. From a little hamlet in the extreme northwestern part of the state. Damn near in Virginia, folks said. An "end-of-the-road" town called Husk, North Carolina. Neither had been outside Ashe County before. Christ the Redeemer Reformed Baptist Church held a bake sale and a raffle to raise the money for their pilgrimage. Flew out of Charlotte on a great silver bird.

They sat side by side in the front row. LO-retta-accent-on-the-first-syllable Himes was an immense woman with dyed, cat-black hair and a penchant for wildly flowered tops. No more than a couple of biscuits and a piece of rhubarb pie from four hundred pounds, she sat there every day, frowning and fanning herself with a white plastic fan that had "Jesus Is Coming" stenciled on the back.

Walter Leroy inherited his height from his father, Delroy. Stoop straightened and ironed out, Delroy Himes would have measured at least six-eight. Maybe more. All sinew and bone, loose inside a clean pair of coveralls. Missing a finger from each hand. Everything knotted and twisted and worn out by a lifetime of struggle, he never said a single word. Let his wife do the talking for both of them. As Delroy was undoubtedly aware, LO-retta was more than up to the task.

Every day after the proceedings, she held forth on the courthouse steps. Rain or shine. Talked about how her boy was "tetched" and shouldn't rightly be on trial at all; cried and told about how Walter Lee, as she called him, "dinna have a violet bone in his body." How he "neva shoulda got so far from them thet loved and unnerstood him." 'Bout how Jesus, whose name she miraculously transformed into a three-syllable word, loved her boy and was "just awaitin' to take him on home."

Another two hours and the Chevy crossed the Columbia River just north of Richland. Running fast and smooth and brown . . . navigable all the way up into Idaho.

They crossed the Snake River at Pasco, then turned onto 12 East. Sign said WALLA WALLA 45. Corso reached over and jostled Meg Dougherty awake.

* * *

To the west, a broad butte ran the length of the valley. Rock, milk-chocolate brown, rising as a gentle mound near the bottom, then suddenly straightening to cliffs for the upper hundred feet. Four antennas were spaced along the flat top, their intermittent red lights blinking against the dense gray clouds. The dark sky silhouetted a pair of red-tailed hawks, who rode the cold currents in lazy circles, heads down, feathered fingers making minute adjustments to the ever-changing wind eddies.

To the east, the Walla Walla River running straight as an arrow and the Blue Mountains barely visible through the haze. Corso checked his watch—12:15. Forty-five minutes before they were scheduled to see Walter Leroy Himes.

They were parked forty yards from the front gate of the Washington State Penitentiary. The walls were thirty feet high, concrete with the original river rock peeping through in places. Topped with a maze of coiled razor wire that somehow gleamed without the aid of sunlight. The enclosure must have been half a mile to a side. At each corner a red octagonal guard tower rose above the battlements.

A steady breeze carried mist from the river and the smells of onions and steel. Bright yellow sawhorses divided the parking lot in two, creating a gauntlet through which arriving cars must pass. Half a dozen helmeted county cops manned each side of the division. On one side, the anti–capital punishment crowd milled about, sipping lattes and waving handmade signs, demanding an end to the killing. All Volvos and fancy outdoor gear, they looked out of place on this side of the mountains.

On the other side milled the "eye-for-an-eye" crowd. Wads of chew. Beaten pickup trucks and motor homes. The damaged and the lonely and the lost. The tattered, gone-broke farmers and the slit-eyed fraternity boys who'd finally found a venue worthy of that red anger they carried inside. No surprise. The murder mavens outnumbered the forgiveness folks at least ten to one.

Dougherty and Corso both rolled down their windows. The civilized crowd was chanting something, but Corso couldn't quite make out the words. On Dougherty's side, Lynyrd Skynyrd blared from a scratchy speaker. "*Sweet Home Alabama . . .*"

The nearest cop detached himself from the lines and made his way over to the driver's window. All boots and black leather, behind a gigantic pair of aviator shades. Lose the white helmet, he could take Dougherty to the prom.

"No visitors today," he said. "They're on lockdown."

"We've got an appointment," Corso said. "Corso and Dougherty from the *Seattle Sun*. We're here to see Walter Leroy Himes."

The cop stepped back a pace, turned his head, and spoke into the microphone on his shoulder. After a moment, he leaned down into the window. Put his black-gloved hands on the window frame. "Lemme see some ID," he said. Corso and Dougherty fished around. Found it. Corso handed it over.

Satisfied, the cop handed the ID back to Corso. "Drive down to the gate," he said. "And take it easy. I don't want you to hit one of my officers." He looked down the tube of milling humanity between the car and the front gate. "I'd put the windows up if I were you. The crowd's a little restless today. Couple hours ago, we had a pair of good old boys sneak over into the peaceful section and kick some ass. Now even the loveniks are spoiling for a fight."

The cop backed up, motioned with his arm. Corso eased the car forward. The minute the Chevy began to move, the crowds on both sides of the aisle began to surge toward the barricades. The cops stepped up, waving batons. On the right, one of the barriers tipped, driven onto two legs by the surge of the crowd. Corso felt his throat tighten. A pair of cops wrestled the barrier back in place. Corso pulled his eyes back to the road just in time to see a full can of Bud Lite land on the hood of the Chevy, stopping their breaths. The spewing can bounced high into the air and disappeared. A half dozen similarly slung weapons arched across the gap in front of the car. Aimed, not at the car, this time, but at the protesters on the other side.

On Corso's side the protesters leaned out to wave their signs in his face. Someone poked at the window with a cross-country ski pole. Corso fed the Chevy more gas. Someone screamed the word "murderer." He made out a sign. It said "SHAME."

Twenty yards from the gate, a beer can burst against the passenger window, which cracked but did not break, pulling a gasp from Dougherty and constricting Corso's throat even further.

Then, suddenly, they rolled past the outermost fence and the crowd was gone. Corso's hands shook as he braked the car at the guard gate. He swallowed twice and looked over at Dougherty.

She was pale and breathing raggedly. The windshield on her side was completely covered with something pink. She looked to Corso, as if for an explanation.

"Strawberry, I think," Corso said.

*   *   *

Death row. Building H of the Washington State Penitentary at Walla Walla, Washington. All the way at the back of the enclosure. Newest building in a hundred-year-old complex about the size of a small New England town. A three-story brick building. Gleaming gray linoleum floors, burnt-orange concrete walls. None of the multiple-radio-station, hip-hop, honky-tonk screaming heebie-jeebie chaos of a regular cell block. Dead-ass silence and lifeless air so thick you felt as if you needed to swim with your arms as you walked along the concrete canyons.

The bullet-headed sergeant who'd met them in reception hadn't bothered with introductions. Just said Himes was a "dead man," so he couldn't leave the row. Said they had a room on the row where the condemned met with their lawyers. If they wanted to see him, it would have to be there. Since then, Corso and Dougherty had been issued badges, passed through three checkpoints, three increasingly intimate friskings, two metal detectors, and were now without shoes, belts, jewelry, wallets, cell phones, and all the other identity accoutrements of modern society. Reduced to visitors eighty-eight and eighty-nine for the day. Names not even optional.

They'd already been through the camera equipment twice, but Bullethead still checked the inspection tags at a small green table outside the entrance to death row, then handed the camera bag back to Dougherty. He punched the intercom button to the left of the orange steel door. "Clear," he said. The door rolled open.

Bullethead walked without swinging his arms. Like he was on parade or something. He led them through the door to the first room on the right, selected a key from a ring attached to his belt, stretched the cable out, and snapped the lock. He pulled the door open and stood aside. "I'll be right outside the door," he announced in a flat, emotionless tone that made it impossible to tell whether he meant it as admonition or reassurance.

The room was about the size of the bathroom in an average city apartment and smelled about the same. Maybe six by eight. That noxious green the government paints everything. A narrow counter ran across the long wall opposite the door. Two ancient oak chairs waited, the varnish on their seats worn away by a hundred years of squirming asses. The air had an acrid quality, as if it were tinctured with adrenaline.

Meg Dougherty's eyes moved toward the door when it snapped shut. Her face looked shiny and stretched in the bright fluorescent light. "You okay?" Corso asked.

She took a deep breath. "You should have told me to wear a suit of armor," she said. "This is . . ." She rolled her eyes. "I had no idea," she said.

"Prisons are the opposite of everything else in the world," Corso said.

Meg slung the camera bag up onto the counter just as the light in the next room burst on. She jumped. Looked to see if Corso noticed. If he had, he wasn't letting on. He was focused on the room next door and fumbling for his notebook.

A mirror image of the room they were in. In between, three inches of wire-reinforced Plexiglas, with a stainless-steel hole in the center, like a movie theater box office, allowing attorney and client to converse with only a fine screen separating them.

Walter Leroy came into the room at a trot. Just because he was wearing ankle irons didn't mean the guards were going to wait for his big sorry ass. In the old days, when prisoners wore chains twenty-four hours a day, men who'd been free for twenty years carried that distinctive shambling trot to their graves.

Himes stood motionless just inside the doorway while a guard checked the room. Satisfied, the guard leaned over the counter and spoke to Corso. "He looks funny to you it's on account of how he shaves everything off," the guy said. "Wouldn't want you thinking we did that to him."

He was right. Not only was Himes's shaved head gleaming, but his eyebrows were missing also. Corso checked the V of the orange coveralls. Hairless. With his bald head, Himes looked like Crusher, the guy Bugs Bunny always wrestled in the cartoons.

"Every Tuesday and Friday. Shaves every hair offa his body." The guard grinned. "Least all the hairs he can reach," he added with a lewd wink. "You ought to see the position he gets in when he shaves his butt crack. You'd never believe old Walter here was that limber. Would ya, Walter?"

"No, suh," Himes said.

The guard used both hands to plop Walter Lee down into the only chair, then turned again to Corso. His lips twisted into a crooked grin. "I was you, mister, I'd keep well back from the window. Old Walter here don't even own a toothbrush." He scowled down at Himes. "Do ya, Walter?" he asked. Himes kept his gaze on the tabletop.

"No, suh," he said.

"Tell 'em why, Walter."

"Suh?"

"Tell 'em why you ain't brushed your teeth in three years."

"Ain't no point." Himes said it like it had been rehearsed.

"Tell 'em why, Walter."

"Ain't no point 'cause you doan need no teeth in heaven. Oniest things to eat are milk and honey. Nothin' but milk and honey for the righteous."

The guard smiled like a wolf, flicked an amused glance at Corso, and left the room.

Walter Leroy Himes looked up. Smiled. One of his front teeth was completely black. The other, missing entirely. Others had partially rotted away and stood now like rancid pilings. He fixed his eyes on Corso. Blinked a couple of times like a mole.

"You the one, huh?" he said.

"I'm the one," Corso confirmed. "My name is Frank Corso."

In the window's glare, Corso could see Meg Dougherty moving on his left, loading a big square camera. The movement caught Himes's eye. He sat back in the chair. Pulled his head back like somebody was waving a weasel in his face.

"What she doin' here?"

"She's a photographer. Her name's—"

"Doan say," Himes said quickly. "Doan wanna hear no name a hers." He pointed with his manacled hands. "Get her outta here."

"Don't you want your picture in the paper?"

"Get her outta here," he repeated. "Doan like 'em like her."

"How do you like them?" Corso asked.

"Not like her."

"What's wrong with her?"

"Got big milkers," Himes said with no hesitation.

Dougherty stopped twisting knobs on the camera. Looked over at Corso.

"Did he just . . . ?"

"I believe so . . . yes," Corso said.

"About my . . . ?"

"Yes."

"Get her out of here," Himes insisted.

Dougherty shot a nervous glance at Corso, who still hadn't taken his eyes off Walter. "No," Corso said. "She stays. You want to get up and walk out, go ahead. But before you go, Walter Lee, you better think about how you've only got three days left and just about the only people in the world who think it's even remotely possible that you might be innocent are sitting here in this room."

Himes pointed over Corso's right shoulder. "Turn out the light," he said.

Corso looked to Dougherty. "Can you work with the light out?"

"Way better than with it on," she said.

Corso took two steps and flicked the switch down. The overhead bulb in the next room cast a dim yellow glow over the counter area, leaving the rest of the room in virtual darkness. "That better?" Corso asked.

"I guess," said Himes.

Corso took a seat. Pulled out his notepad. Himes beat him to the punch.

"So what you give a shit writin' about me and all?"

"It's news," Corso answered.

"Writin' 'bout how I ain't killed them bitches."

"I don't think you got a fair shake."

"And now the retard says I ain't done what she said I done."

Corso could feel movement in the air behind him and hear the clicking of the camera. "Yeah," Corso said. "She's told the police that she lied at your trial." Himes's shiny dome wrinkled as he thought it over. His eyes rolled in his head for a moment. Then rolled back down and stopped with a bounce like slot-machine windows.

"Then they gotta lemme go," he said.

"They may stop the execution or they may not. Lotta people don't like you, Himes. As for you walking out of here, the only way that's ever going to happen is if they've got the real killer."

"Ain't fair," he grumbled.

"There's still the cop who says you confessed to him."

"Lyin' dog. Never said no word to him. Not one. Never said a word."

"You be willing to take a lie-detector test on that subject?"

"Yep," he said without hesitation.

"What about on whether or not you killed those girls?"

"Offered to do that the first time."

"And they turned you down?"

"Nope. I took the test 'fore I ever went to trial. Let 'em hook all them tiny wires all over me." Himes shuddered at the memory.

"So where were the results? I don't recall any mention of a lie-detector test in your trial."

"Weren't none," Himes said. "Never come out."

"You know why?"

Himes spread his huge hands as far as the chains would permit. "Damned if I know." Corso scribbled furiously. "Warn't allowed to talk in court."

"That might have had something to do with the fact that you kept calling the jury cocksuckers."

"What's they were," Himes said stubbornly.

Corso looked back over his shoulder at Dougherty. "You know where I can find his first attorney?" She dropped the camera from her eye.

"I only got through the judge."

"Tomorrow, first thing," Corso said.

Himes's chair squeaked on the floor as he recoiled. "Doan wanna hear her voice."

"What's with you, Himes?" Corso asked. "Why are you always crapping in your own front yard?"

"Huh?"

"Why are you always trying so hard to make people hate you?"

Himes pursed his big rubbery lips. "I had me a bird once," he said after a minute. "An oriole. Found him all tore up by a barbed-wire fence. Took him home and nursed him back to health." Himes's eyes had a distant look. "But you know what?"

"What?"

"Soon as he was getting well . . . soon as he could fly again—just about when I was gonna let him go—he seen himself in a mirror. You know what he done?"

"What?"

"He started flyin' at his own reflection. Just throwin' himself at that other bird in the mirror, like whatever he saw there was surely his own worst enemy. Didn't stop until he'd busted him a crack in the mirror. Little guy kept peckin' until he covered the whole damn mirror with his blood and then fell over, stone dead. Just like that." Himes's eyes locked on to Corso's. "I buried him in the garden. In a matchbox. Later on, I asked my uncle Emmett how come a animal do somethin' like that. What he seen in that mirror that was worth dyin' for. Uncle Emmett, he said he reckoned it was just the critter's nature."

"So . . . you figure this is your destiny. Is that it?"

Himes wrinkled his nose and sneered at Corso. "Doan matter what I figure. People doan care who you are. Doan see nothin' but what they wanna see anyway. Just somethin' bad about you so's they can feel better about themselves. Doan gotta be true, neither. Just gotta let 'em feel superior to somebody else."

"Am I supposed to feel sorry for you?"

Himes smirked. "If you askin' my advice, Mr. Corso, I wouldn't feel nothin' at all. Me . . . I give it up a long while back."

"I want to go back over your trial with you," Corso said. "Starting from the moment you were arrested, until your conviction. Okay?"

Himes said it was. It took forty minutes and nearly filled Corso's notebook. By the time Corso had finished, Meg had her gear packed and was leaning against the wall, in the deep shadows. Corso pocketed his notebook.

Himes got to his feet. Stretched. "They know damn well I neva done them things they said I done. They gonna kill me anyway, huh? Just outta spite."

The room felt thick and damp, as if it had suddenly filled with seawater.

"Could be, Walter. Could be," Corso said without looking up.

He slowly got to his feet. "Anything you need?" he asked Walter Himes. "Can I put some money in your account . . . for cigarettes or something?"

Himes showed his ravaged teeth.

"Ain't no smokin' on the row. Wouldn't want us to get sick or nothin'."

12

Wednesday, September 19
5:40 P.M. Day 3 of 6

The eastern slope of the Cascades loomed like purple pickets. Mara Liasson's voice on "All Things Considered" sounded like somebody was blending margaritas in the backseat. Corso switched the radio off, leaving only the dull hiss of rain and the heartbeat slap of the windshield wipers.

"Thanks," Dougherty said. "The static was driving me crazy." She was huddled against the passenger door, using her jacket as a blanket. The digital dashboard clock read 5:41. Another hour to Seattle. They'd spent the past three hours mostly lost in their own thoughts and listening to National Public Radio. The Kosovo crisis. A guy flogging a book about the creation of *The Oxford English Dictionary*. Advances in fetal surgery. A recipe for peach cobbler.

Corso yawned. "Long day," he said.

She nodded. "Makes you wonder."

"What?"

"Why are we bothering about somebody like Himes?"

"The rationale, as I understand it, is that if we make sure to protect the rights of somebody like Walter Leroy Himes, citizens like us can be pretty damn sure our own rights are going to be secure."

She settled farther down into the seat, pulling the jacket closer around her neck.

"Mind if I ask you a personal question?"

"Yes," Corso said. "Actually, I do."

She laughed again. "So anyway . . . what I want to know is, how can this guy who lives inside this enormous personal bubble, who wouldn't piss on you if you were on fire, how can a guy like that get himself so in tune with other people's tragedies that he can write the kind of pieces you write?"

Her hands moved beneath the coat. Corso checked the rearview mirror and then slid the car over into the left lane, gave it more gas. Passed a tandem Allied Van Lines truck. Ahead, the right lane was clogged with trucks laboring up the slope. He stayed to the left, put his foot in it.

"Are you just going to ignore me?" she asked.

"Yeah," Corso said.

"How fast are we going?" she asked.

"You want to drive?"

"No. Don't change the subject."

"It's like they say . . . if you walk a mile in another man's shoes . . ."

"Yeah?" she prompted.

"You're a mile away, and you've got his shoes."

"Come on."

"What did you think of Walter Lee?" Corso asked.

"You're not going to answer me, are you?"

"No," he said. "Tell me what you thought of him."

As they crested the summit, the rain turned to slush, splatting on the glass, filling the night sky as if they were inside a paperweight. Corso turned the wipers up to high, tried the high beams, but that just made visibility worse. Clicked back to low.

"I'd say Walter's got some issues involving women," she said.

"Don't we all."

"Walter's issues may be a bit out of the mainstream."

"You noticed that, did you? What else?"

She thought it over. "When he was talking about that bird," she began, "suddenly he was like—"

"He was almost human, wasn't he? Like you could see the little kid in him. Carrying that matchbox out to the garden."

"Yeah."

She sighed and turned toward the side window. A reflection of the green dash lights was superimposed over the windswept trees of the summit. Short, thick firs. Nearly all the limbs on the east side of the trees, standing like tattered flags, retaining only those gnarly branches protected by the stout trunks from the howling Pacific winds.

On the left, the bright lights of the Snoqualmie Ski Area flashed by.

"How fast are we going?"

"You sure you don't want to drive?"

Corso couldn't be certain, but he thought maybe she growled at him.

"No wonder you're single," she said.

"Who says I'm single?"

She snorted. "You're not married."

"What—have I got some sort of mark on me?"

She laughed that deep laugh. "I've got the marks. With you, it's the marks you don't have."

"I'm in remission from women."

"Oh . . . nice word choice there. Makes women sound like a deadly disease."

"And your point is?"

She laughed again. "So what passes for your social life these days, Corso?"

"Fishing. And you?"

She made a rude noise with her lips. "Get a clue, Corso. I'm a freak."

"Lots of tattooed people around Seattle."

"Not the kind of stuff that's on me."

They rode in silence for a moment.

"Guy your age, never even got close to being married. Weird, Corso. Statistically aberrant, at best."

"You're not going to quit, are you?"

"Nope," she said. "I'm in therapy. I'm supposed to share."

"Therapy for what?"

"Recovering my lost self-esteem."

"If you ask me, your self-esteem is just peachy. It's your 'other esteem' I've got some questions about."

She snorted and said, "Don't change the subject."

Corso sighed. "Almost . . . once. A few years back." He waved a hand. "Tell you the truth, thought . . . it . . . wasn't so much that I wanted to get married as it was just what seemed to come next in life. Like I'd met her parents and all . . . and, you know, it seemed obvious to everybody but me that the next logical move was to get married . . . so I just sort of went along with the program."

"What happened?"

"My life took a left turn," Corso said.

"New York?"

He looked over at her. She had the coat pulled up over her nose. Her eyes looked like something out of *The Arabian Nights*. "Have you always been this pushy?" he asked.

"Since birth."

"And persistent?"

She dropped the coat below her chin. "I told you; I'm rebuilding my self-esteem. So what happened with the fiancée?"

Corso sighed. "About five minutes after I got fired, she was gone."

The oncoming headlights etched deep shadows in his face.

"Just like that?"

He ran a hand through his hair. "I was working a story in Miami. My editor, Ben Gardner, called me. Said, on account of me, the *Times* was being sued for ten million bucks. Said I was on unpaid leave until things got sorted out. By the time I got back to New York, she was gone. Took her stuff, half of my stuff, and hit the bricks." His mouth formed a bitter smile. "Not even a note," he said.

"What's she doing now?"

"She's a reporter for CNN."

"Really?"

"Cynthia Stone."

"The blonde with the big hair?"

"That's her."

She reached over and clapped him on the shoulder. "See now, you told me something about yourself. That wasn't so bad, was it?"

"Yes," he said.

Sometime earlier in the day, the road had been sanded. The rhythmic ticking of the sand on the undercarriage sounded like a jazz drummer using brushes on the high hat. He steered the Chevy back into the right lane.

"Corso," she said. "Let me help you out here. Now that you've disgorged a tidbit about yourself, this is the point in the conversation where you ask more about me and my story." She settled back in the seat. "Fire away," she said.

Corso sighed. "This morning you said your parents had other plans for you. What did that look like?"

"I was supposed to marry Dickie Wirtz."

"Dickie Wirtz?" Corso mocked. "What's a Dickie Wirtz?"

"His father owned the Drug Store. Four or five of them. All over the state. I was supposed to settle down and mow grass. Raise up a pack of little rat-faced Wirtzes. What about you?"

"What about me?"

"What were you supposed to turn out to be?"

Corso laughed. "My family . . . ," he started, "my family specializes in day-to-day survival. Where I come from, people don't spend any time wondering what you're going to be when you grow up. They just hope you last that long." He looked over at her, hoping for a laugh. Got only silence.

"Another half hour, and we're home," he said finally. He turned the flailing wipers back to regular speed. Then flicked the radio on. Del Shannon singing "Runaway." He turned it up. She pulled the jacket tighter around her shoulders. He could feel her eyes on him as he drove toward the bright lights ahead.

13

He sat on the blacktop with one knee pulled tight to his chest. Rocking back and forth, Moaning. "Busted my goddamn knee," he whined. His ass was soaking wet, but he didn't care.

"You got over the damn wall wid it. Cain't be busted," Jared said. Actually he said "bufted" instead of "busted." Ever since he got that dumbass stud through his tongue, Jared couldn't talk worth shit.

"Shut the hell up. Ain't your goddamn knee. The hell you know about it anyway?" He hugged the knee tighter, glanced over at Tommy, who was standing on a barrel looking over the concrete wall.

"What the hell's he doing over there?"

"Fuckin', I think," Tommy said. "Every once in a while the whole van gets to rocking. Sounds like some bitch is moanin' and groanin' in there and then it stop for a while." Jared rolled a second barrel over next to the fence and climbed up.

"Noffin goin' on," Jared said.

"Wait a minute. It'll start again," Tommy assured him.

He rubbed his knee again and struggled to his feet. Limped over next to Tommy. "Gimme a hand," he said. Tommy reached down, grabbed his wrist, and helped him crawl up onto the teetering barrel. He put his arms over the wall to steady himself. Be lookin' at a little enclosed yard. Businesses on three sides. Shithole hotel on the other. The van come through the alley. Scare the shit outta everybody. Dropped two cans of spray paint on top of the Dumpster he'd been standing on. On the wall above the Dumpster, the flowery *F* of Fury . . . *UR* . . . no goddamn *Y* completing the circle. Damn van showed up. *FUR*—what kind of shit is that?

The van starts to move on its springs. Bouncing like a motherfucker. "Ooooooooooooooooo," from inside the van. Worst damn sound he ever heard, and then bingo . . . it stops and then the van really starts to rock. A sound like somebody puking. And suddenly nothin'.

"Doan sound like no fuckin' I ever heard," Tommy said.

"Wid your mama, you done heard a lot of it too," he said.

"Maybe cops do it different," Jared suggested.

"I tol' you, dipshit—ain't no cop. Ain't no cop drivin' no piece of shit like that motherfucker."

"I seen the hat," Tommy insisted. "Mother either a cop or he in the army. Ain't nobody else be wearin' that kinda hat, man."

"Ain't no damn cop," he said again.

"How he get in frew the gate, if he ain't no cop? You fink of that?"

And then the noise started again. First like somebody humming really loud, then gettin' higher. Then more of the rockin'.

And the sound get worse, like somebody dyin' in there. Then it stop again.

Tommy hopped to the ground. "I'm outta here," he say.

He had to brace himself on the top of the wall and scoot over to the center.

"I ain't leavin' without my paint," he said sullenly.

Jared jumped to the ground. "Let's go over Graffiti City and see what's happening. Gotta be better than this shit."

"What you be wantin' to go over there for?" he spat out. "Who the hell wanna be taggin' shit the city say you allowed to tag? What kinda bullshit is that? Take the heart right out of taggin', man. Ain't got no ghetto in it at all."

"You comin'?" Tommy asked.

"Not without my paint," he said again.

"Catch you later then," Tommy said.

He slid to a sitting position. Pulled his damaged knee to his chest. "No good worthless motherfuckers. No wonder they never gonna amount to shit." When he began to massage his knee, he noticed, for the first time, that his pants were ripped.

Shit! he thought. Gonna have to listen to her shit about the pants. Gonna put on that pissy face and run her lip on me for-sure. "*Shit!*"

His knit hat was soaked through and sliding down toward his eyes. He pushed the cap back on his head and then rubbed his nose with his sleeve.

"*FUR*—what kind of shit is that?"

Dorothy Sheridan massaged her temples with her fingertips. She felt as if her skull were being flattened by a steamroller. Her field of vision had narrowed, and objects were becoming blurry around the edges. Her tongue felt furry and too big for her mouth. On nearly any other day of her life she would have gone home, lounged in a hot bath, and then medicated herself into a stupor. Not today.

No. Today was the day when she got up in front of God and everybody and told them that the press conference that they'd been promised for this morning wasn't going to happen after all. And the whole damn alphabet soup was out there. Fox, CBS, NBC, ABC, CNN, CNBC—all of them. Hell, she'd refused an interview request from Geraldo Rivera's staff.

And that wasn't the worst of it. The survivors were the worst of it. Nearly a dozen of the murdered girls' friends and relatives had already been ensconced in the front row of the media room's spectator seats when Dorothy had peeked into the room at eight-fifteen this morning. Nearly two hours before the scheduled ten o'clock press conference. Sitting there in their Sunday suits, whispering among themselves and wringing their hands.

And she was stuck with it. Originally it was supposed to be a joint conference with the chief, the mayor, and the district attorney. No such luck. One by one they'd had their press people call to say they'd changed their minds. Finally Kesey called and told her to handle it alone. They'd have an announcement ready tomorrow. Handle it.

"You should have taken that job interview with Taylor and Abrams that Monica Stairs offered you," she whispered to herself. "Monica was right. Private-sector public relations has so much more to offer than this. I could have . . ." And then the familiar voices began to drone. The cowardly talk of security and old age and of making sure Brandy had the type of stable environment that she herself had never known.

She was fodder. Thirty-six hours until Himes's scheduled execution and Kesey was sending her out in front of the national media with a "no comment." Dorothy groaned. Something was wrong. Something they weren't telling her. She could feel it in her bones. She massaged her head and wondered whether or not Brandy's braces could be repossessed. They send who? A couple of unemployed Italian orthodontists named Carmine and Guido? Oh, God.

* * *

Half a dozen orange police barriers cordoned the front doors of the *Seattle Sun*. A pair of off-duty King County mounties patrolled the perimeter. Corso shouldered his way past a cameraman, ducked under the barrier. He held his press pass out to the nearest cop. "That's him," a voice said. "Mr. Corso," someone shouted. Suddenly the air was filled with his name. He walked faster. Cameras clicked and whirled. Above the din he heard a vaguely familiar voice call, "Frank." He had the urge to pull his coat up over his head like a Mafia don but resisted. Corso pulled open the glass door and stepped into the quiet of the lobby.

At the sight of Corso, Bill Post absentmindedly began to massage his right hand with his left. Catching himself, he busied his hands with a travel brochure full of palm trees. Corso watched as the brochure stubbornly refused to be refolded, forcing Post to use the heel of his hand to iron a new set of creases.

"Taking a trip?" Corso asked.

The guard gave a tentative grin. "Gonna take Nancy—that's my daughter—Nancy and my granddaughter, Rachael, gonna take 'em both to Hawaii for a little vacation. I been moonlighting down at the hotels in the evenings. Security. You know, banquets, things like that." He gave Corso a wink. "Food's darn good too."

"Been to the islands before?"

"Nope, never. Always wanted to but something always came up. The car always needed work or the house needed a new roof. Always something."

"Isn't that always the way?"

The old guy's eyes narrowed. "They was gonna go once a coupla years ago, when she was still married to that bum DeWayne. He promised he was gonna take 'em but that went by the board, like the rest of his promises."

"How long has the herd been camped outside?"

"I came on at seven and they were already here. So were the rent-a-cops."

Corso turned and headed for the elevator. Waited for the car. Then turned back toward Post. "Sorry about the hand the other day," he said.

Post waved a big paw. "No problem," he said. "Good as new."

The elevator arrived. Corso stepped in and pushed six.

The newsroom was empty. Corso crossed the room to the windows. Only Claire Harris, the arts and entertainment editor, was at her desk. She was about sixty-five. Face like a satchel. Prematurely purple hair and a big toothy grin that reminded Corso of a '57 Chevy. Always hitting on Corso. Always wearing tall boots of some sort: Corso figured she was probably a dominatrix in her spare time. As Corso walked down the aisle, she looked him over like a lunch menu.

"The prodigal returns," she said in a rough, scratchy voice that sounded as if her throat were lined with sandpaper. "I hope you've reconsidered the possibilities of older women." She gave him a lewd wink. Corso couldn't help himself. He laughed.

"I told you before, Claire, I think you overestimate both of us."

Before she could respond, he asked, "Where is everybody?"

"In the lunchroom. Waiting for the news conference."

Corso moved his eyes to the end of the aisle, to Hawes's glassed-in office. Hawes used one hand to press the phone to his ear and the other to frantically wave Corso forward. Hurry up. Hurry up, he gestured. Corso smiled and stood still.

Claire Harris checked over her shoulder to see what was so funny. She narrowed her eyes and waved a bony finger at Corso. "You really shouldn't torture him, you know. He's very high-strung," she rasped.

"We deserve each other," Corso assured her, and started up the aisle.

Corso nodded at Mary Kenny and stepped into the managing editor's office. Closed the door. This morning's paper lay flat on the desk. "Lie-Detector Test?" Meg's photograph of Walter Leroy was unlike any other picture Corso had ever seen of Himes, whose feral visage was generally photographed while snarling or spewing invective. Instead, she'd caught him at a moment of uncertainty, as he was considering one of Corso's questions, and captured a wistful, almost childlike quality in his expression.

"What can I do for you?" Corso asked.

"Another two weeks of stories like today's lead."

Corso figured that was as close to a compliment as Hawes was going to get.

"I got lucky," Corso said. "I was just warming up. Himes coughed up the lie-detector test crap by accident."

"Yeah . . . well . . . get lucky some more. Have more accidents, Circulation's up a hundred forty percent over last week," Hawes growled.

"I'm going to need Dougherty for as long as the story floats," Corso said.

Hawes's eyes narrowed. He seemed surprised. "Okay . . . and?"

"And we ought to pay her at least whatever Newton's getting. No minimum-wage shit."

Hawes sneered at him. "You know what Mark Twain said about using the word 'we,' don't you, Corso?" Without waiting for an answer, Hawes said, "He said the only people who should use that word are the editors of newspapers and folks with tapeworms. I was you, I'd check my stool for a while."

"She's good," Corso insisted. "That's a hell of a picture this morning."

Hawes admitted how it was indeed one hell of a photo. Corso was ready for a fight, but Hawes said, "I'll take it up with Mrs. V."

Hawes tugged the bottom of his vest back into place and adjusted his tie. "Leanne's upstairs with Mrs. V. The cops are coming for her at ten-thirty. Gonna take her downtown for a deposition."

Corso had an image of Leanne Samples sitting in a straight-backed chair under a harsh white light. Two cigar-smoking homicide dicks, sleeves rolled up, leaning in close, breathing smoke and fear into her frightened face. She lasts what? Three minutes. Hell, substitute Richard Simmons for the homicide dicks and she only holds out for five.

"She's going by herself?"

"We got her a lawyer."

Corso breathed a sigh of relief.

"What have you got for tomorrow?" Hawes asked.

"Depends on what they say at the press conference."

Hawes rubbed the corners of his mouth with his thumb and forefinger. Put on a bland expression. "You seen the *PI* or the *Times* today?"

Corso said he hadn't.

"Both features are on you," Hawes said.

"I'll make it a point not to read them," Corso promised.

"Good idea. One of the papers went so far as to refer to you as a 'defrocked journalist.' "

"I've never been defrocked in my life."

Hawes cleared his throat. "So . . . I guess . . . since you're so worried about how she gets paid, then . . . Dougherty is working out okay for you?" Something in his tone put Corso on alert.

"Why wouldn't she?"

Hawes massaged the back of his neck. "Before I'd ever seen her—in the flesh, so to speak—you know, I'd seen some of her work, but I never put the name together with the tattoo story or anything."

"So?"

"So, I sent her out to a society shoot at the yacht club."

"The commodore find her a bit exotic for the yachting set, did he?"

Hawes whistled softly. "Not only that, but she ended up telling the commodore to go fuck himself." Behind his pale eyes Hawes relived the experience. "I mean . . . how the hell was I supposed to know?"

"She's doing fine," Corso assured him.

"What have you got her doing?"

"Finishing up some work at the courthouse."

"Looking for what?"

Corso told him. "I'm guessing we're going to find out Walter Leroy Himes never had a chance. That'll give us an instant backup lead anytime we need it."

Hawes gave him a smile thin enough to pass for a scar. "Nothing like proving yourself right, is there, Corso?"

Corso pretended to think about it. "There's simultaneous orgasms and a good piss when you really gotta go."

Hawes made a "maybe" face and said, "Yeah, but the glow doesn't last as long."

Corso allowed how Hawes had a point and said, "This afternoon I'm going to work on the lie-detector test results," he said. "I made some calls this morning. Tests are ordered by the SPD, but the results are held by the medical examiner's office. They keep it with the rest of the forensic material. I'm going down to ask for a copy."

Hawes emitted a short laugh. "I'll be holding my breath," he said.

"The sooner we start, the sooner they'll tell us it's lost or destroyed and we'll have a story from that end."

The Freedom of Information Act was a joke. Whether it was midtown Manhattan, or Husk, North Carolina, if what you wanted was something the folks in the courthouse didn't particularly want you to have, gird your loins, Bevis, because, like it or not, you were about to dance the bureaucratic boogie. Eventually, after enough attorneys fattened their retirement kitties, you'd get some part of what you'd originally asked for. The rest? Lost. Funny how they never lost parking tickets.

Hawes nodded his approval. "You know about the media circus downtown?"

"I'm guessing they're all over the place."

"Like ugly on an ape. Government Park is bumper-to-bumper remote feeds, do-gooders, and death fiends. You're getting a lot of negative national airtime from that quarter too." He cut the air with his hand. "Dredging up the whole New York thing and all."

Corso shrugged. "It was to be expected," he said.

"You've been getting a ton of calls from the networks," Hawes said. "I had Violet screen your calls and save the media requests separately."

"Thanks," Corso said.

Bennett Hawes waved him off. Walked around to the back of his desk and sat down in the oversize desk chair that he imagined made him look bigger, but which, in reality, had precisely the opposite effect.

"Mrs. V. would like a word with you," he said. As Corso started for the door he said, "Ask her about her chat with the mayor."

Corso took the elevator to the top floor. As he stepped out of the elevator car, Violet looked up from her keyboard. Smiled.

"So how was the room service?" Corso asked.

She frowned and shook her head. "Going to have to get myself right to the gym in the morning," she said. "And every morning for the foreseeable future," she added.

"It go okay with Leanne?" he asked.

"Oh sure," she said. "She's a very sweet girl . . . but . . . you know . . . for a girl her age, that poor thing has been nowhere and done nothing. Never stayed in a hotel room. Never ordered room service. Never been shopping without her mother. Never watched regular television. I mean . . . I'm all for keeping them on a short leash, but . . . really . . . I don't know."

"That's how those damn fundamentalist sects operate," Corso said. "The less stuff the kids are exposed to, the fewer things contradict the crap you're feeding them. You control the input, you control the kid. Self-induced ignorance in the name of religion."

Violet sat back in her chair and took Corso in. "You don't mind me saying, Mr. Corso, but sometimes you sound like you're mad at the Lord," she said.

Corso opened his mouth to protest but, instead, stood staring at the woman, speechless. She bailed them both out.

"I've got a ton of messages for you."

"Maybe later," Corso said.

She arched a thick eyebrow. "Several from a woman at CNN name of Stone, who claims she was formerly your fiancée."

Cynthia. Yeah. It figured. He almost laughed out loud.

"You can go in. Mrs. Van Der Hoven has been expecting you."

The red leather chair Corso had occupied on Monday was now full of lawyer. He was about fifty, with a pair of upturned nostrils the size of dimes. Bald as an egg, tiny ears lying flat against his head, and a set of pinched features gathered in the center of his face like they were having a meeting. The overall effect was an expression of mild revulsion, as if someone had run something rank right beneath his nose.

Mrs. V., from behind her desk, said, "Ah . . . Mr. Corso. Come in."

Leanne was kneeling on a brocade settee, her back to the door, looking out the window at the whitecapped furrows of Puget Sound when Mrs. V.'s voice snapped her head around. She dropped her feet to the floor and hurried to Corso's side. "So there you are," she said. She had a trendy new hairdo and a new set of duds that looked as if they came from The Gap. She also had dark pouches beneath her eyes and scaly patches where she'd been picking at her lower lip.

"Returned from the land of the dead," Corso said.

Mrs. V. waved a hand. "Frank Corso . . . Dan Beardsley."

The men exchanged disinterested nods.

"You've seen Bennett?" she asked.

"What's this about the mayor?" Corso asked.

"I received a rather contentious call from the mayor yesterday. Regarding both the conduct of the paper in general and your conduct in particular. Stanley seemed to feel that we have seriously outstripped the bounds of civilized journalism. He went so far as to remind me that newspapers were, in a sense, public trusts. Can you imagine? That little boot-licking toady preaching ethics to me! He actually suggested that it was my civic duty to clear stories with his office before going to print. He didn't quite say if I knew what was good for me, but it was most certainly floating somewhere nearby."

"Have they issued any public denials to anything we've printed?"

"Not a peep," Mrs. V. said. She made a rueful face. "They have, however, put their machine into motion."

"Yeah, Hawes told me. I'm a celebrity again."

"I've had to hire temps to answer the phones. We've been besieged."

"You wanted them talking about us," Corso reminded her.

"You've received nearly a hundred interview requests."

"Mr. Corso deeply regrets et cetera, et cetera," Corso said.

Leanne took hold of Corso's arm. She smelled like peppermint.

"What have you got for tomorrow?" Mrs. V. asked.

He told her the same thing he'd told Hawes. She looked up at the clock on the far wall. "Three minutes," she said.

"Is there a TV in here?" Corso asked.

"The lunchroom," she said. "Mr. Hawes sent Mr. Newton downtown."

"That's about what he's good for," Corso said. "I'm going downstairs to catch the news conference. Why don't I take Leanne with me? The cops get here, you can send them down." Leanne squeezed his arm tighter. Mrs. V. looked over at Beardsley.

"No problem," he said.

Corso waited until the elevator door slid shut. "How you hangin' in there?" he asked Leanne. She nodded a couple of times but didn't say anything. "Just tell them the truth, Leanne. That's all you've got to do. Your lawyer there will take care of the rest."

The elevator stopped at the second floor. "I'm scared, Mr. Corso," she said.

Corso pushed the Door Close button. He looked her in the eye. "That's because what you're going through is scary, Leanne. You're not making it up. You're not having some sort of paranoid delusion. This would be a stressful situation for anybody. Not just you. Okay?"

She favored Corso with a wan smile, then said, "Okay." He released the button.

* * *

A head poked in the door. "One minute, Ms. Sheridan," she cooed. Dorothy answered with a wave of the hand. Went back to studying her notes. One stinking paragraph. When she looked up, her assistant still stood in the doorway. Leering . . . the way motorists rubberneck at particularly gruesome car wrecks. Sure. Why not? She was next in line, wasn't she? When Dorothy was long gone, forced to sell her ass down by the airport to keep out of the rain, her assistant would have her office. Sure. She'd fill the shelves with those goddamn Beanie Babies she collected. She'd picked up the vibe. The door closed. Dorothy sighed.

Dorothy crossed the room, grabbed the handle, and peeked out through the crack. Standing room only. Her eye fell on the front row, where Malcolm and Paula Tate sat holding hands. They were quiet people. Dairy farmers from Kelso. Their daughter Jennine had been a second-year nursing student when she became the Trashman's third victim. Every week for the past three years, they'd phoned the Seattle Police Department for an update on when they might expect Walter Leroy Himes to get what was coming to him. Just their little low-key way of saying it wasn't over for them until it was over for Himes, and that, for whatever it was worth, they were watching. Dorothy knew because she'd handled the calls. Always polite, always grateful for whatever information or solace she might be able to provide. They looked ten years older than when Dorothy had last seen them.

At the far end of the front row were the Butlers. Neil and Madeleine. Their daughter Sara had been number five. Found by the gulls amid compacted garbage at a city transfer station in south Seattle. Traced back to a Dumpster on lower Queen Anne Hill. Two blocks from the coffee shop where she worked part-time. Neil Butler owned some kind of electronics company, but that wasn't how he spent his time anymore. He'd become a highly visible supporter of appeal limits in death-penalty cases. Made the talk-show circuit. Testified before Congress. Started a foundation in his daughter's name to support candidates who favored an expeditious eye-for-an-eye approach.

In between the Tates and the Butlers sat Alice Doyle, who always wore the same print dress and always carried a picture of her murdered daughter Kelly. Her husband, Rodney, had been a King County police officer. One of those unfortunate souls for whom the rigors of policework had simply been too much. Fifteen years before his daughter's death, Rodney Doyle had put his service revolver to his temple and pulled the trigger.

Then the Nisovic family. All of them. Mother, father, two grandparents, four brothers, and a sister. Albanian refugees whose eldest daughter, Analia, had been the next-to-last girl killed. The father, Slobodan, despite his halting English, always spoke for the family. Always said that his family had seen enough killing for a lifetime. And that, despite having seen the very heart torn from his family, he had no wish to see Walter Leroy Himes put to death. He always asked, in his daughter's name, that the killing stop.

Dorothy squared her shoulders, patted herself down, put her index finger in her mouth, and then used it to smooth her eyebrows. The moment she pulled open the door and started for the forest of microphones, it was as if someone flicked a switch, as the low drone that filled the room quickly faded to breathless silence.

* * *

Cynthia Stone. Leaning against the wall with a CNN microphone in her hand. She never seemed to change. Corso remembered seeing her high school graduation picture and commenting that she even had the same hairdo. "If it works, I don't mess with it," she'd said. "If it doesn't work, it's history." If Corso had only known. Movement behind the bank of microphones pulled his eyes from Cynthia. The Sheridan woman. Looking ill.

"Ladies and gentlemen. I'm going to read a brief prepared statement, after which I will not be taking questions." She began to read. "Unanticipated developments in the case of Walter Leroy Himes have come to the attention of the Seattle Police Department. As we speak, SPD officers are in the process of investigating those developments. For that reason, the press conference that was originally scheduled for this time frame—" The buzz in the room began to rise like an airplane taxiing for takeoff. Sheridan looked around nervously. Corso knew the look well. His college roommate used to feed his pet python white rats. When you first dropped them in the cage they had that same "let-me-the-hell-out-of-here" expression. Sheridan collected her wits. "—which was originally scheduled for this time has been rescheduled for 1:00 P.M. tomorrow. The Seattle Police Department regrets any inconvenience this may cause, but feels it is in the best interest of the community that, in a capital matter such as this, all information be thoroughly investigated before further public statements are issued. Better to err on the side of caution—"

The room went postal. A well-groomed guy in the front row began shouting and waving a fist in Sheridan's face; his wife looked sadly about the room. Tried to pull him back into his seat. A dozen reporters shouted questions at Sheridan, who kept shaking her head and saying there would be no further comment until tomorrow at 1:00 P.M.

"What the hell is the matter with these people?" Bennett Hawes's voice came from behind Corso. "What's the big deal? Am I missing something here? These guys are acting like they got evidence Chief Kesey is the Trashman."

On the screen, the room had erupted into chaos. Sheridan was shaking her head, sidling toward the door. On Corso's left, Leanne Samples looked to Corso for an explanation. "They're not going to let Mr. Himes go?"

"They're not going to do anything . . . until they talk to you."

She pouted. "I already talked to them."

"Officially," Corso said. "They want to take a statement and all." What they wanted was to see if they could bully her into sticking with her original testimony, but Corso wasn't about to tell Leanne anything of the sort. As if on cue, Corso caught sight of Beardsley, Leanne's attorney, and a couple of cops he hadn't seen before standing in the doorway of the lunchroom. He leaned over and put his face close to Leanne's.

"Just tell the truth, Leanne, and everything will be okay. Do you understand me?" She didn't answer. "I'll bet your mama told you that the truth will set you free, didn't she?" She gave him a tentative nod and then picked up the vibe from the doorway, turned toward the cops, went pure white, and then looked back up at Corso.

"Will you come with me?" she asked. "Please."

"I can't," Corso said. "This is for you and your attorney, Mr. Beardsley. I'd just be in the way." Their arms were locked together, but now it was Corso hanging on. "Come on," he said.

She locked her knees and slid the first four feet, then loosened up and walked on her own. "Please," she said to Corso again. Corso shook his head and kept her moving out through the door.

Beardsley put an arm around her shoulder. "It will be fine," he assured her.

The cops stepped forward. "Miss Samples will travel with me," the lawyer informed them. Corso turned and walked back into the lunchroom.

On the screen, local anchor Laurie Dane had intercepted Sheridan before she made good her escape. "According to a story in the *Seattle Sun*, Leanne Samples has told the SPD that she lied during the trial of Walter Leroy Himes?" Sheridan waved her off.

"Other than my earlier statement, I am not able, at this time, to elaborate further."

Her eyes were nearly shut, as if a great weight were pressing down on her head. Behind her, reporters jockeyed for interviews. "Try CNN," Corso shouted over the din. At the front of the room, a woman's hand reached up and changed the channel. A sea of eyes turned to see who had spoken. Corso kept his eyes on the screen.

Cynthia and the well-groomed fist-shaker. "Remind me. Who's that?"

"Neil Butler. One of the parents," Hawes said.

". . . just a further example of the degree of ineptitude of the Seattle Police Department and of the decay of the judicial system," Butler pontificated. He was shaking a finger in Cynthia's face. "In no other civilized country could an animal like Walter Himes . . ."

"Try channel five," Hawes shouted to the front. Same hand.

Another local commentator, Grant Hutchens, was interviewing a couple. They wore matching red-and-black wool coats. Both were fair. Redheads going gray. Almost-white eyelashes. The wife was speaking. "It's hard enough for us to take a day off from the farm. Farms don't take holidays. Animals need feeding and milking whether or not you've got something else planned. We had to hire people to work the place today."

Her husband stepped forward. "But we'll be here tomorrow," he assured the camera. Whatever sense of amiability his otherwise bland face might have suggested was belied by the flat look in his pale blue eyes. "We'll be here for as long as it takes," he said.

"The Tates," Hawes said.

The hand at the front of the room switched the channel. Another local. Interviewing the dark-haired people who'd been sitting front and center. "More parents," Hawes sighed.

"When in doubt, see if you can't get somebody to cry," Corso groused.

"Great sound bites," Hawes offered.

"My fam-i-lee haf faidt een de Amerika systen," the father was saying. Corso's eye was drawn to the grandmother. Beneath the paisley babushka, her weathered face looked like ancient leather. Life-lined and eroded into a serpentine, almost geometrical design of amazing natural complexity. "If dey need us to com bek tomor, ve com bek tomor." As he spoke, his wife, whose dark eyes were filled with tears, whispered a translation to the grandparents, whose faces never so much as twitched. "Ve haf seen nuf keeling." He swallowed. "Nuf keeling," he said again. "De Amerika systen . . . ov justees . . ."

Hawes cupped a hand around his mouth and shouted, "All right, people. The head is officially dead. We've still got a paper to get out here." The hand snapped the TV off. Corso stepped back into the corner and fiddled with the Coke machine as the crowd hustled back to their desks. Their eyes felt like hail on his back. When they'd gone, Corso headed for the door.

"Where you going?" Hawes inquired.

"Gonna get Dougherty and then head up to the morgue."

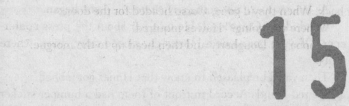

Thursday, September 20
11:40 A.M. Day 4 of 6

Corso listened as the wolf-pack sirens moved closer. Traffic was at a complete stop. Both directions. Despite a thick drizzle, people stood outside their cars, one foot on the doorjambs, scowling up Third Avenue as if to say, For this kind of gridlock, somebody damn well better be dead. Not out loud, though. Much like the weather, nobody talked about the traffic anymore. Sitting for hours breathing catalytic converter fumes had become such a fact of life that taking notice was now considered positively rural.

Meg Dougherty struggled out of her yellow raincoat, threw it over into the backseat, and now sat with a legal pad in her lap. She wore a black long-sleeved blouse. Silk, it looked like. Through the cuff slits, Corso could see more tattoos; thick, green tendrils and leaves entwined both her forearms. From Corso's vantage it was hard to tell, but he thought text of some sort was spaced along the tattooed designs.

"As long as we're not going anywhere . . . ," she began.

"Good idea," Corso said. He told her about the press conference. "If we're gonna do a Himes-got-jobbed story, this is where it fits."

"Then you'll be pleased to know that Himes got jobbed."

The red Honda Accord in front of them had a bumper sticker that read: "I want to die peacefully in my sleep like my grandfather, not screaming like the passengers in his car."

Dougherty thumbed through her notes. "The judge . . . ," she began. "Spearbeck."

Corso turned off the radio. "A slug," she said. "His hours of operation are pretty much standard. It's just that nobody can figure out what he does with his time. Back in ninety-eight, he had the highest backlog of any King County Superior Court judge, an honor he still qualifies for. His backlog is about twice that of his closest competitor, a Judge David Heilman. Soooo," she said flipping the page.

"So," Corso said. "His caseload, then and now, was about twice what everybody else's was."

"Right . . . and that's not the good part."

"Oh?"

"The good part is his rate of overturn." She licked her thumb with a long pink tongue. "The state average is about seven percent overturn. Guess Spearbeck's."

"Fifteen," Corso guessed.

"Eighteen," she corrected. "Almost three times the average."

"So . . . he's not only slow, but sloppy."

She looked up from her notes, waited for the intermittent wiper to clear the window, and took in the gridlock. "Where are we going, anyway?" she asked.

"To the medical examiner's office."

"What for?"

"I want to put in a request for the results of the lie-detector test."

Corso turned up the wipers. People were getting back into their cars. Three blocks up, brake lights were going out and cars were inching forward. Corso put the car in drive and crawled down the street behind the Honda.

"He actually issues fewer contempt citations than most of his colleagues."

Corso could tell she had a punch line, so he kept quiet.

"But I spoke to the proverbial attorney-who-wishes-to-remain-nameless, who says that's because nobody bothers arguing with Spearbeck anymore, because they know they can nearly always get a reversal in appellate court."

"Makes sense," Corso said. "Why mess with contempt citations or judicial complaints if you don't have to? Not to mention, of course, that the client now has to pay you all over again for the appeal."

She looked over at him. "And they say *I'm* cynical."

"What I am is paying attention," Corso corrected quickly.

"You know—" she began.

"Hey," Corso snapped. "What say today we skip the amateur psychoanalysis and stick to the job at hand?" He heard her catch her breath.

"No need to get nasty," she said.

Corso flicked a glance at her from the corner of his eye. "Sorry," he said. "Sometimes I can be a little too . . . I . . ." She'd turned away and was looking out the side window. Part of Corso screamed at him to let it go. He clamped his jaw shut so hard his teeth threatened to crumble, but it didn't help. Next thing he knew, he was talking again. "I'm just not warm and fuzzy. What can I tell you?" The silent treatment. Shit. "I don't make mewing noises whenever I see a baby-something. I think newborn infants look like boiled owls." He threw up his hands. "What can I say? I'm a terrible person. If I could find my inner child, I'd kick his little ass." He'd hoped for a laugh. But no.

When the northbound half of Fourth Avenue broke for a moment, Corso turned the wheel hard to the left, gunned it, and shot through the gap, roaring sharply uphill on James Street. Making all the lights. Under the freeway. All the way to the top of Pill Hill, until he had no choice but to turn left and cut over to Madison.

"You want to hear the rest of it?" she asked in a bored voice.

Corso said he did. He turned left on Madison. Coasted down the hill.

"The prosecutor, Alfred Palin. He's still with the district attorney's office. He's a full-fledged deputy prosecutor these days. The rumor mill says he's thinking about running for judge but is having trouble raising enough money." She wet her thumb again and turned the page. "His office cleared his calendar for him back at the time of the Himes trial. So, for the duration anyway, Himes was his only case. I talked to three lawyers who've recently gone against him. They say he's competent, but nothing special. A law-and-order man. The general consensus was that he was a better politician than lawyer. All three seemed to think his greatest talent was for getting himself assigned to the slam-dunk cases."

"And the defense attorney?"

"Richard Rivers. Mr. Rivers presently lives in Renton and sells adhesives for the 3M Company. Himes was his third and last assignment for the public defenders office. And the only capital case. He was zero for three as a defense attorney. Never stepped into a courtroom again after the Himes trial. I called him this morning and asked for a comment. He hung up on me."

"What about Donald?"

She checked her notes again. "Donald's the courthouse heartthrob. You mention his name to the secretarial staff and they get all dewy-eyed. He's got a filthy-rich wife who he married a mere three weeks after Himes was arrested. She's the former Allison Graves, whose parents have been rich for so long nobody I talked to could remember where the money originally came from. And who, in an amazing stroke of synchronicity, also happens to be Chief Kesey's goddaughter. I'll tell you, Corso, I'm gonna have to check this guy out for myself."

"He's a smooth package," Corso said.

She kept flipping pages backward until she got to the front.

"Donald's partner was a guy named Nance. He retired a couple of months after the Himes trial and lives somewhere down by Scottsdale, Arizona."

Corso took a deep breath. Then ran everything she'd told him around in his head. Decided he liked it.

"Good stuff," he said. "Gives us a lead nobody else has got. Nice work."

He waited for the left-turn arrow, turned the corner onto Ninth Avenue, drove three blocks, and then rolled along the front of Harborview Medical Center to the far end of the building. He parked the car on the corner of Ninth and Alder. About ten feet too close to a fire hydrant and diagonally across Ninth Avenue from the medical examiner's office, which occupied the south end of the hospital's basement. He shut off the car. A silent mist made the windshield instantly opaque. The air inside the car was thick and humid.

"You can stay here or you can come inside with me." He would have bet the ranch that, annoyed as she was, she'd opt to wait in the car, but she surprised him by retrieving her raincoat from the backseat, grabbing the door handle, and getting out, camera bag and all. Slammed the door. No eye contact whatsoever with Corso.

She followed him across the street and down the five steps

into the medical examiner's underground offices. The reception area was a long narrow room running the length of the building. A collection of institutional furniture and tattered magazines was grouped beneath the windows. Four sets of double swinging doors spaced along the far wall. A good-looking young woman with brown, turned-under hair sat at the desk, apparently doing homework of some sort. A sign said her name was Thane Cummings. She looked up and smiled. Closed the book on her mechanical pencil.

"Can I help you?"

"I hope so," Corso said. She was doing some kind of math assignment.

"I want to file a request for information."

"What kind of information?" she asked.

Corso told her.

"Autopsy information requires a court order, and an official request. The lie-detector test . . . I don't know," she said. "I've never been asked for lie-detector test results before." She shrugged and pulled open the bottom drawer of her desk. "There's only one request form, though, so I guess you put your copy requests here and then just check 'Other' "—she pointed to the list of frequently requested materials—"and then put the lie-detector requests here." She ran a bitten thumbnail over an empty patch of the form marked "Other (Explain)."

Corso took his time with the form. No sense giving them an excuse. He continually checked his notes as he worked. He had the eight autopsy dates down pat. It was the lie-detector date that had some play in it. The test was administered somewhere between Himes's arrest and his trial. The spread between February 17 and May 3, 1998, was as close as he could come to pinning it down.

Meg had wandered to the far end of the room. Had a black Nikon out, pointing back in Corso's direction. Decided she didn't like whatever she saw through the viewfinder and began moving closer. Checked the view again. Didn't like that either.

On Corso's left, one of the tall silver doors swung open. A woman, maybe fifty, wearing a long white lab coat, backed out through the swinging door. She was rubbing her hands together as if she was putting on lotion. She had short, curly, salt-and-pepper hair and wore a pair of black-rimmed glasses with thick lenses that made her dark eyes look tiny. A red-and-white name tag on her chest read "Dr. Fran Abbott."

"Oh, Dr. Abbott," the receptionist called.

The woman turned and raised her eyebrows. Rubbing at the backs of her hands now, she took a step in Corso's direction.

"This gentleman was asking about lie-detector test results," the girl said.

"What about them?"

"Do we keep those here?"

"Absolutely," she said. She wiped a palm on her lab coat and offered a hand to Corso. Her grip was moisturized but firm. She peered myopically from Dougherty to Corso and then back to Meg for another go-round. "And you would be?" she inquired.

Corso introduced Meg and himself. Showed the woman his press card. Behind the thick lenses, her eyes got even smaller. "What test would that be?" she asked.

"Walter Leroy Himes," Corso said.

Corso watched as the name went pinballing through her brain. The muscles along the sides of her jaw tightened. She jammed her hands into her coat pockets.

Behind Corso the phone buzzed.

"I'm not sure—" Dr. Abbott began.

"Dr. Abbott," the girl called.

The receptionist held the receiver against her chest. "There's a Sergeant Densmore on the line for you," she said.

Corso watched the color drain from Fran Abbott's face. Watched as she nervously licked her lips and then checked back over her shoulder. "I have to take that," she said. "Please excuse me."

As she turned and headed across the room, Corso strode quickly over to Meg. He pulled the car keys from his pants pocket, grabbed her by the left wrist, and slapped the keys into her palm. She jerked her arm from his grasp.

He leaned in close and spoke in a low voice. "Go get the car. Meet me outside. Turn it around. Make sure we're ready to roll."

Her first inclination was to tell him to keep his damn hands to himself and, while he was at it, to get the damn car for himself too. Something in his eyes, however, caught her attention. The usual vaguely annoyed sneer was missing, replaced by a steely-eyed seriousness she hadn't seen before. She dropped the keys into the pocket of her skirt, switched her camera bag over to her right shoulder, and started for the door.

When Corso turned back, Dr. Abbott was taking notes. "Airport Way," she muttered. Getting directions, Corso figured. Dr. Abbott held the receiver tight to her ear. "Yes," she said. "I understand." She breathed an enormous sigh. Caught herself and turned her back on Corso. "Yes. Twenty minutes. Yes. I'll hurry."

She handed the phone back to the receptionist and spoke to Corso. "I'm afraid I have to go," she said. "An emergency."

Corso watched as the woman bustled through the swinging door and disappeared, leaving only the smell of hand lotion in her wake. Corso stepped back over to the reception desk, signed and dated his request, and gave it to the young woman.

"Thanks for the help," he said.

She smiled. "It's nice to have something to do," she said. "Mostly I just sit around and do homework. Things can be pretty dead around here."

Corso chuckled and said, "I'll bet."

The rain had eased to something more akin to wet fog. Not exactly falling, just sort of hitching a ride on the thick air. Corso felt the unseen moisture gathering on his cheeks as he walked across Ninth Avenue to the Chevy. He raised his collar against the dampness and slid into the passenger seat. "In a couple of minutes, a white van with a yellow light on top is going to come out from that garage door down at the end of the street." Corso pointed down Alder to the ramp and the white garage door at the end of the basement. "Probably going to turn that way," he said, pointing south on Ninth Avenue. "When the van shows, follow it."

"Why?"

"The cop who just called—Densmore—he's the one who wanted to punch my lights out at that meeting I interrupted. He's got something to do with the Trashman case."

"How do you know?"

He told her of asking the desk cops who had been in charge of the Trashman case. "So the young cop says this guy Densmore is the three."

"What's a three?"

"Homicide investigation teams are made up of three detectives. The detective in charge of the team is called the three."

"So?"

"So . . . that's all the guy said to me. That Densmore was the three. I did all my other talking to a Sergeant McCarty."

"So?"

"So . . . ten minutes later, as Donald is giving me the bum's rush out the door, McCarty is reading the younger guy the riot act and pointing at me. Like the younger guy really screwed up or something."

She looked over at Corso. "Weird," she said.

"And then there's the chief talking about how he doesn't want the Himes thing to compromise the ongoing investigation."

"What ongoing investigation?"

"That's a damn good question."

"Weird," she said again.

"What's really weird is how everybody is so uptight. Dr. Abbott in there damn near gets the vapors at the mention of Densmore's name. We've got the mayor making threatening phone calls to Mrs. V. An SPD sergeant seriously thinking about punching my lights out. Canceled news conferences. I mean, what's the big deal? Witness recants. Stop the execution. Get the lawyers together. Figure it out. Everybody comes out looking fair, and humane, and worth whatever ridiculous dole the county is paying them. Seems like a great big 'duuuh' to me."

Half a block away, the white garage door began to roll upward.

"Here we go," Corso said.

The van bounced up the ramp and out onto Alder. Rolled up to the stop sign. Turned right. Dougherty dropped the Chevy into gear. "How far back should I—"

"Just don't run into the back of them and we'll be all right. Stay close. They'll be focused on what they're about to find, not on the rearview mirror."

Corso saw the lightbulb come on behind her eyes.

"This is going to be a body, isn't it?" she said.

"And they said you were just another pretty face."

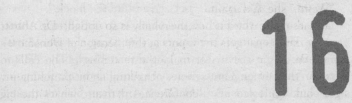

16

Thursday, September 20
12:42 P.M. Day 4 of 6

S outh Doris Street. A little in-grown toenail of a lane, buried
deep within the ten square miles of industrial squalor running south from the Kingdome. Beside the banks of the septic
sump that was once the Duwamish River. The entrance to South
Doris was blocked by orange police barriers. A baby-faced SPD
officer pulled them aside for the medical examiner's van and now
stood miserably in the rain, walking in small circles, stamping his
feet, wishing he'd gotten his teaching certificate.

"Let's drive by nice and slow," Corso said.

Dougherty moved the car forward over the railroad tracks. As
they came abreast of the cop, Corso rolled down his window. The
young cop scowled and swung his arm in the international "move
along" movement. Half a block down South Doris a King County
officer got into his cruiser and backed it out of the mouth of an
alley. The medical examiner's van eased into the space and disap-

peared from view. The cop slid the patrol car back across the alley opening and got out.

"Go straight," Corso said. "Let's go around the block."

They drove to the end of the block and turned right. Auto parts, forklift repairs. A scrap-metal yard along the whole left-hand side of the street. Down to the next block. The Aviator Hotel on the corner. Three stories of crumbling brick. Red neon sign, blinking. Rooms. A filthy South American blanket tacked over a cracked upstairs window. Long-forgotten flower boxes on a rusting fire escape. Rooms.

Another collection of cops was homesteading the north end of South Doris Street. Must have been the artsy-fartsy cop set. They'd added some bright yellow cop tape to their drab orange barricades. "What now?" Dougherty asked.

Corso pointed to the muddy shoulder of the road. A hundred feet in front of the car. "Park," he said. "Bring a camera you can climb with."

She pulled in behind a blue Ford pickup truck with the tail-gate missing. Several greasy tires and rims were strewn about the bed. She pulled the Nikon from the camera bag. They got out. She locked the car and threw the keys over the roof at Corso, who snagged them one-handed and put them in his jacket. "Come on," he said. "Hold my hand, we'll look like a couple out for a walk."

Beneath a row of stunted, moss-encrusted oak trees, they strolled back to the corner, crossed South Homer Street in full view of a dozen recumbent cops, and then disappeared into the deep shade enveloping the east side of the Aviator Hotel. Rooms. Corso pointed to the bottom rung of the fire-escape ladder, about ten feet in the air. He laced his fingers together at knee level. "I'll boost you up."

Dougherty looked dubious. "You sure? You ask me, these cops really don't seem like they want any company."

Corso smiled like a wolf. "What about the public's right to know and all of that?"

She stepped into his hand and reached upward until she had both hands on the bottom rung of the ladder, her boots four feet above the ground.

"Hang on now," he said and let her go. For a moment, she hung, suspended by her arms. Then, with a high-pitched squeal and a hail of dislodged rust, the ladder began to inch toward the ground. When it got low enough, Corso grabbed hold and put his weight onto it, until the metal ladder clicked into the down position and Dougherty stepped to the ground. She brushed herself off and ran her hands through her hair several times. "Yuk," she said as flakes of rust fell to the ground.

She looked up at the rusted metal skeleton, switchbacking its way up the side of the building. "You think this thing is safe?"

"Hell no," Corso said. "Probably hasn't been inspected since the Eisenhower administration. You can stay down here if you want."

"Like hell," she said. "*Après vous.*"

Corso stepped onto the ladder and started up. His weight made the fire escape quiver. On the first-floor landing, he stepped across an overturned flower box, whose spewed soil still supported a vagrant red geranium.

He moved up to the second floor and the blanket over the window, where he noticed that the entire contraption had come loose from the wall, that the bolts which supposedly tied the fire escape to the bricks had pulled loose, leaving the whole thing more or less leaning against the building. He looked down. Dougherty was on her way up. The air smelled of decay. Corso took a deep breath and continued climbing. Moving slowly now, as if he were walking on broken glass.

A pair of putrid cat boxes covered nearly the entire third-floor landing. The rain had filled them to the brim. Clumps of coated cat shit floated in thick, gray water. The sodden air was ripe and rank. Corso used the back of his hand to gingerly push them aside. Shuddered. He climbed the final three rungs holding his breath, stepped over the cornice and onto the roof. Dougherty's head was at cat-box level.

"Careful," he whispered.

"Ohhh," she groaned.

Corso hissed at her and held a finger to his lips. She skirted the cat boxes like they were a land mine. Corso offered his hand. She shook him off and stepped up onto the roof. "That's disgusting," she whispered.

The roof was L-shaped, the two segments separated by a three-foot wall. Mopped-on tar, cracked and grainy. A couple of dozen vents, some just pipes, some with little peaked metal roofs. The tops of the walls were covered by sheet metal, designed to keep the rain from eating away at the bricks. Corso pointed to the far side of the building. "We're going to have to go on hands and knees," he said. She nodded. Pulled the camera from around her neck and shortened the strap. "Ready," she said.

By the time he reached the far side of the building, Corso felt as if somebody were pounding nails into his kneecaps. He sat with his back against the bricks, rubbing his knees with both hands. Dougherty crawled to his side. They took a minute to regroup. She picked gravel from her palms. Let the camera strap out again. Corso kept massaging his knees.

Corso poked his head up slowly, as if expecting sniper fire. Found himself looking into an enclosed courtyard. Ran half the length of the block, in between South Doris and Homer, accessible only by the alley on South Doris. Nobody in sight. Corso grimaced as he rose to his knees. He quickly ducked his head. Caught Dougherty's eye. Pointed straight down. Mouthed the words, "Right under us." Dougherty nodded. She pulled the cam-

era from around her neck and laid it on the roof. Together they
leaned over and peered straight down three stories.

A woman. Dead. Naked. Blood all over her face. Spread-
eagled on her back in a Dumpster. Her lifeless breasts flattened
and falling toward her sides. Her black pubic patch thick with
mist. Her left leg seemed to rest at an impossible angle. Dr.
Abbott and a little Japanese guy in a red windbreaker poking
around her. Densmore and another cop had their notebooks out.
Talking to an elderly African-American guy wearing work gloves
and short rubber boots. Probably the guy who found the body.

Dougherty pulled the lens cap from the camera and set it on
the metal roof flashing. She leaned over the top, twisted the
lens. Corso watched as she ran the telephoto slowly over the
corpse, clicking off pictures as she moved, until she sat back
down with her back to the wall. She used her sleeve to wipe
moisture from the lens. "She's got purple marks around her
wrists, ankles, and throat," she whispered. "And something really
weird stuck to her ear."

"What color?"

"White . . . plastic, I think."

Corso felt a shiver run down his spine. "May I?" he asked.

She pulled the strap from her neck, looped it over Corso's
head, and then handed the camera to him. He aimed the camera
at the far side of the roof and fiddled with the focus, then got to
his knees, leaned over the side of the building, and trained the
lens on the Dumpster below. Focused again. Corso gulped air
and returned to a sitting position. "Did you see it?" she asked.

He nodded. "Oh yeah," he whispered. "I saw it all right."

"What is it?"

"An ear tag," he said. "Ovine. Sheep."

"What's that mean?"

He told her about the holdback of the ear-tag evidence.

"It means they've got more Trashman murders," Corso said. "That's why everybody's panties are in such a wad. They've got a guy on death row, about to meet his maker, and all of a sudden, they've got new murders with the same MO."

"So . . . then . . . this can't be the first new one."

"Exactly," Corso said. "They've been keeping the new killings from the public. And then Leanne Samples shows up with a new story, which, as if it's not bad enough news in its own right, also threatens the official cover-up of the new murders."

Corso rubbed his hands together. "Take pictures," he whispered. "Everything." She rose to her knees and began snapping pictures. Corso pulled out his notebook and began to scribble. 11:20, Densmore calls Abbott. He checked his watch and made more notes. Dougherty plopped back down onto the roof.

"Let's get the hell out of here," Corso said.

She reached for the lens cap on the roof edge but missed, sending the black plastic disk spinning out into space. Corso got to his knees. Watched as the disk floated on the breeze and finally landed on the stiff, directly in front of Dr. Fran Abbott. She looked straight up and made eye contact with Corso. In slow motion, her mouth formed a circle.

She pointed upward with a gloved hand. "Ooooooo," she wailed.

Corso sat back down on the roof. Looked over at Dougherty. A series of shouts and the slapping sound of running feet split the air.

"Oops," she whispered.

Corso gave it a minute, then got to his feet and ambled over to the fire escape. Half a dozen uniformed cops were clustered at the bottom.

"You get your ass down here, right now," one of them hollered. A chorus of threats and remonstrations followed.

Corso stepped back from the edge. "We might as well make it

easy on them," he said to Dougherty. She shook her head. "I need two minutes," she said. "You don't look back this way, and you don't let them up here for at least two minutes."

Corso opened his mouth, but she shouted him down. "Just do it," she yelled.

The fire escape began to vibrate. Corso walked over and looked down. Two-tone brown uniform. A King County mountie with a red face had dragged his beer gut as far as the first landing. He shook his fist at Corso.

"Don't make me come up there," he shouted.

Corso took hold of the uppermost section of fire escape and pushed. The whole thing moved three feet from the supporting wall and waved unsteadily in the breeze before banging back into the bricks. The cop's face went from beet red to stark white. He began to crawl down backward, showing Corso his palms whenever possible.

"This is awful dangerous, fellas," Corso shouted. "You need to be real careful here. Somebody could get seriously hurt."

He started to turn back toward Dougherty. "Not yet!" she whispered.

Densmore wore the same blue suit he'd worn the other day. He had his gun in one hand and the lens cap in the other.

His eyes dilated at the sight of Corso. "You!" he said.

Corso waved toodles with his fingers. "Hi, Andy," he said.

"You son of a bitch. Your ass is mine," he snarled. "I want that camera, and I want you down here right now," he yelled. "Let's go, asshole."

Corso smiled. "That the only suit you own?" he asked.

Behind him, he could hear the clicking of the camera and the sounds of Dougherty moving across the roof. Below, Densmore stuck the automatic back in his belt holster, grabbed the lowest rung of the ladder, and started up.

"Watch out for the flower," Corso shouted when Densmore

reached the first landing. In a show of disdain, Densmore used his foot to sweep the geranium over the edge, scattering the uniforms below. Dougherty appeared at Corso's side.

Densmore had a rhythm going. He jogged up the ladder, crossed the second landing, and started up the final pitch. It was when he reached for the third landing with his left hand that things went terribly awry.

Instead of the metal support, his grasping fingers caught the edge of the nearest cat box, catapulting it completely up and over, sending the collected waste directly down into his upturned face. Instantly, the air was alive with the smell. Dougherty covered her nose and mouth with her hands. Corso winced and stepped back a pace.

Blind now, soaked and choking, Densmore groped upward for purchase, only to have his clawing hands dislodge the remaining cat box, pulling it over the edge, again raining tea and cat crumpets down upon his head. The smell was, by now, nearly unbearable. Densmore began to gag. He slid down the ladder to the second landing. Fell to his knees and dry-heaved a half dozen times before retreating downward. Looking for help that wasn't on the way. Down below, the posse had fanned out. Apparently, as far as local law enforcement was concerned, while bullets were to be considered an everyday occupational hazard, cat shit was way beyond the call of duty.

Corso pulled his cell phone from an inside jacket pocket. Pushed buttons until he found her private number. Auto-dialed. She answered on the third ring. "Yes?"

"It's Corso," he said. "Miss Dougherty and I are about to be arrested."

"Pray tell, what for?"

He gave her the *Reader's Digest* version. A hundred words or less. Heard Mrs. V.'s breathing stop when he told her about the new killing.

"We'll be waiting for you," she said and hung up.

Corso pocketed the phone and turned to Dougherty. "You ever been to jail?"

"No," she said.

Corso had a sudden image of Leanne Samples.

"Mama says there's a first time for everything," he said.

Y ou stink," she said sullenly.

"You're not exactly springtime fresh yourself," Corso countered.

Densmore's drenching had left the fire escape slick and slimy. Despite their daintiest efforts, Corso and Dougherty had picked up a hint of eau de Garfield as they'd climbed down into the waiting arms of the law.

"Why haven't they put us in the regular jail yet?"

Good question. They'd been locked in a windowless underground office in the King County jail for what Corso figured was the better part of two hours. No prints taken. No mugs shot. Just a wooden bench to share and a pair of his and hers jailers stationed outside the door in case either of them needed to take a leak.

"I don't think they want us in with the regular jail population,"

Corso said. "They're probably worried we'll start running our mouths about what we saw today."

Corso checked his watch, and, for the umpteenth time, found it gone. Along with his wallet, his cell phone, the camera, the film, and everything else that was loose on either of them. Strip-searched. Just short of the rubber-glove routine. Corso hadn't asked. He assumed Dougherty'd gotten the same treatment. Probably why she'd been so quiet. He looked at his wrist again. Still gone. Hadda be about two in the afternoon, he figured.

He heard voices in the hall. The door opened. Lieutenant Donald and another cop entered the room. The second man's gold shield hung from his suit-jacket pocket. He had pale blue eyes, wiry red hair, and a humongous cold sore decorating his lower lip. Donald started to close the door behind them, until his nose twitched a couple of times, like a bunny, and he decided to leave it open. He looked at Corso.

"You got some knack for making enemies, man," Donald said.

"It's a calling," Corso said.

"You two better stay the hell away from Densmore," the other guy said, shaking his head. "On good days, he's a pain in the ass. After this . . ." He let it hang.

"This is Sergeant Wald." Nods were exchanged all around.

Donald leaned against the doorjamb. "They took Densmore up to Harborview."

"They're afraid he might have swallowed some of it," Wald said.

Corso held up both hands. "We had nothing to do with it. He's the one brought the shit down upon himself."

"To coin a phrase," Wald said with a wink.

Donald shook his head sadly. "It's all over the precincts. They're calling him Felix. You know, like the cartoon cat."

"Never gonna live it down," Wald said.

"How many new killings have you got?" Corso asked.

The cops lobbed a look back and forth. Corso pushed.

"If you'll forgive me the phrase, fellas, the cat's already out of the bag."

Donald cocked his head, as if to say, What the hell. "This was the second."

"Started about two weeks ago," Wald added.

"Both of them ear-tagged?"

Another look passed between the cops. "Come on," Donald said, gesturing toward the open door. "You're wanted upstairs."

"The gods have assembled," Wald added.

Dougherty got to her feet and followed Donald out the door. Wald stopped, blocking the doorway, and turned back toward Corso. The cold sore glistened with some sort of yellow salve.

"How come on a homicide team with two sergeants and a lieutenant, the lieutenant's not the three?" Corso asked.

"Densmore's a desk jockey from Central. He's our political correctness officer. He's here to make sure SPD gets the glory when we catch the guy. And Chucky . . ." Wald snorted. "Chucky's got no major-crimes experience at all. You don't count the Samples girl throwing herself on the hood of his patrol car, I'm not even sure he owns a felony collar."

"Then why have him on the team?"

"Chief says it's as a liaison. Between the old murders and the new cases."

"What's everybody else say?"

Wald checked the hall. "Everybody else says Chucky is the chief's boy. Say Kesey can't make him captain without he has some high-profile major-crimes time. So, we get him on the team."

"What's that leave you to do?"

"Catch the perp," Wald said with a grimace.

Before Corso could reply, Wald asked, "It true what the matrons say?"

"What's that?"

"That Big Mamma there is tattooed all over?"

Corso felt blood moving to his cheeks. He kept his voice level. "Why don't you ask her for a little peek?"

He nodded at Dougherty and Donald disappearing down the hallway. "Can't nobody compete with Chucky for the ladies," he said with a smirk. "Say she's got some pretty weird stuff all over her."

"I wouldn't know," Corso said.

"Stuff most people wouldn't want on them."

"Sounds to me like one of your bull dykes is dreaming."

"Hmmm," was his only reply.

Corso stepped past him in the doorway and headed down the hall. Donald was showing Dougherty his teeth and holding the elevator door open. Going up. Third floor. Office of the chief of police. At the far end of the hall, Chief Kesey, the mayor, Marvin Hale the district attorney, and Dorothy Sheridan were huddled together like refugees.

Through the wavy glass, Corso could make out Mrs. V.'s profile. Donald opened the door without knocking, stepped aside, and ushered them in. Mrs. V. sat at the far end with Dan Beardsley close at her right hand. Bennett Hawes paced the narrow space behind them.

Corso and Dougherty headed for the friendly end of the table as Wald closed the door. "Are we under arrest?" Corso demanded.

"No," Beardsley said.

"Then let's get the hell out of here."

"There have been developments," Mrs V. said. She looked to the attorney.

"Miss Samples faltered rather badly, I'm afraid," he said.

Corso marinated the idea. "You mean she changed her story again?"

"And again and again and again," Beardsley recited. "Miss Samples's story depended entirely on who was asking the questions and in what tone of voice."

"What am I missing here? Isn't that what you were onboard for—to keep the cops from badgering her?"

Beardsley raised his porcine snout, as if sniffing the air. "I assure you, Mr. Corso," he said with great deliberation, "the young lady did not require coercion. She has, how shall I say . . . a terrific urge to please, which, when combined with difficulty recalling what she said last, makes for quite an interesting witness. Short of invoking her Fifth Amendment rights, I was completely helpless."

The door swung open and Hizhonor marched in. Followed by the chief, the DA, and the Sheridan woman. Beardsley waited for the scuffing of chairs to subside and said, "Mr. Corso has inquired as to whether or not he and Miss Dougherty are under arrest."

"No," said the DA.

"That could damn well change," Chief Kesey said quickly.

"Now, Ben," the mayor chided.

Beardsley made a disgusted face. "Don't be ridiculous. You have neither a complainant for trespassing nor a weapon for assault." The lawyer made a dismissive gesture with his hand. "Unless, of course, it is your intention to issue an assault indictment listing 'feline bowel effluent' as the weapon." Mrs. V. winced at the words.

"Neither of them is under arrest," the district attorney said emphatically. Marvin Hale was an athletic forty-five. Billiard-ball bald. Prone to pipes and sport jackets with elbow patches. "We're here in the spirit of cooperation," he said soothingly.

The chief looked like he was going to puke.

"Well, then . . . in the spirit of cooperation," Corso said, "Miss Dougherty and I want to leave. We've got a story to put together."

A ripple moved through the crowd, like "the wave" at the Kingdome.

Natalie Van Der Hoven sat forward in her chair. "These gentlemen feel strongly that it is our civic duty not to go to print with the story at this time."

"Time?" Corso sneered. "Time is exactly what Walter Leroy doesn't have." He checked his watch. "According to my watch, he's two days from the great beyond."

"You let us worry about Himes," Kesey snapped.

Corso laughed. "Oh yeah, if I were old Walter, you'd be just the bunch I'd want looking out for my well-being."

"After her performance today, the Samples woman can hardly be considered a credible witness," Kesey said.

"As I recall, she was considered credible enough when she was *your* witness," Corso said.

Suddenly the air was filled with threats and denials. Hawes was yelling at the chief, who'd come up out of his chair and was stabbing the air with a finger. Dan Beardsley and Marvin Hale were trading snappy repartee in angry voices. Hizhonor was playing the peacemaker. The Sheridan woman rubbed her temples and stared disconsolately off into space. Meg Dougherty stood in the corner, her hands under her arms, her head swiveling back and forth as if she were watching a tennis match.

"Why in hell didn't you release Himes two weeks ago when the first new body turned up?"

"Because, Mr. Corso, we don't, for a second, believe the killings are related," Kesey said.

Corso was incredulous. "The body I just saw had a tag on her ear."

A knowing look passed among the powers-that-be.

"Different tags," the DA said. "Not from the same batch. The tags found in the latest victims are twenty years newer than those used in ninety-eight."

"MO's not the same either," the chief added. "The new murders have a significantly higher level of violence than the old."

Corso was taken aback. "So you guys are assuming what?"

The chief took over. "We're investigating three angles. I personally think we've got a copycat killer. Somebody who got all excited by the sensational crap he's read in the papers over the past couple of weeks and has decided he wants a little attention too."

"What else?" Corso prodded.

"The possibility that Himes has an accomplice. Somebody who's trying to muddy the waters. Trying to force at least a stay of execution."

"And?"

"We're also looking into some of the more radical members of the anti–capital punishment movement."

"Anti–capital punishment types are killing people?" Mrs. V. scoffed. "Sounds all rather self-defeating to me."

"Unlike newspapers," the chief said, "we have to do our homework before opening our mouths."

The DA leaned across the table. "Now, now. Let's see if we can't fix the problem rather than the blame." His green eyes took in the crowd at the other end of the table. He stopped and let it sink in. "Other than that unfortunate young woman who can't make up her mind whether or not she was raped or by whom . . . do you have anything?"

The room went silent. "Because"—the DA continued—"until and unless somebody shows us one scrap of hard evidence that the original eight murders were not the work of Walter Leroy Himes, we are going to continue to assume his guilt."

"Himes was convicted by a jury of his peers," the mayor added. "He's had three and a half years and several million dollars' worth of appeals."

"You don't think any of this constitutes reasonable doubt?"

Corso asked. He could feel himself grasping for straws. "How would an activist or a copycat know about the ear tags?"

"*You* knew," Kesey said in a tone that suggested that if Corso could find out, anybody could find out. "In any organization the size of the SPD, leaks are to be expected. Considering how many people from the original task force knew about the tags . . . I'm amazed it hasn't hit the papers before."

"We'll be the first to admit that these new developments certainly cast something of a shadow," the DA said. "We are in constant communication with the governor, but as of this moment"—he spread his hands—"we have absolutely nothing that would warrant a request for a stay of execution."

"Not to mention that it's an election year," Hawes growled. "Governor Locke would rather be set on fire than have to stop the execution. He'll take less heat for juicing Himes by mistake than he would for letting him go, even if Himes really *was* innocent."

"And you want us to hold the story of the new murders?" Corso asked.

The chief was suddenly red in the face. "You have to. We'll be inundated. A hundred nuts will confess. We'll get thousands of phoned-in leads. The story will bring our current investigation to a standstill."

"What's in it for us?" Hawes asked.

"What do you want?" Kesey asked.

"We want access to information on all ten murders," Corso said. "We want copies of the field notes from the original detectives. We want copies of the autopsy results and the accompanying photographs, and we want a look at all forensic evidence."

Again the room erupted. Corso shouted them down. "And we want all of it between now and four o'clock this afternoon. If we don't have everything we've asked for by then, we go public."

The district attorney got to his feet and walked over two

places. Put his arms around the chief and the mayor and pulled the three of them into a tight, muttering knot.

Dorothy Sheridan sat openmouthed. Hale straightened up. The chief was the color of an eggplant. The mayor's pallor was more like old custard. They exchanged disgusted looks.

"We keep the holdbacks," the chief said. "We have an ongoing investigation to consider here."

Corso agreed. Kesey worked his lips in and out a couple of times and then looked over at Donald and Wald.

"Donald . . . you and Wald see to it these people get what they need," he said.

Both cops opened their mouths to protest. "We can't let civilians—" Donald began. Kesey raised his voice. "Did you hear what I said, Lieutenant Donald?"

"But—" the cop started.

"Did you?" Louder this time.

"Yessir," Donald snapped.

"What about you, Sergeant Wald?" the chief asked. "Any questions?"

"No, sir," Wald said.

Without another word, the chief and the mayor joined Hale in the full upright position and marched out like Huey, Dewey, and Louie.

"You do have a way about you, Mr. Corso," Mrs. V. said the moment the door closed behind Dorothy Sheridan.

Corso turned to the cops. "How do you want to do this?" he asked.

Donald ran a hand through his hair, which, of course, fell perfectly back into place. He scratched the side of his neck. "Somebody is going to have to go to the medical examiner's office with one of us," he said, "and somebody is going to have to go across the street with the other, I guess."

Wald shook his head. "Densmore's gonna go rat-sh . . ." He

stopped. Flicked a gaze at Mrs. V. "He's gonna lose his mind," he finished.

Natalie Van Der Hoven got to her feet, scowling imperiously down at the detectives. "I'll leave it to you gentlemen to work out the details," she announced. Wald pulled the door open and stood behind it as the *Seattle Sun* contingent filed out. For a second there, just as Mrs. V. swooshed past him, it looked like Donald was going to curtsy.

Like the lady said, the details got worked out. After getting back their belongings, Corso and Dougherty would meet the cops across the street in Tully's coffee shop. Meg was going with Donald. Up to the medical examiner's office. Lie-detector results, autopsy reports, and photos. Corso was going with Wald, across the street to the Public Safety Building for detectives' notes and a look at the hard evidence. Wald stepped out from behind the door.

"Come on," he said.

Donald and Wald got off at ground level. Corso and Dougherty took the elevator all the way to the bottom. Walked down the long basement hall toward booking.

"I'd kill for a shower," Dougherty offered.

"You and me both," Corso said.

Corso bumped her with his elbow. "What'd you think of Donald?"

"Ooooh," she enthused. "That is one fine boy toy," she said.

"You really think so?"

She laughed at him. Women to the left, men to the right. The turnkey dumped the envelope out onto the battered counter. "Check your belongings carefully," he intoned. He pushed a clipboard at Corso. "Sign on line fifty-one."

Corso refilled his pockets and then scribbled his name on the dotted line.

"Sergeant Wald called down," the turnkey said. "Says you guys better go out the garage entrance down here, 'cause there's a herd of media types out front."

Corso thanked him for the tip and then followed his directions to the garage. Dougherty was already there. She had the back of the Nikon open.

"They get the film?" Corso asked.

"No film," she said with a smirk. "It's digital."

"They get the disk?"

"They got *a* disk."

"What's that mean?"

"They didn't get *the* disk," she said.

"What?"

"You heard me. I've still got the shots I took of the body."

"Where—" he began.

She shook her head. "Don't ask, don't tell," she said.

"I hope it was user-friendly?"

"Wouldn't you like to know."

Together, they followed the green exit signs through the bowels of the building, snaking back and forth among the patrol cars and the concrete pillars until they came to a gray steel door labeled "James Street." Dougherty grabbed the knob and stepped out, stopped in her tracks, and then suddenly turned and gave Corso a toothy grin he'd never seen from her before.

"Don't look now, Ken, but I think Malibu Barbie's here," she said.

Corso stepped out into a light drizzle. Overhead, dirty clouds had swallowed the tops of the buildings. Cars had their lights on. He looked uphill. Nothing. Then downhill. Cynthia Stone in a red plastic raincoat, little matching boots and umbrella.

"You still have my number?" Corso asked.

"Yeah."

"Call me when you finish at the medical examiner's office."

Dougherty said she would and then turned downhill, strode past Cynthia without making eye contact, and disappeared around the corner onto Fourth Avenue.

Corso had forgotten how Cynthia walked. That one-foot-in-front-of-the-other thing she did. The delicious way each step rustled with the silken sound of flesh passing flesh, until a guy was overcome and just had to see for himself what was rubbing together.

She held the umbrella tight against her shoulder with her right hand. The left she kept in the pocket of her raincoat. The heels of her red plastic boots clicked as she walked a circle around Corso. "You look good, Frank," she said. "The long hair becomes you."

Corso kept his mouth shut. On the one hand, she looked the same. Same surgically assisted profile and baby-blue eyes. On the other, she looked older than he remembered and more like her mother than he'd ever noticed before. Gonna end up with the same wrinkled, drawstring mouth that she'd be able to cinch up like a sack over everything she found in some way distasteful or disappointing.

"Aren't you going to tell me I look good too?"

"You know how you look, Cynthia. It's what you do."

She looked downhill toward the corner of Fourth Avenue. "Developing a fetish for big girls, are you, Frank?"

"They're easier to hold on to," Corso said.

She made a disbelieving face. "You didn't really think I was going to cling to the hull of a sinking ship, did you, Frank?" When he didn't answer, she said, "What can I say, Frank? When it was good, it was good." She shrugged with one shoulder. "Life goes on."

"You always were a sentimental fool, Cynth."

"I hear she's colorfully decorated."

Behind her, the sounds of car horns bounced off the damp air. The overhanging clouds gave the feeling of being in a low-ceilinged room.

"How'd you know to look for me here?" Corso asked.

She smirked. "I have my sources."

"No, Cynth, you have a *staff* that has sources. You, personally, couldn't find your own ass in the dark."

She twirled the umbrella and stepped in close to Corso. Same perfume as always. "As I recall, you never had much trouble finding my ass in the dark."

"Must have been the zeal of the organs for each other," Corso said.

She raised a sculptured eyebrow. "So you say now," she quipped.

"I've gotta go," Corso said.

She raised the umbrella and leaned her breast against Corso's arm. The insistent mist hissed against the plastic. "You've made quite a comeback, Frank."

He looked into her eyes and remembered what Bo Holland had once said about Cynthia, a couple of years before she and Corso became an item. Back when Corso and Bo shared desk space at the *Times,* and she'd come waltzing through the newsroom, dragging every eye in her wake. Bo'd worked with her before. Someplace in Florida. St. Pete maybe. Said that she was like a beautifully appointed room, its walls lined with a series of doors, which presumably led to other wings of what must surely be a mansion. Surprise was, though, that it didn't matter which door you chose to open, because all doors led to the backyard. What you see is all there is. At the time, Corso had attributed the bitterness of Bo's tone to the pain of a spurned lover. You live and learn.

Corso stepped out from beneath the umbrella. "You come here to help me plot my progress through life or did you want something in particular?"

"I want in on the story, Frank. Because of you, that fish-wrap tabloid you work for has had the story all to itself for the better part of a week. You're all the buzz on every network, but you know it can't last."

"Why's that?"

"Because it's unnatural, Frank. Big dogs eat; little dogs go home hungry. That's just the way it is. You know it, and I know it." She took another step his way, covering his head again with the umbrella, leaning her hip against his. "Come on . . . ," she intoned in her silkiest talking-head tone. "We can still share, can't we? What have you got for tomorrow? I'll give you an attribution." The wind carried her scent to him again. He remembered the smell of her hair and how she liked to sing show tunes in the shower but could never quite remember the words.

Corso couldn't resist. "What I've got for tomorrow, Cynth, will blow those little red boots right off your feet." The raincoat crinkled as she leaned in it against Corso.

"Sometimes you used to prefer I leave the boots on," she said.

Corso opened his mouth to speak, felt a sudden dryness in his throat, and instead turned and allowed gravity to pull him down the hill toward Fourth Avenue.

18

Never heard her comin'. Not till the crash of the door. Scared the shit out of him so bad he come off the bed like a rocket, seein' nothin' but this shape and the new hole in the Tony Hawk poster. Same goddamn place he'd spent a half hour taping up.

"You ain't neva moved," she said. "Your lazy ass is esactly where I left you this morning. Din I tell you to . . ."

Doan know what happened. It's like a dream or something, like suddenly I'm up off the bed standin' in front of her. With my right fist up, all shakin' and shit.

She stepped in closer. Talkin' right up in his face now. Her eyes bulged in her head. "You raise your hand to me? You?" She put hers on her hips. "What all the hell I done for you . . . and you raise your hand to me."

It's like my throat is closed and won't nothin' come out.

"The beatins I took so's he'd leave you be, an you raise your hand to me?" Got spit in the corner of her mouth. "They usta know my name down at Community Health from all the beatins I took on your account."

"I din mean no—" he started.

"Where you learn that shit from, Robert? You learn that from him? Things doan go right, you just slap the bitch around some. You bust her lip, she shut the fuck up. That what 'Big Bobby Boyd' teach you? He teach you like that?"

"I din mean—"

"You neva mean, Robert. Neva. Shit just seem to happen while you mindin' your own buiness, doan it? Big Bobby Boyd neva meant it neither. You axed him, it was like it just slipped out and ended on my face. Come back all sweet and all. 'Sorry, baby, sorry. Neva gonna happen again.' "

He sat down on the bed and rubbed his face with both hands. "I'll tell you, boy . . . may be time for me to revaluate my priorities. Yes, sir." She wandered across the middle of the room. "Doan need no two jobs to take care of myself. No, sir. I get by just fine on my market money."

No way he can tell her what he seen. The eyes on that motherfucker. Neva seen nothin' like that since Randy's big brother took all that fuckin PCP an run facefirst through the shoe-store window. Had his paint cans in his pocket and one leg over the wall when the back doors of the van popped open. Fucker come out, wearin' rubber gloves, went over and opened the top of the Dumpster. Both lids. That's why he didn't split. Wasn't the gloves. He stayed 'cause he couldn't figure why the guy'd need to open both of them. Damn near fell off the wall when that dude come out from the van carryin' somethin' in his arms. Real careful puttin' it in, leanin' in, like arrangin' shit. No way he can tell her about those fuckin' eyes and the feelin' he's had ever since.

He peeked between his fingers to see her looking at him like he'd never seen before, flopped onto his back on the bed, pulled the covers around his shoulders, and rolled over to face the wall. He listened to her labored breathing. Wanted to say something but couldn't force anything through his lips. In a minute, he heard the sound of her shoes on the stairs.

T he cab's headlights punched narrow channels into the dense fog. Dougherty must have had the window open. Corso could hear her voice as she told the cabbie to drive all the way down to the end. Heard the cabbie whine about how he was gonna have to back out blind, and then a minute later he heard the driver's voice again as he told her the fare was $9.75. The interior light flickered for a moment, and she stepped out with a pile of paperwork held beneath her left arm.

"Hey," he called as the cab began to back out of the lot.

The sound of his voice nearly lifted her from the ground. "Jesus—you scared me," she said. With her right hand, she swiped at the fog, as if she could brush it aside.

Corso started across the pavement toward her. "Sorry," he said.

She took several deep breaths. "I guess I'm a little spooked.

Must be what happens when you spend an afternoon with the dead."

She'd changed clothes since he'd seen her last. Motorcycle jacket. Black tights, lycra top. Shorter skirt. Different pair of Doc Martens with thinner soles and shiny silver eyelets. A sorta Janet Jackson meets Morticia Addams look.

"You smell better," he said.

"I'll bet you say that to all the girls."

He laughed. "Yeah, just ask anybody. They'll tell you."

"I stopped at home after the morgue. About the time medical examiners start making it a point to stand upwind of you, ya gotta figure it's time for a shower."

Forty yards north, the fog had enveloped Kamon, the trendy Japanese restaurant at the north end of the lot. Out on Fairview Avenue, yellow cones of light poured down from the street lamps, only to be swallowed whole by the fog before ever reaching the ground. Rush-hour traffic was moving at ten miles an hour. Cold dinners tonight.

Dougherty shivered in the dampness. Used her free hand to pull the jacket tight around her. "I hate this damn fog," she said. "It goes right through you."

Corso nodded his agreement. "Come on," he said. "Let's get out of it."

He took her elbow and led her across the lot and down the ramp to C dock. As he used his key on the gate, she said, "A boat, huh? That's very you, Corso. Very you."

"You think so?"

"Sure," she said. "Like it's all disconnected from everything else. Just sorta like floating on the surface of things."

Corso grimaced as he pulled open the gate. "You really ought to consider a career in radio, you know that, Dougherty? You could do one of those advice shows . . . you know, like Dr. What'shername there."

"That Nazi bitch? As if."

They walked carefully down the dock. Ten feet ahead, the concrete disappeared into the fog. The air was heavy and still. On both sides, masts and rigging appeared ghostly in the filtered light, as if they were strolling among the skeletal remains of a drowned forest. In the empty slips, the water lay still and black, like obsidian. Another thirty feet and Corso's salon lights became visible on the right. He pulled her over in front of him. "Watch your head," he said, pointing at a dark shape ahead in the fog.

"What's that?"

"An anchor," he said. Over the weekend, some drunk had docked a forty-foot Carver way too far into the slip, leaving a sixty-pound Danforth anchor suspended, head high out over the dock. "Nice," she said.

"Home, sweet home," Corso said as he turned into his own slip.

She stopped at the stern. Hugging herself. Hopping from foot to foot. She read the name out loud. *"Saltheart,"* and beneath that, *"Foamfollower."* She furrowed her brow. "Where do I know that name from?"

"It's a name out of a fantasy book I read years ago," Corso said.

She snapped her fingers. "Yeah, those Donaldson books. There's three of them. What's it called . . . ?" she asked herself.

"The Chronicles of Thomas Covenant the Unbeliever."

"Yeah. And the Saltheart character . . . he was like the last of a race of seagoing giants or something."

"That's the one," Corso said.

"Cool name for a boat."

Corso shivered inside his coat. "Come on," he said. "I'm freezing."

He climbed onboard, turned, and offered Dougherty his hand. She plopped the pile of papers into his palm and then hoisted herself over the rail in a single motion.

Corso slid the door aside and then followed her in. "Oh," she said. "It's warm. Feels so good." She rubbed her hands together. Looked around. "Hell . . . it's bigger than my apartment," she said.

He took her coat and laid it on the chart table. Dumped his on top. Corso put together a pot of coffee while she gave herself the grand tour.

"It's definitely you, Corso. All tidy and self-contained," she announced.

"I'm thrilled you think so," he said, handing her a cup. "How'd it go at the medical examiner's?"

"I got everything except the lie-detector test results. They claim they were destroyed or maybe lost. They couldn't seem to make up their minds."

"That figures," Corso said. "Let's see what you've got."

It took a little over two hours and another pot of coffee to sort it all out. To get the paperwork and the photographs into eleven separate piles. When they'd finished, Corso took the primary crime-scene photos and stood them up along the pin rail behind the settee. Piled the paperwork pertaining to each case on the cushion directly below the picture. He left a space between the first eight victims and the more recent casualties.

Dougherty held her cup against her ample chest. She moved her eyes slowly along the row of standing photographs. "God, this is eerie," she said. "Seeing them all lined up like that. Makes me feel like I ought to cover them up so's nobody can see them all dirty and naked like that."

Corso walked over to the first photo. Picked up the crime-scene report. Susanne Tovar. Twenty. Last seen at about ten in the morning on January 7, 1998. Doing her laundry at the Sit and Spin Laundromat on Fourth Avenue. Found by a janitor twelve hours later in a Dumpster behind a bakery in the 2300 block of Eastlake Avenue. Raped, sodomized, and strangled. No fluid residue of any kind. Perp presumed to have worn a condom. Green polyester carpet fibers found beneath her fingernails.

The cops had worked their way back through Susanne Tovar's social life. Found an angry ex-boyfriend named Peter Nilson who looked good for a while. Then Kate Mitchell was found thirteen days later, this time in a Dumpster in Fremont. Same MO. Same fibers beneath the nails. So much for the boyfriend.

The words "serial killer" do not appear in the detective's field notes until the last day of January 1998. When Jennine Tate is found dead in the alley behind the Broadway market. Detective Sergeant Feeney notes that the crimes appear to be both random and stranger-related. Next to the notation he wrote "serial killer?" and drew a circle around the words, as if he was afraid they'd escape.

If Sergeant Feeney still harbored any doubts, they were dispelled when Jennifer Robison disappeared from the Northgate Mall, in broad daylight. Wearing a pair of leopard-skin stretch pants, no less. Told her shopping companion Francine Limuti that she was going to run out to the car for a blouse she wanted to return to Nordstrom. Never seen alive again. Turned up the next morning, three blocks away, behind a Red Robin burger joint, sans the stretch pants.

Sara Butler's picture was the saddest of the lot. Only eighteen years old. The youngest of the victims. Not discovered until she'd made it all the way to the dump. Found by the gulls. Traced back to the Dumpster behind the coffee shop on lower Queen Anne, where she'd worked. Manager said she'd stepped out back for a smoke and never returned. He figured she'd quit—you know how these kids are—and didn't bother to report her missing.

Nine days later, it was Melody Williams. A tourist from Redfield, South Dakota. On her honeymoon. Strolling the Pike Street Market with her new husband, John, who ducked into the men's room, came out two minutes later to find his wife missing.

Cops interviewed nearly a hundred people. Nobody saw a thing. She was found a day and a half later, in a First Avenue construction site less than a mile from where she'd disappeared.

To judge from the stubble, Analia Nisovic had shaved her pubic hair into a heart shape about three days before she disappeared from Westlake Center. The See's Chocolate Shop, where she had recently been promoted to assistant manager, was found unlocked, with the receipts still in the till. Of the eight women, she'd put up the most fight. Her nose and four of her fingers were broken in the struggle.

Then, on the night of April 2, while the city was suffering through the coldest spring in its history, Leanne Samples came staggering down that snow-covered service road and the city heaved a collective sigh of relief. The giddiness lasted for all of three days, until somebody drops a dime and says the body of Kelly Doyle can be found in a trash bin on Sixth Avenue South. Unlike the others, however, the tipster doesn't wait around for the cops to arrive. Dead body number eight was just different enough from the others to cause concern. Could it be they had the wrong guy in jail? Medical examiner said the cold weather made it impossible to pinpoint the time of death. The body was frozen solid. Same MO. Matching ear tag cinches it. Gotta be Himes. Another giant sigh whooshes through town.

Now, damn near three years later, they've got two more. Alice Crane-Carter and the girl they'd seen earlier today. Yet to be identified. Same fibers, different tags. Only difference between the old and new victims was that the level of violence had increased. The new victims had facial contusions. Number nine, Alice Crane-Carter, had suffered a fractured cheekbone and a broken eye socket. No report yet on the unnamed girl.

Corso walked into the galley and put his cup in the sink. Dougherty stood in the salon staring at the photos. "You okay?" he asked.

She shook her head. "I'll tell you what, Corso," she said. "If this is the kind of thing you do for a living, it's no damn wonder you're one weird dude."

"I used to think I'd get used to it," he said. "You know . . . like something inside me would scab over and I wouldn't feel it anymore."

"Did it?"

"No. All I got was the urge to be alone."

He lifted the coffeepot. She shook her head no. "What now?" she asked.

Corso thought it over. "They're running the new murders story tomorrow. Gives me a full day to pull something out of this stuff. So I guess we call it a day and go to bed."

He put his coat on and then held her motorcycle jacket out for her. She thought about snatching the coat from his hands, but instead turned her back and shrugged herself into the jacket. Zipped it all the way up. Corso pulled a set of keys from his jacket pocket. He swung the keys between his thumb and forefinger.

"Sometime tomorrow we're going to have to retrieve the paper's car."

She yawned. "I forgot about the damn car."

"Let's start early," he said. "Himes is getting short on time."

* * *

Corso again dreamed of the cobbled street. He stood on the uneven stones and watched, fascinated, as the three soldiers rudely turned one man after another away from the door. Sometimes providing a rough kick in the pants to speed the victim on his way. Laughing heartily among themselves at the joy of it all. Then—suddenly—the street is empty and the soldiers turn their leaden eyes his way. When he comes forward, the sound of boots and rifles snap around the stone walls. Without a word, they form a line to the right of the door and come to attention. They salute.

As Corso closes the door behind him and begins to climb the narrow stairs, the walls on all sides seem to float away . . . leaving the building sheathed in rags. He steps up. His hands clutching the rails as he moves toward the light at the top of the stairs.

20

9:23 A.M. Day 5 of 6

S top," Corso said.

Apparently this command carried a far greater sense of urgency in North Africa than was customary in south Seattle. The Somali cabdriver locked up the brakes, rocketing Corso and Dougherty forward into the plastic shield separating the front seat the back. Corso glowered at the driver, who was all shrugs and wide-eyed innocence.

Dougherty looked over. "You said stop," she said.

"I meant soon," Corso groused.

"You're never satisfied, you know that?"

The meter read fifteen and a quarter. Corso gave the guy a twenty and told him to keep the change. Corso and Dougherty stepped out onto South Doris Street. With a chirp of the tires, the cab continued west, turned left at the Aviator Hotel, and disappeared.

Dougherty looked around. "And why in hell are we stopping here anyway? The damn car's up around the corner."

Corso jerked his thumb back over his shoulder. The alley gate to the murder scene was open. "Let's have a look."

"No way."

"Come on."

"The last time I listened to you I ended up in jail."

Corso swung a hand around. "All the cop stuff is gone."

"Smelling like cat shit."

"Come on."

The alley ran between a Peterbilt truck-parts distributor and a boarded-up auto-body shop. Ahead in the courtyard, somebody was whistling in between grunts, making it impossible to catch the tune. Dougherty tugged at the back of Corso's coat. Corso kept moving forward until he cleared the buildings.

A turquoise pickup truck from the late fifties was backed up to the rear wall of the Aviator Hotel. Next to the truck, a man knelt on the ground, pouring something from one red plastic bucket into another and then back. Grunting each time he hefted a full bucket. Whistling between grunts.

"Excuse me," Corso said, moving forward.

The man looked up. He was about seventy, a bit bent but still powerful-looking. He wore the same clothes as the day before when Corso had seen him talking with Densmore and Wald, red plaid shirt, jeans, worn through at the seat, short rubber boots, and long rubber gloves. He grunted as he levered himself to his feet.

"I hep you?" he asked.

Corso strode quickly forward with his hand extended. "I wanted to apologize."

"You best not be sellin' somethin'," the man said.

"No, sir. I just wanted to apologize for any trouble or inconvenience we might have caused you yesterday when we . . ." He pointed upward. "The roof."

"That was you they busted up there?"

"Miss Dougherty and I."

The old man gave a hearty laugh. "Wasn't that just sumphin'," he chuckled. "That fella thinkin' I was gonna let him come in the hotel after. Cop or no cop, you ain't comin' in nothin' of mine smellin' like that." Just as suddenly as he'd laughed, his face fell into a frown. "Almost enough to make a body forget about that poor girl . . . layin' there like that. All by herself and such." He pulled the glove from his right hand and shook with Corso.

"Buster Davis," the old man said. "Given name's Clyde, but my mamma took to callin' me Buster, on account of how I always wanted a pair of them Buster Brown shoes I seen on the TV. Wid the kid and the dog inside the shoe. Name just sorta stuck."

Corso introduced Dougherty, then asked, "You the one found the body?"

"Sure did," he said sadly. "Damnedest thing to be findin' that early in the mornin' too. Doin' what I do every mornin', just comin' out see what kinda stuff I gotta paint over and I notice the Dumpster lid's open. I keep 'em shut on accounta the raccoons." He stroked his chin as he recalled the moment. "And there the poor thing was, laying there in her altogether and all. Damnedest thing."

Corso pointed at the gate. Eight feet of chain link with four rows of barbed wire decorating the top. "That gate lock?"

The old man eyed him narrowly. "Wouldn't be much point to it bein' there if it didn't lock, now would it?"

"Whoever left her there must have come through the gate."

"Same thing the cops said and I tell you the same thing I tol' them. Whoever it was musta climbed over and opened it from the inside. Ain't but two keys to that gate. I got one and the security company got the other." He waved a gnarled hand. "For all the damn good they doin' me for the money I'm paying 'em. Can't even keep the kids from paintin' on the damn wall. I got to come out here every damn day and waste my time painting over crap like that." He pointed up at the windowless back wall of the hotel, where someone had taken spray paint and written "FUR" in ornate, sweeping letters.

Dougherty stepped around the men and walked over to the wall.

"Just painted the damn wall, last thing Wednesday night, 'fore I went down to the Eagles for the evening. Get up in the damn mornin', find that poor little thing in there wid the rubbish."

"It's not finished," Dougherty said. Both men turned her way.

"What's not finished?" Corso asked.

"The tag." She pointed up at the letters on the wall. FUR in gold. "It's supposed to say 'fury,' with the tail of the Y making a circle around the whole thing. I've seen this one before. It's all over the place."

"Best not be all over the place for very damn long," the old man said. "City fine you a hunnered-ninety dollars you leave that stuff up on the wall."

"Really?" Corso said. "Even if it's your wall?"

"Specially if it's your wall. Were up to me, I'd just leave it up there. Looks better than them old bricks anyway. Not like anybody gonna see it back here. But the city says no. Got them an ordinance, you know." He threw up his hands. "Which reminds me, I better get myself to work here, 'less it starts rainin' again and I never get the damn thing done." He offered his hand again to Corso, who took it.

"Nice meetin' you folks," he said, nodding at Dougherty. "You-all try to stay out of trouble now," he said with a grin before turning back toward his work.

Dougherty took Corso by the elbow and steered him back

through the gate. They turned left on South Doris and began walking west, toward the hotel.

"Did you hear what he said?" she asked.

"About painting over the graffiti on Wednesday night?"

"Which means the place was tagged sometime before Thursday morning, when he found the girl's body."

"And you're thinking the vandal might have been at work when the murder came down. Maybe saw something."

"No self-respecting tagger would leave his tag unfinished. The tag is their whole trip. It's their artistic identity."

"How is it you know so much about it?"

"I did a photo journal on taggers for *The Stranger*," she said, naming Seattle's most visible alternative paper. "Got to know quite a few of the artists."

"Artists, my ass," Corso scoffed as they reached the corner of South Doris and Homer and turned right under the bare trees.

"Lighten up, Corso. Expression comes in a lot of different flavors."

"Graffiti is hardly art."

"A hundred years ago they said the same thing about photographs."

The Chevy was right where they'd left it the day before. While Corso warmed the engine, Dougherty unlocked the back door, leaned in, and checked her camera case. Satisfied that everything was intact, she slid into the passenger seat.

"What now?" she asked.

"You think you could find the kid?"

"Probably," she said. "I know some people."

Corso wheeled the car around the block, turned left on Airport Way, and headed back downtown. "Where to?" Corso asked.

"It will have to be after dark," Dougherty said. "Taggers aren't morning people. The whole scene is kinda nocturnal."

"You want to come with me? I've got to work my way through that stuff we got from the cops."

Her eyes turned inward. She shook her head. "If I never see those pictures again, it will be too soon. Besides, I've got a treatment on my face this afternoon. Why don't you take me home? Pick me up again at . . . say . . . six or so."

She flipped on the radio. Rob Thomas singing "Smooth" in front of the Carlos Santana band. She began to move in the seat. Corso reached over and turned it up.

Like Mad Fred said: The only thing the dead knew for sure was that being alive was better. Corso sat backward in the teak chair, resting his forearms across the top rail. He moved his head slowly, taking in the dead women one last time, as if, in their final eight-by-ten ignominy, they might yet have a tale to tell.

Outside, the wind had died. The slap of waves against the hull had stopped just after noon. By three, the fog had come rolling in from the Sound, advancing over Queen Anne Hill like a gray-clad army, reducing C dock visibility to twenty feet.

He'd been through it all. Just over two hundred pages. Ten women. All brunettes. The youngest, Sara Butler, had turned eighteen only a month before her disappearance. The oldest, Kelly Doyle, had been twenty-seven at the time of her death. Nine locals, one tourist. Williams, Mitchell, Crane, and Tovar had been married. The rest single. Each of the women still wore her jewelry, but no trace of the clothes or shoes had ever been found. No connection, be it personal or professional, had ever been found among the victims. Husbands, boyfriends, and bosses had been systematically eliminated as suspects. Every known sex offender within five hundred miles had been hauled in and questioned. The first eight ovine ear tags had been of a type not used since the late sixties, a fact that made the tags not only impossible to trace, but which, at the same time, squelched any possibility of a copycat killer. The new tags were sold in forty-four locations in King County alone. The cops were working that angle.

All total, nearly five months of investigation by the SPD, the Washington State Patrol, and the FBI had turned up nothing but some green polyester fibers and half a dozen stray pubic hairs, which any competent defense attorney would argue came from the Dumpsters.

Corso got to his feet. Stretched. Massaged the back of his neck for a moment and then ambled into the galley, where he dropped to one knee and rummaged around under the sink. He came out with a small cardboard box and carried it back to the salon, where, one at a time, almost reverentially, he put the photos and the files facedown in the box and then slid the box back under the sink. He checked his watch: 4:25.

* * *

"The stuff we got from the cops is a hundred-percent useless," Corso said. "I spent the day going over everything." He shook his head. "They've done what they could, but they've got bupkis. This guy's going to have to make a mistake before they get a line on him."

Mrs. V.'s face was grim. "How many more lives is that going to cost?"

Corso shrugged. "The good news is, his level of violence is going up. He's working himself up to a frenzy. It's what these guys do. With each new killing, it takes more and more to get them off. They start to feel invincible. Next thing you know, even the organized ones start to get a little sloppy. Hopefully somebody in charge will be paying attention when it happens."

"Meanwhile . . . Mr. Himes," she began.

"Yeah," Corso said. "Meanwhile, Mr. Himes. We don't come up with a smoking gun, old Walter Lee's gonna buy the farm."

"And you're still convinced of his innocence?"

"Innocent"—he waggled a hand—"I don't know. I go back and forth about that. What I *am* sure of is that he got a bad deal in court. If nothing else, he ought to get a new trial."

A silence settled over the room.

With a sigh, she put her palms on the desk. Got to her feet.

"Guess who's on the payroll?"

"I'll bite, who?"

"Miss Samples."

"Doing what?"

"Subscription complaints. We needed some new help in a hurry. She said she'd like to try. Mr. Harris says she's absolutely marvelous. Totally unflappable. Seems she has a homily for every occasion."

Corso smiled at the thought of Leanne telling some irate subscriber who didn't get his paper how "Mama said . . . all things come to those who wait."

The grin faded when Mrs. V. said, "You wouldn't believe the volume of hate mail we've received in the past eight hours."

"Over what?"

"Over our suggestion that Mr. Himes may not be guilty. It seems that a great many of our fellow citizens are in favor of executing Mr. Himes whether he's guilty or not."

"That's what idiots do, isn't it? Whenever reality fails to match their little preconceptions, they demand that reality forthwith be changed."

"You'd think they'd have *some* interest in justice."

"They can't," Corso said. "They'd have to admit that every day of their lives they're probably rubbing shoulders with the likes of Walter Leroy Himes. They like their villains remarkable. Evil geniuses who want to conquer the world or eat your liver with beans . . . something like that."

"I'm sure you have an opinion on why that is?"

" 'Cause the more remarkable the villain, the farther removed it is from them. They don't actually know anybody like Hannibal Lecter." He waved a hand. "Child-molesting rednecks. Hell, they've got relatives like that. That's what really scares the hell out of them."

She nodded. "What did somebody once say about how the law is practiced in courts, but justice is dispensed in alleys?"

"That's it, exactly," Corso said. "We ought to reinstate public executions." He met her amused gaze. "I mean it. Right out in the town square. Westlake Center. High noon. After church on Sunday. Everybody gets to see the system in action. Gets to let off a little steam. You know . . . bring a lunch. Bring the family. Make a day of it."

"You're terrible," she said with a chuckle.

"No . . . I mean it. It'd be like a weekly cautionary tale. They could wire 'em up for special effects like that Porter guy over in Montana."

She winced at the memory. A couple of years back, triple murderer Stanley Porter had been electrocuted at the Montana State Penitentiary. As horrified witnesses watched, eight-inch flames had burst from Porter's ears. Several sensitive souls had fainted dead away. Turned out they'd had a dead short in the system. Not that it had mattered much to Stanley Porter. He'd had his fifteen minutes. For a while there, seemed like half the cars in Montana had one of those "Stanley Porter is alive and medium-well" bumper stickers.

"Way I figure it," Corso said, "you let a kid see a couple of dozen felons doing their impression of Bunsen burners, and we'll have a lot fewer of the little turds showing up at school with guns."

"I'd like to think we're too civilized for such spectacles."

"That's the problem. We're too damn civilized. We raise these kids out in little isolated patches of suburbia. Buy them any damn thing their diseased little minds can imagine, protect them from all harm, and what do we get? We get these lonely little nerd boys who blow our brains out over breakfast one morning and then go down to the high school and kill everybody who's feeling better than they are."

"You're feeling very passionate about things this afternoon," Mrs. V. noted. Corso rubbed the side of his face. "It's that—what did you call it the other day? That quixotic spark of mine."

"We're imperfect; ergo our systems are imperfect," she said.

Corso ran his hands through his hair. "I had a professor once who said the greatest trait a reporter could possess was a tolerance for ambiguity."

"You think he was correct?"

"Only up to a point. Too much tolerance and you become amorphous. You wake up one morning, everything's so friggin' hunky-dory that you're nobody in particular."

"How so?"

"Because things like intellectual certainty and moral outrage and righteous indignation are the engines of society. Self-satisfied tolerance never accomplished a damn thing except to muddy up the waters of what's right and what's wrong."

He opened his mouth to say something else, but instead merely laughed at himself. "Listen to me. Jesus. I must be tired." Corso turned and crossed to the door. "I've got to pick up Dougherty. We're following an artistic lead."

He tried to muster a final smile, but couldn't get his face to go along with the program. Opened the door and stepped out without a backward glance. Violet Rogers was tapping away at her keyboard. He walked past her desk and pushed the elevator button. Violet looked up. Gave him a wink.

"You know, Violet . . . I've been thinking about what you said the other day. About how maybe I was mad at God and all."

"And?"

"And I think maybe you're right. I think maybe I am."

A muted tinkle announced the elevator's arrival. The door slid open and Corso backed in. Violet shook her head sadly. "You better hope she don't get mad at you back."

Corso pushed the button. Rode to street level, where the little Hispanic guy was behind the security desk. They exchanged silent nods before Corso jerked open the door and stepped outside.

The night air clung to the skin like wet linen. He hunched his shoulders, crossed the sidewalk to where the Datsun was parked in a tow-away zone. Looked up toward First Avenue, where the fog had swallowed even the darkness, leaving the city puffy and whiter than white. He started the engine. Clicked on the headlights. Watched the beams disappear down a black hole about twenty feet out.

* * *

She pulled the leather jacket tighter around herself as she stepped onto the concrete. Corso killed the engine and got out of the car.

"This will probably go better if I go in alone," she said.

He gave her a two-fingered salute. "I'll be right here. You have a problem, you just call my name."

In three steps, she was enveloped by the fog. Corso listened to the fading sound of her boots on the concrete. Overhead, half a dozen orange lights cast a velvet glow. The school was gone, but the playground remained. What used to be the Martha Shelby Middle School was now nothing more than three concrete walls with a basketball hoop bolted to each wall. The city had dedicated the space for graffiti artists and skaters. "Graffiti City" the taggers called it. The de facto agreement was that the cops would leave Graffiti City alone. Smoke your underage cigarettes. Toke on those pipes. Stay out late. Spite your parents. But . . . keep it off the streets and don't wake the neighbors. It starts leaking out into the streets or we get any complaints and the party's over.

As much as Dougherty hated the fog, the cool mist soothed her cheeks and forehead. Her face felt like it was sunburned and about to crack to pieces. The sound of a basketball slapping against the concrete echoed around the walls. To the left, a trio of preteens sat on the ground smoking contraband cigarettes. She heard voices ahead in the gloom. Three more steps and the outlines of two guys emerged. Shrill laughter erupted from somewhere deep in the enclosure.

They were maybe sixteen. One white. One Hispanic. Uniform baggy pants and oversize stocking caps. Plaid jackets buttoned all the way up. Passing a pipe.

"Hey, Cholo . . . look what we got here," the white kid said.

Her mouth suddenly felt as cracked and dry as her face. She knew better than to let them get started on their routine. Let 'em get worked up and they could be dangerous.

"I'm looking for Torpedo," she said.

Torpedo was the street name for one of the kids Dougherty

had photographed for a piece about graffiti artists. They'd gotten
along well. He'd been her guide through the underground world
of taggers and skaters. His tag was the word "Boom" in the center
of the rainbow-hued explosion. Made his taggin' rep puttin' his
mark on cop cars, then made himself a legend tagging the space
needle Christmas Eve, '98.

"I got a torpedo for you, baby," the other kid said.

The first kid stepped in close. He smelled of weed and stale
sweat. He put a hand on her ass and gave it a little tweak. She
slapped his arm away.

"Keep your fucking hands to yourself," she said.

"You hear that?" the Hispanic kid asked. "She gonna kick yo
ass for you, boy." White boy laughed and grabbed his crotch.
Moved his package up and down.

"Come on, baby. Got just what you need right here."

Dougherty felt her throat constrict as she checked out the area
he was fondling and then stared him down.

"At best you got about half what I need right there."

The Hispanic kid bent at the waist and pointed at his friend.
"Hoo hoo hoo."

White boy lost his sense of humor. Started bopping around
like a spastic rapper.

"You got some mouth on you, bitch . . . you know that?"

She felt a finger of fear on the back of her neck. Much as it
pained her, she was about to scream Corso's name when a figure
stepped out of the fog.

"I hear somebody usin' my name in vain?"

Torpedo. Finely wrought features and some of the longest
eyelashes she'd ever seen. Multiracial. A little of everything.
Claimed to have been in seventeen separate foster homes. He'd
grown since she'd seen him last. Tall as she was now. Still wore
the biggest pants she'd ever seen. Obligatory plaid jacket buttoned to the throat and one of those knitted Scandinavian wool

hats with the earflaps. Reindeer cavorting across the front. Festive like.

He stopped. Pointed at her. "The pitcher lady," he said. He walked over and slapped her five. "You gonna makes us famous again?"

"Maybe, if we can get rid of the stoner boys here."

He turned toward the pair. "You heard the lady," he said. "Take your weed-smellin' asses up the road." White boy opened his mouth to speak. Torpedo reached languidly into his pants pocket. Left his hand in there. Everybody got stiff all of a sudden. Had a little E. F. Hutton moment, until Whitey's friend reached over and put a hand on his pal's arm. They passed a look. "No problem," the Hispanic kid said, showing Torpedo his palms. Together, they backed silently off into the gloom.

Torpedo inclined his head to the left and then started walking that way. Dougherty followed. She heard shouts and the clank of the ball on the rim. More dribbling.

Torpedo walked all the way to the east wall. Leaned his back against it. He straddled a puddle. Dozens of bloated cigarette butts bobbed like an armada.

"I been thinkin' 'bout you lately," he said.

"About what?"

" 'Bout how we need some more help to get our story out. To tell people what's really happenin' out here. Not that crap they put in the paper."

"Like what?"

"Like how they givin' kids a year inside for taggin'."

"A year?"

"No shit. I know three kids serving serious jail time for nothin' but taggin'. No dope. No resisting. No nothing but tagging."

Dougherty wasn't surprised. Seattle was as fat and full of itself as it'd been for a hundred years. Anything shabby had to go. You could walk around downtown and point at buildings and say,

"That won't be there in a year." From Dougherty's Capital Hill apartment, the skyline bristled with construction cranes, almost as if the city were under siege. Turned out, affluence was the fifth column.

"What can I do?"

"Get us some space. So we can tell 'em."

"Tell them what?"

"That . . . that no matter how much they tear down, nothin' gonna change. People still gonna be shootin' dope and beatin' their old ladies. Guys gonna lose it behind whiskey and shoot some motherfucker for somethin' that don't make no sense to nobody but him. Ain't gonna be perfect . . . no matter how hard they try, how many poor people they lock up. City just ain't gonna be perfect."

"I can ask around the alternatives and see if anybody's interested."

"Somebody got to tell the story," he said. He pulled out a pack of Merit cigarettes, offered her one, took it himself when she refused. Fired it up.

"What you needin' from me?" he asked.

"The kid who tags 'fury.' "

"What about him?"

"What's his real name?"

"Bobby Boyd."

"I need to find him."

Torpedo bumped himself off the wall. "He doan come down here much. Doan like painting where it's allowed. Kid's a taggin' animal," he said with obvious admiration.

"You know anybody who'd know where I could find him?"

"Sure," he said. "His two main homeboys are Tommy and Jared." He pointed in the direction of the invisible basketball game. "Them two little shits shootin' hoops right over there."

22

Hear the car door. Figure it be that fat Korean she work for. King, Kin, Kim, whatever the hell it is. Stop by sometime to bring her little presents and shit. But there's three voices. Hope like hell it ain't the cops. Can't hear shit through the door. A woman's deep voice say "fury." His mama sayin' how he ain't been out the house at all. They go back and forth, real quick like, but he can't make out the words.

"Robert." The voice. Maybe if he don't say nothin' . . .

"Robert, you come down here, right now."

Shit. Shit. Shit. Must be the damn cops. His stomach contracts and the tears start from his eyes. That bitch judge told him. Gonna get a year inside like Manny, if they catch him at it again. Gonna admit nothin'. Not one goddamn thing. That's where everybody blow it. Listen to that cop crap about how they'll feel better if they tell the truth. End up down in county lockup givin' it up to stay alive. Don't tell 'em nothin'.

He checks himself in the mirror on back the door. Lookin' nappy as hell. He pats at his hair. Just look worse. Shit.

"Robert." Real loud this time.

"Comin'," he calls.

He steps over the hole in the stairs. Take his time. Gettin' his shit together on the way down. No way they gonna see him sweat. All you got to do is just be cool, fool. Just be cool.

Two of 'em. Standin' there in the front room. Ain't no cops neither. Big mean-lookin dude with a ponytail and one of them Capital Hill sun-hater chicks with the black all-over shit. Maybe seen her before somewhere. Hard to tell. All them Addams family hos look the same. "Yeah?"

She's standin' there with her arms folded across her chest, bigtime pissy look on her face. "These people here from the newspaper. Want to talk to you."

"You remember me?" the chick ask.

He don't say nothin'.

"I took pictures of your artwork, last year sometime. Remember?"

"Oh yeah," he say. "You come wid Torpedo."

Before she can say somethin', Pissy Face start flappin' her lip. Right up in Goth Girl's face too. "Don't be talking about no 'art' here, lady." She turn her head and lay the brow on him. Almost as bad as the voice. "What we talkin' about here is vandalism. 'Bout defacin' people's property. 'Bout the kind of choices this young man is making wid his life. Choices if he ain't careful gonna follow him around for the rest of his days. So doan be talking bout no spray can 'art.' Not here in my house, you ain't."

"We're not here to make any trouble," the big guy say.

"Good, 'cause Robert doan need no help wid trouble."

"Why don't you tell us about the yard behind the Aviator Hotel, Robert?" Ponytail say. Felt like all the blood drained down to his feet. Musta looked that way too. Next thing he knows everybody lookin' at him like he hurled or somethin'. She unfold her arms and put a hand on his shoulder. "You all right, Robert? What's this man here talking about? Aviator yard or something."

He's feeling shaky but sacs up. "What about it?"

"About the guy in the black van," Goth Girl say. And now he feels cold all over. Got goose bumps up and down his arms. He don't say nothin'.

She's sweepin' her head around like a searchlight. "What's this van?" she want to know. "This guy?" The big guy ask her if she been watchin' the thing wid that Himes guy on the tube all week. She say "yeah" 'bout what a shame they got to let him go and all. How the likes of that Himes fella ought to be either dead or in the jailhouse.

Big guy say, "We think maybe Robert got a look at the real killer," and all of a sudden, it sound like somebody pulled the plug. Real quiet like. Then she say, "You know what this man's talkin' about, Robert? You see somethin' like that?" He don't say nothin'. Just tryin' not to piss his pants. She gives him the brow.

"You know what he's talkin' about, doan you?"

"This had nothing to do with tagging," Ponytail say.

Goth Girl tell him, "The tag's already painted over."

"Wasn't no tag. Just some damn letters."

" 'Cause you got interrupted," the guy say.

"You know all this shit, why you down here talkin' to me?"

She reach over, slap him in the ear. "You watch your mouth," she say. When he don't say nothin', she get all up in his face. Grab him by the chin, make him look in her eyes. "You know somethin' about this, doan you?"

Ain't no point in tryin' to lie. He nods. She puts the voice on

him. "You better tell these people what you seen." She lets go o
his face. "Maybe all you stayin' out all night finally do some goo
for a change. Go on . . . tell them."

"I seen him," he say, "after he put somethin' in wid the trash
he come around the front and I seen what he looked like."

All of a sudden, they the ones not sayin' shit.

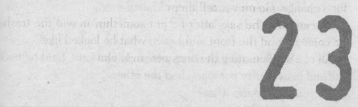

Friday, September 21
8:23 P.M. Day 5 of 6

Skinny little white guy. Weird eyes. Somewhere around thirty-five or forty. Wearing some kind of blue or black uniform. Driving a primer-gray van with quarter-moon bubble windows in back."

"Maybe a cop. Maybe not. Depending on which kids you believe."

Corso nodded as he forked the last piece of hot turkey sandwich into his mouth. They were ensconced in a booth in Andy's Diner, a landmark greasy spoon consisting of an interconnected maze of converted railway cars. Dougherty had long since inhaled an order of meat loaf and mashed potatoes, followed by a humongous piece of cherry pie à la mode. She sat leaning against the wall, squeaking her thumb along the rim of her water glass.

Corso washed the turkey down with a healthy swig of milk,

then gestured toward Dougherty with his fork. "You remember what Buster Davis told us about the gate?"

"He said somebody must have climbed over."

"But all three kids say no."

"So?"

"So . . . he also said that there were only two keys. Said he had one and his security company had the other."

"So you're thinking what?"

"Security guard," Corso said. "It fits with the guy wearing a uniform, and it's consistent with the FBI profile. Not only is it a perfect job for a loner, but it explains how somebody could be familiar with all the different locales where the bodies have been found."

"What do we do?" she asked.

Corso thought it over. "We call the cops. Like the god-fearing citizens we are."

Behind the counter, a short-order cook in a stained white T-shirt was flipping eggs and hash browns. The place was deserted.

"I hate giving that Densmore asshole anything," Dougherty groused.

"No argument there," Corso said. "If Himes wasn't sitting on death row and I wasn't sure this guy was going to kill again real soon, I'd be inclined to let them figure it out for themselves."

"You're right," she sighed. "We can't take the chance. I couldn't live with myself if it turned out to be this guy and he killed again."

Corso dabbed at his lips with a white paper napkin. Pulled his phone from his pocket and pushed a few buttons. Asked for the general number of the Seattle Police Department. Said thanks and dialed again. Asked for Lieutenant Andrew Densmore. Said it was an urgent matter of police business. Waited with the phone held an inch from his ear. Dougherty heard Densmore come on the line. "Densmore," he barked.

"It's Frank Corso."

Silence for a moment, then a bitter laugh. "What is it, ass-hole?" the cop asked. "After tonight's fiasco you still don't think you've fucked things up enough yet?"

Corso wasn't sure exactly what Densmore meant but said, "I think I've got something for you."

"You haven't been listening to me, have you, Corso?"

"I may have a line on the real killer."

"I'm gonna tell you one more time, Corso. If you and circus girl so much as sniff at my investigation, I'm gonna ream the both of you."

"Listen to me—" Corso began.

"No," Densmore said quickly. "You got something to say, why don't you say it to Tiffany Eyre or maybe to her parents."

Corso felt a steel ball bearing roll down his spine. "Who's—" he began.

"We found Tiffany this morning in a Dumpster on Union Street." Corso had to force the phone against his ear.

"Why don't you talk to her parents?" Densmore sneered. "If you think you've got something to say, say it to them. Tell 'em how you and that rag you work for muddied up an ongoing inves-tigation. Tell 'em how we might have had the guy by now if you'd kept your goddamn nose out of it." The line went dead.

Corso sat for a moment, staring at the phone.

"They've got another dead girl."

Dougherty brought both hands to her mouth. "Oh . . . God . . . so soon."

"Motherfucker," Corso said.

The word had barely escaped his lips when he noticed the waitress scowling by the side of the table. Big red hands on half-acre hips. "Earlene," the badge said.

"You kiss your mother with that mouth?" she wanted to know.

"Sorry," Corso said. Across the table, Dougherty grimaced.

The waitress pulled the check from her pocket. "Anything

else?" she asked. When they said no, she dropped the check onto the table and squeaked out of view.

"Well?" Dougherty said.

"He's winding up. The killings are going to get closer together. He's working his way into a murder frenzy."

Suddenly Dougherty's expression froze and she was pointing one of her black-tipped fingers out over Corso's head. He looked back over his shoulder. The cook had come out from behind the counter. He was sitting on a stool, shoveling eggs and hash browns into his mouth, gazing up at the silent TV mounted against the ceiling in the corner of the room.

Split screen. Photo of Walter Leroy Himes. Another of the death chamber. Cut to CNN logo. Washington State Penitentiary, Cynthia Stone reporting . . . gold graphic "LIVE." Cynthia behind her serious face. "We are now less than thirty hours from the event . . ." The screen went black. The cook dropped the remote, wiped his mouth. Spoke to Earlene.

"World'd be a better place without that Himes fella," he said.

"Amen," she said.

* * *

"We've got a problem," Corso said.

"What did I tell you about using 'we'?"

"A serious problem."

Hawes scoffed. "Let me tell you about problems." He waved his arm toward the newsroom. "I've got to be ready. I've got to pretend that Himes might get a stay. Which means I've got thirteen people I can't send home on a Friday night. All of whom had plans and who now hate me, and all of whom I've gotta pay time and a half while they're out there, cursing me under their collective breaths and wishing I was dead."

"I think I've got a serious lead on the murderer."

"So . . . call the cops."

"I did. They don't want to hear about it. Guess what?"

"I'll bite."

"They've got another dead woman. Number eleven."

Hawes sat forward in a hurry. "Says who?"

His face darkened as Corso filled him in. "But the kid didn't actually see a body," he said when Corso had finished.

"No."

"What was your impression of the kid?"

"If I had to guess, I'd say he was being straight with us."

Hawes blew the air from his lungs. "Then we've definitely got to notify SPD."

"I did," Corso said again.

Hawes reached for the phone, stopped his hand in midair. "Maybe Mrs. Van Der Hoven ought to . . . ," he said after a moment.

"You ask me, our mutual popularity is at an all-time low."

"Funny, but subscriptions are at an all-time high," Hawes mused.

"You suppose there's a connection there?"

"I prefer not to think about it."

"We could go public. Save our asses by writing the story."

Hawes rolled his eyes. "And if we're wrong?"

"Then it's like the Atlanta bombing all over again. The poor bastard in the van becomes the new Richard Jewell."

"And if we're right?"

"Then we just gave away one hell of a story."

"At least our asses would be covered."

"That's the Pulitzer spirit," Corso said.

"You got a better idea?"

"We've still got a full day. Maybe Dougherty and I can turn this guy."

"And where is the indispensable Miss Dougherty?"

"I took her home. We've been at it since the news conference yesterday morning."

"The news business is tough that way."

"We've gotta do something."

Hawes rocked in his chair as he thought it over. "You got a plan?" he asked finally. Corso told him what he had in mind.

Hawes winced and nodded simultaneously. He folded his stubby arms across his chest and leaned so far back in his chair his feet came off the ground. Corso watched his lips move in and out as he tried to square the idea with himself. "You know what it's like to go to the American Society of Newspaper Editors conference every year as the managing editor of the *Seattle Sun*, Corso?" Corso said he didn't. "I'm like"—he searched for a word—"plankton. The absolute bottom of the food chain. The bar conversation stops every time I slide onto a stool. The big timers look at me with a combination of pity and something more like terror. As if my presence reminds them of how bad things could actually get." He sat forward. "I stopped going a few years back. Got to the point where if one more of those guys gave me that patronizing little smile, I was going to pop him one." He looked up at Corso. "This year's event is in Denver, right after the Pulitzers in April. I was thinking this morning that I might just go. Maybe do a little smiling of my own."

"Then we better hope like hell I'm not right and that he doesn't kill again between now and tomorrow night."

Hawes folded his arms even tighter. Full straight-jacket hug.

"Bite your tongue," he said.

24

Yuppies love brunch. Especially on weekends, when, having survived yet another week in their cubicles, they come lurching out of their high-priced hovels to migrate purblind toward the bistro du jour, where, after an hour or so of waiting in the rain, they're awarded a table at which they languish well into the shank of the afternoon, sipping oceans of latte and picking at divine goat cheese omelets.

Julia's Bakery was packed to the rafters. Headline on the *Seattle Times* read "Judgment Day." The *Post Intelligencer* blared: "And One to Go!" The clock on the wall read 9:21 before Corso and Dougherty squeezed inside, shuffled their way through the service line, and then, for want of a table, back out the side door into the parking lot.

Corso set his coffee atop a blue mailbox and zipped his coat. The fog had disappeared. Leaving acrylic-blue skies, marred only

by occasional patches of fast-moving clouds. "You look remarkably status quo today," he offered. Beneath her full-length black
leather coat Dougherty wore a white blouse and a pair of blue
jeans tucked into black cowboy boots. She'd changed her lip and
nail colors from the usual black to fire-engine red. She looked
like a bigger version of fifties pinup girl Betty Paige.

She glared at him and grunted.

He retrieved his coffee. Blew away the steam. She rolled her
cup between her hands. "Where do we start?"

"Four crime scenes each." He recited the list from memory.

"What about the other locations?"

"We'll do this one together. Just to make sure we're on the
same page."

"This one?"

"Yeah, remember? Susanne Tovar, the first victim, was found
out back of here in the bakery's Dumpster."

"What about the hotel?"

"Buster Davis is our control group. Since he's the one got us
started on this thing, I want to call him last. That way, whatever
we find out today won't be tainted by what we already know."

She stopped a strip of cinnamon roll just short of her mouth. "I
don't understand."

"If we call Buster first and ask him what security company he
uses, then we'll have that company implanted in our heads while
we're out there knocking on doors. It's better to do it blind. It's
just human nature to try to prove what you already know. When
we're all done, we'll see how many duplicates we get, and then
we'll call Buster."

He gestured with his cup. "Come on."

They crossed Eastlake Avenue and stood on the sidewalk looking back at the bakery. Corso pointed north. "We're going to have
to do everything commercial within a square block of each dump
site."

Dougherty stuffed the last of the roll in her mouth. Held up a finger as she chewed and swallowed. She spread her arms. "Across the street like this too?"

"Yeah. If it's a neighborhood like this, you know, mostly residential with its own little business district, try to do every storefront. We've got one woman found three blocks from the Northgate Mall. If it's like that, wall-to-wall businesses for ten blocks all around, then we're going to have to do the best we can."

Together they walked to the far end of the block. Holiday Travel on one corner, Rory's pub across the street. Corso opened the door to Holiday Travel and stepped aside, allowing Dougherty to enter first. A young woman. Thick, wheat-colored hair, held back from her face by a tortoiseshell clip. Tapping away at the computer. She swiveled a one-eighty in her chair. Found a big smile.

"I'll bet you two want to get out of the rain," she said hopefully.

"Sounds great to me," Corso said. "But unfortunately, right at this moment, I don't think time is going to allow."

"I've got seven days, eight nights in Mazatlán . . . airfare, hotel, continental breakfast . . . four forty-nine ninety-five, double occupancy . . . plus tax, of course."

He gestured toward Dougherty. "My friend and I were thinking about renting that vacant storefront up at the end of the block."

"Oh," the woman said. "I hadn't noticed anything was empty."

"Up past the Italian restaurant," Dougherty said.

"We were wondering whether or not the building owners provide security or whether it was something we'd have to pay for out of our own pockets."

"Oh no," she said. "We can barely get the real estate corporation to fix the plumbing. Security comes out of the individual merchants' pockets."

"Who do you use?" Corso asked.

She pulled out a sliding shelf in her desk. A business card was taped to the wood.

"Reliable Security. In Shoreline. Same as everybody in the building. They supposedly give us a group discount." She waved an unbelieving hand. "Supposedly gets us a discount from our insurance companies too. So, I guess it probably evens out in the end."

Corso thanked her. She pulled a business card from a silver holder on her desk.

"Holiday for all your travel needs," she said.

Corso thanked her again, stuffed the card in his jacket pocket, and followed Dougherty out onto the sidewalk. "At this point," he said, "a week on a beach sounds pretty good."

Dougherty's laugh was anything but amused. "Yeah. I'll break out my thong."

"Don't be so hard on yourself, Dougherty. As far as I'm concerned, you're the very flower of American womanhood."

"I'm the whole goddamn garden."

"I'm serious," he said.

"So am I," she said. She bopped him on the arm. "But thanks for the thought, big fella. What now?"

Corso pointed across the street. "Let's start over there."

They split up. Corso did the florist, Dougherty the tavern. Corso the pizza joint, Dougherty the café. It took an hour and fifty-five minutes to work the neighborhood. Corso pulled the car keys from his pocket and held them out. "You take the car. I'll cab it." He checked his watch. "Where do you want to meet?"

"This is going to take forever," she said.

Corso pointed north along Eastlake Avenue. "Half a mile up the road there's a place on the left called Bridges."

"I know it."

"How late are the stores open?"

"On a Saturday night? Till nine probably."

"Let's meet at Bridges at nine-thirty."

5:56 P.M. Day 6 of 6

"Move to the front of the cell." The voice clattered through the concrete and steel, like a dry stick drawn along a fence. Walter Leroy Himes rose from his bunk and shuffled toward the light. He remained expressionless as he leaned his back against the cell door and stuck his arms out through the bars. Practiced hands snapped a cuff around each wrist. "Clear," a metallic voice called.

The door at the opposite end of the cell slid open on greased wheels. A guard came in carrying a tray, which he set down on the bunk. "Here's what you wanted, Walter Lee. Two bacon cheeseburgers, fries, and a couple of Cokes." He gave Himes a grin.

"Enjoy," he said.

The cell door closed behind him with a click. "Clear."

Himes stood still for a moment after the cuffs had been removed. Waiting for the sound of the footsteps to fade before ambling over and sitting next to the tray.

Forty yards away, in the red-zone security area, a pair of corrections officers stared at a grainy black-and-white picture. "Watch him," one said. "He'll touch everything on the plate, then check the room before he eats."

As if on cue, Himes used his right forefinger to probe the items on the tray. Seemingly satisfied, he got to his feet again and took a leisurely lap of the cell, moving from corner to corner, peering here and poking there, finally checking inside the toilet before returning to the bunk.

"Like there's somebody hiding in there with him," the other said.

"Old Walter always acts like somebody's gonna run up and take his grub from him. Just hates anybody watching him eat."

"Ain't gonna have that problem much longer, is he?"

Himes reached over and delicately slid a single french fry from its white paper wrapping. He put the end in between his lips and sucked it in like spaghetti, then grabbed the nearest burger and bit it in half. His jaw muscles worked like pile drivers as his mangled mouth mashed the burger. As he was about to swallow, Himes cast his eyes upward at the camera, and, mouth still full, opened his mouth. Wide.

"Jesus," said one of the guards. "That's disgusting."

"I count myself as a decent Christian, but I can't say I'm gonna be too sorry to see him go," said the other.

9:40 P.M. Day 6 of 6

On the opposite shore of Lake Union, the defunct ferry *Kalakala* lay beached in the gloom, like some festering carcass run aground by the tide. Once the pride of the Puget Sound ferry fleet, the old Art Deco vessel now lay derelict, listing hard to starboard, her hundred-car deck yawning out at the lake like an invalid bird waiting to be fed.

Corso got the waiter's attention. Pointed at his cup. The front door burst open and Dougherty came striding in. She swiveled her head, caught sight of Corso sitting in a booth overlooking the lake. She slid in opposite Corso. He showed the waiter two fingers. "How'd it go?" he asked.

"I had no idea there were so many security companies in one city," Dougherty said. "I stopped counting at forty."

"The paranoia business is booming," Corso said.

"Or how many people just flat wouldn't discuss it with me."

"Let me guess . . . for security reasons."

"Amazing, huh?"

"Or how many businesses don't have any type of security at all."

She nodded. "I must have had a dozen people tell me that since the rest of the strip mall was paying for security, they figured they'd just ride along on the other tenants' coattails." She threw a dozen or so pages of notes onto the table.

Corso read from his notes. "Lockworks, First Response, ADT, Homeguard, Proline, Washington Emergency Services, Entrance Controls, Security Link."

Dougherty retrieved a page of her notes and took over. "Intelligent Controls, Silver Shield, Protection Technology, Allied, Northwest, Lock Ranger. It goes on and on. How in hell are we going to sort all this out?"

"What we need to know is whether any of the companies appear on all ten lists." He tore the first page of notes from his notebook and slid them over the table toward Dougherty. "Here's the one we did together this morning. Now we've each got five."

The waiter set a mug of coffee in front of Dougherty and refilled Corso's. "Get you anything else?" he asked. Dougherty shook her head. Corso told him no, then took another sip from the cup and started working on his notes. Alphabetizing each site. Making it easier to compare notes. Then going back looking for matches.

Corso finished first. Ten minutes later, Dougherty made a couple of final scribbles and looked up.

"So? How many did you get?" he asked.

"Three."

"Me too."

She covered her paper with her hand. "You go first."

"No. You go."

"You first," she insisted.

"Indian poker," he said. "Together."

Dougherty laughed out loud. "You're getting silly on me, Corso."

"Ready?"

"Okay . . . on three."

"One . . . two . . . three . . ."

They each held their lists up over their heads. Dougherty's read: Reliable, Metro, Silver Shield. Same as Corso's. "Bingo," she said.

" 'Let's see what our studio audience has to say,' " Corso intoned.

He crossed the room to the pay phone and jimmied the directory from its metal moorings. Rasta Boy behind the counter opened his mouth to protest, but Corso waved him off. "I'll put it back in a minute," Corso said.

Corso slapped the book onto the tabletop. Turned to the beginning of the yellow pages. Worked his way back to H. Hotels. The Ambassador. The Atrium. The Aviator. Six-eight-two, four-five, eight-five. He pulled his phone from his pocket and dialed.

"Mr. Davis," he said. "This is Frank Corso. I spoke to you yesterday." Corso listened. "Yeah, the guy from the roof. Yes, sir. Yes, sir." Again he listened intently. "Just wanted to run a quick question by you, sir. Yes . . . thank you. The other day you said that the only other key to that gate was in the hands of your security company. Yes, sir. Yes. What company is that?" Corso winked at Dougherty. "Yes, sir. I sure will. Thanks again."

"Well?"

"Survey says . . . Silver Shield," Corso said.

"I'll be damned."

Corso fingered his way deeper into the yellow pages. Security. Flipped two pages. Moved his finger down the page: "Silver Shield Security, See our add on page 1,438." Corso thumbed back one page. Half-page ad. Red border. "Nationwide—America's first choice for security. Over three hundred offices across America. For instant response, call . . ."

Corso dialed.

"Silver Shield. This is Kramer. Your address, please."

"This isn't a security matter," Corso said quickly.

Kramer sounded disappointed. "How can I help you?"

"I'm looking for some information on a Silver Shield employee."

"You'd hafta call the people in personnel. On Monday. The number is—"

"I can't wait that long," Corso said.

"Then you're out of luck with me, buddy. Nobody but personnel—or maybe Mr. Gabriel himself—could tell you anything personal like that."

Corso mustered a hearty laugh. "Gabriel," he intoned enthusiastically. "Why, I had no idea Sam Gabriel owned Silver Shield. Thanks a lot, Mr. Kramer. I'll give Sam a call at home."

"Whoa, whoa," Kramer said. "I don't know who this Sam guy you know is, but before you get going off half-cocked, it's Vincent Gabriel who's the owner here."

"Jeez. Thanks for stopping me. I could have made a real fool of myself there." He hung up.

Dougherty raised an immaculate eyebrow. "It's scary how well you lie."

"Owner's a guy named Vincent Gabriel."

"What good does that do us?"

Corso pulled up the phone book and worked his way back to the G's. Two Vincent Gabriels. One down by Southcenter with a Military Road address. A strip mall wonderland. Strictly red necks, white socks, and blue-ribbon beer. The other was hard by the lake in Madison Park. Big-time, old-time, high-rent district. He remembered the yellow page ad, "Nationwide—America's first choice for security."

25

Dorothy Sheridan was keeping her mouth shut. She had no doubt about it. She was there to take the fall. She wasn't sure exactly when or how they were going to shift the blame her way, or, for that matter, what blame there was to shift. She was, however, certain it was going to happen.

Kesey tugged at his collar. "The governor is adamant. No smoking gun . . . no stay."

"He's right," the mayor said. "Even if, god forbid, Himes turned out to be innocent, the backlash would be less than if he stopped the execution without cause."

"I've gotta go," the DA said. "I've got a flight at ten-fifteen."

"You better take Sheridan here with you," the chief said. "She's been the survivor liaison the whole time. You handle the press, and she'll handle the survivors for you."

It took everything Dorothy had not to groan out loud. Prison.

An execution. Where in her job description, she wondered, did it say anything about maximum-security prisons and lethal injections?

Hizhonor scowled. "What survivors?"

"The victims' families," the chief said. "We've got . . ." As usual, he looked to Dorothy for a number.

"Eight," she said.

"We've got eight family members scheduled to witness the execution," he finished.

"Shit," said the mayor. "I suppose that Butler asshole is one of them."

"You can count on it," said Kesey.

"Himes's mother is there too," Dorothy said. The mayor looked horrified. "To watch?"

"No, sir," she said. "To say good-bye . . . you know, last respects and all."

10:00 P.M. Day 6 of 6

"Ain't neva give none of you-all a hard time. Not all the years I been here."

"We got procedures, Walter."

"Ain't neva asked none of you-all for nothin'."

"No . . . you haven't," said the new one they called Smitty.

"Wanna see my mama like a man. Not chained up like some cur dog."

Smitty looked up at the sergeant, who pursed his thin lips and shook his bullet head. "Gotta chain you up, Walter. It's the rules," Smitty said.

"Ain't right," Himes said. "You gonna let them freak people come in here and watch me die, but you won't let me see my mama like a man."

Smitty reached to slide the waist chain around Himes's middle. "Wait," the sergeant said.

Smitty stopped, genuflected, with the chain dangling from his hand.

"Clear," the sergeant said suddenly.

The cell door rolled open. "Come on, Walter," he said, stepping aside. "Let's go down the hall and see your mama." Himes looked down at his ankles as he shuffled out of the cell, at first short-stepping out of habit, then lengthening his stride as he left his cell without ankle chains for the first time in about three years.

Himes had nearly mastered his unencumbered gait when he stopped outside the second door on the right. Smitty pulled a key from his pocket and unlocked the door. Pulled it open. Himes stepped inside. Smitty shut the door behind him. Snapped the lock. The sergeant gave Smitty a bored look that said, What the hell?

Loretta Himes had her face buried in a wad of tissues as Walter slipped into the worn wooden seat. He leaned close to the screen. "Mama," he said gently.

She looked up. Her eye makeup lay in pools on her cheeks.

"Doan neva let 'em see you cry," he said.

10:10 P.M. Day 6 of 6

Scared, Dorothy knew. For fourteen years, she'd watched denying defendants as their facades had finally flickered. Seen them in that moment right after sentencing when the bailiff takes them by the arm. When they peer at their lawyers like furtive children begging to be held tightly and assured it was all a bad dream.

Yeah. She knew the look all right, and the pilot had it.

"A little foggier than we usually fly in. But . . . I understand it's an emergency, so we'll just take our time getting out of here. Weather's supposed to be clear on the other side of the mountains." He'd said it hopefully, but without conviction, before he'd disappeared inside the cockpit.

Across the aisle, she saw Marvin Hale peer out the tiny window into the gloaming. These days it didn't actually get dark; it merely segued to deeper shades of gray. She'd called home. Left a message for Brandy. She'd stopped just short of telling her how much she loved her. Afraid something in her voice would give away her terror.

Classic no-win situation. Either she was going to be forced to watch an execution or . . . What should she call it? What was the proper euphemism for something like this? Should she call it . . . a change in plans? Technical difficulties? A glitch? What?

The pilot revved the port engine, spun the plane on its axis, and started toward the invisible runways. For the first time in a week, her head was comfortably numb.

10:21 P.M. Day 6 of 6

The circular driveway ran slightly uphill, curving steadily left beneath arches of ancient oaks as it wound its way toward the shimmering lights a hundred yards ahead. Corso brought the Chevy to a halt in front of a three-story French Colonial mansion, whose elegant stone facade and slate-roofed turrets spoke eloquently of another age.

Dougherty whistled softly. "Aren't we just swell," she said.

A tall blond kid wearing a green Silver Cloud Valet Service jacket skipped down the front stairs and pulled open the driver's door before Corso got his seat belt unfastened.

"Evening, sir," he said.

Corso left the car running as he eased himself from behind the wheel and stepped out onto the driveway. Somewhere in the castle, a door opened and closed, allowing a slice of music and laughter to escape momentarily into the night. Along the front, the light from a dozen tall, transomed windows cast a golden glow down upon the entryway.

The sight of Dougherty stepping out onto the bricks seemed to startle the kid. His head swiveled from Corso, to Dougherty, to the house, and then back to Corso.

"Excuse me, sir. Don't mind me asking, but are you guys sure you've got the right place?"

"This the Gabriel residence?" Corso asked.

"Yes, sir . . . it is." His voice was tentative.

"You happen to know what Mr. Gabriel does for a living?" Corso asked.

"Some kind of security thing."

"Then we're in the right place."

The kid looked embarrassed. "You-all came for the reception, then?"

"What reception?"

"The wedding. Mr. Gabriel's daughter."

Corso handed the kid a ten-dollar bill. "Keep it handy," he said. "We're not going to be long." He turned to Dougherty. "You bring your gown?"

"As if . . . ," she huffed and headed for the door, where she grabbed the brass knocker and gave it three sharp raps. Inside the house, what sounded like a four-piece combo was playing Horace Silver's "Song for My Father."

Out in the driveway, the kid had made no move to park the car. He stood, slack-jawed, resting his forearms on the Chevy's roof. The front door opened.

Blond Margaret Thatcher hair. Her taut face suggested thirty-five, but the guile in her green eyes said fifty. She wore an ankle-length silver sheath. Silk. Understated and elegant. Highlighted by a double string of perfectly matched pearls. The minute she blinked them into focus, she swallowed the toothy welcome smile. Took her time looking them over, as if she couldn't decide whether she should call the cops or an exterminator.

"Yes?" she said icily.

"Very sorry to intrude," Corso said.

"How can I help you?" Her tone suggested she would have liked to add the words "off my front steps" but was far too well-bred.

"I need to speak to Vincent Gabriel."

She folded her arms against the chill. "I'm Mrs. Gabriel."

Corso handed her his press credential. She scanned it and handed it back.

"Whatever it is will have to wait until Monday." She stepped back and began to close the door.

"It could be a matter of life and death," Corso said quickly.

She searched his eyes for irony. Took in Dougherty again. Frowned.

"You're serious, aren't you?"

"Yes," he said. "I'm afraid I am."

"If this is about one of his security clients, you should—"

"It's not," Corso interrupted.

"My daughter . . . ," she began. Then stopped and heaved a sigh. "Life and death," she said again. Corso confirmed this.

She rubbed her upper arms as she stepped out onto the top step. "Go around that way . . . that side of the house," she said, pointing. "The solarium door is open. Wait in there. I'll get my husband."

Corso and Dougherty followed a flagstone path around the north end of the house. As they reached the corner and turned right again, Lake Washington came into view. Across the lake, the high-rises of Bellevue flickered like candles in the night, their fractured reflections dancing piecemeal across the rough surface.

The solarium ran perpendicular to the house. All glass. Round on top like a Quonset hut. Corso pulled open the door, stepped aside, and allowed Dougherty to enter first. In the center of the space, a palm tree nearly brushed the twenty-foot ceiling. A forest of exotic potted plants were scattered around, giving the impression that someone had strewn lawn furniture about the jungle. Overhead, a pair of brass ceiling fans twirled languorously.

Dougherty turned in a circle, taking it all in. "Great room," she said.

Before Corso could agree, Vincent Gabriel stepped into the room. A powerful-looking man in a tux he sure as hell hadn't rented. What used to be called swarthy. Six-two, maybe two-ten or so, with a thick mustache and a head of wavy salt-and-pepper hair he was never going to lose. His bearing and stride gave off an air of tightly controlled aggression. He crossed the room to Corso and Dougherty with a champagne glass in his hand and a scowl on his face.

"What's this?" he demanded.

"We're very sorry for the intrusion," Corso said.

Vincent Gabriel's expression suggested they were about to get sorrier.

"And who might you be?"

Again, Corso handed over his press credential. Unlike his wife, Vincent Gabriel read every word. Front and back. "Corso, huh?" he said. "You're the one who's been writing the Himes story for the *Sun*."

"Yes. I am."

"The one used to be with the *New York Times*."

"That's me," Corso said.

Gabriel waited, as if affording Corso an opportunity to defend himself.

Instead, Corso inclined his head and said, "This is my associate, Meg Dougherty."

Vincent gave her a curt nod. "I've got ninety-five guests inside, Mr. Corso. So, real quick here, you better tell me what is it you find so damned important that it requires interrupting my daughter's wedding reception."

"The Himes story," Corso said.

Gabriel stiffened, then reached over and set his champagne on a glass-topped table.

"And what might that awful mess have to do with me?"

"We've come across a piece of information that"—Corso chose his words carefully—"that suggests it might be possible the real killer is a security guard."

"What piece of information might that be?"

Without naming the Aviator Hotel, Corso told him the kids' story. The locked gate, the taggers. The van. The supposed guy in uniform.

"You're here on the word of vandals?" His tone carried an understood "you idiot."

"No, sir," Dougherty piped up. "We're here because we took what the kids told us and ran with it."

"Ran with it how?"

"We divided up the murders and canvassed the neighborhoods where the bodies were found." She gave him the blow-by-blow. Halfway through, he checked his watch and interrupted. "I still don't see what this has to do with me."

"Only three security companies had clients in the immediate neighborhoods of where all eleven bodies were found," she said.

"Reliable, Metro Link, and you—Silver Shield," Corso added.

Vincent Gabriel made a disbelieving face. "I'll bet you could canvass any three square commercial blocks in the Pacific Northwest and get much the same result. Reliable, Metro, and

Silver Shield are the three biggest players in this part of the
country."

"Then Corso called down to where this whole thing with the
kids started," Dougherty said.

"The guy who says the only key other than his belongs to his
security company," Corso prompted.

"And where the kids swear the guy had a key to the gate."

"And he's a Silver Shield customer?"

"Yessir," Corso and Dougherty said in unison. For the first
time, Vincent Gabriel's tanned face showed concern.

"Interesting," he said, picking up his champagne glass. "Tell
you what. You two come down to the office on Monday morning
and we'll see if—"

Corso interrupted him. "That could be too late, Mr. Gabriel.
Have you read the paper today?"

"What? No . . . with all the—"

"He killed another young woman yesterday afternoon," Dougherty said.

"The killings are getting closer together," Corso added. "It's
only three days since the last one."

Gabriel's complexion lost some of its glow. "You can't expect
me to—"

Before he could finish, the door connecting the solarium to
the house swung open. The bride, looking internally radiant in
that way in which only brides are capable.

She looked like her mother. Same height. Same hair. Same
frank green eyes. Her gown trailed across the terra-cotta tile floor
to Vincent's side.

"Is everything all right?" she asked her father.

He patted her arm and assured her that everything was just
peachy.

"Well, then, come on," she pleaded. "The Lunquists want a

picture with us." She tried to tug him along by the forearm, but he stood his ground.

"Tell them I'll be in in a minute."

When she started to protest, he put a finger delicately on her lips. "Just a minute, Princess," he said softly. "Tell them I'll be right there."

She kissed him on the cheek, leaving a silver-pink signature on his face, shot Corso and Dougherty a quizzical look, and flounced out the way she'd come. Her father watched her cross the room and close the door behind herself. He stood for a moment staring at the air in her wake, as if she'd left a vapor trail.

"I can't imagine losing her," he said.

"Most people can't imagine it even after it happens," Corso said. "Something in them refuses to believe it's possible to outlive a child."

"I don't know what I'd do," he said. "What I'd get out of bed for in the morning." He waved his arm around the room. "You get to a point in life where you've got everything you thought you wanted and when you think about losing a child or a wife . . . it's like all of a sudden you realize none of it really means a damn thing to you. That only the people in your life are worth a god-damn thing. All the rest of this . . ." His voice got husky as it trailed off. "I have to go," he said almost apologetically, as if suddenly embarrassed and overwhelmed by the magnitude of his blessings. "I can't—"

"One minute," Corso said. "Give me one minute."

As Vincent started for the door, Corso kept on talking to his back. "The FBI profile of this guy says he's a white male, somewhere between twenty-five and thirty-five. A loner. The kind of guy who eats lunch by himself and has a hard time getting along with his fellow workers. Bad interpersonal skills. Single, but

probably lives in a dependent relationship with a woman—
maybe a sister or a cousin, something like that. Maybe has a history of petty crimes. Fires, assaults, things like that. He may have
some sort of strict religious background. The Bureau thought
there was a ceremonial element to the way the bodies were left.
And, if the kids are to be believed, he drives a primer-gray Dodge
van, with quarter-moon bubble windows in the back."

Vincent Gabriel had stopped with his hand on the door handle. When he turned back toward Corso, his face was like concrete. "That's it?" he asked tentatively.

"He's probably had some stressor in his life lately. Something
that's set him off on another murder spree," Corso added.

Gabriel blew air through his pursed lips and then ran a hand
through his hair.

"Sound like anybody who might work for you?" Dougherty
asked.

Vincent Gabriel shrugged. "Could be," he said in a low voice.
"Not what he drives or anything . . . but I might—" He stopped
himself. "I'm not usually involved in the day-to-day operations."
He shrugged. "Tell you the truth, most of the time, I couldn't tell
you who works for me and who doesn't, let alone what they drive.'

"But . . . ," Corso pressed.

"But lately . . . the local office . . . had . . ." He searched for
the right phrase. "They had a really weird scene."

"Weird how?"

Gabriel stared at his patent-leather shoes and nodded almost
imperceptibly.

"Guy that's worked for us for years. I get a call from his supervisor. Says the guy's been getting increasingly weird lately. Says
he's concerned . . ." He looked up at Corso. "You know—the
guy's a gun nut. What with all the workplace violence . . . the
supervisor thinks this guy might be dangerous or something. So
he calls me."

"This guy have any unusual stressors in his life lately?" Corso asked. "Something that could push him over the edge?"

"Yeah, the guy I'm thinking of . . . he has," Gabriel said. "Two, in fact."

He absentmindedly touched the lipstick on his cheek and then looked from Dougherty to Corso, as if pleading for absolution. "His mother died a month or so back and then . . . two weeks ago"—he looked up at the twirling fans—"I fired him."

"What for?" Dougherty asked.

Vincent Gabriel took a deep breath. He looked tubercular. "Threatening to kill another employee." He spread his big hands. "He was completely out of it," he said. "He kept claiming the guy was stealing from his locker."

"Any chance he was right?"

"We don't have lockers."

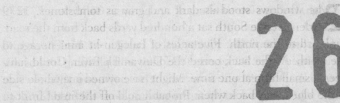

Saturday, September 22
11:02 P.M. Day 6 of 6

"Got no damn use for no preacher," Himes said to the sergeant. "Don't be bringin' his sorry ass in here."

"You sure, Walter? I seen him bring comfort to a lotta men."

Himes laughed. "He doan come in here to comfort the likes of me. He comes in so's he can comfort the likes of you-all. So's you can go home tonight, have dinner wid the Mrs. tellin' yourself there's some kinda difference between the killin' you-all do and the kind they say I done."

The sergeant folded his arms and looked over at Smitty. "Walter's got a point there," he said to the other man. "Not a whole lotta difference . . . not from Walter's end anyway, is there?"

"No, sir," said the younger man. "I guess there isn't."

The windows stood as dark and gray as tombstones. 1279 Arlen Avenue South sat a hundred yards back from the road. Junkyard to the north. Five acres of halogen-lit mini-storage to the south. At the back oozed the Duwamish River. Could have been a small farm at one time. Might have owned one whole side of the block, way back when. Probably sold off the street front to make ends meet. Nothing left now but a driveway easement and a narrow strip of ground along an acrid river.

From the end of the muddy drive, a single yellow porch light revealed a peeling two-story facade cowering beneath a stand of mossy oaks. The clapboard siding now forming a shallow V as the structure sagged inexorably downward. In the distance a siren wailed its plaintive song. Closer, a junkyard dog picked up the note and rolled it into a long miserable howl.

"That's gotta be it," Corso said.

"What are we doing here, anyway?" Dougherty asked.

"I've got to be sure."

"What? You think he's going to have a sign or something?"

"I'd settle for a van with bubble windows."

"You're nuts."

Corso shrugged. "All we've got so far is a big maybe. I want to be sure."

He gave the Chevy some gas. Rolled past the driveway and parked in front of the junkyard, between a battered flatbed truck and an orange VW beetle. He killed the engine and the lights. Grabbed the door handle. "Come on," he said.

"What if he shows up while we're walking down his driveway?"

"Then we claim to be broken down and stupid. We saw a light and were looking for help."

"You're out of your goddamn mind," Dougherty whispered.

"Come on. The driveway's empty. Let's just poke around a little."

"What if he's parked behind the house?"

"If it's a van, we hot-foot it out of there and call the cops."

"No way."

"Okay," he said. "Wait in the car . . . I'll be right back."

She grabbed him by the elbow. "You're not leaving me out here alone," she said.

"Come on, then."

"I hate you."

"Take a number."

She punched him in the arm. Hard. "You go first," she hissed through her teeth.

Corso pointed to the grass-covered berm running between the worn tire ruts. "Up here."

The ditches on either side of the drive were a forest of dead dandelions, the unmowed summer stalks standing stiff and still in the unnatural light as Corso and Dougherty edged their way up the driveway toward the house.

As they came abreast of the house, it became obvious that no vehicle was present. Corso felt his breathing become deeper and more regular. Despite feeling like his throat was full of dirt, he managed to swallow a couple of times.

The end of the drive was worn in a circle. A well-trodden path led from the circle to the back door. To the right, what had once been a long outbuilding running across the back of the property now lay collapsed upon itself. Fallen to the left, with its walls and roofs fanned out along the ground like playing cards. At the far end, the tines of a rusted hay rake lay like the rib cage of some ancient metal beast.

The weed-covered backyard sported a pile of partially burned furniture. Corso walked over to the pile. Probed it with his toe. In the dim light, he could make out the soot-covered remains of a brass bed. A partially burned mattress and box spring, their floral prints scorched in some places, melted in others. Blankets and bedclothes. A couple of lamps and shades. Smashed picture frames. An end table, maybe two. A charred collection of old women's clothes and underthings. All piled together in a smelly heap. Corso reached gingerly into the pile, pulled aside the pieces of a broken picture frame, and extracted the picture between his fingers. Turned it over. A color rendition of Christ expelling the moneylenders from the temple. Carefully, he put the picture back on the pile.

He dusted his palms together as he crossed the lawn to the back door. Grabbed the handle on the screen door. The rusted spring shrieked as Corso pulled open the door. In the junkyard, a trio of dogs began to bark. Corso rapped on the door with his knuckles.

"Hello," he called tentatively.

The door swung inward.

"Did you . . . ," Dougherty sputtered.

He raised a hand. Scout's honor. "I just knocked. It opened on its own."

"Hello," he sang again.

She read the gleam in his eyes. "Don't even think about it."

He elbowed the door open. Poked his head in. "Anybody home?" he called.

Silence. Corso turned a dull red as he stepped across the threshold. Dougherty poked her head in the door. She could see past the room they were in, up the hall and into what must be the living room. Everything was a familiar red. "Darkroom bulbs," she whispered.

They were in the kitchen. The room smelled of rancid milk and decay. The old-fashioned sink was piled high with dirty dishes. The counters awash in paper plates, takeout containers and empty beer cans. Rainier Lite mostly.

Corso started forward. She grabbed him by the belt, but he kept moving, towing her over the threshold and through the kitchen into what probably had been the dining room. A window on the left had been covered from the inside. Rough-sawn plywood had been nailed over the opening, the edges dented and split from the force of the hammer blows. To the right of the window, a gun case sat catty-corner. Full. Maybe a dozen weapons. All chained together through the trigger guards. From among the shotguns and deer rifles poked the priapic banana clip of an AK-47.

Corso moved forward. Peeked into the living room. Thrift shop furniture along the perimeter. Knicknacks on the shelves. A rag rug on the floor. Big color portrait of Jesus—blond-haired and blue-eyed—over the mantel. Everything shipshape. Same red bulb burning overhead. Same window treatment. Half-inch plywood and ten-penny nails.

"Let's get out of here," Dougherty whispered.

Corso headed toward the stairs. "Let's have a look upstairs." Before she could protest, he said, "A quick cruise upstairs and then we'll be gone." He held out his hand. Dougherty released her grip on his belt and laced her fingers through his.

The stairs popped and groaned as they climbed, moving quickly now, like children running home after dark. No plywood over the windows up here. Tattered curtains over old-fashioned shades.

One bedroom on either side of the second-floor landing. Two rooms of some kind down the hall. Corso opened the door on the right. Hit the lights. Regular bulb. The room was bare. Completely empty, right down to the pine boards covering the floor. He pulled Dougherty across the planks, pulled open the interior door. Found the light switch to the right of the door. A bathroom. Similarly empty. Spotless and smelling of chlorine bleach.

Still pulling Dougherty along by the hand, he retraced his steps across the room, crossed the landing, and pulled open the opposite door. About half the size of the master bedroom across the hall, the room was military spare. A single bed along one wall was made to a precision seldom seen in civilian circles. Shoes stood in a perfect line in the mouth of the closet, where each hanger was precisely equidistant from its mates. The walls were bare except for a single marine corps poster: "The Free, the Proud, the Brave."

Dougherty balked in the doorway, so Corso let go of her hand and crossed to the bookcase. What must have been every issue of *Soldier of Fortune* ever printed. Gun manuals. *Police Digest. Guns and Ammo.* Police manuals. The NRA newsletter. "A regular Charlton Heston," Corso said under his breath.

"What?" Dougherty said from the doorway. Corso didn't answer. Just moved from the bookcase to the dresser.

The top of the dresser was arranged with the same precision. A silver comb and brush set perfectly aligned. A candy dish full of change. Pennies, nickels, dimes, and quarters, each in its own little space. Exactly in the center of the coins sat a brass skeleton key. Six huge bullets, fifty-caliber at least, stood like teeth along the back edge. At the right, half a dozen condoms, stretched out straight and neat in red foil packs.

"Corso," Dougherty hissed from the doorway. "Come on."

He nodded and returned to her side. She followed him down the hall. Another bathroom. Same precise arrangement. Bright, gleaming fixtures. Towels so neat the bathroom looked like one in a motel. Corso pulled open the medicine cabinet. Lined up like little soldiers stood a dozen or so pill bottles. Corso scanned the labels: Risperdal, Zyprexa, Haloperidol, Clozapine, Olanzapine, Sertindol. "What's all that?" Dougherty whispered.

"Antipsychotic medication," Corso said.

Back on the landing, they skirted the stairwell to the door of the remaining room. Locked. Corso shook the knob. Then stepped back and lowered his shoulder.

"Don't you dare," she said, wagging a fist in his face.

Instead of arguing, Corso turned and jogged back to the furnished bedroom. Dougherty stood transfixed. He reappeared a few seconds later with an old fashioned brass key in his hand. He put the key in the lock, turned it one way—nothing—then the other, and the lock snapped. He pushed the door open. The room was dark. Over Corso's shoulder, Dougherty could see a plywood-covered window.

He reached inside, groping for the light switch. Found it. The room lit up like a ballpark. A dozen track lights hung from the ceiling along three sides of the room, spilling fans of white light down along the bare walls and boarded-over windows. Corso walked out into the middle of the room and looked around. On his left, a floor-to-ceiling curtain hung bunched in the far corner. His eyes followed the aluminum track around the room. Back to where Dougherty stood in the doorway. To her left sat a brand-new leather lounger and an oak end table. On the table, a crystal ashtray glinted in the harsh overhead lights. Beneath the odors of stale smoke and nicotine, something sickly sweet hung in the air.

Corso gestured toward the chair. "So, what? Somebody comes in here, pulls back the curtain, sits in their favorite chair, puts their feet up, lights up a smoke, and then what, stares at the walls?"

Dougherty took three steps into the room. "Weird," she said. "It's like a home theater or something, except there's nothing behind the curtain."

Corso walked to the far wall. Running his hands over the rotting plaster and splintered plywood, feeling for something no available to the eye. Nothing. He turned to Dougherty and shrugged. "Beats me," he said.

"Let's go," she begged.

Corso started for the door. Then suddenly stopped. Tilted his head. "Or maybe," he said tentatively, "maybe you come into the room and close the curtain."

He walked to the corner, grabbed the edge of the curtain, and began to pull the heavy material along its overhead track. As he walked along the wall, he heard Dougherty catch her breath. And then again, as he moved along the far wall, rounded the corner, and turned back her way, something stuck in her throat.

She began moving toward the center of the room as if she were remote-controlled. Corso let go of the curtain and looked around.

Clothes. Women's clothes. Complete ensembles. Pinned neatly to the inside of the curtain. Outerwear on the left. Underwear on the right. Nine complete sets, with room for at least one more.

Corso pointed to the set directly in front of him. "Victim number four. Jennifer Robison," he said. Matching black bra and panties. A black, sleeveless blouse, silk maybe, and a pair of leopard-skin stretch pants. "That's what she was reported to be wearing when she disappeared from the Northgate Mall."

"You catch this?" Dougherty asked, pointing upward.

Written along the top of the curtain in bold black letters: "Behold the ten brides of Christ . . . who having strayed from his ways are now returned to the fold of our master, like lost sheep." Then it started over. "Behold the ten . . ."

"Jesus," he said as he moved around the room. The garments were attached to the curtain with little color-coordinated safety pins.

"Can you smell it?" Dougherty asked. She rubbed a white

sports bra between her fingers and then held the fingers to her nose. "Smells like my grandfather."

Corso leaned in close to the closet set of clothes. Recoiled. Then leaned in again. "Old Spice," he said.

Dougherty looked ill. "You don't suppose he—"

"Let's get the hell out of here," Corso said.

They moved quickly now. Doused the light and relocked the room. Hurried down the hall. Turned left into the occupied bedroom, crossed the room, and set the key carefully in the bowl of change.

Abandoning any pretense of stealth, they thumped down the stairs. They went the way they had come, to the back door. Corso peeked out. The yard was empty. He grabbed Dougherty by the hand. As they double-timed it around the house and back down the driveway, Corso pulled the phone from his pocket and dialed

He kept it short and sweet. Didn't give Densmore the chance to say anything other than his name. "Densmore . . . this is Corso. You listen to me, goddamnit. We got him. Dead to rights He killed all of them. Past and present. His name is Patrick Defeo." Corso spelled it. "He lives at twelve seventy-nine Arlen Avenue South. The driveway between Arlen Auto Parts and the Cascade Self-Storage yard. Call the chief and get the execution stopped and then get down here. Hurry. And bring the goddamn marines. He's armed to the teeth. Lotsa backup. You hear me?"

He pocketed the phone.

Dougherty was dragging him now. Pulling him headlong over the rutted tracks. Ten yards from the end of the drive, Corso heard the squeal of tires, tried to stop and listen, but Dougherty wasn't buying. She dropped his hand and began to run, her long strides eating up the ground. Good thing she was wearing boots If she'd been going any faster, she'd have plowed facefirst into the gray van that slid to a stop in the mouth of the driveway.

27

The van's engine shuddered slightly at each revolution. The rhythmic tick of a bad valve seemed to be the only sound moving in the air. Behind the nearly black windows, the figure leaned to his right, as if fetching something from the glove compartment. From where he stood in the driveway, Corso could see the rear bubble window puffing out like a blister from the van's flat profile.

Dougherty was backing toward Corso, who began moving quickly toward the van. He swallowed and put on his best Jim Rockford smile.

"Look, honey, we got lucky."

Dougherty's expression suggested she was not familiar with English. Corso hooked her around the waist and forced her forward. Skidding her over the grass.

"What . . . you can't read the sign?" Defeo said in a nasal tenor.

He couldn't have weighed more than a hundred fifty pounds. A pipsqueak. "Somethin' about the sign you two didn't understand?"

Corso kept smiling. Mr. Jovial. "What sign is that?"

Corso had no intention of squinting into the headlights. He kept moving, forcing Defeo to step aside as they made their way past the van, out into the street. The guy smelled of Old Spice. Corso nearly gagged. Defeo's hand trembled as he pointed to a tattered sign hanging askew! "No Trespassing."

"Sorry," Corso said. "It was dark as hell when we walked down. I never even saw the sign." He turned to Dougherty. "Did you see it, honey?"

She managed to stammer out, "No."

"Well, what the hell are you doing here anyway?" Defeo asked. He walked around Corso, taking him in from all angles. "Nobody comes down here at night no more. No reason to." He made eye contact for the first time.

You had to pull your eyes from the twitching muscles around his mouth before you could process the face. Patrick Defeo appeared to have been made of spare parts. His right eye was fully an inch higher than its counterpart. Same thing with his cab-door ears. Offset. Angular, the effect was of a head that had been welded together. The expression lost and desperate, like one of those long-ago *Life* black-and-whites of gaunt Dust Bowl refugees.

He wore a blue baseball cap. "FBI" in big gold letters. The hat was sized down as far as it would go, leaving a four-inch piece of strap sticking out the back. Otherwise it was all camouflage. Fatigues with a pack of Marlboros rolled into the left sleeve. Tiny spit-shined boots. Pants tucked into the boots. Marine insignia on his chest. Special Forces patches sewn on his narrow shoulders.

"We broke down," Corso said. "Up the street." He pointed

toward the Chevy. "We were going along just fine and then just like that"—he snapped his fingers—"it quit."

Dougherty regained her wits and said, "We saw the house light and thought maybe you'd call a tow truck for us."

It wasn't just his mouth. Defeo was twitchy all over, as if his limbs had a life of their own. He seemed to be incapable of standing still. Constantly moving from one foot to another, shifting his weight, as if he was about to walk off and then suddenly changed his mind. He folded his arms across his chest to keep them still. Beneath his arms, his fingers fluttered like wings.

"Can't imagine what might have happened. Always been a real reliable car. Nothing like this ever happened before."

Defeo rolled his neck, like he was working out a kink. "Just quit, you said."

"Just like that," Corso said. "I'm terrible with cars. Don't know a thing about 'em. Never have."

Defeo looked Corso over like he was measuring him for a suit. "What was you doing down here anyway?" he demanded. "The old woman sent you two down here to spy on me? Still can't keep her damn nose outta my business."

Dougherty began to stammer, "Oh . . . no . . . we . . . not to spy . . . we—"

"We just took a wrong turn somewhere," Corso said quickly.

Defeo cocked his head, as if listening to distant voices. Rolled his neck again.

"Lemme have a look at this broke-down car of yours," Defeo said, gesturing up the road with his chin. "Lemme see it."

"We were desperate," Dougherty said as they moved toward the Chevy. "Yours was the only light on the whole street."

Defeo's eyes rolled in his head like a horse's. "Nobody out here no more," he said. He swung his arms in an arc. "Used to be nothin' but farms." He pointed at the mini-storage yard. "That was Jorgenson's dairy." He looked up at Corso. "Will be again too.

Someday. When the final turnaround comes. Everything's gonna be like it was before."

He looked from Corso to Dougherty and back, as if daring them to disagree.

Suddenly, Defeo stopped walking. Reached over and grabbed Dougherty by the arm. Squinted at the gold bracelet tattooed around her wrist and the red letters in the palm of her hand. "What the hell you go and defile yourself like that for?" he asked. "That's a hell of a thing. Let a woman defile herself that way." He dropped her arm and looked to Corso for an explanation, as if to say, "You let her do that to herself?"

Corso kept grinning and walking.

Dougherty hung back now. Rubbing her arm where he'd touched it. Corso pointed to the Chevy. "Here it is," he said. Defeo looked the car over as if he were going to salvage it for parts. "All parked nice and neat," he commented. "You push it in here?"

"Just rolled it right in," Corso said.

"Get in. Pop the hood," Defeo said.

Corso slid into the driver's seat. Found the hood release. Pulled it. Dougherty slipped into the passenger seat and locked the door. Still massaging her arm.

Defeo fiddled around for a moment and then opened the hood.

Dougherty shot Corso a panicked look. He made a "stay calm" gesture.

"Try it," Defeo said.

Instead of turning the key to the right, Corso turned it to the left. Got a series of electrical clicks. "Nothing," he said out the window.

"Try it again," Defeo called back. Corso did it again.

"You sure you turning it the right way?" Defeo asked.

"Positive," Corso assured him.

They kept repeating the process for what seemed to Dougherty an hour, until finally Defeo dropped the hood. He walked around to the driver's side and leaned down. Peered into the car. Gave Corso his version of a smile. "I'm gonna run up the house, get my toolbox," Defeo said. A muscle in his cheek fluttered like a butterfly.

He looked back over his shoulder twice as he hustled back to the van. Smiling all the way, like he'd just heard a good joke and couldn't wait to tell it to somebody else. The van began to roll. Corso checked his watch. Thirteen minutes since he'd called Densmore.

"Did you smell him?" Dougherty asked.

Corso nodded. "Let's get the hell out of here. From now on he's Densmore's problem." He turned the key in the ignition. Nothing. Tried it again. Still nothing. His stomach was suddenly ice cold.

"He . . . ," was all Dougherty could get out.

He grabbed the door handle. "Come on."

In the junkyard, the dogs were growling along the fence. He grabbed Dougherty by the hand and sprinted diagonally across the street, running along the fronts of the buildings, trying doors, looking for a place to duck in and hide, finding nothing until, fifty yards up the street, they came to a narrow alley separating a welding shop from something called Fircrest Fabrication. A pair of fifty-five-gallon drums were chained together in the mouth of a grimy alcove. One barrel was marked "Oil." The other, "Solvents." He peered over the top into a narrow space between the recycling drums and the metal wall behind. Maybe three feet wide. Big enough.

He grabbed Dougherty by the elbows and lifted her completely over the drums. Set her gently on the littered ground.

"Get down," he said. "Stay down."

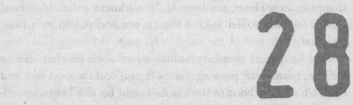

Saturday, September 22
11:38 P.M. Day 6 of 6

His knuckles glowed white around the phone. Again, he paced over and peered down the driveway. Nothing had changed. The van still sat facing the street. Lights on. Engine running. The tired yellow bulb over the front door carved the same deep shadows into the yard.

"Come on," he muttered to himself.

Corso jogged back to the alley. Dougherty sat huddled against the north wall, her usually ruddy face now the color of cement.

"What if they don't come?" she wheezed.

"They'll come," he said, with a good deal more conviction than he felt. He checked his watch. Sixteen minutes since he'd hung up on Densmore. Four since Defeo went for his tools. This time of night, if they were coming, it shouldn't be long.

He ran to the edge of the driveway and looked down. Status

quo. On his way back to Dougherty, he heard the sound of studded tires snapping on the pavement. He turned. No lights. The snapping drew closer, until out of the darkness a dark blue Ford Crown Victoria rolled around the corner and pulled to a stop, with the front half of the car blocking the driveway. Wald was driving. Densmore shotgun. Donald in back, behind Wald. Densmore was out of the passenger door the second the car came to a stop. Circled the hood of the car. Got right up in Corso's face.

"Where's the backup?" Corso asked.

"You just don't know when to quit, do you?" he said.

"The guy's got automatic weapons, fellas. You guys are gonna need some serious help here. Lots of it."

Behind Densmore's back, the two cops exchanged worried looks. Densmore held up a moderating hand. He turned to his fellow cops. "We don't even know if this is the guy. All we've got is the say-so of the world's most notorious liar here."

"Still, Andy . . . we better—" Wald began.

Densmore was having none of it. "Last I looked, Wald, I was still the three. You got any complaints, you better take it up with somebody downtown."

Corso stared disbelievingly at Densmore. "Did you call the chief? You didn't, did you?" He turned to the other cops. "Did he call about Himes?"

"What makes you think this is the guy?" Donald asked Corso.

Dougherty was out of the alley now, walking across the pavement toward the men, her eyes the size of hubcaps. "He's got the victims' clothes on display. He's got, like, this really sick little shrine set up in there," she said.

The cops exchanged another long look. "And you know this how?" Wald asked.

Dougherty covered her mouth with her hand, looked to Corso.

"We were inside the house," he said.

Densmore bared his teeth. "You broke into . . . ??" he barked.

"It wasn't locked."

"You realize . . . you asshole"—he stomped in a tight circle—
"you realize you've tainted every piece of evidence inside that
house, don't you? We're not going to be able to use anything in
there."

Densmore jabbed a finger, first at Corso, then at Dougherty.
He had a smile on his face. "You two are under arrest. As soon as
we get this sorted out, I'm having you transported downtown on
charges of—"

Whatever charges Densmore had in mind were lost when
Donald suddenly said, "We've got movement up at the house."

He was right. The light over the front door had been turned
off, leaving only the headlights and the ghostly purple reflections
of the mini-storage yard to illuminate the scene. As Corso
squinted into the gloom, Defeo clicked on the high beams. No
doubt about it. He could see the cop car across the front of the
driveway. After a moment, he threw open the door of the van,
jumped out, and ran back into the house.

"He made us," said Donald.

Wald popped the trunk on the cop car and began shouldering
himself into a Kevlar vest. Donald stood dumbfounded for a
moment and then hustled over and followed suit; his long delicate fingers shook as he pulled the Velcro fasteners tight across
his chest. By the time Wald had the vest settled over his suit, he
was alternately thumbing shells into a shotgun and peering nervously down the muddy track toward the van.

Densmore fixed Corso with a final feral stare, stepped around
Donald, and leaned into the trunk. Instead of a vest, he came out
with a bullhorn.

"Call for backup, Chucky," Wald said.

Donald had gotten one step toward the front of the car when
Densmore snapped, "No, we'll handle this."

Wald started for the radio. "Fuck you, Densmore," he said. "You want to risk your own ass, that's okay by me. But—"

He didn't get to finish. Up at the house, Defeo was back in the van. Wald squatted in front of the driver's door, holding the shotgun in his left hand. Thumbed off the safety.

"The van's moving," Donald chanted.

He was right. The van was rolling forward down the drive. The bright lights and dark-tinted windows made Defeo completely invisible.

The van stopped. Seventy yards from the cop car. Densmore arranged his gold shield over his heart like it would make him bulletproof. He got to his feet and faced the van over the hood of the car. He held his service revolver in his left hand and the bullhorn in his right. He straightened his spine and brought the bullhorn up to his lips like a carnival barker.

"Jesus, Densmore, get down," Wald said, tugging at his partner's pant leg. "Are you fucking crazy?"

Densmore's electronic voice crackled through the darkness.

"This is the Seattle Police Department. You are surrounded. Turn off the car and put both hands out the window."

Defeo raced the engine. Corso thought he might have heard high-pitched laughter. Wald got to his knees, in firing position. Donald rested his forearms on the roof as he aimed at the windshield. His face was taut. His mouth hung open.

"This is Detective Sergeant Andrew Densmore of the Seattle Police Department. Turn off the car and—"

Defeo came up through the sunroof. Fired half a dozen rounds before anyone could move. The force of the slugs moved Densmore backward, like he was on tracks. Moon-walking in reverse. The bullhorn arced back into the darkness. Corso threw himself into the ditch beside the driveway. The assault weapon began to spit bullets in sixes and eights. Tearing the windows from the car, sending the glass showering down onto the pavement. The force of the multiple impacts rocked the car on its springs. Gaping holes appeared on the far side as flattened slugs began to punch their way through the sheet metal. And then it stopped.

Donald crouched behind the rear tire, his arms thrown over his head.

Wald kept the engine block between himself and the van. Densmore lay in the road, one foot twitching, his arms outstretched above his head, as if he were basking on the beach. His service revolver lay in the middle of the street. Corso thought of trying to drag him from the line of fire, but, before he could force himself into action, the assault began anew. Again the flat sound of the muzzle filled the night air. The cop car began to disintegrate as the bullets tore the metal to pieces. Pieces of metal began to fall noisily to the street. The car squatted on its rims. Then silence again.

"He's coming," Donald shouted. The roar of the van's engine filled the air. Corso jumped to his feet, took one step to the right, and retrieved Densmore's revolver from the pavement. When he turned, the van was no more than fifty feet away, its worn fan belt screaming as it rocketed down the rutted track.

Wald was on his feet, pumping the shotgun. The windshield of the van was a shattered mess. Corso raised the revolver and began pulling the trigger. Over and over as the van lurched onward. He was still pulling the useless trigger when Wald dove out from behind the car and tackled him back into the ditch.

The van hit the police car doing about forty miles an hour, nearly lifting the Crown Victoria up onto its side. Six tons of scrap metal hovered in the air for a moment and then slammed back to earth. An eerie silence settled over the scene. Only the soft ticking of cooling metal was audible above the buzzing of the streetlights.

Wald scrambled up from the ground, keeping the shotgun trained on the van as he worked his way between the two cars, inching toward the driver's door. The van's windshield had torn loose from the frame and was about to collapse inward. Except right above the steering wheel, where a red dimple of impacted glass bulged outward like a boil.

"Put both hands out the window," Wald screamed.

Corso gulped air, snapped his head around looking for Dougherty. She lay fifteen yards to his left. Facedown in the ditch. Unmoving. His legs were loose-jointed and seemed to have a will of their own as he covered the distance and knelt by her side.

"Hands out the window," Wald screamed again.

Corso took her by the shoulders and carefully turned her over. Her eyes popped open in terror. She raised a hand to strike out, recognized Corso and instead threw her arms around his neck and pulled him down upon her.

"Is it over?" she breathed into his neck.

Corso said it was. "You okay?" he asked. She said she was. Corso disentangled himself and got to his feet. He took her hands and pulled her from the ground.

"We're going to jail, huh?" she said. Corso looked back over his shoulder.

Wald had the driver's door open. He rested the shotgun on his hip while he felt for life on the driver's throat.

"Maybe not," Corso said.

"Is he?" she asked.

"I think so, yeah," Corso said, taking her by the elbow and turning her away. She wobbled, like the heels weren't connected to her boots.

"Perp's dead," Wald announced. The sound of his own voice seemed to bring him around. He swiveled his head. "Chucky," he hollered. "Andy."

The force of the collision had driven Donald all the way across the street. He rose from the grass wiping at a nosebleed, his trousers blown out to reveal a pair of peeled, bloody knees. His unfired gun was still in his hand. "Over here," he yelled.

Wald was breathing heavily through his mouth. His lip was bleeding; his bright yellow tie had escaped the vest and now lay flopped up over his shoulder. The shotgun hung from his limp right arm. He found himself looking at the soles of Densmore's shoes and stopped in his tracks. He gulped air and shouted to Donald on the far side of the street.

"Chucky! Call for an aide car. Officer-down call."

Donald holstered his gun. "For Christ's sake, Wald . . . come over here and look at the poor bastard. He doesn't need an aide car. Half his head's gone." As if sickened by his own words, he suddenly began to retch, sending the contents of his stomach spewing out onto the pavement in a dozen raspy spasms.

Donald was right. Densmore's head was gone from the eyebrows up. Nothing but a couple of shiny gray dreadlocks hanging down over the ears. What was left of his skull looked like a broken lava lamp.

"Listen," Corso said.

Wald looked confused. "What?"

Corso gestured with his hand. "Listen, No sirens. No nothing."

"So?"

"So Dougherty and I are getting out of here."

"No," Wald said. "You can't . . . we—"

"This scene doesn't play with us in it."

"He's right," Donald croaked. "We keep this simple. An anonymous tip. We follow up on a phone tip and walk into a hornet's nest. We've got a hero. We've got a villain. All nice and simple like."

Corso jumped in. "Otherwise, somebody's gonna want to know why an experienced cop like yourself found himself facing a mass murderer without backup. Especially after you'd been told what to expect."

"Jesus," Donald muttered. "We're fucked here, Wald. This is a career killer."

"Same people are gonna want an explanation of why Lieutenant Donald here never managed to get off a shot."

Wald shot a disgusted glance at Donald and then returned his gaze to Corso.

"You think I'm betting my ass—my career—on you two keeping your mouths shut?" Wald sneered.

"There's nothing in this for either Dougherty or me, except some time behind bars. We broke and entered. We interfered with an ongoing investigation. Tainted evidence. Maybe even recklessly endangered. It's as much in our own best interests to keep our mouths shut as it is for you two."

"We beat it, and you guys tell the story any way you want." He hesitated. "If not for your own asses, then maybe do it for Densmore."

Wald looked down at Densmore. Winced. "God knows he paid for his lunch."

"Paid in full," Donald said.

Wald swiveled his head. Donald nodded.

"Somebody gonna call about Himes or what?" Corso demanded.

Wald pulled a phone from his inside jacket pocket. Checked his wrist.

"What you say is in that house is in there?"

"I swear."

Wald opened the phone and dialed. "This is Detective Sergeant Steven Wald. I need to be patched through to Chief Kesey, immediately." He began to shake his head. "Don't start that not available crap with me. This is an emergency." He looked up at Corso. "Wald," he shouted into the phone, exasperated now. "Detective Sergeant Steven Wald. Don't tell me you can't—" He listened for a moment. "Get me a supervisor," he snapped. He covered the mouthpiece with his hand. "She says all the circuits are busy."

"Oh, Jesus," Donald moaned.

Wald looked at Corso again. "Get outta here," he said, then turned back to Donald.

"Make that radio call, Chucky."

Corso moved quickly, grabbing Dougherty by the hand. "Let's get the hell out of here."

He didn't have to ask twice.

Saturday, September 22
11:38 P.M. Day 6 of 6

It was like a small-town carnival. Bright ballpark banks of mercury vapor lights threw an unholy purple glare on the overhead coils of razor wire. The blaring music made the ominous front gate of the Washington State Penitentiary look like the clown's-mouth entrance to the fun house. Closest to the wall, an irregular midway sported food stands, T-shirts, souvenirs, and sno-cones. The remaining commercial sprawl was spread haphazardly about the parking lot, as if the vendors had been unable to agree on any pattern of arrangement whatsoever. Farther back in the shadows, a herd of motor homes grazed placidly among the bands of vans and packs of pickups. Maybe a dozen remote TV feeds, parked hip to hip inside the first chain-link fence, pointing their blank white eyes at the sky. The seething crowd was nervous and constantly on the move. Hard to count. Two, three thousand anyway, Dorothy figured. The air was electric.

Warden Danson was a short, contentious-looking man with eyes like rivets. He'd met them just inside the west gate, his breath rising toward the orchard of stars in the night sky, his small hands massaging each other for warmth.

Without bothering to introduce Dorothy, Marvin Hale had pulled Danson aside. They'd spent the past five minutes forty feet away, gesturing like spastic mimes and hissing at each other in stage whispers.

What, from the outside, had appeared to be a single stone wall was actually two parallel walls, with the guard towers spanning the gap at intervals. A prisoner scaling the inside wall, instead of facing a mere half dozen steel fences, two of which were lethally electrified, found himself trapped between the proverbial rock and the hard place of song and story. Almost wasn't fair.

Hale used one hand on Dorothy's elbow and the other to point to the right. Dorothy looked down his arm. At that moment, a red light came on over the door at the far end. "Go down to that door," Hale said. "They're expecting you. Whoever's there will take you to witness orientation."

Dorothy pushed the little button on the side of her watch and the dial lit up: 11:40. Twenty minutes to go. Without a word she turned and began marching toward the light, stepping along, her arms swinging smoothly at her sides, her chin held high. Inexplicably, "Onward, Christian Soldiers" began to play in her head.

                              11:40 P.M. Day 6 of 6

I seen seventeen of 'em go now," said the sergeant. "You see enough of them, you learn to tell the difference." Smitty looked reverentially at the sergeant. This was Smitty's first execution. He'd requested the death-watch assignment because they said it was quiet in the death house. None of that screaming-in-their-sleep babble of the cell blocks. Everybody said, Hell, the state of Washington never offs anybody anyway. Easy duty, they'd said. Now Smitty wasn't so sure. During the past week his dreams had turned increasingly gruesome. Turned to nightmares of such severity that, on three occasions, some primal instinct had been forced to intervene, shouting at him from the darkness of sleep, "Wake up; you don't have to die; it's just a dream," catapulting him upright in bed, his lungs empty from gasping, his cheeks washed with tears.

"Seen the big mouths who talk a good game. They're always the ones we got to stop halfway down the mile and hose out their pants for 'em. Seen the mealymouth little bastards you gotta carry the whole damn way. Little fuckers get so strong at the sight of the table, takes eight of us to strap 'em in."

"How do you figure old Walter's gonna go?" Smitty asked.

The sergeant chuckled. "Walter's gonna walk down that hall like he's goin' out for an ice cream cone."

"You really think so?"

"Count on it, kid," the sergeant said. "That guy's known nothin' but hate his whole life. No way he'd give anybody the satisfaction of seeing him crawl. He'll jump up on that damn table like Cindy Crawford's waiting up there for him."

For reasons he couldn't explain, the image made Smitty feel better.

11:52 P.M. Day 6 of 6

Please remember that Mr. Himes has a right to make a final statement," the woman was saying. "We have no control over the content." She looked up from the page in her hand and noticed Dorothy for the first time. "Are you . . . ," she began. Eight heads turned Dorothy's way. Two Butlers, two Nisovics, two Tates, Alice Doyle, clutching a picture of her daughter Kelly in her lap, and on the far left, John Williams, come all the way from South Dakota in search of something without a name. Dorothy waved a hand at the woman, as if to tell her to carry on, which she did. "Sometimes inmates express contrition, sometimes not." She checked the crowd. "You'll need to be prepared for whatever he might say."

She looked from person to person again. "We insist that you refrain from saying anything to the inmate. Although I am given to understand that Mr. Himes will not have family members in attendance, I believe his ACLU attorney, Mr. Adams, will be there. So for the sake of Mr. Adams, at least . . ." She let it go.

She turned the paper over in her hand. "On the back," she said and waited for her stunned audience to follow suit, "on the back is a description of the inmate's final hours. "At ten-thirty this morning, Mr. Himes was transferred to a segregation cell adjacent to the death chamber. At six o'clock this evening, Mr. Himes had a final meal of cheeseburgers and French fries. Between ten o'clock and eleven, he spent an hour with his mother. Subsequently, Mr. Himes was afforded the opportunity to consult with clergy . . . an opportunity which Mr. Himes rejected." She checked her watch. Dorothy did too. Ten minutes.

"So that you'll know what to expect, let me tell you what's going to happen." Again she paused to let the audience catch up. She began to read from the sheet. "In the state of Washington, lethal injection comes in three phases. The inmate is first injected with thiopental sodium which many of you know as sodium pentothol, or truth serum. The first injection immobilizes the inmate."

The first injection would immobilize a rhinoceros, Dorothy thought.

"One minute later the inmate is injected with Pavulon. Pavulon is a curare derivative that immediately halts the diaphragm."

Mrs. Butler's shoulders began to shake. Her husband rubbed the back of her neck. Whispered in her ear.

"One minute later the inmate is injected with potassium chloride, at which point the heart can no longer beat. Inmates generally emit an audible gasp at this point." She checked the crowd again. "A minute later the inmate is pronounced dead."

Sounded almost serene. Except that Dorothy had once heard a couple of medical examiners discussing the process.

"They make it look like the guy's just gone to sleep," one of them said.

The other had laughed out loud. "Are you shittin' me? All three of those drugs have a pH higher than six. Must feel like the fires of hell are being injected into your veins. If they could, they'd sit straight up and make noises like nobody's heard on earth since the Spanish Inquisition."

The other guy had nodded grimly. "Except, strapped down, with the lungs immobile, the closest you can get to a scream is that one little gasp they all let out."

"Yeah," said the first guy. "In the end, all they leave you with is the whimper instead of the bang."

And then, on the other side of the glass, Himes stepped into the death chamber. Standing there. Bald. No eyebrows. He cast a contemptuous glance at the white-covered gurney and then stood glaring at the viewing window.

"You all got your popcorn ready?" he asked.

Warden Danson now entered. "Mr. Himes would like to exercise his constitutional right to make a final statement," he said.

Himes stepped closer. "I ain't neva killed nobody," Himes said. "So I know where I'm goin' from here." He took them in again, moving only his eyes. "Probably the same place you-all think you goin'. So if we both right, old Walter Lee'll see you when you get there." He showed the stubs of his teeth. "And if we ain't . . . I'll see you-all in hell."

Alice Doyle got to her feet and pressed the picture of her daughter Kelly tightly against the glass. She turned back toward Dorothy, her pouchy eyes streaming.

"I want this to be the last thing he sees. The very last thing," she cried.

Somewhere in the room somebody was making noises like a gored animal.

Dorothy turned and ground her face into the wall.

30

C orso dreamed of that cobbled street again. Of the soldiers and the door intended solely for him. Only this time, in the moment when he closed the door behind himself, before putting that first foot on the tread and watching the walls fall away . . . this time someone began knocking on the door. The knocking got louder. He hesitated, foot in the air, torn between the insistent sound at his back and the bright promise waiting above.

Corso sat up in bed. More knocking as he struggled into a Mariners T-shirt and a pair of black sweatpants. Slipped on boat shoes. Up three steps, into the galley.

Corso checked the clock over the nav station: 10:15 A.M.

With a yawn, he pulled open the door and stepped out on deck, rubbing his eyes. The wind was up. Overhead, the sky was electric blue. No clouds at all. He checked the tops of the masts.

Six, eight knots from the south. All over the marina, loose halyards banged against masts like drunken tinkers.

Wald and Donald. Cleaned and pressed. Showered, shaved,
and swapped suits.

Hadn't helped Donald as much as it helped Wald, though. On
Wald, the extra lines seemed to disappear into his already pouchy
face. Donald, on the other hand, looked like he'd been snorting
speedballs for a week. For some reason, Corso was cheered by
the sight.

"A little early for protecting and serving, don't you think?"
Corso said.

"We never rest," Wald assured him.

"You seen the papers?" Donald asked.

"Not yet."

"I'll bet you missed our press conference too."

"Next time I'll set the alarm."

Both cops checked the area. "We kept it simple," Wald said.
"Phone tip. We go out for a look-see and, out of the blue, the guy
attacks us. Densmore and Defeo get offed in the struggle."

"Works for me," Corso said, rubbing his face with his hands.

Donald stepped in closer to Corso. His blue eyes were fili-
greed with red. "You sure?" he asked. "Last night isn't going to
show up in a book or something, is it?"

Corso looked him over. "I don't know what you're talking
about. I spent last night right here." Corso yawned. "Read till
about midnight."

"Nothing like a good book," Donald said.

Corso agreed and then yawned again. Covering his mouth
this time.

"You ready for a little mirth?" Wald asked.

"I love the smell of irony in the morning," Corso said.

"The lab says Defeo had a bullet in his head."

"Couldn't happen to a nicer guy."

"They say the bullet's the cause of death."

"So?"

"They also say the slug came from Densmore's piece."

"No shit," Corso said.

"Who taught you to shoot? I may want to take lessons," Donald joked.

"I learned from the KGB," Corso said with a straight face.

"We told 'em Andy must have gotten a salvo off on the way down," Wald said with a grimace.

"Was that before or after the top half of his head got vaporized?"

"We opted for before," Donald said.

Corso shrugged. "It'll look better on his record than on mine."

Wald shook his head. "Amazing, ain't it? Densmore makes every mistake a cop can make, damn near gets us all killed, and he comes out of this thing looking like Rambo."

"Radio said Himes had already said his final words when the call came from the governor," Corso said.

Wald whistled silently. "Six more minutes and your boy Himes was history," Wald said.

"He's fired his ACLU attorney and hired Myron Mendenhal," Donald said, naming Seattle's most successful personal-injury specialist.

"He's gonna get millions," Wald offered.

"Got a press conference called for this afternoon."

"What about you guys?" Corso asked.

Wald looked as if he was going to puke. "I'm getting promoted to lieutenant. Chucky here's getting a commendation for valor."

"The public does *so* like a happy ending," Corso sneered. He got to his feet. Stretched. And then sidestepped up the slip, past the cops.

The good weather had the weekend warriors out. Four boats up, a red-haired woman he'd never seen before was scrubbing the deck of a Morgan Out-Island. Farther along on the far side, a couple of boatyard types were replacing the roller furling on a Catalina thirty-six. The new cable and fittings ran nearly the length of the dock. Half a dozen other boats had people crawling over them. Sunday on the dock.

"What about this Defeo guy?" Corso asked.

Wald shrugged. "The usual. School record full of shrinks and counselors. Been through the mental-health system and back. Diagnosed as schizophrenic when he was sixteen. Applied to the Seattle and King County police departments, about three times each. Took the tests for all four branches of the armed services. Nobody wanted any part of him."

"A regular super criminal," Corso said.

"His current doctor and his therapist are both playing hardball. Claiming doctor/patient privilege. Holding out for court orders. It'll be a week or so before we can be certain, but we're pretty damn sure Defeo must have told his mama what he was doing back in ninety-eight."

"Either that or she figured it out on her own," Donald added.

"You guys see that pile of burnt stuff in the backyard?" Corso asked.

"His mama's stuff," Wald said.

"Interesting relationship there."

"Freud'd have a field day," Donald agreed.

Wald rolled his eyes. "Anyway . . . instead of dropping a quarter on her own flesh and blood, Mama took away his genuine lambs of God ear tags, got him on medication and into therapy. Which, if you don't count eight murders, worked just peachy until she died a couple of months back."

"At which time, he, of course, stopped taking the meds," Wald added.

"And the killing started again," Donald finished.

"You find the rest of the clothes?"

"One set was still at the dry cleaners. He had 'em all cleaned before he mounted them. Thoughtful of him, don't you think?"

"We've identified six sets for sure," Wald said. He ran down the list from memory. Kate Mitchell, Analia Nisovic, and Jennifer Robison from ninety-eight. And all three recent victims, Alice Crane-Carter, Denise Gould, and Tiffany Eyre. "The other four we're working on," Wald concluded.

"Five," Corso said.

"Five what?" Donald demanded.

"The other five sets of clothes. You said you'd identified six. That leaves five." He looked from cop to cop. "There's eleven victims, right?"

"We've got ten sets of clothes," Wald said. "Nine from the house and one from the dry cleaner."

"Where's the other set?" Corso asked.

"You read the shit in that room, didn't you?" Donald said. "That crap about the ten brides of Christ. He only needed ten sets."

"Which," noted Wald, "our Bible-toting brethren in the station house assure us is a notion not to be found in the Bible."

"So there's a missing set of clothes, then?"

"Who the hell knows?" Donald said. "Maybe they got torn up during the attack. With that crazy bastard anything could have happened."

"The dry cleaners only cleaned ten," Wald said.

On the Catalina, one guy was winching the other guy up the mast in a yellow canvas boson's chair. "Pretty weird," Corso noted. "You'd think with Defeo so fixated on his ten brides of Christ thing . . . you'd think he could keep track of the damn number."

Donald moved toward Corso with a stiff-legged gait. His face suddenly red. His voice suddenly loud. Along the dock, all work stopped.

"What the fuck is the matter with you, Corso? What is it? The only way you can get up in the morning is if you feel superior to everybody else? You can't feel good about yourself unless you see something that nobody else sees? Is that what floats your boat, Corso?" Donald was close now, crowding Corso.

"Just wondering," Corso said affably.

"You know what I think? I think you're a big-time loser. I think you're such a loser, you don't even have sense enough to know when you've won, and that's the biggest kind of loser there is."

"Hey, hey," Wald was saying. "We're all on the same side here." He stepped between the two men, stood facing his partner.

Corso kept his eyes locked on Donald. "Wald," he said, "you better take the lieutenant here home for his nap. He seems to be a bit out of sorts this morning."

Donald made a show of trying to swim his way past Wald to get at Corso.

"You're a loser," he was yelling. "A loser."

Corso stood his ground, smiling as Wald began shoving Donald down the dock. Halfway down, right after Donald took to walking on his own, Wald stopped for a moment and threw a long quizzical look back Corso's way, then turned and followed his partner toward the gate and the ramp beyond.

* * *

"Two Killed in Trashman Battle." Big as headlines get. Picture of Wald and Donald standing beside the bullet-riddled car in their spiffy Kevlar vests. A sidebar on Densmore and his career. Corso folded the paper beneath his arm, pulled open the front door of the *Seattle Sun*, and stepped into the lobby.

Behind the security desk, Bill Post looked up and smiled. "Hey, Mr. Corso," he said. "You seen they got him, huh?"

Corso crossed the room. Leaned on the desk.

"I saw," he said. "I hear Himes is already out."

Post nodded. "I'm workin' security at the Hilton this afternoon.

Himes and his new mouthpiece are havin' them a press conference."

"A guy can always use a little extra Hawaii money," Corso said.

"Yeah," he beamed. "Leavin' next Wednesday. Ten glorious days and nights on Maui."

Corso said, "Congratulations," and started for the elevator. Post waddled out from behind the desk, following Corso down the hall. "You shoulda seen my granddaughter's face when I told her. Never seen the kid so happy before. Nancy says she's already packed and ready to go."

Corso stopped his finger just short of the Up button. Turned to Post. "Where do the people who answer the phones work? What floor is that?" he asked.

"Down two," Post said. "That's basement, B."

Corso thumbed the Down button. "If I don't see you again," he said to the guard, "have a mai tai for me."

"Thanks," Post said. "I'll make it a couple." They shook hands.

The door slid open silently. Corso stepped into the car. Pushed B. Post waved.

Basement B was just that. A windowless room filled with cubicles. The dull roar of a hundred conversations rolled like waves just below the ceiling. Corso had to ask three times before he found the right row. Three desks up. Leanne Samples wore a white plastic band in her hair. She was making conversation with the stout African-American woman at the next desk when Corso turned the corner.

"Mr. Corso," she squealed when she saw him.

She tried to jump to her feet but the cord on her headset wasn't nearly long enough and jerked her right back into her chair.

"Oops," she said, dropping the headset to the desktop and throwing her arms around Corso's waist. "It's all done, huh? They got the guy."

"They got the guy," Corso repeated. Changed the subject. "You're looking great. I hear you're a regular whiz at your job."

She took him by the hand and led him to the next cubicle. "Georgeanne, this is my friend Mr. Corso." Georgeanne, whose last name turned out to be Taylor, allowed how it was a great pleasure to meet the famous Mr. Frank Corso and how she faithfully read his column. Leanne dragged him on. They zigzagged the length of the room in a frenzy of rushed introductions and hurried handshakes. Fifteen minutes later, they stumbled out of the maze, directly in front of the elevators.

She pulled at his elbow. "And you must meet my friend Ellie over here . . ."

Corso resisted. "I've gotta go," he said. "I need to have a few words with Mr. Hawes."

Her eyes widened. "Oh . . . ," she said. "We mustn't keep Mr. Hawes waiting." She was suddenly flustered. Looked around the room as if she'd never seen it before. "I probably ought to get back to work myself." She managed a wan smile. "After all, they're not paying me to stand around and talk to famous writers, are they?" Corso managed a smile of his own. They shook hands. Changed their minds and hugged. Said good-bye and then hugged again.

Corso turned and rang for the elevator. "Mr. Corso," Leanne said, "thank you for everything." He nodded. "Everything is different in my life now. Better. It's like, for the first time, I actually have a life of my own."

Corso held up a hand. "That's your doing, not mine," he said.

She started to argue, but he cut her off.

"You know what *my* mama used to say, Leanne?"

"What?"

"She used to say, 'If a miracle takes place within five miles of you, take credit for it.' That's what she used to say." Corso stepped into the elevator, pushed six.

The car slid upward. Corso watched the numbers turn red

until the car bounced to a halt on six. Corso held the door open with his arm. The newsroom. Normally, on a Sunday, they'd be down to a skeleton crew and the building would be silent. Last night's developments cost people another day off. He stepped out of the car and started up the aisle toward Bennett Hawes's glassed-in office, leaving silence in his wake as phone conversations suddenly ended and coffee cups stopped short of lips. Claire Harris waved. Corso gave her a salacious wink.

"Hey, Claire," he said, stopping by her desk.

"I'll tell ya, kiddo . . . whatever your other failings may be, you sure know how to set the woods on fire."

"Thanks, Claire."

"You're not going to upset poor Bennett, are you?"

"I'm too tired."

Hawes gestured him in with a nod of his head. Corso continued up the aisle toward Hawes. Pulled open the door and stepped in. He dangled a set of keys from his thumb and forefinger for a moment before tossing them across the desk. Hawes snatched them out of midair and put them in his top drawer. "Once and for all," Corso said. "Here's your car back."

Hawes rocked back in his oversize chair and took Corso in. "Seems your security-guard angle was right on the money."

"A lucky guess," Corso said with a smirk.

Hawes searched his eyes for a story. "Am I missing something here?" he asked.

"Yeah," Corso said. "And it's gonna have to stay that way."

Hawes furrowed his brow. "Were you—"

Corso held up a hand. "I can't," he said.

"Dougherty's okay?"

"She's fine," Corso assured him.

A silence settled over the room. "You make your reservations for the American Society of Newspaper Editors conference?" Corso asked.

"Sent the registration form in yesterday."

"If it wasn't for me, you'd sure as hell get a Pulitzer nomination."

Both men knew it was true. Small papers that break major stories are usually rewarded with Pulitzer nominations. Corso's presence on the story, however, made that impossible. As far as the committee was concerned, nominating Frank Corso for a journalism award would be like nominating Jeffrey Dahmer for a culinary medal.

Hawes shrugged. "I've got no complaints."

"Everybody's got the story they want. Big shootout at the O.K. Corral. At great personal cost, brave cops kill despoiler of virgins. What else could anybody ask for? It's positively mythic."

Corso walked over to the desk and stuck out his hand. Hawes got to his feet. Made eye contact and took Corso's hand in his. "I stand corrected," Hawes said.

Corso raised an eyebrow.

"About you," Hawes said. "You ever get tired of writing books and want to get back into the newspaper business full-time, you be sure to give me a call."

"Tell Mrs. V. I'll give her a jingle one of these nights," Corso said.

Hawes said he would. "What's for you now?"

Corso thought it over. "Finally got some decent weather; I think I'll wash my boat. Maybe putt over and pump the heads and top it off with diesel."

"Sailing off into the sunset?"

"Something like that."

* * *

A dock is a special type of community. Diverse beyond reason. Filled with everything from millionaires who barely remember they own a vessel to lifetime live-aboards who have every dime they own tied up in the rig. Moguls, morons, and misfits, all of whom find common ground in the mystique of the water. All of whom, it seemed, wanted to drop by and chat of a sunny Sunday afternoon as Corso washed *Saltheart*. Everyone mentioned the weather, of course, and then immediately segued into how they'd heard there'd been some excitement down here this morning. Corso handed out quite a few Heinekens but precious little information.

Others bitched about the Carver's anchor hanging out over the dock. Wanted to call management. The guy in the green Cruisa-home wanted to push the Carver back in the slip and retie it with a springline, but nobody would lend a hand. You just don't touch another man's lines.

Corso had worked up a full sweat. He'd started in the dinghy with the sun hot on his shoulders. Paddling himself around, scrubbing the hull. Worked his way back onboard, where, as the last rays of the day had begun to slide behind Queen Anne Hill, the wind quickly died and the fog appeared from nowhere to take its place. As the mist settled on his bare shoulders, Corso moved the broom in a single-minded frenzy. He'd been at it so long the soft blue bristles had begun to hum in his head, like a mantra. A low Gregorian chant. "Behold the ten brides of Christ . . ." it intoned, ". . . who having strayed from his ways are now returned to the fold of our master, like lost sheep. Behold the . . ."

31

Sunday, September 23
1:57 P.M.   Day 6 + 1

Why, she used to wonder, would survivors subject themselves to this? She knew why *she* was here. That was easy. She was covering her ass. Making sure when Chief Kesey called she'd be able to say, "Yes, Chief, as a matter of fact, I did hear what Himes and his attorney had to say. Actually, I was there in the hotel for the press conference, Chief. And you?" On a Sunday too.

But them. The Tates and the Butlers, Mrs. Doyle and the Nisovics. Right there in the front row again. After the week they'd had. Dorothy Sheridan shivered, because, after fourteen years and a daughter of her own, she finally understood. Same as her, they were covering their asses. They were doing everything they could. Making certain that no stone was unturned, no step untaken, no opportunity to remember lost. Fruitful . . . futile . . . it didn't matter. Because somewhere down the road, when the headlines and memories had faded, nothing was going to be more vital to their long-term survival than being able to tell themselves they'd done everything humanly possible.

She'd made up her mind. First thing Monday morning she was calling Monica and setting up an interview. Anything had to be better than this. What good was security if it killed you? First thing Monday.

She was still lost in thought when the buzz in the room suddenly subsided, pulling her attention to the dais. She'd never seen Myron Mendenhal in person before. Only on TV. Not that he looked particularly good either way. The man was a gnome. A bandy-legged troll with a head about four sizes too big for his body. Bald on top, grown out long on the sides. Big Moscow snow-cutter eyebrows.

Mendenhal tapped at the bank of microphones. Flashbulbs twinkled all over the ballroom. TV cameras began to hum. "Ladies and gentlemen," he began. "It seems my client has been unavoidably delayed, so why don't we begin." He had a wet mouth. Everything he said sounded a little juicy. "As most of you well know, my client Walter Leroy Himes was unjustly convicted and sentenced to death for the series of murders commonly known as the Trashman killings. Whether this gross miscarriage of justice was a matter of official ineptitude or indifference will be decided in a court of law. What cannot be denied, however, is that even at this late date, it is not too late for some measure of justice to be done."

Dorothy allowed his voice to settle into a drone. Her head no longer throbbed. Instead, the pain had become a cold river of pressure flowing directly behind her eyes, making her feel as if her eyeballs might unexpectedly pop from their sockets like champagne corks. She massaged the bridge of her nose with her thumb and forefinger.

Mendenhal stopped talking as the buzz in the room began to rise. Himes, in maybe the worst suit in the world. An orange-plaid pattern that could have been used as the international symbol for bad taste. Way too small. Oh, god, look at his ankles.

Himes pulled out the other chair on the dais and sat down hard enough to make the bank of microphones belch. Weaving back and forth. Obviously shitfaced drunk. Sitting there surveying the crowd with this big loopy grin on his face.

"As I was saying," Myron Mendenhal continued, "on behalf of my client Mr. Himes"—whom he acknowledged with the smallest of nods—"I have today, in state superior court, filed a lawsuit alleging willful and malicious prosecution in the amounts of . . ."

Thirteen million. If they got even half of that there'd be big-time layoffs. Might get all the way down to her. She pressed at her eyes, as if to keep them in place. She heard the scrape of a chair and then another belch from the mikes.

Himes leaning over the microphones. "Now that them no-good bitches got what they deserved . . . now old Walter Lee gonna get somma what he deserves for a change."

Mendenhal whispered furiously in his client's ear. Himes sneered and kept on talking. "Gonna buy me evathin' I want. Might even git me a little"—he winked—"you know . . . a little . . . poontang."

Malcolm Tate rose from his front-row seat. He pointed at Himes.

"Don't," he warned. "Don't you dare."

Himes pointed back at him. "I seen you there. Eva time, in the front row, with your clean clothes and your old woman and all . . . up there in the good seats."

"You shut your mouth," Tate warned at the top of his voice.

All around the room, security guards hustled toward Malcolm Tate. His wife pulled at his pant leg, then rose to put herself between her husband and the dais.

"I'll bet one of them bitches was yourn, wasn't she?" Himes taunted.

Paula Tate put both palms on her husband's chest and gently tried to force him back into his chair. Malcolm Tate, however, was having none of it. Instead, he stepped around his wife and wagged a blunt finger in Himes's face. "You shut your filthy mouth," he said.

Himes leaned forward over the table, grinned at the audience, and then spit on Tate's blue denim shirt. A collective intake of breath was followed by dead silence. Malcolm Tate's mouth fell open as he stared down at the yellow glob of phlegm now welded to his shirtfront.

"Ladies and gentlemen, please, ah. . . ." Myron Mendenhal sputtered. "Could we perhaps . . . at this time—"

Tate went berserk. With a bellow, he lurched forward, toward Himes. His fingers extended like talons, as if he intended to go for the eyes. Tate took a single stride and then attempted to hurl himself upward onto the dais. He'd have made it too, except that his trailing foot became entangled in the maze of cables running along the front of the platform, stopping his ascent in mid-flight, jerking him down onto the cluster of microphones. Myron Mendenhal fell backward from his chair. An electronic shriek tore the air.

A female security guard arrived first, grabbing Tate by the belt and jerking him to the floor. Malcolm Tate got as far up as his knees before he was buried beneath an onrushing pile of uniforms. The amplifiers screamed like a jet on takeoff. The audience was on its feet, hands cupped over ears as if playing some deranged version of Simon Says. Without willing it so, Dorothy Sheridan found herself hurrying toward the front of the room. "Malcolm," Paula Tate cried. "Oh . . . please, Malcolm."

By the time Dorothy arrived, Tate had been pulled to his feet and was being led stiff-legged down the central aisle by four rent-a-cops. Somewhere in the scuffle, he'd suffered a cut on the bridge of his nose, sending a single crimson rivulet rolling down over his upper lip and into his mouth. "Mr. Tate," Dorothy said. "Please, Mr. Tate."

He bellowed at the ceiling, launching a spray of blood and spittle as he was muscled past her down the aisle. She turned and trotted along behind Paula Tate, who repeatedly called her husband's name as he was dragged from the room. Dorothy patted at the pockets of her dress until she found her SPD ID badge.

Out in the hallway, Malcolm Tate had been forced to his knees. The female guard had disengaged and was whispering into a handheld radio. Holding her SPD ID badge before her, Dorothy Sheridan ran to Malcolm Tate's side. "Don't hurt him," she said.

The nearest guard turned his sweaty, pockmarked face her way. "Listen, lady, why don't you—"

She waved the ID in his face. "Don't hurt him . . . you hear me? Don't."

Malcolm Tate hiccuped once and then vomited onto the carpet. The security guards released their grip and scrambled to their feet as his body convulsed, over and over again, until he was empty, left with nothing but a single silver strand connecting his lower lip to the carpet below. His wife knelt at his side. Put her hand on his back.

"Malcolm," she said again.

Dorothy pointed to a bench against the wall. "Put him there," she said. The pockmarked guard started to protest. "Do it," she screamed.

Carefully avoiding the puddle, two of the guards helped Malcolm Tate to the bench, where he sat heavily, holding his head in his hands.

Someone brought a glass of water and some paper towels.

Ten minutes later, Paula Tate was till dabbing at her husband's face and whispering in his ear when a pair of uniformed SPD officers came jogging around the corner and down the hall.

Dorothy held up her ID and met them halfway. As she explained the situation, they began to relax. "Poor guy," the younger one said.

"Would you please help them to their car?" Dorothy asked.

"Sure," they said in unison.

Paula Tate looked Sheridan's way with red-rimmed eyes. "Come on," Sheridan said. The Tates rose from the bench together and shuffled over. "Are we . . . is Malcolm being arrested?" Mrs. Tate wanted to know. Dorothy shook her head. "These officers are going to see you to your car," she said. Paula Tate's eyes filled with tears. "Did you hear what that man said?"

Dorothy said she had.

"How could this happen?" Paula Tate asked, as much to herself as to Sheridan. "I don't understand."

"I'm so sorry," was all Dorothy could come up with. "If there's anything I can—"

Paula Tate turned away. Her words echoed in Dorothy's head as she watched the officers lead the couple up the stairs and around the corner.

Dorothy walked over, eased the ballroom door open, and stepped back inside. A trio of techies were putting the microphones back in order. Myron Mendenhal was still straightening his suit. Himes sat there, looking pleased with himself, rocking his chair up onto its back legs and then letting it slam back down.

A voice on her right asked, "Everybody all right?" Another guard. Fat and fifty. About to burst the buttons on a Hilton security uniform that obviously didn't belong to him. Handwritten name tag read "Bill Post."

"Fine," she said.

He made a gesture as if he were mopping his brow. "Gotta

leave that kinda rough stuff for the young guys," he said. "Me, I'm just moonlighting for a little vacation money. Didn't expect anything like that. No, sir, I didn't."

Mendenhal was talking again. Same thing he'd said before the excitement. Thirteen million. Civil suits to follow. "How do you compensate a man for three years of his life?" he asked. "Is there some dollar figure that can repair the heart of a man who has lived for years under the specter of his own imminent death? Who has lain upon the table of death? I think not. Can we—"

Dorothy held her breath as Himes leaned toward the mikes.

"If it ain't me or him, just gonna be somebody else, you know."

"Excuse me?" a big-haired blonde along the wall said.

"Said there's always gonna be somebody out there killin' bitches. Bitches and mo' bitches is gonna be dyin' all over the damn place, till you-all up to your damn ass in dead bitches."

Up front, Slobodan Nisovic slowly got to his feet. Brushed at his face, then turned his back on Mendenhal and Himes. The little man leaned over and appeared to whisper in his mother's ear. She nodded and handed him something.

On Dorothy's right, Bill Post muttered, "Holy shit," under his breath and started hustling toward the front of the room with an awkward, rolling gait.

When Slobodan Nisovic straightened up, he was holding an automatic in both hands. He had tears in his eyes as he looked out over the crowded ballroom.

"No" was all he said before turning toward the front of the room and pulling the trigger. The roar of the gun ripped the air. Dorothy stood transfixed as, all around her, people threw themselves to the floor. Screams and more shots. Himes was down on his side on the dais, his chest a mass of red. Nisovic turned to face the crowd. He stuck the gun in his mouth and pulled the trigger. Dorothy watched the side of his face explode and waited for him to crumple to the floor.

To Dorothy's amazement, however, Slobodan Nisovic flinched but didn't fall. He just stood there jerking the trigger, over and over. Nothing happened. Not even a click. Just the silent finger flexing and unflexing inside the trigger guard, until old Bill Post hit him with a flying tackle and drove him to the floor. First thing Monday. Call Monica.

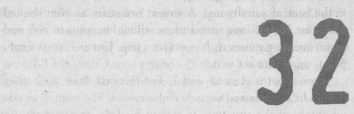

"Guess what's missing?"

He pointed to the series of photos pinned to the drapes. Victim number two. Kate Mitchell. Dougherty checked her watch and scowled. She wanted to punch him in the mouth. He looked so goddamn pleased with himself. Standing there in the salon, moving from one foot to the other, like some smart-ass schoolboy who'd stolen the answers to the algebra final. She stepped in close, poked him in the chest with a long red finger-nail.

"What gives with you? I finally get last night's disaster out of my mind and sleep for the first time in forty-eight hours and what happens? You call me at one in the morning. Then, without being consulted, next thing I know, there's a cab calling me from down-stairs. What kind of shit is that? You think I'm your dog or some-thing?"

Corso tried to look as if his feelings were hurt, but she ignored him. "In return for being dragged out of bed, I get fifteen minutes in the back of a drafty taxi, driving at two miles an hour through the worst fog I've ever seen and you think I'm going to play god-damn guessing games with you. Get a grip, Corso. If you've got a point, you better get to it."

"How about a glass of wine?" For the first time since she'd known him, he looked vaguely embarrassed. She wanted to take advantage of the situation, to stay in his face, to puncture that veneer of his but couldn't muster the energy. Instead, she sighed and said, "White. Dry." He hesitated, waiting for her to step aside. She held her ground.

Corso squeezed by her, slowly, belly to belly, slipped into the galley, and opened the refrigerator. Dougherty slid the coat from her shoulders and threw it over the back of the teak desk chair. Aware of her unencumbered body moving beneath the dress, she folded her arms across her chest and leaned back against the built-in bookcase. She tried to focus on Corso pulling the cork, but couldn't keep her eyes from drifting to the glossy black-and-whites of Kate Mitchell. From the way her arranged body seemed to fall away from its center. From the knot of angry bruises encircling her narrow throat. From the rubbery film covering her eyeballs like milky sandwich wrap. She pulled away. Hugging herself harder now. Her mouth felt as dry as wood.

"I can't believe you dragged me down here in the middle of the night to look at photographs," she groused. "This thing is over. The good guys finally won."

"Nobody won," Corso countered. "Himes is up in Harborview sitting in bed, stuffing his face and telling anybody who'll listen what he's going to do with the money he gets from the state. Old man Nisovic's the closest thing we've got to a hero and that poor bastard couldn't even blow his own brains out. Sticks a gun in his mouth and only manages to shoot off half his jawbone. Not only that, but whenever he gets out of the hospital, he's going to have to stand trial for trying to off Himes. Excuse me if I'm not feeling all warm and fuzzy over this one."

"What's your problem, Corso?"

"Ten brides. Eleven bodies," he said while pouring wine. "Do the math."

"You saw that place. Defeo was a hundred-percent stone nuts. What makes you think anything he did has to make literal sense?"

"He seemed pretty firm on the number ten to me."

She thought about it and, although unwilling to admit it to Corso, couldn't help but agree. The amount of trouble Defeo had gone through to play out his deranged "lambs of God" and "brides of Christ" scenario, no matter how loony it might seem to the rest of the world, suggested that he probably wasn't going to be confused about the size of his flock.

"So how come you're the only one bothered by the disparity?"

"The cops have already got what they want. They've got themselves a serial murderer, a martyr, and a couple of heroes. Cue the memorial service and the awards ceremony. End of story."

Corso came back into the salon offering a glass of wine. She took it. Stuck her nose into the glass. Okay, not fruity. She took a sip. Then another, sipping halfway down the glass. Just the way she liked it, but she wasn't telling him that either.

"Okay?" he inquired.

"Um," was all she said. She waved at the photos. "So what is it I'm supposed to notice is missing?"

The glint in his eye said he was going to try to make her guess.

"Don't," she warned. "I'm not in the mood."

He took her seriously, tucked his lower lip in, and said, "The ear tag." He reached down onto the settee cushion, picked up the list of the items in Kate Mitchell's evidence bag. He read the list: " 'One watch, Timex. One gold bracelet. One gold cross and chain. Two toe rings. One plastic ear tag, ovine,' " he intoned finally. Corso let the list float back to the cushion, then pointed to Dougherty's photos of the evidence. Pointed.

"No tag," he said. "Not in any of them."

Dougherty drained her glass and handed it to Corso. She put one knee on the cushion and stuck her nose close to the pictures. Picked up the list and mouthed the words as she slowly scanned the pictures. He was right. No ear tag in any of the prints.

When she looked back over her shoulder, Corso had refilled both glasses. She stood upright, plucked the glass from his fingers. "So . . . what? You think I made a mistake? You think I missed something, don't you? That's why you dragged me down here at one o'clock in the morning, to tell me I missed something."

"Matter-of-fact, I don't think any such thing," he said. "I think you got everything that was there."

"Which means what?"

"Which means somebody removed it from the evidence room."

"Stole it?"

"Yep."

"Why in God's name would anybody want to steal an ear tag?"

"Good question."

"For a souvenir, maybe?" she offered.

"Hell of a risk for a trinket."

Grudgingly, she agreed. "What then?"

"Damned if I know."

"You're paranoid. You know that? You could find a conspiracy at a yard sale, Corso."

He didn't say anything. Just stood there rolling his wineglass between his palms, staring back at the photographs.

"How could someone get into the police evidence room and . . ." She stopped herself. "Unless the person was—"

"Somehow associated with the Himes case," he finished for her.

"You mean in some kind of official capacity?"

"Absolutely. The SPD evidence room isn't part of the building tour."

"Maybe they used it for testing purposes or something."

"If they did, it'd be noted in the file. Besides which, they'd never use up one whole tag. They take little pieces from all of them."

"And all the rest of the victims still have their tags?"

"Yep."

"You still have the rest of the files?"

"Yep."

"Lemme see."

She watched from the far side of the salon as Corso retrieved the cardboard box from beneath the sink and then, once again, covered the pin rail with glossy visions of murder most foul. She handed him her glass and knelt on the cushions, studying the prints. Moving a fingertip from list to photo and back. Halfway through the gallery, she heard the muted pop of a cork. He was right. Except for Kate Mitchell's missing ear tag, the evidence lists matched the photos she'd taken on Thursday. Kate Mitchell's crime-scene photographs, however, clearly showed the tag in her left ear at the time when the body was found. Now, her tag was gone. Ergo what?

Corso slipped her glass between her fingers. "So?" he said.

She took a swallow. "So . . . then . . . what you're saying is that maybe one of the women wasn't killed by Defeo after all. She was killed by somebody connected to the original investigation, who then arranged it to look like she was just another victim of the Trashman."

"You're a quick one, you are," Corso said.

"And you think the odd victim was Kate Mitchell."

He shook his head. "It can't be her."

"Why not?"

"Because Defeo had her clothes."

"They know that for sure?"

"It's the outfit she was reported missing in. The dry cleaners by Defeo's house has records for cleaning all ten sets of women's clothes found by the cops. They've identified five sets of the clothes. Mitchell's was one of them."

"Can't be one of the new victims," she said out loud to herself. "That wouldn't make any sense at all."

"If there's something haywire with any of the original victims, it's gotta be the Doyle girl," Corso said quickly.

"The one they found after Himes was already in jail?"

"Gotta be."

"Mother carries the picture with her all the time."

"Yep."

"Why her?"

"She's the only fly in the ointment. Found two full days after Himes was arrested. Frozen solid, so time of death couldn't be pinned down. The only victim where whoever called the cops about the body didn't stick around until they got there."

"If you ask me, that's pretty damn weak."

His expression said he wasn't prepared to argue the point.

"I suppose you think you know who did it."

"Not a clue," he said with a flicker in his eye that said maybe he did.

Dougherty made a rude noise with her lips. "You're a regular engine of conflict, you know that, Corso? Where others find answers, you find only questions."

"It's possible that—" he began.

She waved him off. "I'm not onboard here, Corso. I've gone along with the program. Haven't I gone along with the program?" He nodded but didn't speak. "I've been shot at, shit on, thrown into jail." She looked at the floor. "I saw a man get killed last night," she said in a low voice. "All in the name of getting to the bottom of this thing. But"—she hesitated—"this is way too out there." She waved a hand. "Let well enough alone, for criminey sakes. Win some friends. Influence some people."

Her hand dropped to her side with a slap. "It's like you're always striving . . . looking for some sort of moral high ground or something. Like you don't think anybody but you can possibly get things right."

He stood silently, his eyes turned inward, looking tired and lonely.

She turned her back on Corso, ran her eyes over the pictures again, shivered, and looked away. She felt Corso's eyes moving over her back like long fingers. Without turning, she said, "Get rid of those pictures, will you, Frank? They're giving me the damn willies."

He said, "Sure." As Corso busied himself with the photos, she pulled the right half of the aft door aside and stepped out onto the stern. Unbelievable that a glorious day like today could end like this. Like being closed in a box of cotton. The air was stark white, floating seamlessly around the boat like chowder. She looked up. Not even the tops of the masts were visible. Then down. The water beneath the swim step was flat and still, like black ice.

From somewhere within the fog . . . the sharp sound of shoes and then the voice. A woman's voice. "Frank?" And the hesitant clicking of high heels.

She watched as Corso reached above the navigation station with his left hand. With a single twiddle of his fingers, he simultaneously activated the boat's exterior spotlights and doused the cabin lights. "Frank." The voice again.

Corso turned Dougherty's way. Put a finger to his lips. She nodded in the darkness. And then peeked around the corner, toward the bow. The spotlights made it possible to make out the iceberg outline of the cruiser in the next slip. Nothing else. Corso's head poked out into the fog just as a figure appeared at the end of the slip. Cynthia Stone. Same red plastic raincoat she'd been wearing the other day.

"How'd you find your way down here?" he asked.

"I told you, Frank. I have my sources."

She had this way of squirming around while standing still. Like she had ants in her dress or something. "Aren't you going to invite me onboard?" she asked. She didn't wait for an answer. Stepped up onto the dock box, threw a leg over the rail, then the other, until she had Corso pinned against the doorway with her crotch.

Corso took his time escaping. The raincoat cracked and crinkled as he backed slowly out of the doorway. "What do you want, Cynth?"

She slid the door closed behind her. "Do I have to want something to see my ex-fiancé?"

"Pretty much. That's the way it works. Yeah," Corso said.

"You're getting to be such a cynic, Frank," she teased.

Corso shook his head. "Nah," he said. "Cynics think they know all the answers. I'm not even clear on the questions."

"That's remarkably humble," she cooed. "Especially for you, Frank."

"I was just buttoning things up for the night, Cynth."

She stepped up close to him again. "I'm leaving in the morning."

"Where to?"

"D.C.," she said. "The Hartman hearings."

"Lot of good dirt there."

She leaned against him now. "Speaking of which, Frank."

"Yeah."

"You know what my downtown source told me tonight?"

"It's late, Cynth."

"The story is that you and Officers Donald and Wald had quite the spat earlier today. Right here on this very dock. In front of God and everybody. The way I hear it, if Detective Wald hadn't intervened, you and Donald might have actually come to blows."

"And your point is?"

"My point is that you've been one step ahead of the rest of us for the past week and a half and, when I heard that story . . . I don't know . . . suddenly I had this niggling feeling that you *still* know something the rest of us don't." She put her arms around his waist and searched his eyes. "Come on, Frank. Talk to Mama."

"I don't know what you're talking about, Cynth. You know me. I've never been good with authority figures. Especially cops."

She smiled and began to pick at the belt of the raincoat. "A trade," she wheedled.

"One good turn deserves another." She gave him a piranha-like smile and pulled the coat back to reveal scanty red silk underthings. "You used to like it when I surprised you like this." She swayed from side to side, as if dancing to silent music. "Remember?"

From the darkness of the stern, Dougherty's hands clenched as she watched Corso's Adam's apple bob a couple of times before he spoke. "I remember," he said.

Her dancing had turned her back to Dougherty. Corso looked out over Cynthia Stone's head. Found Dougherty's eyes. Covered his mouth with his hand.

"You haven't been sleeping with that cow, have you? She's had her shots, I hope. You haven't caught anything dreadful?"

"Maybe you should ask her."

Corso pointed toward Dougherty in the stern. Stone turned her head.

"Mooooo," Dougherty said from the darkness.

Cynthia Stone's mouth dropped so far open her fillings gleamed in the dull light. She spun back toward Corso. Pulled back her right fist and let it fly. Corso caught it in midair. She brought up a left, but Corso caught that one too. When she tried to knee him in the balls, he deflected the blow with his thigh and pinned her against the sink.

"Don't," he said evenly. "Way I see it, Cynth, you don't have a free one coming from me. You hit me and I'm going to knock you on your ass." He let go of her hands and stepped back.

"You son of a bitch," she spat out. "You're a loser . . . you know that, Frank? A small-time loser. You and your freak there . . . you two . . . you deserve each other."

Cynthia Stone crossed the galley, jerked open the door, and stepped out on deck.

Dougherty walked back into the salon, closing the door behind her.

"That we deserve each other is the best she can do?" she asked.

"She works best from a script," Corso said.

Cynthia Stone's high heels pounded a frantic staccato beat on the slip. Then came a sound, like the dull ring of a cracked bell . . . followed by the rustling of plastic and a sudden sob. Dougherty raised her eyebrows, looked to Corso. His thin lips curled into a smile.

"The anchor," he said.

Dougherty loped across the boat, pulled open the door on the opposite side of the galley just in time to see Cynthia Stone's murky silhouette struggle back to its feet. The apparition swayed for a moment and then began crabbing down the dock. Slowly, placing one foot at a time on the concrete, holding her forehead with one hand while using the other to probe the fog for other unseen impediments. A moment before disappearing into the fog, she stopped and wobbled, as if she might lose it and fall in the lake. Dougherty felt Corso tighten against her back. "Shouldn't we . . . ," she began.

Then Stone was moving again, moaning slightly with each measured step.

Mewing under her breath as she disappeared from view.

"Nah," they said in unison and laughed out loud.

They stood close in the doorway, listening to the scrape of her shoes.

"If she'd hit you, you were going to pop her one, weren't you?"

"Absolutely," he said without a hint of reservation.

"Some folks wouldn't think much of that."

"Some folks don't know Cynthia Stone."

"She was really something in those red undies."

"If you don't think so, just ask her."

"You think you'd have been so holy if I wasn't here?" she asked.

He chuckled. "I'm a slow learner," he said. "But not that slow."

"Hmmm."

They stood in the narrow doorway until they heard the metallic clank of the gate. Dougherty slid the door closed. Corso's breath tickled the back of her ear. She turned and put her palm on his chest. She watched his eyes fall down the slope of her neck and stop at the top of her breasts. He brought his eyes up. Put his hand on top of hers. She took a breath. Sharp, quick. Tried to pull her hand away, but he held on. She felt the movement of her flesh beneath the dress. How long had it been?

"Don't screw with me, Corso."

A slow smile inched its way across his face, sad and lonely. He reached up and touched her hair. "I don't screw with anybody," he said.

She searched her mind for a sentence. Something with thorns. About how just because Stone had gotten his dander up didn't mean she was going to step into the breach. She opened her mouth to speak but couldn't get past Corso's eyes or the way his hand felt against her hair. She wanted to move away but instead moved closer. Wanted to hide, without relinquishing his gaze.

"Corso . . . it's been . . ." She felt her lips moving closer to his. His hands moved around the back of her neck and pulled. "Corso . . ." Her voice was lost in his mouth. In the crush of lips and teeth, she nearly forgot herself. Pulled away. "If you want me to stop the amateur psychoanalysis, all you have to do is ask," she said. Then his mouth was on hers again. She felt his hands run down the curve of her breasts, felt his fingers at her waist. She tried to call out. To tell him to wait. But her voice faded to a whisper. He looked into her eyes and wrapped his fingers around the top button of her dress. One button. Two buttons.

She gulped a bucket of air. "The lights," she said. Corso released her. Reached up. Snapped them into total darkness. In the black, she searched for his lips and pressed herself against him. Their hips met, folded into one another. She felt her body move in the slow give and take of passion. Corso grabbed her hips and backed her against the wall.

Without warning, her knees buckled and she began to slide down the wall. He seemed to have too many hands. He moved with her, rolling the dress from her shoulders as they slid to the floor. She felt her arms pulling free of the fabric, felt his hands reading the tattoos like Braille. Felt the pads of his fingers pause over the occasional welts, trying to follow the design. She groaned.

She raised her hips; the dress disappeared and suddenly they were on the floor, with his lips tracing the etchings on her flesh, moving across the arch of her right breast. Somewhere in the gloom a car alarm began to bray. She felt his breath on her belly and his hand along the inside of her thigh. Her pelvis reached up to meet his touch, pressing her warmth against the soft pad of his hand.

She pushed her hand into Corso's crotch, worked her fingers through the button fly of his jeans. His breath came faster. Louder. He moved against her hand.

She thought she might have called his name. She couldn't be sure. Next thing she knew she was unbuckling his belt, raising her mouth again to his, aware of nothing but the tangy burn between her legs and the continuous shiver shooting past her navel.

Stronger, faster, louder than the shock of memory. She squeezed her eyes shut, almost pushed him off. And then, he slipped between her thoughts. Inside her, and suddenly she thought of nothing but the slow swing of his rhythm. Felt nothing but the moment's pulse and the skin of a man dancing close to hers.

33

S he put on the big-time pissy face when he say he doan
wanna go to no damn whistle-blower ceremony. "What you
mean, you doan wanna go?" Like she got a earwax problem or
something. Start puttin' the voice and the brow on him at the
same time. "You goin', Robert. You just get that in your mind right
now. You goin'. And you getting up there and acceptin' that award
all nice and polite like. You hear me, boy?"

He doan say nothin'. Doan help. She keeps on wid the voice.

"For once in your life you do the right thing. Do somethin'
make somebody proud of you and you think you ain't going." She
wave a finger all up in his face. He feel like breaking the goddamn thing off, chewing it up, and swallowing it.

"You goin'," she say. Like he didn't hear it the first fifteen times
she say it.

She told every damn neighbor on the block. "My Bobby getting an award from the mayor himself. Gonna be on TV and all. Two thousand dollars. In the papers. Hepped 'em catch that Trashman guy. Gonna get him a whistle-blower award. Right down at the courthouse. Wednesday morning at ten. Havin' them a big ceremony just for him."

Called Grandma down in Riverside too. Told her the same damn shit. Tell her how that fat Korean, King, Kin, Kim, whatever the hell it is, gonna give her the morning off so's she can go. Said he gonna pay her for the time too, 'cause of having a hero in the family. She promised she'd take pictures and send them on down south to Grandma soon as she got 'em developed.

Shoulda never told Goth Girl and the tall dude nothin'. Assholes sent all them damn cops over here wantin' to know every motherfuckin' thing he saw that night. Askin' the same shit over and over like a bunch of fuckin' retards can't remember what he told 'em five minutes ago. Makin' him sign a paper full of his own words. Shit.

And now she out shoppin' for clothes. So's he'll look like a gentleman, she say. He say he ain't going. She say, "Fine, I'll buy 'em widout your ass." Shit. Shoulda gone with her. Might maybe could have talked her into some of that Tommy Hilfiger stuff like the downtown brothers always sporting. Shit may be lame, but it at least got some ghetto to it.

Screw that whistle-blowing, stoolie-of-the-year, rat-out-your-damn-friends award. Who needs that goddamn thing anyway. Whistle-blower my ass.

34

A husband and a daughter... both dead and gone. Alice Doyle wasn't planning on losing anything else. Herds of furniture crammed the rooms. Leaving only narrow, plastic-covered trails to navigate as one moved from place to place. In the living room, the furniture and lampshades had likewise been sealed in plastic like leftover stew.

While she'd busied herself in the kitchen, Corso had toured the room. A million knickknacks and trinkets. Half a dozen photos of Kelly. None of which Corso had seen before. Several of which showed her in a different light than the "Little Miss Vivacious" shot the papers had all been using... unsure of herself. Maybe even a bit melancholy.

Two pictures of her late husband, Rodney. One as a young police officer in his dress blues. Another as a middle-aged man in a cardigan, holding a pitchfork, scowling into the lens. The man had changed but the chin remained the same. "Disappointed" was the word that came to mind, as if here was a person who felt slighted because time and circumstance had, for reasons unknown, conspired to grant him less than his allotted share.

His badge lay on the shelf next to the pictures on the wall. Corso had reached to pick it up, but it was stuck to the surface. He'd reached for the glass cat on the shelf above. Same deal. He'd crossed the room and tried elsewhere. Everything was glued to the shelves. Yeah. Alice Doyle was keeping what she had left.

Corso sat back on the couch. He brought the cup to his lips and sipped. Tea. Didn't taste like much of anything. Like the pipes were rusty, maybe.

"Roddy wasn't happy," she was saying. "Not for a long, long time."

They were on their second pot of tea. He hadn't had to ask a question in half an hour. Apparently, Alice Doyle didn't get many visitors.

Corso inhaled just enough tea to wet his teeth. "Not since the war," she went on. "Never had a happy day in his life since he came back from that godforsaken place."

He'd heard it all before. More times than he could count. Something about Vietnam had poisoned half a generation. Taken their visions of heroic charges across open ground and mutated them into long-drawn-out, duck-and-cover jungle skirmishes, around bends in the road and across the rivers, up the sides of slippery hills, which they were ordered to "take" in the face of snipers and mines and machine guns. As if the ground really mattered and they weren't just going to walk back down later, fewer than before.

"You could see . . . as soon as he got back. He was different. Angry. Like somebody I'd never seen before." She set the cup in the saucer in her lap and stared off into space. "I remember once . . . right after he got back. We went to a dance in Volunteer Park and this man said something—maybe to me, maybe to Roddy, I don't remember—and Roddy just went off on him. I can still see the man covering his head and trying to crawl under a car while Roddy kicked him and spit on him and called him a son of a bitch. I can still see the blood on the man's yellow shirt and his pocket change spilled out on the pavement where he lay." She sighed. "Just like it was yesterday."

"How old was he when he . . ." Corso let it hang.

"He was thirty-nine. Kelly was fourteen." Her eyes clouded over. "He took his revolver, went out by the compost heap, and shot himself in the head. No note. No good-bye of any kind. No anything. We got half his pension. The station house took up a collection. Paid off the house for us."

"How did Kelly take it?"

She set her cup and saucer on the table. Sighed. "Like girls that age take things like that, Mr. Corso. They blame themselves. She grew up too fast. Got a lot wilder. For about five years there, I hardly knew my own daughter. It was the only time in our lives we weren't close."

"So . . . at the end . . . you and Kelly were close again?"

"Like sisters," she said.

"She'd never been married?"

She shook her head and smiled. Started reciting the lines she'd said so many times before. "She was so demanding. She knew just what she wanted and wasn't going to settle for anything less. My Kelly was a girl who knew where she was going."

Corso took another sip. "At the time of her death, was Kelly involved with anyone?"

She shook her head. "She'd been between boyfriends for months. She said she was fed up with relationships that weren't going anywhere."

"You sure?" he asked gently. "You know, sometimes . . ." He waggled a hand. "Sometimes people don't always share everything with their parents."

She cast Corso a pitying glance and began to clean up. "There was no reason for Kelly to keep anything from me. I didn't try to run her life for her. She was a grown woman." She put Corso's cup and saucer on the tray and got to her feet. "I didn't care who she dated, as long as she was happy." She headed for the kitchen. "She always knew she could have brought home a doctor, a lawyer, or an Indian chief and I'd be happy as long as she was." She turned around to back through the swinging door. She cocked an amused eyebrow at Corso. "As long as it wasn't a cop. There's nothing but sorrow being married to a cop. Ask me. I know."

She came back through the door wiping her hands on a black-and-white dish towel.

"You've let me prattle on for over an hour. You're quite a listener."

Corso smiled.

"In your business, that must be quite an asset. So tell me, Mr. Corso, do you mind if I ask a question?" He said he didn't. "So why . . . at this late date . . . what interest is any of this to you now? The story's over, isn't it?"

"I thought I might write a book about it," Corso lied.

She brought a hand to her throat. "Lord knows it had enough twists and turns."

"It sure did," he agreed. "A few more than anybody needed," he added.

She had a faraway look in her eyes. "A book would be good," she said. "When it's written down, people don't forget so easily."

"Did she have a best girlfriend? Somebody her own age she was close to?"

Alice Doyle took a deep breath. "Paula Ziller . . . I suppose. They'd known each other since middle school."

"You know where I might be able to find her?"

"She's moved away," she answered absently. "Down to Portland somewhere."

"That's Ziller." He spelled it. She nodded.

"Ah," she said softly and left the room.

When she returned, she carried a Ziplock freezer bag full of greeting cards. Lots of snowflakes and mangers. Alice Doyle sat in the chair opposite Corso, the bag in her lap. "She sent me a card last year," she said, pawing through the bag. "Paula's a nice girl. The kind who remembers to send cards," she mused.

She pulled an oversize red card from the bag and handed it to Corso. The return address sticker had been snipped from the envelope and scotch-taped to the front of the card. Paula Ziller— 1840 Harrison Street, Portland, Oregon. Noel.

"You used to be a journalist," Alice Doyle said suddenly.

"At one time, yes."

"Did you ever cover a war?"

"Yes, ma'am. The Gulf War."

She paused to collect herself. "What was it about that Vietnam War that sent them all home so damaged?" she asked finally. "So damaged."

"I think all wars are like that," Corso said. He looked up into the woman's liquid brown eyes. "My family talks about how whatever was kind or decent about my father must have gotten lost in some Korean foxhole. About how the only thing the army shipped home was his whiskey thirst and his mean streak."

"I'm sorry," Alice Doyle said.

"Don't be," Corso said. "He wasn't worth it."

35

Maybe losing a friend to a monster permanently heightens the senses. Or maybe she was merely prudent by nature. Either way, Paula Ziller was an exceptionally careful young woman. She stopped the red Ford Taurus well back in the driveway, pushed the garage-door opener, and waited, allowing first the low and then the high beams to play over the empty interior of the garage before easing slowly forward.

Once parked inside, she took her time. Corso watched her eyes play over the rearview mirror as the garage door slid down behind her. A full minute passed before the side yard lit up like a ballpark. Only then did she scurry from the side door of the garage to the back steps, her purse clutched in one hand and her keys at the ready in the other. Little white Mace canister dangling from the key chain. In door. Out lights.

The radio in the rented Ford Explorer had already been tuned to the Portland NPR jazz station when Corso got it from the airport. He'd left it that way. Tuesday-night blues program. Hank Crawford and Jimmy McGriff jamming on "The Glory of Love."

Corso groaned as he stretched. His back was tight. He thought of Dougherty. Remembered the taste of her mouth. And again felt the imaginary draft he'd felt all day on the back of his neck, as if he'd left a door ajar somewhere and the wind had suddenly found access.

Corso checked his watch: 7:40. Two hours since he'd knocked on the front door and then peeked in the side window of the garage and found it empty. He counted to a hundred. And then again. Enough time for a careful girl to get settled and maybe take a leak. Not enough to climb into bed.

1840 Harrison Street was a small, postwar starter home. One story, probably two bedrooms, with a detached garage. The kind of no-frills home once intended to shelter returning GIs and their expectant families.

Corso stepped up onto the front porch and knocked twice on the screen door. He heard the padding of feet and then suddenly the front porch lit up like a runway. He remembered the Mace and moved as far back from the door as possible without stepping off the porch. Held his press credential out in front of him. Winced.

He hadn't noticed the intercom speaker mounted over the front door. The electronic "What do you want?" startled him.

"I'm Frank Corso, from the *Seattle Sun*. I got your name and address from Alice Doyle." He waited, holding the card in front of him like a supplicant and squinting into the spotlights.

A series of snaps and pops and then the inside door opened on a security chain. She was short and had at least one brown eye. Maybe five foot three in her stocking feet. Red hair the color of an orangutan. "What do you want?" she said again.

"I'd like to talk to you about Kelly Doyle."

"Put your ID up against the door so I can see it," she said.

Corso stepped forward and pressed the card against the glass of the screen door.

"I'm going to call Mrs. Doyle," she said and closed the door.

Corso could sense that she hadn't walked away. A minute passed; the interior door opened. She reached out and flipped the lock on the screen door.

"If that didn't send you scurrying off, you must be who you say you are. Come in," she said. Corso stepped into the vestibule.

She was built like a gymnast. Not quite stocky, but hard all over. Big close-set ears, big brown eyes, little tiny nose. Maybe a little surgery, Corso figured.

She picked apologetically at her battered flannel nightgown. "Sorry about the frumpy," she said. "I had a bad day at work. I was going to nuke something to eat and then get in bed and read."

"It's stunning," he assured her.

She looked down at the orange sweat socks on her feet. "Especially the socks," she said. "Very haute."

"My thoughts precisely," he said.

She looked him over. "Are you always this easy to please?" she asked with a teasing twinkle in her eyes.

"I'm a prince," Corso said. "Ask anybody."

"Yeah." She laughed. "I'll just bet you are. Come on."

She led him down a central hall to the brightly lit kitchen at the back of the house. Yellow fifties dinette set. Bright blue dishes and glasses inside four-pane kitchen cabinets. New appliances and sink, old linoleum and light fixtures. Ethan Allen meets Ikea.

She gestured toward one of the chairs. Corso said he'd rather stand.

She leaned back against the counter. "You said you wanted to talk about Kelly."

"If you don't mind."

"But . . . I saw on the news that . . . the police killed the guy."

"They did."

"Then what's to talk about?"

"It's pretty complicated . . . but to make a long story short, I'm not altogether sure I think Kelly was killed by the same person who killed the rest of the girls."

Her dark eyes flashed. "They said there was no doubt about it."

"Who said?"

"The Seattle police."

"You spoke with them?"

"I sure did."

"When was this?"

"Over three years ago. As soon as I heard Kelly was dead. I called to tell them what I knew, but they said they had evidence that made it certain Kelly was killed by the same person who'd killed all those other poor girls."

Corso spread his hands. "I'm not sure," he said.

"Neither was I," she said. "That's why I called and sent the letter."

"What letter?"

"About Kelly's mystery man."

"Maybe you better start at the beginning."

"Coffee?" she asked.

He said no.

She poured herself a cup, and again leaned back against the counter. "You have to understand Kelly, Mr. Corso." Paula Ziller sighed. "Kelly had a knack for losers. I never understood why. She was beautiful and smart and vivacious and everything most girls wish they were and yet . . . if you put her in a room with a dozen men, she'd always pick the loser. The guy who hadn't had a job in five years . . . the guy with five kids who claimed he wasn't married. Every time." She waved her coffee cup. "Like on some level or other she was looking for something she just couldn't find."

"Like a father, maybe," Corso suggested.

She nodded. "I never thought of it that way. But . . . yeah . . . maybe," she said.

"So anyway."

"So . . . it was right at the time I was in the process of moving from Seattle down here to Portland. Kelly had this hot and heavy romance going on with some guy." She made a wry face. "Very hush-hush. Her mother couldn't know about it or anything. I figured the guy must be married. One of those 'My wife doesn't understand me, we'll be divorcing soon' types."

"Mrs. Doyle says her daughter shared everything with her."

"That was one of the weird things about the whole deal. Usually she did. Kelly dated African Americans. She was engaged to a Chinese guy for a while." She made a face. "All of which was okay with her mom. But not this one. For some reason, this one was strictly off-limits to everybody . . . even me."

"Then how come you know?"

"Because it started to get ugly."

"Ugly how?"

"Ugly like all of a sudden, out of the blue, he says he's going to marry somebody else. He says it was some sort of family obligation or something. Like he had no choice. Like he had to do it or else."

"And?"

"Kelly was crazy about him. Desperate."

"So?"

She raised her eyebrows. "She told him she was pregnant."

"She wasn't."

"How do you know?"

"I've read the autopsy report."

She looked away for a moment and then took a long sip from her cup.

"Then she told him she was going to his girlfriend. When she told him that, I guess he came unglued and threatened her. Said he wasn't going to let her ruin his life. Said he'd put a stop to her if she tried."

"How?"

"I don't know. That's all she said."

"And you have no idea who this guy was?"

She shook her head. "A name . . . no . . . but I think I may have seen him once," she said. "Right before I moved. I stopped in some little hole-in-the-wall deli in Wallingford. Inside that old school they renovated into a shopping center."

Corso said he knew the place.

"She was sitting at a table with this guy I'd never seen before. A fox. They were arguing. You could feel it in the air. The other people in the place were embarrassed for them." She let a hand drop noisily to her side. "I backed right out the door. I felt like I was intruding on something."

"And you never mentioned it to her?"

Her eyes clouded over. "That was the last time I ever saw her alive." She turned and emptied the dregs of her cup down the drain. "I'll tell you though, Mr. . . . ."

"Corso," he filled in.

"I've carried Kelly and what happened to her with me every day of my life since then." She searched him with her eyes. "I've never quite felt safe since."

Corso knew the feeling. The moment when the last remnants of childhood optimism finally disappear down the drain like tepid coffee.

"So when she turned up dead, you notified the police."

"I called and sent a letter."

"You have a copy of the letter?"

"Somewhere."

Corso reached into the inside pocket of his jacket, pulled out a handful of newspaper. Folded both the headlines and the captions over, so only the photographs remained visible.

"The guy in the deli. Was it any of these guys?" he asked, turning the first picture her way. She shook her head. He showed her another picture. Same result. Then the third. She nearly put her nose on the paper. Pointed.

"Second guy from the left," she said.

36

Wald slipped onto the stool next to Corso. Ordered a cup of coffee and an English muffin from the gold-toothed counterman.

"What? There weren't enough shit-hole eateries downtown? You had to drag me all the way out to hell and gone?"

"I figured you might not want to be seen with me."

"At last," Wald said, "an area of agreement." He took in the place. Sighed. "Nice ambience. Kind of retro–industrial waste."

Hector's Lunch was nestled in the shadow of the West Seattle Highway. Catering to the longshoremen of pier eighteen, it opened at five and closed at two. At 11 A.M. on a Wednesday, they were too late for breakfast and too early for lunch. Except for a bearded senior citizen snoring in a booth over by the men's room, they had the place to themselves.

The counterman set Wald's order on the counter and disappeared through the door to the kitchen. "So . . . you and your girlfriend decide you don't want to go along with the program anymore?"

"Nope," said Corso. "A deal's a deal."

Wald took a bite out of his English muffin. Washed it down with coffee.

Corso slid the picture across the counter at Wald. Crimescene photo. Head shot.

"Kate Mitchell. Victim number two."

Wald gave it a cursory glance. Bit off another piece of muffin. "So?"

"Notice the lovely ear tag."

"The accessory no girl should be without."

"Here's the SPD list of what's supposed to be in the bag: 'one watch, Timex; one gold bracelet; one gold cross and chain; two toe rings; one plastic ear tag, ovine.' Here's Dougherty's picture of what's *actually* still in Kate Mitchell's evidence file. Day before yesterday. Two toe rings. A gold cross and chain, and a gold bracelet, and a wristwatch." He waited. "No ear tag."

More muffin, more coffee. "She musta missed it," the cop insisted.

Corso plopped two more pictures on top of the first. "Here's two other angles. No ear tag. She didn't miss it."

This time Wald studied all three photos, then turned them upside down on the counter. "Anything could have happened. Maybe it got sent for testing and never got returned. Maybe it's in somebody else's file. Who the fuck knows?"

"Whoever took it out of the file knows."

Wald's posture stiffened. The implication was clear. The SPD property room wasn't exactly the public library. "Now why would anybody want to do a thing like that?"

"So they could accessorize Kelly Doyle with it."

Wald stopped mid-munch. "To what purpose?" he asked tentatively.

"To make damn sure she was listed as a Trashman victim."

"Who says she wasn't?"

"I do."

He finished chewing. Finished the coffee. Looked Corso in the eye.

"You got somebody specific in mind? Or you just talking out your ass?"

"I'll tell you a little story, and then you tell me."

"Have at it."

"I talked to a woman named Paula Ziller last night. She's a securities analyst, lives down in Portland. Used to be Kelly Doyle's best friend." Wald stopped swirling the dregs of his coffee and locked his eyes on Corso, as if daring him to continue. Instead, Corso pulled two pieces of folded paper from his coat pocket. Held them between his middle and index fingers and offered them to the cop. Wald pulled his head back, as if Corso was trying to hand him a weasel. Then finally reached out and plucked the pages from Corso's fingers. Flattened them on the counter and began to read. He read both pages once and then started at the beginning and went through them again.

"Sound like anybody we know?" Corso asked.

"Sounds like a whole lotta people."

"That letter isn't in Kelly Doyle's file."

"How—" he began.

"I've got a copy of the file, remember? You and I xeroxed it with our own little hands."

Wald went silent.

"You know her father?" Corso asked.

"The Doyle girl?"

"Yeah."

"He was just before my time. I hear he went sideways with his piece."

"The Ziller woman says Kelly Doyle dated most of the known world and none of it was a problem for her mother. Both she and the mother claim they were real close. Shared everything."

"I'm touched. I really am, but you got a point here, Corso?"

"Mama Doyle told me there was only one kind of man her daughter best never bring home."

"What kind was that?"

"A cop."

Wald shrugged and turned away. "Who can blame her? I'm bettin' my wife feels the same way about our daughters."

Wald winced when Corso pulled a newspaper photo from the same pocket.

"I showed the Ziller woman this."

Wald looked like he wanted to close his eyes and put his fingers in his ears.

"She says the second guy on the left is the guy she saw Kelly Doyle arguing with, a week before she died."

Wald shot the photo a quick glance and then pulled a napkin from the dispenser and dabbed at his lips.

"What did I ever do to deserve you?" he muttered.

"I want to see the property room log books for the two days between when Himes was arrested and Kelly Doyle was found."

Wald blew a long whistle. Scratched the back of his neck.

"You realize what you're asking me to do?"

"I'm asking you to put a murderer where he belongs."

"Says you."

"We can sure as hell find out, now can't we?"

"There's gotta be some other explanation."

"I'm all ears, Wald. What you got in mind?"

He used his forefinger to pick at the sore on his lip. "Lotta people have access to the property room."

"Do they all sign in?"

"As far as I know."

"And they have to sign out for specific items. Just like you and I had to do the other day."

"Far as I know."

"Then why not have a look?" Before he could object, Corso went on. "If you're right and you have a look and his name's not there, then we can let this whole thing settle. If you find what I'm saying you're going to find, then it's a grounder, right? I mean . . . what are the chances? We've got a two-day time window from the day Himes was arrested till the day Kelly Doyle was found. How many people can have signed out for that particular piece of property, within that period of time?"

"And if it's there?"

"Then have a look at the sign-outs for Kelly Doyle's file. If we get a doubleheader, then it's a slam dunk. We explain all the ten brides stuff. We explain the missing set of clothes. We explain the missing tag and the letter. Neat as can be. End of story. Our boy inherits Himes's seat on the gurney."

Wald wiped the corners of his mouth with his thumb and forefinger.

"This is bad juju, Corso," he said. "In case you forgot, we got a funeral for a dead cop this afternoon." He wagged a finger Corso's way. "A cop who, at the time of his death, was my partner." He paused to let it sink in. "We got a general public still wants to fry Walter Himes. A million people who don't give a rat's ass we took the real perp down. They still want Himes dead. Period." He waved a thick hand. "Instead, they turn on the tube and there's Himes sitting up in Harborview on their dime. Stuffin' his face and talking to the press about what he's gonna do with all the money he gets from the city." He waved again. "Downtown is like a fucking circus. Kesey tried to fire a secretary for dripping coffee on his desk. Everybody is out of their minds.

Scared shitless." Wald looked away. "I've got eighteen years of my life into this. I'm thirty-six hours from being promoted to lieutenant when I really ought to get fired or sent back to foot patrol and, all of a sudden, the whole department looks like a joke. A sideshow. Like we're the fucking Keystone Kops or something."

"You know I'm right," Corso said.

"Oh . . . you're a mind reader now too. You know what I'm thinking."

Wald's face was blank, but the tips of his ears were bright red.

"Holy Mary mother of God," he said. Checked his watch.

He threw a five-dollar bill on the counter. Pinned Corso with his glare.

"Shift changes at twelve-thirty. I'll have a look then, but I'm telling you, man, I hope to God you're wrong," he said.

"Tell you the truth, Wald, I kinda hope so too. This story doesn't need any more twists and turns."

Wald jammed his hands in his overcoat pockets. "Gimme a number. I'll call you after the funeral."

Corso watched him leave. Pulled the phone from his pocket and dialed Dougherty's number again. Same deal. Just rings forever. Unplugged.

The counterman reappeared; he pulled a gray plastic tub from beneath the counter and set Wald's dishes inside. "How's the chili?" Corso asked the kid.

"Canned," the kid said with a glint.

"Gimme a bowl and a large glass of milk."

37

Butler Parking Garage. All the way down to the bottom, he'd said. Five floors. As close to three o'clock as he could make it.

The oily grit on the floor caused Corso's shoes to slip with nearly every step. The place smelled like they'd used urine instead of water to mix the concrete. The only parked car was a '69 Pontiac convertible. Red. Ghetto sled extraordinaire. All fins and flourishes. The four flat tires and the inch and a half of dust suggested it had been a while since this baby had cruised the Malt Shoppe.

Two thirds of the way down his esophagus, the glass of milk was losing a titanic battle with the chili. Felt like he had a candle in his chest. Shoulda held the onions.

It was seven after three when a dim green bulb came on over the elevator. The door slid back with a bump, but nobody stepped out. From where he was, Corso could just make out the tip of a toe holding the door open.

The sound of his slipping shoes ricocheted around the walls as he made his way over. Wald. Standing at the front of the elevator car. Fresh from the funeral in his dress blues. Sick expression on his face.

"I want two promises from you," he said.

"Like?"

"First I want to make damn sure I'm clean on these." He waved a large manila envelope. "They're clean from my end. You make sure they stay clean from yours. It gets out I had anything to do with this, I might as well just transfer to internal affairs with the rest of the rats."

"You have my word on it. What else?"

Wald stared at Corso long and hard. "I want to hear that I won't be seeing you again. Or hearing from you. Or anything. This needs to be the last time I ever lay eyes on you."

Corso grinned. "You could hurt a guy's feelings talking like that, Wald."

The cop stiffened. "I'm not in the mood, Corso. I buried a fellow officer this afternoon. The fact that I didn't much like him or that you didn't much like him or that he wasn't much of a cop . . . you know . . . somehow, when it came to putting him in the ground, none of that mattered. He still had parents and a sister and her kids sitting there. And his dying still"—he searched for a word—"diminishes . . . his death diminishes all of us. Individually and as a department." He held out the brown envelope. Grimaced. "And now I'm going to contribute to this debacle," he said disgustedly. "As if we don't look bad enough already."

Corso took hold of the envelope. Wald hung on. The envelope swung between them, like one of those old pictures of the Great White Father and the Indians signing a treaty and then holding it up for all to see.

"I thought about lying to you. Telling you it wasn't there. But you're so goddamn insistent, you'd just get somebody else to check it out for you. I thought about tearing out the pages. Burning them. Telling you to go fuck yourself."

"So . . . what stopped you?"

"I don't know," he said after a moment. "I really don't."

Wald released his grip on the envelope. Corso let it fall to his side. Wald opened his mouth to speak, thought better of it. Punched the button.

* * *

She picked it up on the tenth ring.

"Yeah."

"Hey," he said.

"Hey yourself."

"How you doin'?"

"Fine. You?"

"I'm a little sore," he said. "Musta used a few muscles I haven't used in quite a while."

She laughed. "One in particular."

"That one's fine. It's the rest of me that's broke down."

"Must be middle age," she teased.

A crackle of static ran through the line and then faded to silence.

"I've been calling—" he began.

"I had it unplugged."

They both spoke at once; he heard her laugh.

"About the other night . . ." she began.

"What night was that?"

"Don't start with me, Corso."

"You always say that."

"I don't generally drink that much."

"Do we have to talk about it?"

"Yes, Corso . . . I know it's your worst nightmare, but we do."

"Then let's do it in person," Corso said. "I'd feel better about it that way."

"I've got a lot to do today."

"Dinner?"

Pause. "Where?"

"Depends on what you're in the mood to eat."

"Red meat," she said. "And thick red wine."

"Metropolitan Grill. Eight o'clock."

"Corso . . . you know, just because we . . . we . . . you know . . . doesn't mean we have to make like we're going steady or anything."

Longer pause. "Look . . . if you don't want to . . ."

"I didn't say that."

"Eight o'clock."

* * *

"Hawes."

"Corso."

"What—you've had a change of heart and want to get back into the newspaper game?"

"Maybe we get you that Pulitzer nomination after all."

"How so?"

"Maybe help your boy Newton make his bones while we're at it."

"I'm all ears."

Except for a single "holy shit," muttered about halfway through, he stayed that way until Corso finished talking.

"Wait a second," he said. A series of clicks came over the line. Two minutes passed. Then Hawes's voice again. "Mrs. V.'s on with us," he said.

"And you've got all this documented?" she wanted to know.

"Big as life. I've got copies of the evidence room sign-out

sheets for both files. He signed the Mitchell woman's file out the day after Himes was arrested. He's checked the Doyle file nearly twice a month for over three years."

"Will your source come forward, if necessary?" she asked.

"No. My source is untouchable. If we're not prepared to go to the wall to protect the source, then we should drop a quarter and give the story away."

They thought it over. "What did you have in mind for breaking the story?" she asked.

Corso told her. Hawes whistled. "You are a troublemaker, aren't you?"

"It's more dramatic that way. They always field questions at the end. All the local affiliates will have a team there. That way, Newton's face ends up all over the evening news. Get his name in the lead paragraph in every paper, coast to coast."

"And what do you get out of this?" Hawes asked.

"I get to crawl back under my rock."

"I wish we had more," Mrs. V. said.

"Don't we always."

"You're doing that 'we' thing again," Hawes said.

"I've got an idea, though."

"Shoot."

"Let me ask you a question, Hawes. If you were stepping out on your wife, how would you handle it."

"I'd double my life insurance. Louise ever caught me—"

"Seriously. If you were conducting a little liaison on the side, where would you meet your sweetie? Would you find a little love nest, where nobody knows either of you and stick with it? Meet there all the time? Or would you move around from place to place, for a little variety?"

"I'd find a place and stick with it."

"Me too," said Corso.

"Wallingford."

"That's it. Send Newton and anybody else you can spare. Have them show pictures around. Especially the hotels and motels. She lived with her mother. He was creeping around on his girlfriend. They had to be doing the hokeypokey somewhere. Chances are that if the Ziller woman saw them together, so did somebody else."

"You know, Mr. Corso . . . whether Mr. Newton or anyone else breaks the news, the smart money is going to figure the story came through you."

"They'll have to find me."

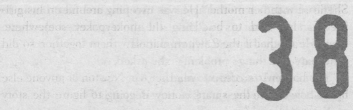

38

Thursday, September 27
9:23 A.M. Day 6 + 5

At the Fairway buoy, less than fifty feet of water slipped beneath the hull. He reached up and set the autopilot for 3:39. Magnetic. The twin Lehman diesels purred at two thousand RPMs. Turning into the wind at a stately twelve knots, the bow plowed contentedly into endless rows of rising green waves, which curled but did not break. Overhead, the sun looked like a tarnished nickel trying desperately to assert itself in a silver sky. The water ahead shimmered with silver light.

The depth sounder began to question itself as the bottom fell away. Sixty-five feet and then a hundred and five. One-fifty. And then suddenly the sounder lost touch. Its ultrasonic impulses no longer able to bounce off the rapidly retreating bottom.

To the east, the Magnolia Bluffs loomed white against the haze. He lifted the binoculars. Picture windows and planter boxes. Glass-topped tables and furled umbrellas. Hawaiian torches around the patio. An empty hammock hanging thick and wet between two trees.

The sounder chattered again at two hundred feet, began to spew random numbers and then slid into a sustained electronic beep. He reached up and switched it off.

"What's that thing's problem?" she asked.

"The bottom's too deep to read."

"So how do you keep track of how deep it is?"

"You read the chart."

She sat and peered at the chart for a moment, then pointed with a long fingernail. "Is this where we are?"

He bent and looked down at the chart table. "Yeah. The depth is the black numbers."

"Six hundred feet," she said tentatively.

"That's about right," he said. "It falls away in a big hurry."

She rolled open the starboard door and gazed out at the blots of half-million-dollar houses covering the side of the hill, half a mile away. "You think they know?" she asked. "You know, that they're like sitting there and right out here under the water it's like the end of the world. Like the abyss."

"Nah," he said. "They're just pleased to have front-row seats for the surface of things."

They were across the shipping channel now, pointed directly at Kingston and the Kitsap Peninsula, where a pair of ferries looped gracefully around each other. She got to her feet and put an arm around his waist, slid her hand down inside the right-hand pocket of his jeans. He moved his left hand up under her hair to the back of her neck. With his right hand, he disengaged the autopilot. Took the wheel, aiming at an imaginary point in the silver foam between the ferries.

39

Dorothy Sheridan straightened the red-white-and-blue bunting, tapped the microphones one last time, and then stepped down from the stage. The interview with Taylor and Abrams had gone well. Monica had called Tuesday night to say T. and A., as she liked to call them, were going to make Dorothy an offer, but it was Thursday, and she hadn't heard anything. A timid voice in her head kept saying that maybe it was all for the best.

She checked her notes. First it was the kid. Robert Boyd. He was Seifort's baby. The mayor's Whistle-blower's Award. Stanley'd say a few words, hand the kid the plaque and the check, and then it was her turn with the Post guy. Good Citizen Award. That was easy. She'd seen it for herself. Been there when he'd tackled poor Mr. Nisovic. Give him the check and the medal and then hand off to Chief Kesey. Promotion for Sergeant Wald and a valor commendation for Chucky Donald. She shook her head in wonder. The only thing funnier than a *Seattle Sun* employee getting an award from the mayor was Chucky Donald getting anointed for valor.

* * *

"What if somebody see me," he demanded, "lookin' like a goddamn FBI agent?" Put on the pissy face right away. "Those down-at-the-heel little bums you hang out wid." She bust up laughing. "Tommy Hutton's mama din bring so many 'uncles' home, him and his sisters woulda starved years ago. None of them you hang out wid got any room to talk. Them people oughta be happy jus havin' somethin' new for a change." She laughed again.

Bitch really think she funny this morning. True about Tommy's mama, though. Woman ought to have her one of those little red dispenser things like in the bakery. Numba nineteen. Nineteen. He put a hand over his mouth so she couldn't see his lips. They hadn't talked about the money yet, neither. Know she gonna want him to put it in the bank . . . for college or some such shit. He smiled behind his hand. Check gonna be made out to him, though, so there's hope.

* * *

Her fingers worked at his throat.

"Daddy, we have *got* to fix that tie."

Bill Post squinted into the bathroom mirror. "What's the matter with it?"

"It only comes halfway down your shirt, for Pete's sake. It's supposed to reach the top of your belt buckle. You look like Oliver Hardy."

"Is that the fat one or the skinny one?"

"The fat one."

Rachael ducked between his pants legs and came up under

the pedestal sink. With the three of them jammed into the tiny bathroom, all Bill Post could do was turn in a circle. Nancy slid the tie out from under his collar. Tied it around her own neck and then slipped it over his head. She turned up his stiff collar. "You look like a conductor," she said.

"Railroad?"

"Orchestra."

She rearranged the collar. Slipped the knot into place at Bill Post's throat. "There," she said, patting his jacket into place. "Now you look like a hero."

* * *

It was going well. The police auditorium in the Alaska Building was only about a quarter full, which was fine with Dorothy. She figured the recent hurricane of excitement had kept the crowd down. No parents of survivors, either. Thank goodness.

She'd done the introductions without flubbing anything. Seifort was working his way up to handing the Boyd kid the loot. Dorothy Sheridan pulled a single blue notecard from her pocket. Bill Post. Post no Bills came to mind, and she smiled.

"What we need, ladies and gentlemen," Hizhonor was saying, "is more young men like Robert Boyd. Young men with a sense of purpose and a sense of community." The kid sat there scowling into his lap. "It is with great pride that I introduce the recipient of this year's Whistle-blower Award—Mr. Robert Boyd."

The mayor offered the plaque. The kid reached over and grabbed the check instead. He carefully stashed the check in the inside pocket of his sport coat and then accepted the plaque from Stanley. Big photo-op handshake. The kid exits stage left. His mother's been saving a seat for him at the end of the third row. She throws an arm around his shoulder, drawing him close. He looks embarrassed. Just like Brandy.

"And now, ladies and gentlemen, to present our next award, Seattle Police Department spokesperson Dorothy Sheridan."

* * *

Seems the big old doofus tackled some guy with a gun. Same guy shot that liver-lips Himes asshole. She sayin' he might have saved the lives of a whole room fulla people, but he can't figure out why they make a fuss about anybody for saving that piece-of-shit Himes. Oughta give the fucker wid the gun the medal. Oughta give me the money.

She ain't said nothin' about the money, but that sure as hell ain't gonna last. She kept tryin' to talk in his ear but he's making like he's digging every word they say onstage and can't listen to her right now.

The red-headed lady was saying, "On behalf of the Seattle Police Department and the people of King County, I would like to present the Good Citizen Award to Mr. Bill Post."

Doofus bust a move up to the front, grab his loot, thank about three hundred fucking people and then, finally, they're applauding again.

We should go now, he's thinkin'. No reason to sit through this cop shit. He looks up at her. She's reading his mind. Pissy look. Shit.

* * *

Bill Post hung the silver medal around Rachael's neck. She pulled it back off and dropped it on the floor with a clang. He grunted as he bent to retrieve it. He dropped it in the breast pocket of his sport coat. She'd been sitting quietly for a long time now and was getting itchy. He pulled her into his lap, where she squirmed like a fish. Just about done. Both cops had gotten their awards. Chief Kesey was going on. "Without the efforts of dedicated professional law-enforcement officers such as these, we would no longer have a society in which we could reasonably have any hope of realizing our dreams or the dreams of our children." Rachael slid onto the floor and began playing with her shoes. The applause rose and then faded as the police spokeslady, whose name Bill Post couldn't, for the life of him, recall at the moment, came forward and called for questions. What was the current status of Slobodan Nisovic? Mr. Nisovic was still in Harborview Medical Center. In serious but stable condition. Charges? Charges would be decided by the district attorney's office. What about Himes? Was either Donald or Wald being reassigned? Another half a dozen questions and then a lull. Post picked Rachael up and bounced her on his knee. Nancy grabbed her purse from the floor.

"If there are no further questions," the woman said, "I'd like to thank you all—"

A pink-cheeked guy rose from the audience. "Blaine Newton from the *Seattle Sun*," he said. "I have a question for Chief Kesey."

A POUND
OF CURE

God only knows what he was thinking. There must have been eighty people in the room. Forty of them cops. Maybe the collective pressure just got to be too much for him and he slipped a cog or something. Or maybe, as rumor around the department had it, he'd had a sudden vision of what his life in prison was going to look like. Either way, anything would have been better than what he did.

Chief Kesey stepped up to the microphone. Blaine Newton turned a page on his clipboard, cleared his throat, and said, "Chief Kesey, I was wondering if you were aware of the fact that at the time of her death, victim number eight, Kelly Doyle, was conducting an affair with Lieutenant Charles Donald?"

Kesey went white. "Excuse me, what did you—"

"I asked you if you were aware of the fact that Lieutenant Donald and Trashman victim number eight, Kelly Doyle, were conducting an affair at the time of her death, in nineteen ninety-eight."

The Sheridan woman stepped forward. "Surely, Mr. . . . ."

"Newton."

"Surely, Mr. Newton, there must be some more appropriate venue for these sorts of unfounded allegations, than a moment such as—"

Newton had begun to sweat profusely. His voice rose an octave. He was reading now. "You might be interested to know that the *Seattle Sun* has obtained depositions from nine past and present employees of the Emerald Inn on Stone Way attesting to the fact that in early nineteen ninety-eight Detective Donald and Kelly Doyle met for afternoon liaisons on an average of three to four times a week. Sometimes more."

"You're a damn liar," Kesey shouted.

Every camera in the room was grinding. Newton wiped his brow with his forearm. Kesey turned away from the audience. Said something. Neither the microphones nor the cameras picked up what he said. Those on the stage at the time later agreed that he'd been talking to Donald. "Tell him he's a god-damn liar," he'd said.

Newton was talking again. "Copies of the Seattle Police Department's evidence room log books reveal that—"

At that point, Donald lost his marbles. Grabbed the Sheridan woman by the back of her hair, pulled her to his chest, and put a gun in her ear. "Keep away from me," he said as he backed down the stairs, dragging Sheridan along with him. Her eyes were squeezed shut. Her lips moved as if in prayer. "Keep away from me," he said again, grinding the pistol into the woman's head.

"Let her go," someone screamed.

"Now," another voice shouted.

Most of the civilians were either huddled on the floor or sprinting for the doors at the back of the room. The rest of the crowd had guns out. The screaming to let her go came now from a dozen throats as Donald began to back down the aisle.

That's when the Post guy got to his feet and started for Donald.

Musta thought his shiny new silver medal made him bulletproof or something. "Now listen here . . . ," he said, reaching a big red hand out for Donald.

Donald shot him once in the heart. The old guy clutched his chest in disbelief, staggered backward into the row of folding chairs, and went down in a clatter. A woman dropped to her knees beside the old man. A little girl in a pink dress and white tights began to cry. A chorus of shouts. To put down the gun . . . to let her go now . . . roared, octaves below the girl's high-pitched wail.

From there on, it was like a collage. Each of the three television cameras in the room was focused on something different. The local ABC affiliate stayed with Donald as he continued to edge toward the side door of the auditorium, with the Sheridan woman locked behind his forearm. He reached back and grabbed the door handle.

Some instinct in the Sheridan woman told her she'd be better off in a room full of cops. For the first time since the ordeal began, she opened her eyes. What she saw was the black nostrils of a dozen gun barrels pointed her way. Her reaction to the sight saved her life. She fainted dead away. Dropped to the floor so quickly that Donald was left staring down in disbelief at her motionless body.

Except for Donald, everybody in the room who was holding a gun used it. Sounded like some sort of salute. Donald was dead before he hit the floor. Calls for aide wagons and backup were being shouted in from all over the room. Cops were herding civilians and news crews out the back of the room. The woman and the girl pitched a fit, wouldn't leave the old man. The cops let 'em stay.

Outside in the hall, CBS filled its feel-good quota with pictures of Robert Boyd—recipient of the mayor's Whistle-blower's

Award—with his arms around his sobbing mother, patting her back and reminding her that they were both all right.

NBC was still inside the auditorium when the first gurney arrived and was waved toward Bill Post. NBC swung his camera in time to see a pair of EMTs push their way through a circle of cops to reach Dorothy Sheridan's side. They quickly checked for wounds. Found none. Pulse. Strong. One lifted up Sheridan's head. The other ran something under her nose. She frowned and shook her head. Ran a hand over her face and then suddenly sat up. She looked over her shoulder. A circle of feet obscured Donald's mangled body. She hiccuped once and covered her mouth.

When she turned back, Chief Kesey had taken one of her hands. The camera mike wasn't close enough to pick up what she said, but even amateur lip readers could plainly make out the words. "I quit."

When he swung back to Bill Post, they were performing CPR. Fifteen and a breath. Fifteen and a breath. Serious head shaking. Fifteen and a breath. Fifteen and a breath. Suddenly the chest compression guy stopped. Put his hand flat on the chest. Then replaced his hand with his ear. "He's breathing again," he announced.

His partner clapped an oxygen mask on Bill Post's face and then began carefully separating the folds of the old man's clothes. Gently probing for the wound. Sport coat unbuttoned and parted. Same for the shirt. Undershirt ignominiously pulled up along his torso and bunched beneath his southernmost chin. The EMT frowned. He looked up at his buddy and said, "Nothing. Not a mark on him."

The other guy checked his pulse and then listened to his heart. "He's doing fine."

Together they carefully rolled him over. Same deal. They pulled his undershirt back down and rolled him onto his back.

Felt around in the shirt. Then in the sport coat. The chest compresser's hand came out of the coat with the silver Good Citizen Award in it. The once-symmetrical silver disk had been warped into the shape of a wavy potato chip.

"Bullet hit this," he announced. "Saved his life."

By the time they had Bill Post strapped to a gurney and rolling toward the doors, his eyes were open and the room was empty. Most of the throng had followed Donald's body out the door. The stragglers left with Post. An officer poked his head in.

"We need to seal the room," he said.

NBC nodded, gathered his stuff. As he stepped into the hall, the Boyd kid came sauntering over. "Left my jacket in there," he said.

"Sorry . . . you'll have to—" the cop began.

"Robert here won the mayor's Whistle-blower Award today," NBC said.

"Did you, now?" the cop said.

"Sure did," the kid replied.

The cop smiled down at Robert. Pulled the door open. "Hurry up, now. Go get it." The kid ducked inside.

"It true what they say? We had cops killing cops in there?"

NBC nodded. "You wanna see it?" he asked.

The cop looked around the chaotic hallway. "Sure," he said.

NBC turned the camera on. Rewound to when Kesey stepped up to answer the question, then turned the screen to face the cop. His face sagged as he watched the three minutes of tape.

"Jesus," he said.

The door opened and Robert Boyd appeared, wearing a brown-plaid wool jacket. As the door eased closed, NBC noticed a sudden flash of gold, like a fish rising in a stream. He watched Robert Boyd kindly take his distraught mother by the arm and help her down the hall to the corner, where he looked back with a barracuda smile before steering his mom toward the front doors.

NBC pulled open the auditorium door and peered inside. Right between the state seal and the city seal. Big, thick, gold letters. The tail of the *Y* looped around to make a circle.

BLACK RIVER

To Bill Farley—
master of all things mysterious
and bookseller extraordinaire

In the country of the blind, the one-eyed man is king.

—H. G. WELLS

1

Like nearly everyone born in the tin shacks that line the banks of the Río Cauto, Gerardo Limón was short, dark, and bandy-legged. A textbook cholo, Limón was less than a generation removed from the jungle and thus denied even the pretense of having measurable quantities of European blood, a deprivation of the soul which, for all his adult life, had burned in his chest like a candle. That his partner, Ramón Javier, was tall, elegant, and obviously of Spanish descent merely added fuel to the flame.

Gerardo shouldered his way into the orange coveralls and then buckled the leather tool belt about his waist. A sticky valve in the truck's engine ticked in the near darkness. Twenty yards away, Ramón spaced a trio of orange traffic cones across the mouth of the driveway leading to the back of the Briarwood Garden Apartments.

The kill zone was perfect. The driveway had two nearly blind turns. This end of the building had no windows. To the north, half a mile of marsh separated the apartments from the Speedy Auto Parts outlet up the road.

"You wanna pitch or catch?" Gerardo asked.

"Who was up last?" Ramón wanted to know.

"We turned two, remember?"

Last time out, they'd encountered an unexpected visitor and had to play an impromptu doubleheader. Ramón's thin lips twisted into a smile as he recalled the last time they'd worn these uniforms. As he settled the tool belt on his hips, he wondered how many times they'd run their "utility repairmen" number. Certainly dozens. He'd lost count years ago.

Ramón Javier liked to think he might have become a doctor, or a jazz musician, or maybe even a baseball player if things had been different. If his family had made it to Miami the first time. If they hadn't been dragged back to that stinking island and treated like pig shit for five years.

Ramón settled the yellow hard hat onto his head and checked the load in the .22 automatic, screwed the CAC22 suppressor carefully onto the barrel, and then slipped the weapon through the loop in the tool belt generally reserved for the hammer.

He checked his watch. "Three minutes, " he said. "What will it be?"

"Whatever you want," Gerardo said. "I don't care."

"Don't forget, we got orders to lose the truck," Ramón said.

Gerardo shrugged. "You pitch. I'll catch."

Wednesday, July 26   5:24 a.m.

The kitchen floor squeaked as he made his way over to the refrigerator. He removed a brown paper sack, set it on the counter, and checked inside. Two sandwiches: olive loaf and American cheese on white. A little salt, a little pepper, and just a dab of Miracle Whip. Satisfied, he grabbed the plastic water bottle from the refrigerator, stuffed it into the pocket of his jacket, and headed for the door.

Overhead, the Milky Way was little more than a smear across the sky. Too many lights, too many people, too much smog for the stars. He used his key to open the truck door. The '79 Toyota pickup, once bright yellow, had oxidized to a shade more reminiscent of uncleaned teeth.

The engine started at the first turn of the key. He smiled as he raced the motor and fiddled with the radio. The ON-OFF knob was going. You had to catch it just right, and even then, first time you hit a bump, it would switch itself off, and you had to start all over again.

He caught two bars of music. Chopin, he thought, when the light in the cab flickered. As he sat up, a movement caught his eye. He looked to his left, thinking it was that sorry ass troll who lived in the basement. Guy never slept. Never washed either.

Wasn't him, though. No, it was old hangdog himself. Standing there with his hands clasped behind his back, staring in the truck window like he's the messenger of doom or something.

He rolled down the window. "You want something?" he inquired.

"How do you live with yourself?" the guy asked. "Have you no shame?"

He raced the engine three times and then spoke. "Don't you ever give it up, man? It's over. What can I say? Shit happens."

Given a second chance, the driver probably would have chosen his words more carefully. As last words go, *shit happens* left a great deal to be desired. Those three syllables were, however, the last mortal utterance to pass his lips, because, at that point, old hang-dog pulled a gun out from behind his back and shot the driver four times in the face.

As he stood next to the truck, trying to absorb the gravity of his act, the truck radio suddenly began to play classical music, scattering his thoughts like leaves. He looked uncomprehendingly at the weapon in his hand; then he lobbed it through the window into the driver's lap and slowly walked away.

Wednesday, July 26   5:26 a.m.

"What was that?" Ramón asked.

"Shhh." Gerardo held a finger to his lips.

The pulsing yellow light circled them in the darkness.

"Sounded like shots to me," Ramón whispered.

Gerardo slipped the gun from his tool belt and held it close along his right leg as he worked his way along the side of the building all the way to the back, where he could see out into the parking lot. He peered around the corner and then came running back.

"He's sitting there warming up the truck, just like always."

"Musta been backfires," said Ramón, without believing it.

They'd been following him for a week. Memorizing his schedule. Getting to know his habits. Gerardo checked his watch. "One minute," he whispered.

Whatever his other failings, and the quality of his life suggested they were many, their victim was always on time. Left his cruddy apartment just before five-thirty each morning. Warmed up his truck for three minutes and then left for work in time to arrive at five minutes to six. The only time he'd varied from his schedule was Friday night, when he'd stopped for gas and groceries on the way home.

Gerardo's thick lips began to tremble as he stared at his watch and counted time. "Thirty seconds," he whispered. "Twenty-nine . . ."

Wednesday, July 26   5:31 a.m.

He signed his confession, checked his watch, and then dialed nine-one-one. "There has been a killing at the Briarwood Garden Apartments. Twenty-six-eleven Marginal Way South," he said. "In the back parking lot. I'll meet the officers there."

"Let me have your—"

He hung up on the dispatcher. Then he smoothed his confession out on the counter and read it over. It began: *This morning, July 26, 2000, I killed a man who deserved to die. For this act I am prepared to suffer whatever consequences society sees fit to impose upon me.* It was followed by his signature. He'd thought of explaining his crime but felt certain they wouldn't understand. They knew so little of honor.

The more he looked at the word *consequences*, the more convinced he became it was spelled incorrectly. To be thought a killer was one thing; to be thought ignorant was another.

Wednesday, July 26   5:34 a.m.

66 He's late," Gerardo said.

This time it was Ramón who scurried up to the corner of the building and peeked around. In the ghostly overhead light, he could see the mark sitting behind the wheel, hear the sounds of music and the engine running. He wondered if perhaps the driver had fallen asleep at the wheel. Something about the situation didn't feel right.

When he looked around, Gerardo had doused the emergency light and was throwing the traffic cones into the truck. He hurried along the side of the building.

"He's still sitting there," he whispered to Gerardo. "Maybe we should wait a few more minutes."

Gerardo's face was grim. "Something's wrong," he said. "Get in."

Ramón hopped into the passenger side just as the truck sprung to life.

"You play center," Gerardo said. "I'll play third."

They'd done it so many times before, nothing more needed to be said. Gerardo gunned the truck up the narrow drive, swung left around the parking lot, and slid to a stop with the bed of their pickup blocking the mark's. Both men leaped from the truck and ran to their respective positions, Ramón out onto the grass in front of the truck, where he assumed the combat position, holding his silenced automatic in two hands, pointing directly at the dark windshield, Gerardo a half pace to the rear of the driver's-side window, where by the mere extension of his arm he could place the end of the suppressor behind the victim's ear.

"What the fuck is this?" Gerardo said.

When Gerardo returned his weapon to his belt and leaned down to peer in the window, Ramón hustled across the grass to his side. The mark sat open-mouthed. Four separate rivers of blood ran down over his face and disappeared into his collar. He'd been shot twice high on the forehead, once in the right eye and once again just to the left of the nose.

"Somebody shot him," Gerardo offered, in that literal manner of his that drove Ramón crazy.

"No shit," Ramón said. He pointed down at the .22 target pistol in the dead man's lap. "Shooter dropped the piece," he said.

"What the fuck are we gonna do? *We* was supposed to shoot the guy. What kinda fuck would do something like this?" Gerardo demanded.

"Lemme think, will ya?"

Ramón looked around the parking lot. Nothing. Apparently nobody had heard the noise. "We gotta finish this thing," he said after a minute. "Just like the plan."

"But we didn't pop him."

"Don't matter," Ramón said quickly. "We still gotta finish." He checked the area again. Still nothing. "We finish . . . just like it was us who offed him."

"It ain't right," Gerardo said. "We was supposed to do it."

Ramón knew the muley look. He pointed the silenced automatic through the window and shot the lifeless corpse twice in the side. The body toppled over in the seat.

"There . . . we shot him," he said. "You feel better now?"

Gerardo didn't answer. Just stared sullenly off into space.

"Go ahead," Ramón said. "Give him a couple."

Gerardo shook his head. "It's not right," he said again.

"Go on," Ramón coaxed.

Gerardo hesitated for a moment, gave a small shrug, leaned into the cab, and shot the body three times in rapid succession.

Ramón began to move. "I'll drive his truck. You follow behind. We do it just like we planned."

"What if—"

Ramón cut him off. "You gonna go back and tell the man we struck out?" he asked. "You gonna tell him how we was sitting on our thumbs out front while somebody else was earning our money for us?" They both knew the answer was no. In their present position, failure was not an option.

Ramón pulled open the driver's door and used his foot to push the body down onto the passenger-side floorboards. "Let's go," he said. "Nice and easy like always."

Gerardo hustled over to their truck and moved it forward, allowing his partner to back out into the lot. He began to sweat, as he followed the flickering taillights down the drive, around the corner, and into the street, where they drove north at forty miles an hour.

A mile down the road from the Briarwood Garden Apartments, flashing lights appeared in the distance, blue and white. Both men tensed at the wheel, watching the lights grow closer, until a pair of white police cruisers came roaring by in the opposite direction. Both men smiled with relief and watched their rearview mirrors as the lights disappeared into the darkness.

Wednesday, July 26   5:41 a.m.

The swirling light was captured in the iris of a single orange eye. Then, a moment later, the static crack of a radio scratched the air, and the heron began rushing forward through the water, curling its long neck for flight, beating indignant wings against the cold night air. He watched as the great bird forced itself upward into the black sky and then pulled his confession from his jacket pocket and read it once again. He stayed in the shadows as he made his way toward the pulsing blue-and-white lights ahead. At the final corner, he stopped. Everything was as he had imagined it would be—a pair of police cruisers sat in the middle of the lot, doors open, light banks blazing; four policemen stood in a knot in front of the cars, the harsh glare of their headlights turning their legs to gold—everything but the truck and the body.

The yellow truck was gone. He leaned back against the building to steady himself. Then he looked again. Still gone. He blinked his eyes in disbelief and then, afraid he might have fallen asleep, checked his watch. Five forty-two. Eleven minutes since he'd called nine-one-one. No way the pervert had lived and driven off. No way the cops had towed him off so quickly. His pulse throbbed in his temples and his knees were weak. He'd never been more confused in his life. Without willing it so, he began to move. As if in a trance, he pocketed his confession and hurried back the way he'd come.

2

Tuesday, October 17   9:43 a.m.

He could hear the blood. Above the rush of the traffic and the whisper of the breeze, the rhythm of a thousand hearts came to his ears with a sound not unlike the rush of wings. Between the towering buildings, he could see whitecaps rushing across Elliott Bay and the dark shores of Bainbridge Island floating in the distance, but of the impending crowd there was only the sound.

It wasn't until he reached the corner of Seventh and Madison that the assembled multitude came into view. The entire block was surrounded by orange police barricades. Mounted officers cantered back and forth between the crowd and the federal courthouse. The helmeted blue line stood shoulder to shoulder, batons at the ready. A dozen satellite trucks squatted in the street, aiming their wide white eyes at the sky.

Corso stopped for a moment and looked up at the clouds, grateful for a break in the relentless rain. Overhead, a swirling sky held the promise of more, and the air was heavy with water. Fall had arrived as a silver river, slanting down from the sky, day after day, for weeks on end. Even a brief respite from the deluge lessened the gloom.

Taking a deep breath, Corso shuddered inside his overcoat, before crossing Seventh Avenue and starting over the freeway bridge. Ahead, the crowd rippled like a snake. He stopped on the corner. Shouted questions pulled his gaze to the left, where an ocean of photographers suddenly raised their cameras above their heads and began snapping away. Atop the satellite trucks, cameramen scrambled to their feet and began squinting through viewfinders.

Two men and a woman were striding south on Sixth Avenue: the federal prosecution team. Corso's mind began to flip through the pages of their dossiers, as he watched them stroll up the street. The guy in the rumpled trench coat was Raymond Butler. He was the gofer, the research guy. An AGO lifer, Butler went all the way back to Balagula's first trial in San Francisco, before they understood what kind of animal they were dealing with. They found out the hard way when their star witnesses, a pair of construction superintendents named Joshua Harmon and Brian Swanson, disappeared from a Vallejo motel and were subsequently found floating in San Pablo Bay, alongside the pair of Alameda County sheriff's deputies who'd been assigned to guard them. This turn of events left the judge in the first trial no choice but to declare a mistrial. The public outcry for justice prompted the feds to seek a change of venue: north to Seattle where, they hoped, a second trial could be conducted beyond the reach of Balagula's tentacles.

The guy without the overcoat was Warren Klein,

current golden boy of the U.S. Attorney General's Office. A real Horatio Alger story. A poor boy who graduated fourth in his class at Yale, deemed too rough around the edges for major law firms, he signed on with the AG's office and hit it big when a string of successful organized crime prosecutions down in Miami propelled him from relative obscurity to the lead position in what figured to be the most public trial since O. J. Simpson. Off the record, his colleagues found him cold and conniving and, behind his back, whispered that his appointment as lead counsel had surely put him in over his head. Corso's sources thought otherwise. Word on the street was that Klein had something up his sleeve. Rumor had it that he'd turned a witness, somebody who could tie Nicholas Balagula directly to the Fairmont Hospital collapse. If it was true, rough edges or not, Warren Klein was about to enjoy the lifestyle of the rich and famous.

On the inside, closest to the narrow boxwood hedge, was Renee Rogers, lead prosecutor in the last trial. Once the best and brightest, her star had dimmed considerably when, last year in Seattle, Balagula's second trial had ended in a hung jury. That the trial had been held amid the tightest security in state history, and had also been among its most costly, had further fueled the fire of public outrage when an anonymous sequestered jury had failed to agree on what every legal pundit in the country had assumed to be an open-and-shut case. The likelihood of jury tampering and persistent whispers of a drinking problem had carried away any chance for Rogers's further advancement with the AG's office. This time around, she was in the second chair and rumored to be shopping the private sector.

Lost in thought, Corso watched the paparazzi move along the sidewalk like a meal going down a python. A sudden click of heels pulled his attention to his side. The name tag said Sunny Kerrigan. The logo on the camera and the hand-held microphone read KING 5 News. He'd seen her before. She was the second-banana weekend anchor.

"Mr. Corso," she said, "could we have a few minutes of your time?" The cameraman took a step forward. She pushed the mike up at Corso's face. He stepped around her and started across the street. She trotted along at his heels like a terrier.

"Is it true, Mr. Corso, that you're acting as a consultant to the prosecution, and this is why you're the only spectator allowed in the courtroom?"

Corso lengthened his stride and veered off to the left. He was halfway across the street when she hustled around him and tried to block his path. "Could you tell us, Mr. Corso, whether or not—"

He sidestepped her again, slapped the camera out of his face, and kept moving. "Hey," the cameraman whined, as he fought to balance the camera on his shoulder. "No need for that."

"Mr. Corso . . ." she began.

Whatever she had to say was drowned out by a roar from the crowd. At the south end of the block, the police lines parted, allowing a black Lincoln Town Car to roll along the face of the building. The air was suddenly filled with the click of lenses and the whir of automatic winders. The crowd surged along with the car, creeping down the block as the Lincoln moved slowly along. Kerrigan shot him a disgusted look before she and the cameraman hurried off and disappeared into the melee. Corso breathed a sigh of relief.

He picked up his pace, moving the opposite way, toward the area just deserted by the crowd. He walked along the helmeted line of cops until he spotted a sergeant standing behind a barrier. He held up the laminated ID card. The sergeant stepped up, reached between a pair of officers, and plucked the card from Corso's fingers. He looked from Corso to the card and back. "Okay," he said, after a moment.

The barrier was pulled aside and Corso stepped through.

"Quite the spectacle," Corso offered.

"It's crap," the sergeant said. "California ought to clean up its own mess instead of sending it up north to us."

He had a point. This had all started three years ago when, following a minor seismic tremor, the west wall of the newly completed Fairmont Hospital in Hayward, California, had collapsed, killing sixty-three people, forty-one of them children. Subsequent investigation revealed the structure had been built amid a web of extortion, falsified bids, and assorted frauds, including substandard concrete, nonexistent earthquake protection, and fabricated inspection records. They also found that all roads, however tenuous and well disguised, led to one Nicholas Balagula, a former Russian gangster who had, over the past decade, carved out a substantial U.S. criminal empire beneath the noses of the California authorities. As the bulk of the hospital's financing was provided by a federal grant, the case was deemed to be within the federal jurisdiction and assigned to the federal prosecutor's office.

"Oughta just take that Balagula guy out and shoot him," the sergeant said.

"I'm with you there."

Forty yards north, the crowd now filled the entire northbound lane of Sixth Avenue. The Lincoln's tail-lights blinked twice and then went out, as it stopped in front of the rear entrance to the courthouse. Both rear doors popped open.

First out was Bruce Elkins, Balagula's attorney. He carried an aluminum briefcase in one hand and a brown overcoat in the other. He was a short barrel-chested specimen who, these days, favored Armani suits and hundred-dollar custom-made shirts. On two separate occasions, he had attempted to resign from the case. The courts, however, mindful of a defendant's right to the counsel of his choice, had respectfully disagreed.

Next out was Mikhail Ivanov, Nicholas Balagula's longtime right-hand man. He was a nondescript man of sixty-three with a full head of gray hair and an unreadable face as bland and blank as a cabbage. In the last fifty years, Ivanov had helped Balagula cut an unparalleled criminal swath across three continents, picking up scraps as Balagula amassed a personal fortune rumored to be in the hundreds of millions of dollars. Faithful as a dog, on two occasions with the law closing in he'd saved his boss by stepping forward and confessing to the crimes. He'd served seven years on the first occasion and four the next. These days, he billed himself as Balagula's financial planner. Sources said he'd been squirreling money away lately, in foreign banks. Looked like he might be about ready to retire.

Ivanov turned in a full circle to survey the scene and then leaned down and spoke into the car.

Nicholas Balagula emerged from the limo at a lope. His shaven head reflected the dozens of flashbulbs that were firing all over the street. For court, Balagula dressed strictly off the rack, wearing a blue Sears, Roebuck suit that made him look every inch the beleaguered building supply dealer his attorney painted him to be. He acknowledged the snarling crowd with a small wave. The air was filled with shouts of his name and the whirring of cameras as he hurried across the sidewalk and disappeared through the doors, with Mikhail Ivanov bringing up the rear.

Elkins had bellied up to the barricades to work the media. For the past week, during jury selection, he'd been a fixture on the evening news, claiming that the seating of an anonymous jury behind a one-way Plexiglas screen was a clear violation of his client's right to face his accusers and that bringing his client to court a third time was little more than vengeful retribution by a defeated and embarrassed prosecution, whom, as everyone knew, he was going to best for a third and final time.

"Frank!" a woman's voice called.

Corso turned toward the sound. Six feet tall without the big Doc Martens, Meg Dougherty was striding along in front of the cops. One camera dangled from her neck, another was slung over her shoulder. Everything black: clothes, hair, nails, everything—a cross between Morticia Addams and Betty Paige in a full-length black velvet cape.

"What a zoo," she said, with a grimace. She stopped a pace away from the line of cops. "You suppose you boys could step aside for a minute, so a girl could give a guy a hug?"

Corso glanced over at the sergeant, who pursed his lips in thought.

"She stays outside the barrier," he said.

Dougherty nodded okay. The sergeant checked the crowd and said, "Give the lady a little room." The two cops directly in front of her stepped out into the street.

Corso and Dougherty stepped into the breach and shared a hug, a hug long enough and hard enough to embarrass them both and send them reeling away from one each other like opposite poles of a magnet. Corso brushed at his coat, while she tugged her sleeves back down over the tattooed words and leaves and tendrils that spiraled their way around her arms.

"There seems to be a barrier between us," he joked.

"There always was, Frank."

They hugged again, and he remembered the smell of her, something like vanilla and cinnamon. After a moment, they stepped back and stood in silence, taking each other in.

"How're things going?" he asked.

"Same old," she said. "And you?"

"Busy."

"I saw you on television the other night."

He shrugged. "Got a new publicist. She's a real go-getter."

She gestured up the street. "Way too many bodies for me," she said. "I never had much taste for full-contact photography."

"What else are you working on?" Corso asked.

"The usual. Freelancing for anybody with the cash.

Trying to put a new show together." She offered a wan smile. "Always hoping to come up with that one big story that will put me over the top and turn me into the next Frank Corso."

He opened his mouth to protest, but she kept on talking.

"You seen the papers?"

He shook his head. She checked her watch.

"So you haven't heard what they found buried in the bridge footing?"

"What?"

"A truck."

"I've missed you," he said, out of the blue.

She shifted her weight and looked up at the steel-wool sky. Up the street, Bruce Elkins had abandoned the crowd and smiled his way inside.

"Me too," Dougherty said finally.

"I think of you a lot. Maybe we could—"

"Don't," she said. "We agreed . . . remember?"

"Way I recall it was more like *you* agreed."

"Whatever," she snapped.

Corso's lips tightened. He turned away.

She winced and put a hand on his arm. "I didn't mean it like that . . . like it sounded." When he didn't respond, she stepped in closer and lowered her voice. "It was too much for me, Corso. It felt like beating my head against a brick wall."

He looked at her over his shoulder. "At least it wasn't boring."

"What it *was* was exhausting. I always felt I was on the outside looking in." She waved a hand in the air. "You're like a stone. I shared myself with you, Frank." She slashed the air again. "Willingly . . . blissfully . . .

and seven months later I didn't know any more about you than I did when I started."

She stepped around in front of him and took his face in her hands.

"Besides . . ."

The cop on Corso's right turned his face away, as if embarrassed to be listening.

Corso cleared his throat. "Maybe we should do a nice platonic dinner or something. Catch up on old times and all that."

"Besides," she said again, louder this time, "I've got a boyfriend. It's been over a year, Frank."

Corso's pale eyes flickered.

"People pair up. That's what happens here on earth. It's how we keep the planet populated."

"I didn't say anything," Corso protested. "Did I say anything?"

"You didn't have to. Besides . . . he'd go crazy if I went without him. I've told him all about you."

Corso made a rude noise with his lips. "I know you. You've been rubbing his nose in my famous-author status, haven't you?"

She laughed. "Only when he really deserves it. He's read all your books. He says you're a passable stylist."

Corso's face arranged itself into something between a sneer and a smile.

"He's super jealous of you, but at the same time, another part of him really wants to meet the famous author I used to hang with." She bopped Corso lightly in the arm. "You know how childish guys are."

"Sure . . . bring him along. We'll all be chums."

"You'll like him."

"No I won't, but bring him along anyway," Corso said.

Again she laughed that deep laugh of hers and poked him in the chest with a long black fingernail. "This gonna be one of those bullshit I'll-have-my-people-call-your-people things, or are we really gonna get together?"

To help Corso make up his mind, she reached inside the cape and came out with a small black leather notebook. She stood pencil poised, a determined expression on her face.

Corso heaved a sigh. "How about Saturday night at the Coastal Kitchen?" he said. "Like around seven or so."

She wrote it down with a flourish and looked up. "You'll be pleasant."

"Don't worry. I'll make nice to the boyfriend."

"You could bring somebody. Maybe that would—"

He was already shaking his head. She sighed.

"You've gone back to being a hermit, haven't you?"

Corso shrugged. "You know me. I'm relationship-challenged."

"It would really help if you didn't hate everybody."

"I don't—" he began.

"Uh-oh," Dougherty said, "I think your cover's blown."

Sunny Kerrigan and her cameraman were leading a knot of media types down the street in their direction. "Shit," Corso muttered.

Dougherty stepped back from the barrier. The cops closed ranks. She got up on tiptoe and yelled over their heads, "Saturday! Seven!"

Corso nodded and turned away. He could hear the Kerrigan woman talking into her microphone. "This is Sunny Kerrigan, KING Five News, reporting live from the first day of the Nicholas Balagula trial, where reclusive author Frank Corso . . ."

He pulled his collar up around his ears and hunched his shoulders as he started up the street. That night, news footage would show a headless apparition in a black overcoat pulling open the courthouse door and disappearing inside.

3

Renee Rogers flicked her eyes toward the stairs just in time to see Corso mount the last three steps to the mezzanine. He was even better looking in person than he was on TV, she decided: six-three or -four, somewhere in the vicinity of forty, wearing a black silk shirt and jeans under what must have been a three-thousand-dollar cashmere overcoat. A man of extremes, she thought, as he strode across the marble floor in her direction. Probably what got him in so much trouble, way back when.

While he didn't exactly swagger, his walk was ripe with attitude. Something in his movements suggested he didn't much care what other people thought. She wondered what he was covering up with all the physical bravado.

He walked across the marble floor and stopped by her side. He held out his hand and said, "Frank Corso."

She took his hand in hers and was surprised at how rough it was and how small her own hand seemed in comparison. "Renee Rogers," she said.

Over his shoulder, she watched Klein and Butler come out of the men's room together. Klein's narrow eyes widened for a moment when he caught sight of Corso. He straightened his vest and came quickly across the floor in their direction.

Renee Rogers had a good idea what was coming. When Klein had received the memo stating that an exception to the no-spectators rule was being made for a writer named Frank Corso, he'd gone ballistic. While a quick reprimand from the AG herself had closed his mouth, it hadn't had any effect on his anger.

He pulled up by Corso's right elbow. Corso again offered his hand. Klein didn't so much as look at it. Instead, he stepped between Corso and Rogers, as close to nose-to-nose with Corso as a guy eight inches shorter could get.

"I don't know what kind of strings your publisher pulled to get you in here, but whatever it was doesn't carry any weight with me."

"He went to college with the Attorney General," Corso offered.

"And those Ivy League types do stick together, don't they?"

"You should know," Corso said.

Klein's neck was beginning to redden. "I went to Yale on a scholarship. I didn't have a rich set of parents picking up the tab. I bussed dishes and swept floors."

"Well, then, you'll have skills you can fall back on if you lose this case, won't you, Mr. Klein."

Klein did a bad job of suppressing a smirk. "Not gonna happen, smart guy. I've got that SOB dead to rights, and I'm not gonna let you or anybody else get between me and putting Nicholas Balagula behind bars. He may have subverted the justice system on other people's watches, but he's not going to do it on mine."

Over Klein's shoulder, Corso saw Renee Rogers's face blanch at the words. Raymond Butler looked down at the floor and adjusted his tie.

"The only thing that would make me happier than seeing Balagula in prison would be seeing him in the electric chair, which as far as I'm concerned is where he belongs," Corso said.

Klein threw him a barracuda smile. "Then you've got a front-row seat for the game." He reached out and tapped Corso on the chest with his index finger, three times. "But a seat in the front row is all you've got. "

Corso eased his hands from his pockets.

"It's all I want," he said.

Renee Rogers felt the crackle in the air. Klein reached toward Corso again.

"Don't," Corso said quietly.

Klein's extended finger stopped in midair, about an inch from Corso's chest. The lawyer narrowed his eyes as he looked up. "Are you threatening me?"

"Perish the thought," said Corso. "I'm merely expressing my heartfelt desire not to be touched again." Smiling now. "I mean—after all—who knows where that finger has been?"

Raymond Butler hid his mouth with his hand and turned away. Renee Rogers was openly amused. Warren Klein looked from one to the other, nodded, as if the moment had confirmed something he already knew, and strode off. Butler threw Rogers a grin and followed along in Klein's wake.

"Don't mind Warren," Renee Rogers said. "He's a

bit overwrought. His shining moment has come at last, and he doesn't quite know what to do with it."

"I hope he's right about his case," Corso said.

"He's got Balagula by the balls for the Fairmont Hospital collapse. One of his investigators turned a witness who can link Mr. B to both the faulty concrete and the falsified core samples."

Corso gave a low whistle. "Pity *you* didn't have the guy last time."

She rolled her eyes. "The guy was a suspect. Ray talked to him half a dozen times. Claimed Harmon and Swanson were lying about him being part of the conspiracy." She waved an angry hand. "And, of course, they were no longer around for rebuttal."

"Then out of the blue . . ."

"Klein sends somebody around in my tracks, and all of a sudden this same yokel says he can put Balagula in the room when the core sample scam was discussed."

"Why the change of heart?"

"He says the thought of all those dead children started wearing on him. That he was never going to be right again unless he told the truth." She caught the bitterness flowing into her voice and clamped her mouth shut.

Corso watched her jaw muscles flex and flutter. "Maybe it *is* better to be lucky than good," he offered.

She made a face. "Wouldn't have mattered. Balagula'd already compromised the jury." She arched an eyebrow at Corso. "As you so well know."

"*I* got lucky," Corso said.

She held his gaze. "What you've got, Mr. Corso, are very good sources."

"Gosh and golly," Corso said, with a smile.

"It's not funny," she insisted. "It's not right that some guy who writes true-crime books should be able to come up with better and more accurate information than the Attorney General's Office."

"Narrative nonfiction," he corrected.

"I'll never forget when my secretary handed me that *TIME* magazine article you wrote. If I'd had a gun and known where to find you, I'd be in prison today."

Enraged by the hung jury, Corso had made it his business to find out how fourteen nameless, faceless citizens had been identified and then compromised. Fourteen souls culled from a pool of over five thousand King County voters. Jurors were interviewed from behind screens. No questions that might reveal identity were permitted. In the end, neither the feds nor the defense had known the names of those who were chosen. Twelve jurors and two alternates were selected and immediately sequestered for the duration of the trial in a downtown hotel under the tightest security imaginable, and still Balagula had managed to get to somebody. Only question was how.

Weeks later, while reviewing the trial transcript, Corso came upon the precise moment when he believed the Balagula camp got its hands on the master jury list. Right at the end of the first week, everything changed. Overnight, Elkins switched his defensive strategy from an aggressive attempt to discredit and deny to a strategy of stalling for time. He flooded the judge with motions. Claimed to be ill. Claimed Balagula was ill. All in all, he managed to add what Corso figured was three weeks to the trial, a delay that turned out to be more than enough time for the defense to work its magic.

The Balagula camp first took the list of five thousand names to Berkley Marketing, a boiler-room telemarketing firm operating out of a leaky warehouse in South Seattle. Paid them to make voice contact with every person on the list. In only three days Berkley had reduced the list to thirty-three persons whose whereabouts could not, in one manner or another, be verified.

They then sent the names of the thirty-three possibles to Allied Investigations, an enormous nationwide security agency, who pounded the pavement for a week and reduced the number of missing persons to sixteen.

Next up was Henderson, Bates & May, a law firm specializing in "jury profiling." In addition to consulting with well-known mental health professionals looking for weak personalities, they also pried into everyone's financial history through a mortgage bank they owned named Fresno Guarantee Trust, in hopes of finding a weak link, which quite obviously they had managed to do.

The trail wasn't hard to follow, because none of the parties had broken the law and were, at least at the outset, cooperative. When the feds turned up the heat, and it became apparent that they were into something sticky, Berkley Marketing and Allied Investigations revealed the jobs had arrived by fax and the money by mail, leaving only Henderson, Bates & May as a possible source of information. Unfortunately, attempts by the AGO to lay hands on the "juror profiles" created by Henderson, Bates & May were rebuffed by HB&M on the grounds of attorney-client privilege, an assertion that was upheld in several higher courts.

"You ever find out where he got the jury list?" Corso asked.

She grimaced. "Ray's pretty sure it was a secretary in the county clerk's office, but we can't prove it."

"What's to stop them from doing it again?"

"Absolutely nothing. All we can do is make the jury pool as large as possible, keep them anonymous, and sequester them out of his reach. There's nothing we can do about leaks at the state and county level."

"Be a good idea if this was over in a hurry," Corso said.

"That's Warren's plan." She made a dismissive gesture with her hand. "That's why it's a single indictment. Only the Fairmont. Sixty-three counts of murder two."

"Chancy."

"And unpopular," Rogers added. "The good people of Alameda County want somebody to pay for their deputies."

"What if he wiggles out again?"

"Then he walks. There's no way we can possibly try him again for anything. We don't get him this time, we don't get him at all."

"And if you get him?"

"Then he gets life plus twenty-five and everybody's happy".

"Rogers," Klein called from the far end of the mezzanine. He tapped his watch with his forefinger.

"He sure likes to tap things, doesn't he?" Corso said.

She smiled. "Gotta go. Nice meeting you, Mr. Corso."

Corso assured her that the pleasure was his. She could feel his eyes on her as she walked away and disappeared down the stairs.

Tuesday, October 17   3:41 p.m.

"**Y**our Honor, I must again protest."

"That's what you get paid for, Mr. Elkins. Protest away."

Bruce Elkins spread his arms and then dropped them, allowing his hands to slap against his sides in a show of disgusted resignation. "I don't see how we can possibly go on with this proceeding, when Mr. Balagula is being denied his most basic . . . his most fundamental . . . constitutional rights."

"What rights would those be?"

"His right to face his accusers. His right to make eye contact with the very people who will decide his fate."

Judge Fulton Howell waved his gavel in the air. "As you well know, Mr. Elkins, The Fourth Circuit Court of Appeals has recently disagreed with you. They have ruled that the extenuating circumstances surrounding this trial warrant extraordinary measures to ensure the integrity of the judicial process. The matter is not open to discussion. Please proceed with your case."

"With all due respect, Your Honor—"

The judge waved him off. "As we discussed at length this morning, Mr. Elkins, the court will not be party to any unnecessary delays. Either proceed with your case or I will appoint another attorney to represent your client."

Elkins had been at it for over three hours, claiming that every piece of the prosecution's case was, in some manner or another, a breach of his client's rights and, as such, should not be introduced as evidence. He was prospecting for reversible error, forcing the judge to rule on so many motions that some higher court somewhere would be bound to disagree with at least one of the rulings and thus create grounds for appeal.

Elkins was good. Animated and theatrical, he accepted the stream of negative rulings from the bench with a show of profound disappointment, like a kid on Christmas morning who finds there's nothing under the tree with his name on it and tries to be brave. What Elkins knew for sure was that, one-way glass or no, after a while the jury was going to start feeling sorry for him.

Nicholas Balagula watched it all with an expression of bemused detachment. A man of the people in a cheap suit and a Timex watch, he sat sipping from a glass of ice water, which he periodically refilled from the government-issue plastic pitcher on the defense table.

"Proceed, Mr. Elkins," the judge said again.

Elkins returned to the defense table, where he extracted a document from one of the brown file folders that littered the top of the table. He held the piece of paper at arm's length and by a single corner, as if it were septic.

"Surely, Your Honor will agree that last-minute additions to the witness list must be considered prejudicial to the defense." Judge Fulton Howell's face said he didn't agree to any such thing. Undaunted, Elkins waved the document and began to play to the jury box. "After twice having failed to prove my client guilty of so much as a misdemeanor, after nearly three years of litigation and the squandering of untold millions in public funds"—he spun quickly, waving the document in the direction of the prosecutors—"these people would have us believe they can suddenly produce a witness whose testimony is sufficiently compelling as to permit his last-minute inclusion on their witness list. Sufficiently earth-shattering as to justify the blatant disregard for the most basic rules of evidence and discovery."

Klein was on his feet now. "Your Honor—"

Elkins raised his voice and kept talking. "As if the malicious and mean-spirited persecution of Mr. Balagula were not travesty enough—"

"That's enough, Mr. Elkins," the judge said.

"As if the emotional damage and financial ruin visited upon Mr. Balagula and his family were not blot on our system of justice—"

"Your Honor!" Klein again.

The judge's jowls shook as he banged the gavel three times.

"That's quite enough, Mr. Elkins," he said.

Now Elkins looked contrite. Caught with his hand in the cookie jar. He used his manicured fingernails to flick the document in his hand. "Victor Lebow is a disgruntled employee. Your Honor. A man with a grudge. A man with a score to settle." He raised a finger and played to the crowd. "A man, I might add, who was facing the very real possibility of spending the foreseeable future in a federal penitentiary, until . . ." He paused for effect, his face a mask of righteous indignation.

"Your Honor," Klein pleaded.

". . . until these people agreed to give Mr. Lebow total and complete immunity from prosecution, in return for his testimony against Mr. Balagula."

Klein's face was red. "If I may," he began.

"A man who"—Elkins walked to the rail and confronted the invisible jury, invisible behind the one-way screen—". . . a man who is being paid for his testimony."

Judge Fulton Howell leaned forward in the seat, resting his forearms on the bench. He heaved a sigh and waved his gavel at the jury box. "The jury will disregard Mr. Elkins's outburst." He got to his feet and checked his watch with an air of sadness and then pointed the little hammer at Elkins and Klein. "Mr. Elkins, Mr. Klein: in my chambers." He checked his watch and sighed again. "Court is adjourned until ten o'clock tomorrow morning." *Bang!*

Corso watched as Klein and Elkins followed the judge through the door behind the bench. To the right, Raymond Butler pulled a cell phone from his coat pocket and wandered over to the wall. Renee Rogers began sorting papers and putting them back in their proper folders. When he swiveled his head the other way, Corso saw Nicholas Balagula and Mikhail Ivanov whispering together and staring intently in his direction.

* * *

"It's no wonder they believe in God," Nicholas Balagula said. He looked around the courtroom with thinly disguised contempt. "What else but divine intervention can explain how such fools as these could have prospered?"

Mikhail Ivanov leaned closer, hoping his proximity would encourage Balagula to keep his voice down, but it was not to be.

"How else can they justify this silly legal system?" Balagula waved a hand in anger. "It is for children and fools. It punishes only those foolish enough to put themselves at its mercy."

"They have more people in prison than the rest of the world combined," Ivanov reminded him. He could feel the eyes of the jury on them.

"They have the coloreds and the poor in prison." Balagula shook his big head, as if in disbelief. "In Russia, we lock people up for their politics. Here, they lock you up for your class. For your culture." He looked Ivanov in the eye. "Marx was right."

Desperate for a change of subject, Ivanov nodded toward the far side of the room. "Our Mr. Corso is in attendance again." Few subjects got so predictable a rise out of Nico as did the subject of Frank Corso. Despite years of glaring media coverage, Nico rarely took offense at anything generated by the media storm. *The dogs of capitalism,* he called them, and neither read the papers nor watched the news. Mr. Corso, however, was another matter. Anything written about him by Mr. Corso he wanted to see immediately.

"He looks like some . . . some hippie."

"Don't be fooled, Nico," Mikhail Ivanov whispered. "He's a most dangerous man."

Nicholas Balagula curled his thick rubbery lips. "And we are not?"

Ivanov sighed. All too often lately, Nico seemed to feel as if he were invincible. As if the pair of hard-won mistrials had somehow guaranteed his future infallibility.

"That's not the point, and you know it, " he said. "What's the point of baiting the bear unnecessarily?"

"He's been nipping at our heels for years. Harrying us. All those stories and articles. I want to take his measure for a moment." He hunched his shoulders and spread his big hands. "A little talk. That's all."

"A little talk is often a dangerous thing."

Nicholas Balagula emitted a short dry laugh. "If danger was what I had in mind, Mikhail, I'd send Gerardo and Ramón, and then our nosy Mr. Frank Corso would know what danger is all about."

Ivanov opened his mouth to object, but it was too late. Nico was already on his feet, already stepping out from behind the defense table and walking across the silent courtroom. His hands swung at his sides as he strolled toward the lone spectator at the other end of the room.

Behind his stone face, Ivanov inwardly grimaced and then began moving in the same direction, vowing, as he walked, that when this was over and they were both finally free and clear, he would retire to his villa in Nice. Maybe take a mistress. Perhaps a woman with children, upon whom he could dote in his old age.

At the far end of the room, Raymond Butler stopped talking and pressed the phone hard against his chest. Renee Rogers stood statue-still as Nicholas Balagula walked past the prosecution table and then began to veer toward the rail . . . toward Corso.

Balagula stopped at the rail, six feet from the chair in which Corso sat.

"You would be Mr. Frank Corso," he said.

Corso got slowly to his feet. He was four inches taller than Balagula but gave away at least fifty pounds to the older man. "Yes," he said. "I would be."

"You've been making quite a hobby out of me," Balagula said.

"In your case, I like to think of it as a job," Corso replied.

The pair of bailiffs who flanked the judge's bench began to move toward the men.

"I am but a poor émigré to your country. I have—"

Corso cut him off. "In your country you were a murdering piece of shit, and now you're a murdering piece of shit here."

Balagula pressed his thighs against the rail and leaned toward Corso. "I have used better men than you as if they were women," he said.

Corso smiled, took a step forward, and leaned down into Balagula's face. "And afterward, they sent flowers. Right?"

"You should learn to mind your own business."

"Like those babies in Fairmont Hospital?"

Mikhail Ivanov stepped between the men. He used his arms to push Balagula back a step. "The car is ready," he said. "We must go."

Balagula kept his gaze locked on Corso as the bailiffs stepped into the gap between the two men. "We'll meet again, Mr. Corso. I'm sure of it."

"In hell," Corso said, as Ivanov steered his boss through the hinged gate and toward the doors. No one moved until the door closed behind the pair.

A massive sigh from Renee Rogers pulled Corso's attention from the door. "You do have a way with people," she said, as she snapped her briefcase shut. Against the far wall, Ray Butler leaned, chatting into the phone, oblivious to the confrontation. "After twenty-odd years of marriage and three kids, Ray and his wife Junie just bought their first house. In Bethesda. They're like teenagers all over again."

"Must be nice," Corso said without meaning it.

She inclined her head toward the pair of bailiffs. "These gentlemen have kindly agreed to escort me out through the parking garage. I'm told we can avoid the media that way. Would you care to join me?"

Corso stared up the aisle toward the door. "Sure," he said, without looking her way.

Stopping at the top of the aisle, Nicholas Balagula looked back at Corso and the prosecution team. His color was deeper than usual. Ivanov could tell that his friend's encounter with Corso had left him feeling peevish and unfulfilled, and thus Ivanov had an inkling of what was to come next.

"Tonight," was all Balagula said.

"I've had to make alternative arrangements," Ivanov said.

"Oh?"

"Our customary provider has refused to continue."

"There are others, I'm sure."

"He objects to the condition in which the goods were returned."

"Surely there can be no shortage."

Ivanov shrugged. "Your tastes are difficult."

"Tonight," Nicholas Balagula said again.

5

Tuesday, October 17   4:09 p.m.

She pulled the olive from the red plastic sword, popped it into her mouth, and chewed slowly. "So, what is it about the Nicholas Balagula saga that so captures your attention, Mr. Corso?" she asked, when she'd finished.

"What do you mean?"

They sat on opposite sides of a scarred oak table, four blocks west of the courthouse. Twenty years ago, Vito's had been the favored watering hole of Seattle's movers and shakers. These days it was just another remnant waiting for the wrecking ball. Seattle at the millennium. If it wasn't glitzy, it was gone.

Renee Rogers downed the final swallows of her second Bombay Sapphire martini and wiped her full lips with her cocktail napkin. "You've been following this case from the beginning." She ate the other olive and gestured to the bartender for another drink. "I remember you sitting in the first row of the balcony during the San Francisco trial. I'd see you up there every day and wonder who you were."

"Balagula offends my sense of the natural order of things."

"How so?"

Corso thought it over. "I guess there's a part of me that believes something corny like *What goes around comes around.* That things are intended to be a certain way, and if you deviate too far you suffer the consequences."

"A moral order."

"Something more organic. More like a river, maybe," Corso said. "One of those rustbelt rivers where they poured so many toxins into the water it finally caught fire. And then—you know—all they had to do was to stop the dumping, and a couple of years later it went right back to being a river again. Nothing Balagula touches is ever the same again. It's like he spreads pestilence or something." He made a face. "Sounds stupid when I say it out loud."

"I understand," she said. "I know the type. I've spent the last seventeen years putting them behind bars."

"Not guys like him. Most people kill because they don't see any way out, or in the heat of passion, or because they've got a blood lust. Balagula's used murder as a business strategy from the beginning, even when the stakes were small."

"Since the day he arrived."

"All the way back to when he first surfaced in Brighton Beach fifteen years ago, claiming to be a wholesale jeweler. Next thing you know, the four biggest wholesale jewelers in Brooklyn go missing within the same six-month period and Balagula ends up with all their business."

When she smiled, he could see the lines in the corners of her gray eyes. He wondered if the color was natural or contact lenses.

"Do I detect a streak of self-righteousness in the famous writer?" she asked.

"My mama used to say I had enough moral indignation for a dozen preachers." Corso took a sip of beer and checked his watch.

"I understand you're a year late with the book."

Corso raised an eyebrow. "A book needs an ending."

She leaned back in the chair, rested the base of the martini glass against her sternum, and shook her head sadly. "The end to this one's been a long time coming." She sighed.

"I'm pretty sure my publisher would agree."

"You've got enough clout to make them wait."

"It's not about clout," Corso said. "It's not about the quality of your work or the love of words. It's about money, pure and simple. If you're making them money, they'll put up with you. If you're not, you go back to your day job."

She winced. "I always looked at publishing as something romantic." She waved the martini glass in the air. "Something almost mystical," she said.

"And I used to think truth and justice would just naturally prevail," Corso said, with a shrug. A silence settled around them as he poured the remains of the Tsingtao into his beer glass. "Who knew?" he added.

The bartender appeared at her elbow with another martini. She waited for him to leave and then picked up the glass. "Here's to shattered illusions."

Corso raised his glass. She took a sip, reached over and clicked his glass with hers, and took another sip. "This is my last case for the AGO," she said.

"So I hear."

"I've got seventeen years in."

"Life goes on. You're a survivor."

She offered a wry smile. "Coming from you, I'll take that as a compliment."

Corso laughed. "I've certainly had my ups and downs."

"About ten million of them, as I recall."

"The paper settled for six million and change."

"How'd you do it?"

"Do what?"

"Go on."

"I'm like one of those Thomas Hardy characters. I just keep on keeping on."

"Seriously," she said. "I haven't worked in the private sector since I had a job at a root-beer stand. I'm damaged goods."

Corso chuckled. "And now you find yourself sitting across the table from one of the most notorious pieces of damaged goods on the planet, and you figure you might as well get a little advice on plague dispersal."

She wrinkled her nose and laughed into her glass. "Something like that."

"You got any offers?"

"A few."

"I had exactly *one*. One publisher with a failing family newspaper who decided she was so desperate to save the paper that she'd hire the Typhoid Mary of the newspaper business just for the publicity."

"And?"

"And one thing led to another. We hit a couple of big stories. The paper righted itself. I wrote a book. Turned out to be a big seller. So I wrote another one." He shrugged. "Life went on."

"Did you feel exonerated?"

"You mean like, 'You had me down and look at me now'?"

"Yes."

He shook his head. "It's too arbitrary for that."

"Arbitrary how?"

Corso thought it over. "My whole life was aimed at being a reporter. Not just a reporter but the best reporter. I was going to win a Pulitzer. I was going to win the Nobel Prize. As far as I was concerned , it was my destiny." He looked down at the table and then up at Renee Rogers. "You understand what I'm saying? That was my path. The rest of this"—he waved a hand—"everything that's happened since is just me stumbling around the woods. It's not like I planned any of it. It just happened. It's arbitrary."

"You see the *Post Intelligencer* yesterday?"

"No. Why?"

"They did a big story on you: RECLUSIVE LOCAL WRITER SURFACES. About how you were going to be the only spectator allowed in the courtroom. About you getting fired by the *New York Times* for fabricating a story, about the lawsuit and the settlement, how you've since become a bestselling author and all that." She ate another olive and took a sip of the martini. "They said you'd never told your version of the *New York Times* story. They said you have a standing offer from Barbara Walters. Is that true?"

"Yeah."

"Why's that? Most everybody wants to tell their side of the story."

"Because nobody in their right mind would believe me if I did."

"Try me."

"No, thanks."

"No fair," she teased. "You know my story. How I let a guy with a history of jury tampering compromise a jury of mine."

"You show me yours, I'll show you mine?"

Her eyes held a wicked gleam. "Something like that," she said.

Corso heaved a sigh. "I got hustled," he said. "I got overconfident and started reading my own press clippings about how I was destined for a Pulitzer. Next thing I knew, I was hot on the trail of a guy a lot like Balagula, and everything was going my way. Witnesses were coming out of the woodwork to sign depositions. Everything was falling into place for what was going to be the exposé of the century. The biggest story since Watergate."

"And that didn't ring any bells with you?"

"I was so full of myself, it seemed like it was my destiny."

She nodded. "I remember the feeling," she said sadly. "I was absolutely certain that nobody could get to my jury." She sat and watched as he rolled his glass between the palms of his hands. Finally she asked, "Why is it newspapers have trouble printing your name without the word *reclusive* as part of the package?"

"I've had my fifteen minutes. It's somebody else's turn."

Corso downed the rest of his beer. The cold liquid did nothing to stem the dryness of his throat.

"I gotta go," he said. "Time and deadlines wait for no man." He reached into his pocket, but she waved him off. "I've got it covered," she said, with a smile. "Look at it as your tax dollars at work."

"Thanks," Corso offered. "I'll see you tomorrow."

He got to his feet and retrieved his coat from the rack by the door. He could feel her eyes moving over him like ants as he shrugged his way into the coat and stepped out through the stained-glass doors.

Outside, the promise of rain had been kept. Huge silver raindrops exploded on impact with the asphalt. Cars sloshed down Fifth Avenue, swept along inside silver canopies of mist. Corso pulled the coat tight around his neck and began walking uphill.

6

Tuesday, October 17   4:13 p.m.

Half his index finger was missing. Water dripped from the squared-off tip as he pointed toward the far end of the lot at a pair of buildings, barely visible through the rain.

Fifty-something with a narrow face that hadn't seen a razor in a week, he wore rubber boots and a sewer suit, the ensemble topped off by a drooping army camouflage hat.

"Building on the right!" he shouted above the din. "Name's Ball, Joe Ball. He's the foreman. If anybody can help you, he's the guy."

"Thanks!" Meg Dougherty yelled out the car window.

When he nodded you're-welcome a river ran from the brim of his floppy hat, splashing down onto the ground at his feet. He shook his head.

"Been around here twenty years!" he shouted. "Don't ever remember it raining any more than lately."

"Me neither." Shattered raindrops wet Dougherty's left cheek. She had her finger on the window handle but hesitated.

"Not this hard, this long!"

"It's almost biblical," she agreed.

He smiled, revealing a set of tombstone teeth, tilted and oddly spaced along his gums.

"That's what my old woman says," he said. "Says the Day of Judgment is at hand. Says we're all gonna pay for our sins this time around."

"I sure hope not," was all she could come up with.

He showed his teeth again. "You and me both, lady," he said. He turned and walked to a battered Chevy pickup, where he offered a final wave and climbed in.

Dougherty rolled up the window, pulled the shift into drive, and started bouncing down the gravel track toward the buildings in the distance.

The raindrops were huge, pounding the little car's sheet metal as she drove the quarter mile. The flailing wipers barely broke even. From fifty yards, she could finally make out the buildings. A pair of old fashioned Quonset huts, EVERGREEN EQUIPMENT painted on the front of each. A black sign on the door of the right-hand building read OFFICE. NO ADMITTANCE.

Dougherty parked the Toyota parallel to the front of the building, as close to the office door as possible. She shut off the engine, pulled the hood of her cape over her head, and then sat for a moment, working up the courage to step out into the torrent. With a sigh, she elbowed the door open, stepped out, and made a dash for the office.

The office was old and hot and empty. In the right front corner of the space, a gas-fired stove poured too much heat into the room. Behind the scarred counter, an orange NO SMOKING sign loomed over a pair of gray metal desks, whose tops were awash in a rainbow of paperwork. The walls were covered with yellowed posters. Several had come partially loose and curled at the edges: CATERPILLAR, PETERBILT, BRUNSWICK BEARINGS. An Arcadia Machine Shop calendar featuring a spectacularly endowed blonde wearing little more than a surprised expression and a red polka-dot thong. At the back of the room, another door stood ajar.

"Hello!" she called. She waited and then called again, louder this time. Nothing. The spring-loaded gate squealed as Dougherty pushed through. "Hello," she called a third time. Still nothing. And then, from somewhere in the bowels of the building, she heard a noise. Not words, more like a squeal. A dog, maybe.

She walked behind the desks and pulled the rear door open. Big as an airplane hanger, the building smelled of old grease and cheap cigars. The walls were lined with workbenches and tool cribs. The floor was littered with machinery in various stages of repair. Along the far wall sat a road grader, its blade removed and lying next to the huge tires. A pair of dump trucks were parked bumper to bumper in the center of the space. Across the way, a rusted bulldozer lay in pieces, its parts scattered about the floor like the skeleton of some ancient beast.

The noise reached her ears again, high-pitched and unintelligible. She waited a moment for her eyes to adjust to the gloom and then began to pick her way forward, moving toward the sound, stepping carefully around the debris on the floor. Skirting the dump trucks, she opened her mouth to call, then heard the word and swallowed it.

"Please," someone blubbered. "Please."

She stood still. The fear and desperation were palpable. She could feel the tension on her skin, as she steadied herself on a filthy fender and took another step forward. She was close now. She heard a hiccup and then a sniffle.

She peeked around a pile of oil drums. He was in his mid-forties. Bald. Kneeling in the middle of the floor, twenty yards away, his hands clasped in silent prayer. His lips quivered as he mouthed some silent litany. And the tears. His cheeks were wet with tears. "For God's sake, man, I got three kids," he whined.

"Shoulda thoughta that before," another voice said.

"Before you fucked up your end," yet another voice added.

The kneeling man waved his folded hands in front of his body like he was ringing a bell. "How was I supposed—"

"You take money to bury a truck, the truck better stay buried."

"You fuck up, you become a loose end," the second voice said.

"We leave loose ends, we become loose ends," said the third.

"Please," the guy chanted. "Please."

"Shut up."

"No way I coulda—"

Dougherty heard a single flat report. Saw the kneeling man rock backward. Watched as his clasped hands came undone and his arms spread like wings. She gasped as the small red flower bloomed in his right eye and a single rivulet of blood ran down across his face. She stood transfixed as he fell over onto his side, his lips silent now, his single lifeless eye staring down at the floor.

She clamped a hand over her mouth and began to backpedal.

"Strike him out," the second voice said.

She heard a grunt and two more silenced shots. As she spun on her toes and began to run, her arm hit something and sent it spinning off into space. She didn't wait for it to land.

7

Ramón Javier stepped forward, placed the silencer against the back of the victim's head, and pulled the trigger twice. The head rocked back and forth as if saying *no* to the floor. Satisfied, Ramón pulled a handkerchief from his pocket and began to wipe the weapon clean when he heard the sounds. The sound of metal hitting the floor and then the unmistakable scrape of a shoe.

They moved in unison. Ramón held the automatic up by his right ear and started moving toward the noise. Gerardo required no prompting. He ran for the car.

Ramón eased along the oil drums, keeping himself covered in case the intruder was armed. He squatted and peeked around the corner. Got just enough of a look to see it was a woman, before the shadow disappeared behind the truck.

He abandoned his caution now and broke into a full sprint; his long legs propelling him forward into the gloom. By the time he reached the center of the room, he realized he'd been too careful; she was halfway to the office door.

Have to take her on the fly, he thought. No problem.

He began sidestepping to his left, looking for a better angle of fire. Detached and calm, he waited for her shadow to appear in the halo of the office door. He could hear the slap of her boots on the floor. He smiled as he raised the gun. And suddenly there she was, awash in the office lights, wearing some sort of black cape. He saw her face, the wide eyes as she glanced over her shoulder into the darkness, the deep-red lipstick. He sighted down the barrel. Exhaled.

And then his left foot came down on something metal and irregular, and with a pop his ankle rolled beneath him, sending bolts of agony shooting up and down his lower leg. The pain sent him lurching forward, hopping on his good foot. Ahead in the gloom, the office door slammed the wall and then ricocheted itself closed again. He cursed himself and hobbled after the retreating shadow.

Reduced to quarter speed, he gimped the distance and threw open the office door. His ankle was on fire as he hobbled around the counter. The exterior door flapped in the wind, its metal blind clanking to and fro. Above the roar of the wind and rain, he heard an engine start. He cursed again and limped out the door, silenced automatic held with both hands.

Five yards to his left, a peeling blue Toyota fishtailed in the muddy gravel, its rear end swinging out of control as the tires fought for traction. Ramón could barely make out the shape of the driver through the fogged rear window. He aimed and squeezed off a shot. The rear window shattered and disappeared. He could see the back of her head clearly now, the black hair bouncing as she fought the wheel, trying to keep the careening little car on a straight line.

Bitch don't get lucky twice, he thought to himself.

He aimed carefully. The little car was going nowhere, its tires spinning in the mud. Fifteen feet to the back of her head. He smiled, exhaled, and began the slow pull of the trigger, just as the rear end of the car swung back to the left. Suddenly finding firmer ground, the spinning tires spewed a hail of mud and gravel back into his face, choking him, blinding him, sending his silenced shot sailing off into space.

Ramón wiped his face with his sleeve and then choked as he spit out a small rock. Again, he pawed at the debris on his face but managed only to spread the glop around. His right eye was filled with mud, his left a mere slit. Mouth awash in grit, he was still trying to clear his vision when Gerardo slid the Mercedes to a stop.

"Come on, man!" Gerardo screamed. "Come on!"

Ramón limped around the front of the car and threw himself into the passenger seat. Gerardo tromped on the accelerator, rocketing the car forward, slamming the passenger door, forcing Ramón to brace himself with his bad foot. He groaned in pain.

Gerardo held the accelerator to the floor. The Toyota was fifty yards ahead, speeding toward the gate, throwing up a rooster tail of mud in its wake.

"We gotta get her," Ramón said through clenched teeth. "No matter what."

The Toyota became airborne as it bounced out the gate. The Mercedes had already made up half the distance. Ahead, a half mile of access easement connected

the construction yard with the collection of warehouses
and loading docks that ran along the east side of Western Avenue. Nothing needed to be said. They had to get
her before she made it out to the traffic on Western.

The Mercedes only needed the first two hundred
yards to close the remaining gap. Gerardo's mouth
hung open as they roared up to the Toyota's rear end.
Ramón braced himself on the dashboard as Gerardo
drove the front bumper into the rear of the speeding
Toyota, sending the little car careening left and right.
For a moment it looked as if she would lose control
and either roll the car or slide down into the marsh,
where they could easily finish her off. Instead, the Toyota swung wide and then suddenly righted itself for a
final dash to the warehouses ahead.

Ramón leaned out the window, tried to steady his
arm on the mirror, and fired two shots. Nothing. He
cursed the rocking of the car.

"Get her," he said, as much to himself as to Gerardo.
"Get her."

The Mercedes was fifteen yards behind and gaining
fast when she crimped the wheel and tried to turn the
Toyota left at full speed. They watched in anticipation
as the Toyota began first to slide sideways into the
building, then as the car began to raise two wheels to
the sky. Through the filthy windshield, Ramón caught
a glimpse of the undercarriage as the car began to roll.
Gerardo stood on the brakes, sliding the Mercedes
around the corner in a controlled power slide. Both
men felt certain they had her now. Gerardo babied the
gas pedal, ready to move in close. Ramón switched the
gun to his left hand and put his right on the door handle, ready to jump out and finish the game.

Suddenly, a feather of sparks appeared. Instead of flopping over on its side, the Toyota's roof hit the cinder-block wall, sending the little car bouncing back onto its wheels, careening down the narrow alley like a drunk.

Again, Gerardo floored the Mercedes. The big car roared forward, throwing Ramón back into the seat. Ramón pushed himself forward. He stuck his head out the window, just as the Toyota turned right at the end of the building, bounced off a fence, and disappeared from view. The rain stung Ramón's cheeks, as Gerardo slid the car between the building and the fence. And then the world went red and blue.

A Nationwide moving van was backed up to a loading dock, its massive red-and-blue trailer completely blocking the way. Ramón could see her eyes in the rearview mirror, which explained why she never hit the brakes.

The Toyota plowed into the trailer at full speed. Gerardo stood on the brakes. Ramón braced himself on the window frame and watched as the nose of the little car ducked under the trailer, as suddenly, yet seemingly in slow motion, the Toyota's windshield exploded and the car's top began to peel back like a soup can.

Gerardo spun the Mercedes in a complete circle, leaving them pointing back the way they'd come. He looked over at Ramón. White spittle had collected at the corners of his mouth. "Go finish her," he said. "Strike her out."

Ramón felt a slight discomfort in his ankle as he jogged toward the Toyota but couldn't, at that moment, remember what had happened to cause the pain. The remains of the car steamed in the downpour. Somewhere in the wreckage an electric fan still whirred. The windshield was dust. The top had been peeled completely back onto the trunk, leaving only the shattered body of the car wedged beneath the trailer.

He was no more than a dozen feet from the rear of the car when he heard voices. On the far side of the truck, somebody said, "Holy shit."

"Robby, call nine-one-one!" shouted another.

Ramón began to backpedal. When a pair of legs hurried toward the front of the truck, he turned and hustled back to the Mercedes.

Gerardo wasted no time getting them back around the corner.

"You finish her?" he asked.

"No," Ramón said. "We got tourists."

Gerardo stopped the car and looked over at his partner, who, for one of the few times in their twenty years together, looked shaken.

"She hadda be dead," he offered.

"Took the top of her head clean off," Ramón said.

"You seen it?"

"Yeah."

A long silence ensued. Finally, Gerardo spoke. "What now?"

"We better clean up our other mess," Ramón said.

Gerardo dropped the Mercedes into DRIVE and started rolling.

8

The rain fell in volleys, arching in from the south like silver arrows, blurring the windows and hammering the hull with a fury. The gimbaled ceiling lamp squeaked as *Saltheart* rocked back and forth. A fender groaned as the boat mashed it against the dock.

The sounds pulled Corso's attention from his keyboard. He got to his feet and stretched. Although he'd lived aboard for years and seldom noticed the boat's movements, tonight he could feel the rocking. As the wind buffeted the boat about the slip, he yawned, walked forward into the galley, and dumped his cold coffee into the sink.

He poured himself a fresh cup, doctoring it with a little cream and a spoonful of sugar. He looked up again just as the alarm buzzer went off. The last twenty feet of C dock were covered with bright green Astroturf, ostensibly to provide better traction but in reality to hide a web of pressure-sensitive alarm wires that warned Corso of the approach of visitors.

They were leaning into the wind, using a quivering

umbrella like a battering ram. Even in semidarkness, through rain-sheeted windows, he had no doubt about these two. These two were cops. He grabbed his yellow raincoat from its hook and stepped out on deck.

Outside, the wind and rain roared. The air was alive with the sounds of slapping waves, groaning timbers, and the *tink-tink* of a hundred loose halyards, flapping all over the marina. At the top of the swaying masts, the anemometers whirled themselves blurry in the gale.

They stood shoulder to shoulder on the dock, sharing the umbrella: the new breed of cops, a pair of stockbrokers with thick necks, squinting in the tempest. The one on the left sported a helmet of sandy hair that trembled in the breeze. The other guy wore a black wool cabbie's hat. They were both about thirty and accustomed to walking in people's front doors without an invitation. Standing as they were, six and a half feet below Corso's boots, they found themselves in an unaccustomed position of weakness, and Corso could sense it made them uncomfortable. He smiled. From waterline to deck, *Saltheart* had nearly six feet of freeboard. Without the boarding stairs, there was no getting on deck gracefully. It was strictly assholes and elbows and hoping like hell you didn't fall between the boat and the dock, where you'd be trapped and, on a night like this, would either drown in the frigid water or be ground to jelly between the fiberglass hull and the concrete dock.

"You Frank Corso?" Hair Helmet asked.

"Depends on who wants to know."

The question sent them digging around in their coats. Coming up with a pair of Seattle Police Department IDs. They held the IDs at arm's length. Corso leaned down over the rail. Detectives First Class Troy—the hair—Hamer and Roger—the hat—Sorenstam.

"What's this about?" Corso asked.

"Margaret Dougherty," Hamer said.

"Meg?"

"Yeah," said the other cop.

"What about Meg?"

They exchanged a look. Hamer hunched his shoulders against the wind and gestured toward the boat. "You think maybe we could—"

"What about Meg?" Corso insisted.

"She crashed her car over by Western Avenue," Sorenstam said.

"Into a Nationwide van," added Hamer.

"She okay?"

"We're investigating the accident," Sorenstam said.

"Is she okay?" Corso said, louder and slower.

"Why don't we step inside and—" Hamer tried again.

"What's going on?" Corso said.

"If you don't mind, Mr. Corso—"

"I mind."

"She's up at Harborview."

Sorenstam made a sad face and waggled a hand. "Docs say it's touch and go."

Corso felt his insides go cold. Felt so much like somebody's palm was pressing on his chest that he actually looked down, as if to remove the offending hand.

He sighed, folded back the hinged section of rail, lifted the stainless steel boarding ladder from its place on the side of the pilothouse, and turned and hooked the steps over the bulwarks. "Come on aboard," he said.

Corso led them in through the port door. Sorenstam thoughtfully left the umbrella on deck before stepping inside and looking around.

"Nice," he said. "Nice setup you've got here."

"It suits me," Corso said.

"Helluva view of the city," said Hamer, as he began to unbutton his overcoat.

Corso held up a hand. "Whoa, don't get too comfortable. I'm going up to Harborview. You've got between now and when the cab gets here."

He grabbed his cell phone from the navigation table, dialed nine, and pushed the talk button. After a moment, he recited his phone number, then his name and address. He left the phone turned on and set it back on the table.

"Car in the shop?" Hamer asked.

"Don't own one," Corso said.

"Not a black Mercedes?"

Corso stuffed his wallet into his right rear pants pocket. "I own a one-third interest in a Subaru Outback. Coupla other people here on the dock and I bought it together. Parking's a pain in the ass and none of us needs a car full time, so we went in together."

"Pretty unusual," Hamer commented. "Famous guy with a lotta money like you doesn't own a car of his own."

Corso pulled his overcoat from the narrow closet. "Guess I'm just an unusual guy," he said. "What's this about a black Mercedes? Was it involved?"

"We're at an early stage of our investigation. We—"

Corso cut him off. "You guys want to stop jacking me around here or what?"

The phone rang. The electronic voice said the cab was waiting.

He shrugged his way into the coat. Stuck the phone in the pocket. They stood stone-faced as Corso grabbed a Mariners baseball cap from a hook over the door, pulled his ponytail out through the hole in the back, and settled the cap on his head.

He slid the door open. Gestured with his hand. "After you," he said.

Corso followed the pair down the steps and onto the dock. Hamer stepped forward. Got right up in Corso's face. "I'd think a real friend of Miss Dougherty's would be more anxious to help bring this matter to a close."

"I'd think a couple of cops would have better things to do on a night like this than blow smoke up my ass."

"And what's that supposed to mean?" asked Sorenstam.

"I'm supposed to believe a couple of dicks are down here on a night like this over a traffic accident?" He gave an exaggerated shrug. "What? Things have gotten so slow they're assigning traffic cases to detectives? Is that it?"

Sorenstam reached in his pocket. Pulled out a black leather notebook and flipped it open: *Corso. Sat. 7 pm. Coastal.* Dougherty's handwriting.

"There's this," Sorenstam said.

Hamer moved even closer, crowding Corso now. "And a witness who says he saw a black Mercedes on the scene. Says he saw a guy with a gun get in the Mercedes and drive off. He says the guy was tall and dark. Had a ponytail."

"Now you add that to coupla fresh bullet holes in the

trunk of her car," his partner said. "And you've got pause to wonder."

"Pause to wonder," Hamer repeated.

Sorenstam read Corso's mind. "Car was a rust bucket," he said. "The holes are clean as a baby's ass."

"And that brings you down here to me?"

"You've got two priors." Sorenstam said it like he was sorry it was true. "Assault one and assault with intent."

"Against members of the press," Hamer added.

"Meg's a friend."

"Her diary says it was more than friends."

"We had a thing going for a while."

"She dump you?" Hamer asked.

"It was mutual," Corso said. "Until this morning, I hadn't seen her in six or seven months."

They tried to stonewall it, but Corso could see the surprise in their eyes.

"This morning?" Hamer said.

"Around noon. Maybe a little before."

"Where was this?"

"The federal courthouse."

"So you two just ran into one another?"

Corso shrugged. "We were both doing what we do."

They looked blank.

"The Balagula trial," Corso said. "I'm writing a book about it. She was there taking pictures. We ran into each other."

"Just coincidence, huh?" sneered Hamer.

"After all these months," his partner added.

Corso opened his mouth to speak, changed his mind, and turned and walked away instead. At the far end of the dock, a pair of mallard ducks quacked angrily as they paddled around in the flotsam and jetsam driven ashore by the storm. Corso pulled open the gate and started up the ramp toward the parking lot. Above the bluster, he could hear the cops jogging along behind as he strode to the top.

Corso was one stride onto the asphalt when Sorenstam stepped in front of him, forcing him to come to an abrupt stop. "Happened around four o'clock," Sorenstam said. He was so close, Corso could smell his breath mints. He looked over his shoulder. Hamer was tailgating him hard. Corso took a deep breath.

"Let me make this easy on you fellas. At four o'clock this afternoon, I was having drinks with a federal prosecutor named Renee Rogers."

"Where was this?"

"Vito's on Madison."

The cab's headlights appeared behind a crystal curtain of rain.

"She's staying at the Madison Renaissance," Corso said. "Give her a jingle." He sidestepped out from between the cops and walked away.

9

When Corso slipped through the door, there were three of them in the room with her.

Dougherty lay on her back, tilted halfway up in bed, her head bandaged up like the Mummy. Her black cape hung from a hook on the wall, like some nocturnal flier wounded and brought to ground. There must have been half a dozen tubes coming out of her. Corso winced at the sight.

Standing with her back to the bathroom door, chewing on a knuckle, was a girl of about sixteen, wearing a white uniform and a red-and-white striped apron. Next to the bed stood a pair of orderlies, a yoke of late twenty-somethings, losers spending their boogie nights emptying bedpans. One of them, a redheaded guy already sporting a nice case of male pattern baldness, stood with his hands in his pants pockets, squinting down at the bed, where his partner lifted the side of Dougherty's hospital gown with the tip of a pen.

"Take a look at this shit," he whispered to Redhead. "It's filthy."

Corso felt his despair turn livid. He crossed the room in four long strides, grabbed Redhead by the collar, and jerked him off his feet, sending him sliding backward across the room on his butt. Another step, and Corso grabbed a double handful of the other guy's kinky black hair and lifted him to the tips of his toes

The guy screeched like an owl as Corso slid him across the linoleum and slammed him face first into the back of the door. By the time Corso dragged him back and pulled open the door, the guy's knees had gone slack and the screeching had turned into little more than a wet gurgle. With his left hand still in the guy's hair, Corso grabbed him by the belt and lofted him out into the hall on a fly. When the door swung shut, a red stain decorated the inside.

Corso pointed at Redhead and the candy striper. "This is no freak show," he said. "I see anything like that going on again, and it's you motherfuckers who're gonna need intensive care. You hear me?"

Between gulps, Redhead managed a tentative nod. Candy Striper was now sobbing and gnawing on her entire fist.

"Get the fuck out of here," Corso said.

They kept their eyes locked on Corso and their backs against the wall as they sidestepped their way out the door.

Corso walked to Dougherty's side. Her eyes were still beneath the lids. The way the bandage clung to her head told him they'd shaved off her hair. Yellow fluid had leaked from her skull, staining the top of the bandage. He touched her cheek with the back of his fingers and then tried to settle the hospital gown around her body. Dissatisfied, he lifted a blue cotton blanket from the foot of the bed, shook it out full-sized, and covered her with it.

As he stared down at her, the door burst open: big black security guard waving a can of pepper spray, followed by a nurse. She swam her way around the guard and stood with her hands on her hips. She wore a forest-green cardigan over her crisp white uniform. Her plastic name tag read RACHEL TAYLOR, DIRECTOR OF NURSING SERVICES.

She was about forty. Trim, with a round face and a big pair of liquid brown eyes. Probably a runner, Corso thought. Her face was flushed, her anger a pair of red patches on her cheeks.

"Leave this room immediately," she said. "This woman is in critical condition. Your presence here is endangering her life."

"Not until I get some assurances."

"You assaulted one of my people," she said. "The police are on the way."

"But it's all right with you that your *people* debased and humiliated this woman. That works for you, does it, honey?"

"Which of my people would that be?"

"Those two morons and the candy striper."

"What are you talking about?" she demanded.

Corso told her. It didn't take long, but by the time he'd finished, Nurse Rachel Taylor's face had lost the ruddy glow of anger and taken on an ashen cast.

She opened her mouth and then closed it. Something in his manner told her it was true. She turned and spoke out into the hall. "Morgan, ask Dr. Hayes to fix Robert's face, pronto. Then I want to see the three of you in my office. You wait until I get there. You hear me?"

She turned back to the room and looked up at the security guard. "It's okay, Quincy. You can go. See if you can't call off the posse."

Quincy wasn't happy. He fixed Corso with what he imagined to be his most baleful stare. Something in Corso's eyes made him nervous. "You sure?" he asked, without moving his hooded eyes from Corso. She said she was sure, and, with a great show of reluctance, Quincy left the room, one halfhearted step at a time.

"I'm afraid I owe you an apology," she said. "That sort of unprofessional behavior has never been tolerated by this institution. I can assure you that those involved will no longer be affiliated with this hospital."

Corso nodded and walked over to Dougherty's side. "She'd hate being dressed this way," he said. He looked back over his shoulder at the nurse. "You have anything we could cover her up with?"

"Like what?"

"Like something with legs and sleeves."

She thought it over. "Scrubs," she said, after a minute. "There's long-sleeved scrubs."

"That'd be great."

"I'll call down for some."

"She'd really appreciate it," Corso said.

"I'll take care of it," the woman said. Something in her tone told Corso she didn't think modesty was going to make any difference.

They stood in silence, the question floating in the air between them.

"How bad is it?" Corso finally asked.

"Hard to tell."

Again, silence settled over the room.

"Prognosis?"

She folded her hands. "The protocol for an injury such as this is to offer neither hope nor despair. There's simply no way of telling."

"Why's that?"

"Anything could happen. She could sit up tomorrow afternoon and ask for ice cream, or she could never sit up again. There's just no way of telling."

"Anything I can do?"

"You religious?" she asked.

"No."

She shrugged. "Then I guess you're doing everything you can."

She stood and watched as Corso stared out the window, out over Pioneer Square and the mouth of the Duwamish River toward the lights of West Seattle in the distance.

"The brain itself shows no visible signs of damage, but there is quite a bit of swelling."

"Which means?"

"Which means if the swelling continues, they'll have to relieve the pressure by cutting a hole in her skull."

When he looked out the window again, she asked, "Did you know her well?"

"Yeah . . . for a while."

"Did she have the tattoos then?"

"Yeah."

He knew what she was going to ask before she worked up the courage. "Why would anyone . . . ?" she began.

"She didn't volunteer," Corso said. "Somebody did it to her."

He heard her breath catch. "Oh," she said. "She's the one who—that guy—he doped her up and . . ."

Corso nodded. "Yeah. She's the one."

A few years back, Meg Dougherty had been a successful young photo artist. Already had a couple of hot local shows and was beginning to attract a national following, she was dating a trendy Seattle tattoo artist; guy who kinda looked like Billy Idol. They were *the* trendy couple. You'd see them all the time in the alternative press: big loopy smiles and sunglasses at night, that kind of thing.

Unfortunately, while she'd been developing photos, he'd been developing a cocaine habit. When she told him she wanted to break it off, he seemed to take it well. They agreed to have a farewell dinner together. She drank half a glass of wine and—*bam*—the lights went out. She woke up thirty-six hours later in Providence Hospital: in shock, nearly without vital signs, and tattooed from head to toe with an array of images, designs, and slogans designed to render her body permanently obscene.

She spent a month in the hospital and, over the past couple of years, had endured endless sessions of laser surgery and dermabrasion to remove the Maori swirl designs from her face and the graphic red lettering from the palms of her hands. The rest of the artwork she was pretty much resigned to living with.

Corso turned from the window and faced her. "You'll see to it they leave her alone. That her privacy will be respected."

"You have my word, Mr.—"

"And get her those scrubs."

"Consider it done."

He reached inside his overcoat and came out with a business card. His name and cell phone number. "If there's any problem, any change in her condition . . ."

"I'll personally let you know." She glanced down at the card and furrowed her brow. She stared at the card for a long moment and then figured it out. "You're the writer," she said.

When she looked up, Corso was gone.

Tuesday, October 17   11:22 p.m.

Mikhail Ivanov had once read in the *San Francisco Chronicle* that he had killed over forty men with his own hands. He knew this to be an exaggeration. Although he had never kept count, he felt sure the actual figure would be no more than half that number.

Numbers aside, Mikhail Ivanov harbored few regrets. In his mind, he'd merely done what he did best. He had no head for business. Nico took care of that. Even as a child, Nico had had an extraordinary eye for profit. Where others saw a trickle of coins, Nico saw a torrent of cash. It was as if he had been born with an eye for advantage. As Ivanov saw it, taking care of the details had merely been his part of the business arrangement.

Of the many tasks he had performed over the years, only one left him feeling cold in the bowels. Perhaps, as Nico often suggested, he was a prude at heart. Little more than a foolish American Bible Belter. Or perhaps, as he had begun to think in recent years, some things were fundamentally against the laws of nature and, as such, had an uncanny way of connecting violators to the universal darkness of the soul.

Either way, dealing with flesh peddlers made his skin crawl. Tonight's specimen had come not with recommendation but with a warning. They said he carried a knife and was prepared to use it at the slightest provocation. Faced with the angry withdrawal of their normal source, Ivanov had no choice.

Standing side by side in the hotel corridor, they looked like father and son. The man was past forty, with the thin face of a penitent and a pair of narrow eyes that never stopped moving. "You the Russian?" he asked.

Ivanov said he was and pulled the door open, allowing them to enter. The boy wore a red raincoat and matching boots. He was probably twelve or thirteen but small for his age. He had been shaved and scraped to make him look ten, but Nico would be neither fooled nor pleased. Ivanov sighed. "Okay," he said.

The man took the boy by the elbows and set him in the chair closest to the door. He took off the boots and then stood him on the carpet. Starting at the bottom, he unfastened the six black clasps holding the coat closed. He folded the coat and laid it on the seat of the chair and put the boots on top.

The boy now wore nothing but a rhinestone dog collar and a pair of black vinyl underpants. Ivanov inclined his head toward the adjoining door in the far wall and then walked soundlessly across the room and knocked. After a guttural sound from within, he opened the door and ushered the boy inside and closed the door.

The man stood with his hands in his pockets until

Ivanov pulled out a roll of bills and began to count. "Anything he breaks, he pays for," the man said.

Ivanov kept counting.

"I heard some ugly shit," the guy said.

Ivanov continued to count.

10

Mikhail Ivanov stood in the doorway and watched the flesh peddler. He'd pushed the elevator button three times now, and still it hadn't arrived. He kept glancing from Ivanov to the boy and back. He whispered something to the boy but got no response.

From inside the suite, the sound of the shower hissed in Mikhail Ivanov's ears. He wondered how many showers it would take before he himself felt clean again. Before the stench of perversity managed to work its way out his pores, so he could wash it down the drain once and for all. He sighed.

A muted *ding* announced that, at last, the elevator car arrived. The flesh peddler stepped inside. The boy hesitated, looked back down the hall at Ivanov. His small face was knotted like a fist. A hand reached out and pulled him out of sight.

Ivanov turned away. He closed the door and walked back into the suite. His stomach churned. Standing in the middle of the room, he breathed deeply and thought of his house in Nice. Of the bright blue

Mediterranean visible from every window. Of the smells of sand and sea. And of how, before long, he would be free of all this.

Wednesday, October 18   1:24 p.m.

Warren Klein started with an artist's rendering of Fairmont Hospital, one of those idyllic airbrushed liknesses that appear prior to construction and make the viewer feel as if, illness notwithstanding, he'd like to move right in.

"This is what the public was promised," Klein intoned. "A modern state-of-the-art facility of which the community could be proud. A facility whose pediatric surgical expertise could be expected to be a model for future facilities nationwide."

Elkins began to rise. Judge Howell waved him back into his seat.

Klein used an old-fashioned pointer to indicate a section of text at the bottom of the page. "Ladies and gentlemen of the jury, I call your attention to this section of promotional copy at the bottom of the picture." He turned toward the black glass jury box. "You have been provided with a copy marked PEOPLE'S EXHIBIT ELEVEN."

The sounds of the jury shifting in their seats and the rustling of paper filled the air in the nearly silent courtroom. Klein waited for a moment and then began to read. "The design of Fairmont Hospital will include next-generation construction criteria virtually guaranteed to prevent collapse or serious damage in the event of seismic activity."

Klein let the tip of the pointer fall to the floor with a click. "Ladies and gentlemen of the jury, the state will show that Fairmont Hospital, which sat less than ten miles from the San Andreas Fault, was in fact constructed without the slightest regard for either seismic activity or human safety."

Elkins was on his feet now. "Your Honor, please. . . ."

Klein raised his voice. "In one of the most seismically volatile areas in the world, this man"—he aimed the pointer at the defense table—"this man, Nicholas Balagula, in order to line his own pockets, falsified both construction and inspection records, putting the lives of nearly four hundred people at constant risk—"

The judge banged the gavel. "Mr. Klein."

"—and eventually leading to the untimely deaths of sixty-three people, forty-one of whom were children." Klein stood stiff and still, the pointer aimed at the defense table, allowing the gravity of his words to sink into the invisible jurors.

Satisfied that he'd made his point, Klein reached toward the easel.

Elkins looked wounded. "If the court please."

"Yes, Mr. Elkins," the judge said.

"I wish to renew my objection to any further inflammatory images. As you know, I have—"

The judge cut him off. "As *you* know, Mr. Elkins, *I* have already ruled on the matter of the photographs."

"Yes, Your Honor, but I'm afraid I must take exception to—"

"Your exception is noted, Mr. Elkins." The judge turned his attention to Klein. "Proceed."

Once again, Klein addressed the jury directly.

"Ladies and gentlemen of the jury, before I proceed, I feel an obligation to prepare you for what is to follow. The images you are about to see are, to say the least"—he pretended to search for a word—"harrowing," he said finally. "I apologize for their graphic nature and for any undue discomfort which they may cause you." He was pacing now, working his way from one end of the jury box to the other. "But I can assure you that any pain or discomfort you may experience will pale in comparison to the suffering of the loved ones of those who perished and is virtually insignificant when compared with the final moments of the sixty-three unfortunate souls who died in the collapse of Fairmont Hospital."

He walked over to the prosecution table and handed the pointer to Raymond Butler. As he made his way back toward the easel, the room crackled with tension. He gestured toward the idyllic rendering of the hospital. "This is what the good people of Alameda County, California, were promised." In a single motion he pulled the picture from the easel and leaned it, face in, against the jury box. "This is what they got," he said, in a loud voice.

A ground-angle shot, three feet by four feet, in living color, the crumbled rear wall of the hospital slightly out of focus in the background. A sea of broken concrete, ribbons of twisted electrical wire, and a single strip of filthy gauze all pulled the eye toward the bottom of the picture, where—poking up from beneath the rubble—was a leg and tiny foot, soft and pink and fat, the ankle encircled by a blue-and-white beaded anklet that read MICHAEL.

From inside the jury box came a hiccup, quickly followed by a sob. Someone moaned. Rogers and Butler looked away. The judge's face was ashen. The bailiff at the far end leaned into the jury box and then walked over and whispered in Judge Howell's ear.

The judge's lips were pressed tight as he banged the gavel. "The jury has requested a recess. Court will reconvene at two-thirty this afternoon."

Warren Klein beamed as he sauntered over to the prosecution table.

"For Christ's sake, Warren, cover that picture up," Renee Rogers whispered.

His smile was replaced by astonishment. "Why would I want to do that?" he asked. "I want them to—"

"You've made your point, Warren. Leaving it uncovered is overkill."

"She's right," Butler added. "There's a thin line between getting the jury's attention and offending them."

"What a pair of shrinking violets," Klein scoffed. "No wonder you couldn't put him away." He looked over at the Balagula contingent. "With an animal like that, you've got to fight fire with fire."

Renee Rogers opened her mouth to argue, changed her mind, and instead pushed past Klein, walked over to the easel, and covered the picture. Klein followed her, his neck getting progressively redder as he crossed the room.

His whisper could be heard all over the courtroom. "Are you forgetting who's in charge here?" he demanded.

"With you reminding everyone, Warren, one could hardly forget."

She stood her ground. Klein stepped in, nose to

nose. "I'm going to put that little foot right up Balagula's ass," he said. "You just watch me." He curled his lips into a sneer, turned, and walked back to the table, where he gathered his notes into his briefcase. "Lunch?" he inquired.

When Rogers and Butler looked at him like he was crazy, he laughed out loud.

"No wonder he kicked your ass," he said. "Neither of you has the stomach for the job." He strode from the room, swinging his briefcase and whistling.

Renee Rogers wandered over to Corso. "Warren's looking for lunch company."

Corso shook his head sadly. "I'll have to take a rain check," he said. "Dead babies tend to put me off my feed."

"I could use a drink," she said.

"Or ten," Corso added.

"Afterward. Vito's."

"I can't today. I've got something I want to run down."

She raised an eyebrow. "Something to do with Seattle PD calling me to make sure we were together yesterday afternoon?"

Corso told her about Dougherty.

"How is she now?"

"I called before I came down this morning, and they said her condition was unchanged."

She put her hand on his arm. "I've got a terrific urge to say something stupid. Like how she's going to be all right or how it will surely work out for the best."

Corso nodded his thanks. Her hand was warm and vaguely comforting.

"Why would anybody want to kill a photographer?"

"I don't know," Corso said, "but I'm damn sure going to find out."

* * *

Nicholas Balagula watched the drama taking place at the prosecution table.

"It appears our Mr. Corso has become a member of the inner circle."

"Miss Rogers and Mr. Butler probably wish to assure themselves of sympathetic treatment in his book," Mikhail Ivanov said. "These Americans thrive on celebrity."

"I think he's in her pants," Balagula said.

Their conversation was interrupted by Bruce Elkins, who leaned down between Ivanov and Balagula. "Do you two think you could look like maybe some of this affects you somehow? It would help me considerably if you didn't sit there looking at pictures of dead children like you were taking a walk in the park. The jury notices things like that, don't think they don't."

"Of course you're right—" Ivanov began.

Balagula cut him off. "You take care of your end," he said to his lawyer, "and the rest will take care of itself."

Elkins shook his head. "One of these days, Nico. One of these days your arrogance is going to come back to haunt us all."

"Not today," Balagula said with a smile.

Elkins stood still. "Is there something I should know here?" he demanded.

"Like what?" Ivanov asked.

"You tell me," Elkins said. "I have no intention of

being party to anything unethical. Am I making myself understood?"

But Nicholas had Balagula turned away and was now staring intently at the prosecution table.

Mikhail Ivanov watched in silence as Elkins gathered his belongings and headed out the front door for his daily dance with the media. "He's right, you know," he said, after a moment. "Arrogance is a dangerous thing."

Nicholas Balagula ignored him. "Have Gerardo and Ramón follow our Mr. Corso. Let's find out where our nosy writer friend goes to roost."

"Whatever for?"

"Because I said so," Balagula said. He turned his hooded eyes toward Ivanov. "That's all the reason you need, is it not?"

Ivanov could feel the burning in his cheeks. "I'll take care of it," he said.

He walked to the door and peeked out. Not because he was interested in what Elkins had to say but so Nico would not be able to see his face.

11

Corso kicked a rolled newspaper aside, stepped over the threshold into the apartment, and closed the door behind himself. He stood for a moment in the narrow entry hall, staring down at the silver key in the palm of his hand. He heaved a sigh. When Dougherty hadn't bothered to ask for her key back, he'd figured it was because she'd changed the lock. That's what he would have done. The fact that the key still worked saddened him and left him feeling hollow and cold.

He pocketed the key and walked down the green carpet runner into the living room. Everything was as he remembered—the burgundy oriental rug and the bright green couch, the nest of rosewood Chinese tables, the framed posters. All of it—except for the photographs. The places that had once held pictures of him . . . of them . . . now showed a sandy-haired guy with a close-cropped beard and glasses, laughing, lounging, leaning his head against her shoulder.

He turned away from the photographs and pulled

open the mahogany door to what had once been a walk-in closet: an eight-by-eight space that Dougherty, before the advent of digital photography, had used as a darkroom and that now served as her makeshift office. At the back, a built-in desk held her computer. A trio of battered file cabinets lined the left wall. Overhead, a pair of shelves overflowed with books and magazines.

The cops had been through her files, leaving the drawers open and the folders scattered about like leaves. A black-and-white picture of himself lay on top of the pile: standing on a rock at the apex of Stuart Island, the entrance to Roach Harbor barely visible in the distance. He reached out and turned it over. She'd written *Frank Corso, Stuart Island, 11/9/99.* Must have been what sent the cops scurrying to his door.

He sat in her chair and ran his hands along the arm-rests. He remembered the week on the island. No phone, no electricity, no nothing . . . except each other. Walking in the woods and digging clams down on the beach. Watching darkness fall from the deck and then retiring inside. And the nights filled with low moans among the rustle of the trees and the ragged songs of the night birds.

Corso got to his feet. Ran one hand over his face and another through his hair. A voice in his head was getting louder, telling him to get to work, to stop spacing out and start looking for something that might give him a clue as to why somebody would want to do her harm. He gathered the folders that littered the desktop and tapped everything back inside before returning them to the file cabinet.

The cops had her little black notebook, but that was just what she used when she was out on a shoot. At home, she kept track of her life in a series of six-by-eight journals she bought from Urban Outfitters. Her idea books, she called them.

She went through two or three a year and never threw them out. The entire top shelf above the desk was filled with old journals, purple, red, blue, and green. Like the files, they were a mess. The brick she used as a bookend had been moved. A dozen journals lay sprawled on their sides. He stood them up, put the brick back in place, and eased out the purple book on the far right. Inside the front cover she'd written *1/00–7/00 Post-Corso Journal Number Two*. His fingers felt thick and stiff as he thumbed through the pages. It was awash in her bold, looped handwriting. It also was full, which meant she'd started another.

He went through the office slowly, looking for her current journal, cleaning up as he went along. There were only three possibilities: either she had it with her in the car and the cops had it, or the cops had taken it when they went through the apartment, or it was still here someplace. Took him five minutes to satisfy himself that it wasn't in the office.

Finally, he sat down in her chair again and pushed the button on the keyboard of her candy-colored iMac. A symphonic tone filled the little space. He waited for the computer to boot, then went directly to Adobe PhotoShop. Clicked his way to MY PHOTOS and surveyed the field of labeled and dated folders. Near the right margin, a folder read MAGNOLIA BRIDGE 10/17/00. He double-clicked the icon. She'd taken thirty-two pictures of the construction site. He opened a picture of the truck still embedded in the hill, zoomed in twice on the license plate, and found it too mud-encrusted to read. Five pictures later, the fire hoses had cleaned the plate enough for Corso to be able to make it out: Washington plate 982-DDG. He pulled his notebook from his pocket, wrote the number down, and then picked up the phone and dialed.

"Licensing," a man's gruff voice said.

"Ellen Gardner, please," Corso said.

"Hang on," the guy said.

A putrid instrumental version of Bob Marley's "Three Little Birds" forced Corso to hold the phone away from his ear. Halfway through the second chorus, the music stopped. "Gardner."

"It's Frank."

"And what can we do for you today Mr. Jones?"

"Washington plate: Nine-eight-two-DDG."

"Five minutes."

"Different number." He recited from memory. "Ring it once and hang up. I'll call you back."

"Why certainly, sir. You have a nice day too." *Click.*

Nine minutes later, having searched the tiny kitchen, he stood in the doorway to the bedroom, unable to force his foot across the threshold, bracing himself against the doorjamb with both hands, like Samson about to bring down the temple, when the phone rang once and then went silent. With a sigh, he propelled himself forward into the room, like a ski racer pulling himself out the gate.

The black-and-gold bedspread was dented where she'd been sitting. He stood by the side of the bed and dialed the phone. This time, Gardner answered.

"It's me."

"Registered to Donald Barth. Twenty-six-eleven Marginal Way South, Renton, Washington. Nine-eight-one-oh-nine. Mr. Barth is employed by the Meridian School District in the maintenance department."

"The check's in the mail."

"Why, thank you, sir," she drawled.

Corso pulled open the drawer in the nightstand, and there it was. Shiny black, with a bright blue elastic holding it shut. He pulled the elastic aside and opened the book to where her pen was stored. The final page of the journal read *Consolidated, Rough and Ready, Baker Brothers, Evergreen, Matson and Mayer*. He read the list several times. Backward, then forward. The names sounded vaguely familiar, but he couldn't put them in context.

He leafed back another page. Times. The bridge. *D/L 2:30*. Then another. *Airport—David—Tues. American 1244*. Nothing. He went back a full week, but nothing among the notations suggested anything that could have led to such dire consequences.

He returned the journal to the nightstand and walked back out into the living room. In his mind, he retraced his steps through the apartment. Looking for something he might have missed or misinterpreted. Nothing came to mind.

He was still deep in thought when the lock clicked and the door swung open. The sandy-haired guy in the pictures, reading the newspaper headlines, briefcase slung over one shoulder, dragging a wheeled suitcase along behind like a stubborn puppy. He stopped in his tracks at the sight of Corso and lowered the paper to his side.

"What are you . . . ?" he began, before a glimmer of recognition swept through his eyes. "You're—"

"Frank Corso. You must be David."

David gave no sign that he'd heard. Instead he slid his luggage into the hall leading to the bathroom and threw the paper on top.

"How'd you get in?" he demanded.

He couldn't have been much more than thirty: five-ten, slim. His beard was redder than his hair, but not as red as his face. He repeated his question.

"Meg's been hurt," Corso said.

"What—just because you're this famous writer, you think you can walk around other people's apartments without an invitation?" He pointed toward the door. "Get the hell out of here, right now."

"Listen," Corso started.

The younger man cocked a fist and took a quick step forward. Corso straight-armed him to a halt.

"Take it easy," he said quietly. "She's in Harborview Hospital. She was—"

He didn't get a chance to give him the particulars. Without warning, the kid telegraphed a looping over-head right at Corso's chin. Corso moved his head. As the punch came whistling by, Corso grabbed the kid's arm and used his forward motion to send him stagger-ing out into the living room. Now Corso had his back to the yawning door. "Take it easy, man," Corso said. "She needs you to have a calm head here. She's—"

This time the kid rushed him, head down, his arms grasping like horns, in an all-out tackle. Again, Corso sidestepped like a matador. This time, however, he sent a short right hand the kid's way, clipping him along-side the jaw as he rushed past, sending him lurching head first into the door across the hall. The hall echoed with a hollow boom. David lay still at the base of the door.

Corso reached down and touched the guy's throat. His pulse was fast and heavy. With a sigh, he stepped into Dougherty's apartment and began to pull the door closed. That's when he spotted the series of pictures on the front page of the *Seattle Times*.

Upper left was a picture of an embankment, washed away by the rain. Halfway down the embankment, the front end of an automobile poked its nose out of the dirt. The next picture showed a fire truck using its high-pressure hoses to loosen the hill's grip on the vehicle. The third picture captured the very moment when the buried truck came loose from the hill and began its freefall to the ground below. He turned the page sideways. Picture credit read: M. DOUGHERTY.

The squeak of a door pulled Corso's attention from the page. Across the hall, a bald-headed guy had his door open on a chain. His eyes moved back and forth between Corso and the body on his doorsill. David groaned and rolled over on his back.

"Whenever Junior wakes up, tell him Meg's up at Harborview. Room One-oh-nine in the Intensive Care Unit. Okay?"

The guy gave a minuscule nod and quickly closed the door. Corso refolded the paper and took it with him as he walked down the hall and out into the street.

Outside, the trees swayed in the wind and the sky was flecked with blowing leaves.

Corso turned left out the door and started up Republican Street toward the Subaru. At the far end of the block, a halo of exhaust swirled around a dirty black Mercedes, obscuring a pair of low-rider silhouettes.

12

Wednesday, October 18   4:41 p.m.

"Things are a goddamn mess is what they are."

He was about fifty, wire-thin, with an Adam's apple the size of a Ping-Pong ball. His narrow, unshaven face was twisted into a sullen mask. "We got every damn piece of equipment we own down at the bridge site. We got the city offerin' to pay us double-time to keep workin' all night, and the boss ain't no-goddamn-where to be found."

Corso unbuttoned his coat and slipped it from his shoulders. The office was like a sauna. "Gone home?" he asked.

"Hell, no. His missus ain't seen him since yesterday morning. Poor woman's near outa her mind. Called the cops last night when he didn't make it to supper. Cops come and rousted me out at a quarter to three. Got my old woman over there sittin' with her till we got some idea what in hell's going on."

"What do the cops say?"

He slashed the air with his hand. "Those dumb shits don't know nothin' more than what I tol' 'em. Wanna know if he's got a woman somewhere. I tol' 'em half a dozen times: Joe Ball's a family man. Just bought him a house a few months back. Ain't got no floozie stashed someplace. Joe Ball ain't here at seven sharp they's somethin' big-time wrong, mister. And you can take that to the bank."

"When'd *you* see him last?" Corso asked.

The guy heaved a sigh. "Tell you the same thing I tol' them. Last time I laid eyes on Joe was about three-thirty yesterday. Right in this here office. I'd been out at the site for fourteen hours. Joe was here when I come back and punched out." He turned a palm toward the leaden sky. "Tol' me he'd see me in the mornin'."

"He was alone?"

" 'Ceptin' for the girl who come later."

"Girl?"

"I was up by the guard shack fixin' to go home. She come by just as I was packin' up. Said she was a reporter. Doin' a story on the bridge repairs. Wanted to know about the equipment we had down at the job site. I sent her down here to see Joe."

"Black hair?" Corso used his finger to draw a line across his forehead. "Cut straight across like this?"

The guy nodded. "That's the one."

For the third time in the past hour, Corso failed to suppress a shudder. He'd experienced the first when, fifteen minutes after leaving Dougherty's apartment, he finally got around to scanning the fourth photograph.

She'd used a long lens to zoom in on the macabre figure sitting behind the wheel of the buried truck. The fire hose had cleaned the windshield enough to reveal the ivory grin of the decomposed body that sat slouched in the driver's seat, his head thrown back as if sharing some cosmic joke with the sky.

The news copy told how construction crews attempting to repair a washout of the foundations supporting the Magnolia Bridge had come upon the yellow Toyota pickup buried a dozen feet down into the hill.

According to the *Seattle Times*, police were speculating that the truck must have been buried some three months earlier, when torrential rains had first threatened the bridge, necessitating an emergency repair operation of equally monumental proportions.

It wasn't the massive sinkhole or the remnant driver that sent a cold chill running down Corso's spine like a frozen ball bearing. It was the cement truck and the logo. Two intertwined *R*s: ROUGH AND READY CONCRETE.

He'd slid the Subaru to the curb, hurried over to the pay phone on the corner of Fifteenth and Republican, and thumbed his way through the frayed yellow pages to Construction Equipment. Like he figured, they were all there: Consolidated Trucking, Rough and Ready Concrete, Baker Brothers Cranes, Evergreen Equipment, Matson and Mayer Pile Driving. Shudder number one.

A quick perusal of the company's addresses revealed that Evergreen Equipment was located on a piece of reclaimed marshland adjacent to Western Avenue. Right where the cops said she'd crashed. He remembered what she'd said about chasing the story that would put her over the top and shuddered for a second time.

The guy leaned over and rested his hands on the

Subaru's window frame. Half his right index finger was missing. He eyed Corso suspiciously. "You know somethin' about this, mister?" Before Corso could answer, he went on. " 'Cause Joe's old woman would be most appreciative iffen you could shed a little light on what's goin' on here. I know she surely would." The guy leaned farther in the window. He smelled of mildew. "Girl ain't missin' too, is she?"

Corso shook his head and told him about her crash. About the witnesses who said she was being pursued by a black Mercedes, and about how he'd surmised that Dougherty was chasing the story of how the truck got buried in the hillside. The guy shifted his weight from foot to foot and rubbed his chin as Corso spoke.

"You think Joe comin' up missing and the girl's accident are related?" he asked, when Corso finished.

"I wouldn't jump to any conclusions, if I were you," Corso said.

The guy thought it over. "I don't like it," he said finally. "You can set your watch by Joe Ball. Him not bein' here at a time like this . . . and then the girl . . . I don't like it."

"That makes two of us, buddy," Corso said. He dug around in his pocket. Came out with a business card. "Anything comes up you think I ought to know about, give me a call. Okay?"

"I don't like it," the guy said again.

"I don't like it," Gerardo said. "What the fuck's he doing down here, anyway? Boss says he's just some nosy writer dude. He got nothin' to do with this shit."

"Take it easy. We just gonna do what we was told," Ramón said. "We gonna stay on him and find out where he lives."

Although his voice was calm, Ramón was worried too. Ever since they'd found the guy dead in his truck, nothing had gone quite as planned. Somebody'd offed the mark before they got the chance. The truck had become unburied. The girl walked in on them while they were cleaning up. Tourists showed up and prevented them from making sure she was dead. Nothing but loose ends and sloppy work.

"We gonna tell the boss where he went?" Gerardo demanded.

"We tell 'em that, we gotta tell 'em about the girl."

Gerardo thought it over. "Maybe we shoulda told 'em the guy was dead when we got there. Maybe then none of this other shit woulda happened."

"I don't think so," Ramón said. "We tell 'em we lied about the hit, they's gonna be somebody tailing *our* asses."

"I don't like it," Gerardo said again. "Maybe we oughta just pop this writer guy's ass and be done with it."

"Here he comes," Ramón said.

The green Subaru wagon was rolling down the access road, heading back out onto Western Avenue. Ramón waited until the car turned right at the farthest warehouse and disappeared from view, then dropped the Mercedes into DRIVE and took his foot off the brake. "Let's see where he goes next," he said, as much to himself as to Gerardo.

13

"**W**e have no vacancy," the guy said. "We have a vacancy, I put a sign out in the street. Apartments here never vacant long."

Southeast Asian. Couldn't have been much over five feet tall, standing ramrod straight in the door of his apartment. Mid-sixties. Close-cropped hair and a pair of black eyes that could stare a hole in a brick.

"I didn't come about an apartment," Corso said. "I came about a former tenant named Donald Barth."

"Ah," the man said. "Quite sad. The police came yesterday."

"Mr. . . . ?"

"Pov," he said quickly. "Nhim Pov. I am the manager here."

Nhim Pov stepped out onto the tiny concrete porch and closed the door behind himself. "What about Mr. Barth?" he asked. "What business of yours is his unfortunate death?"

"I'm a writer," Corso said. "And I'm trying to figure out what it was about his life that induced somebody to shoot him nine times and then bury him and his truck in the side of a hill."

"I told the police. Mr. Barth was very quiet, a very private man. I know nothing personal about him whatsoever."

"How long did he live here?"

"Five years, I think. I come here as manager three years ago. Mr. Barth was married then. Then last year this time she left, and he live here by himself."

"He have any problems with any of his neighbors?"

"He make trouble, he would not be living here still." He offered a small smile. "I run what you Americans call a tight ship, Mr. Corso. People who make difficulties do not get their leases renewed."

"He pay his rent on time?"

Again the little man smiled. "Same answer. The county has a long waiting list. People can no longer afford to live around here. They get old. They have no money. Where else can they go?"

Nhim Pov was right. The emerald city had become so glitzy that a little two-bedroom fixer-upper was the better part of three hundred grand. A decent apartment was a thousand dollars a month. It had gotten so the people who made the city work could no longer afford to live there. Not just blue-collar folk, either. Across the lake in trendy Bellevue, the new mayor, who was bringing down a cool hundred and fifty thousand a year, applied for and was granted another hundred grand as a housing allowance, because Bellevue has an ordinance that says the mayor has to live within the city limits, and without the extra stipend he couldn't afford to do so.

"When did you first realize that Mr. Barth wasn't coming back?"

"A few weeks after he left," he said. "Mr. Barth always paid his rent on the first of the month. Always. So I look in the parking lot and see his truck is gone. I have no need to go in and make sure he is okay, right? I think maybe he is away somewhere. Maybe have an emergency." He waved a hand around. "Some of these people very old. If I don't hear from them I call. They don't answer, I knock on the door. Sometimes they're sick. Sometimes they're dead."

"So after a couple of weeks, you start to wonder."

"I go in his apartment." He shrugged. "Everything is just as he left it, I guess. I never been in there before."

"Then?"

"Then I wait for the rest of the month. When he still doesn't come, I move his furniture out to the shed, clean up the apartment, and rent it to Mr. Leng."

"You still have his stuff?"

"What else am I to do with a man's life, sell it?"

"Lotta people would."

"Many people have no honor."

"Could I look through his belongings?"

"Police already been all through it."

"Just a short look. I won't take long."

Nhim Pov thought it over and then suddenly stepped back inside his apartment. Through the crack in the door, Corso could see a print of Buddha on the far wall and a small shrine set up in the corner.

In a moment, Mr. Pov was back on the porch, holding a set of brass keys in one hand and a dictionary in the other. "What is this word *induce* you said before?" he asked Corso.

"Did I?"

"You say you wanted to find out what would *induce* somebody to kill Mr. Barth and bury the body."

"It means to lead or move, by persuasion or influence."

Pov found the word in his dictionary. His lips moved slightly as he read the words. "So then . . . the force comes from without," he said.

"Yes," Corso said. "You're quite a student of the language, Mr. Pov."

"Nice of you to say," he said. "I have worked hard on my English."

"You're quite good."

The little man beamed. "Thank you." He bowed at the waist. "From a writer, I take that as highest honor."

He slipped a red felt bookmark into the page and set the dictionary on the floor inside his front door. He closed the door, tried the knob to make sure it was locked, and then turned to Corso. "Now, Mr.—" he began.

"Corso. Frank Corso."

Nhim Pov was smiling now. "Mr. Corso, you have kindly *induced* me to show you the remains of Mr. Barth's belongings."

Corso followed the little man down the sidewalk and then across the wet grass between buildings. They emerged onto a grassed-over area running along the edge of the marsh. Nihm Pov stopped and pointed out over the water. "At night . . . sometimes . . . the moon and the water—they remind me of my homeland."

"It's what's left of the Black River," Corso said.

"Oh." He looked up at Corso. "How so what's left?"

Corso walked over to the edge of the water. "The

Black River used to be the major drainage for Lake Washington. All these little creeks running in, feeding the lake, and the Black River draining it out into the Cedar River and then the White and the Green, until they all got together as the Duwamish and emptied into Puget Sound."

"What happened?"

"People just couldn't leave things alone. When they dug the Lake Washington Ship Canal, they lowered the water level of Lake Washington by nine feet and suddenly the Black River was gone." Out in the middle of the marsh, several dozen ducks bobbed about on the rippled surface, asleep, heads tucked under their wings. "Except that the Black River wouldn't die," Corso continued. "It went underground." He swept his hand around. "It pops up as marshes and seepage all over this part of the county. They can't build on it, so they've turned it into bird sanctuaries."

"It is a river's nature to remain a river," Nhim Pov said.

"Yes," Corso agreed. "It is."

"That is the beauty of America, is it not?" Pov said, as they turned away from the water.

"What's that?"

"That a man such as myself can arrive on these shores and create a life for himself and his family without having to give up his beliefs and customs."

"How long have you been here?"

"Ten years."

"From?"

"I came from Thailand, where I was in a refugee camp for nine years."

"From where originally?"

"I am Cambodian. I am in America now, but I will always be Cambodian. Like this Black River, I will always be what I am."

They rounded the corner of the final building. A line of half a dozen sheds stood along a row of trees. Nhim Pov strode over to the nearest shed, slipped a key into a shiny silver lock, and slid the door aside. He stepped inside, reached up, and pulled an unseen cord. A single bulb illuminated the interior with weak yellow light.

Nhim Pov stepped back outside and gestured with his head. Corso stepped inside. The air smelled of fresh earth and mildew. Donald Barth's possessions had been piled on either side of a narrow central aisle. Corso walked to the back wall without touching anything and then turned and walked halfway back.

In the center of the couch a Dole pineapple box held half a dozen framed photographs. Probably the stuff he had hanging on the wall, Corso figured. An old photo of a woman in a patched housedress, her narrow expressionless eyes squinting into the sun: maybe his mother. Another of a thin young man wearing a set of marine dress blues.

A crude wooden frame held an oval picture of a handsome couple, smiling and holding hands on an arched garden bridge. He was a good-looking fellow, with a thick head of dark hair and a noticeable cleft in his chin. She was younger, a pretty girl with a small mouth and even features. Corso held the picture up. "This Mr. Barth?" he asked.

Nhim Pov nodded. "And Mrs. Barth."

Corso leaned the picture against the side of a box and picked up another. Inside a black metal frame, a young boy of seven or eight sat in the sand wearing a green bathing suit. Laughing in the gentle surf, with what looked a lot like the Santa Monica Pier in the background.

Corso pulled the picture of the couple on the bridge from the box again and held it up next to the picture of the boy. The resemblance was unmistakable. Corso showed the picture to Pov.

"His son," Pov said.

Corso was about to put both pictures back in the box when he noticed the disparity in the color of the paper. Although decades newer, the picture taken on the bridge was yellowed and brittle looking.

Corso returned the boy's picture to the box. He turned the photo of the couple over. A rectangular piece of cardboard was held in place by six wire nails.

He looked over at Mr. Pov. "Mind if I take this apart?" he asked.

"As long as you put it back," the man said.

Corso set the frame face down on the couch. He rummaged in his pants pocket and came out with a handful of change, from which he extracted a dime. He used the dime to pry the nails up, then used his index finger to bend them back and out of the way, until he could lift the piece of cardboard free and set it aside.

He scratched one corner of the picture loose and peeled the whole thing up off the glass. It was a wedding invitation, framed in such a way as to allow only the picture to be visible. Below the picture, it read: *Marie Ellen Hall and Donald J. Barth invite you to share the joy of their coming nuptials.* WHERE: *Blessed Sacrament Church, 5041 9th Avenue NE, Seattle, Washington, 98107.* WHEN: *Saturday April 3rd, 1993. Reception to follow in the Parish Hall.* RSVP: *206-324-0098.*

"Be all right if I took this with me?" Corso asked Pov. "I'll bring it back as soon as I'm finished."

Pov nodded. "Okay," he said.

Corso spent another twenty minutes going through the remains of Donald Barth's life. "I guess that's it," he said finally, dusting his hands together.

Mr. Pov pulled the chain on the light and they walked outside together. Overhead a full moon ducked in and out of a starless steel-wool sky. Mr. Pov slid the door closed and snapped the padlock back in place.

"A philosopher once said that a man's true worth is not measured by the extent of his possessions but by the paucity of his needs," Corso said.

"Ah," Pov said. "What is this *paucity*?"

Corso told him and then spelled it.

"If such is true, then Mr. Barth was a wealthy man indeed."

Corso thanked Mr. Pov for his help. The men shook hands and parted company. Nhim Pov turned left, toward his apartment, and Corso went right, toward the hissing purple lights of the parking lot.

* * *

Gerardo was outraged. "What the hell's he doin' here for a damn hour, anyway? He don't got nothing to do with this. Every place we go, this guy's pokin' his nose in our business."

"He's got some connection going for himself."

"What connection is that?"

"Between the girl and the guy in the truck."

Gerardo scowled. "Like what?"

"Damned if I know," Ramón said.

"Maybe he knows the Ball guy buried the truck for us."

"How would he know that? He's just supposed to be some nosy-ass writer who's always talkin' shit about the boss."

"Here he comes," Gerardo said, pointing out through the darkened window. As they sat in the gloom, the Subaru rolled out from behind the Briarwood Garden Apartments and bounced into the street. Gerardo started the Mercedes's engine. He waited until Corso was halfway up the block before turning on the lights and following.

"We maybe better figure out where this guy fits into the picture," Ramón said, as they followed the Subaru up the freeway entrance ramp.

"Soon," Gerardo agreed. "Real soon."

14

"Stop," Ramón said.

Half a block up Ninth Avenue, Harborview Hospital rose into the night sky like a stone rocket ship on a launching pad. Gerardo and Ramón watched as Corso stopped at the gate, plucked a ticket from the automatic dispenser, and wheeled the Subaru out of sight.

Gerardo pulled the car to the curb in a tow-away zone. "You goin' in?"

"Yeah."

"What for?"

"I dunno. I got a feeling."

"What kinda feeling?"

Ramón checked his watch. "He's gotta be visitin' somebody."

"Like who?"

"That's what I'm gonna find out."

"You want in the trunk?"

"I'm just goin' to look."

A hospital security guard left the entrance and began limping their way.

"Rent-a-pig gonna tell us to move," Gerardo said.

Ramón popped the door and stepped out into the street. "Take it around the block," he said. "I'll catch up with you in a bit."

The guard was still coming. "Oughta blow his fat ass up," Gerardo groused, but Ramón didn't hear. Ramón was already jogging up the sidewalk, cutting through a flower bed to the corner of the building, where he stood and watched as Corso crossed the parking lot and entered the back door of the hospital. Ramón hopped over the shrubbery and stood on the sidewalk, watching Corso stride down the shining hallway.

Wednesday, October 18   9:29 p.m.

The room was quiet, the burnished metal stillness broken only by the underlying hum of machinery somewhere deep in the building. Nurse Rachel Taylor leaned over Dougherty's bed, adjusting the flow of an overhead IV. Tonight's cardigan was bright red. Corso cleared his throat. The woman looked back over her shoulder, smiled, and held up a finger. A minute turned to two before the woman walked across the room to Corso's side.

"Don't you ever go home?" Corso asked.

"Not according to my daughter," Rachel Taylor said, with a sigh. "To hear Melissa tell it, my insistence that we remain fed and clothed amounts to abandonment."

"How old?"

"Fourteen."

"Great age for girls," Corso offered.

"Yeah . . . if you don't mind their brains being controlled from outer space."

Corso walked to the side of the bed and looked down. Dougherty lay on her back. Yesterday's stained bandage had been replaced, but she was still little more than an inanimate maze of tubes and wires, stiff and unmoving beneath the crisp white covers.

"How's she doing?" Corso whispered.

"Her vital signs are better, but the brain swelling is worse."

"What now?"

She took Corso by the arm and moved him toward the door. "Come on," she said. Corso followed her out into the hall. "I hate to talk about comatose patients as if they're not there," she explained. "I always have this feeling that on some deeper level they may be listening." Corso nodded his understanding.

"What next?" he asked.

She wrinkled her nose. "Next we iron out a couple of administrative matters."

"Such as?"

"I had a very unhappy financial administrator down here this evening."

"And?"

"And he wants to move Miss Dougherty up to Providence Hospital."

"Why would he want to do that?"

"Because we're chock-full of patients and Providence is only sixty percent full, and because neither Miss Dougherty nor the young man with whom she lives has any kind of health insurance."

Corso trapped the words in his throat. What started as a profane protest came out as little more than a low growl. He closed his eyes for a moment and rubbed the bridge of his nose with his thumb and forefinger. In the darkness behind his eyelids, he could see the endless halls of the veterans' hospital where his father had coughed out his last breath. Where he and his mother and his brother and sister had traveled every Tuesday night for seven years to pay homage to a man they barely knew—a man who left whatever decency he might once have possessed lying in the bottom of a frozen Korean foxhole and came home with little more than an unquenchable thirst and an ungovernable temper. Corso's nose stung with the smell of stale urine along the maze of scuffed hallways. He could see the ghosts sitting outside their rooms in the late evening, mouths agape, stubbled black-tooth chins resting on stained gowns. The burned and the legless, the lame and the disjointed, the shakers, the droolers, and the goners, all lined up along the halls like sentinels.

When he opened his eyes, the nurse held up a moderating hand. "It's standard procedure," she said. "Providence is a full-service—"

Corso cut her off. "Providence is a dump. I want her to stay here."

"If she stays here, she's going to have to move to a semiprivate room."

"A ward."

"There are no"—she made quotation marks in the air with her fingers—"*wards* anymore. The most patients we have in a single room is four."

"She wouldn't like being in a room with other people."

Rachel Taylor made a resigned face. "Sometimes, Mr. Corso—"

"I'll take care of the bill," Corso said suddenly.

The nurse took a step back, looking at Corso as if for the first time. "Do you have any idea how much money we're talking about here?"

"No," he said, "and I don't care. Whatever it is, I'll take care of it."

"Her present bill alone. . . . You're serious, aren't you?"

"I don't have many friends," he said. "I can't afford to lose any."

The sadness in his eyes told her he wasn't kidding. "You have to work it out with the business office."

"How do I do that?" he asked.

She took him by the elbow. "Come down to the nurses' station, and I'll get you started on the paperwork," she said. Before he could move, she gripped his arm tighter. "If you don't mind me saying it, Mr. Corso, she's a very lucky woman to have a friend like you."

Corso grunted and started down the hall.

* * *

Ramón was backed into a service alcove, a collapsible wheelchair on either side of him, as he peeked down the hall toward the red-sweater nurse and the nosy-writer man. He'd watched as they came out of the room together. Watched as they talked and then disappeared down a hall to the left. He checked the area. Nothing. Nobody. He stepped out and started down the hall. His shoes squeaked with every step as he made his way down the gleaming corridor. Still nobody in sight as he used his right hand to push open the door of Room 109.

In the green glow of the life-support machines, he could make out a single heavily bandaged figure lying propped halfway up in bed. As he started to step into the room, he glanced to his left and caught sight of a long black cape hanging on the wall. His breath suddenly lay frozen in his chest. He could feel the bile rising in his stomach. His mouth tasted like sheet metal.

He stood, one foot in the room, the other still in the corridor, when a voice said, "Excuse me." Startled, Ramón turned quickly toward the sound. A thick little Japanese guy, looked like a doctor: all in blue, stethoscope flopped up over one shoulder, wearing a fruity-looking shower-cap thing.

"Wrong room," Ramón said with a smile.

"You better check in at the nurses' station," he said. "This is the ICU. We can't have you wandering around in here."

Ramón pulled his foot out of the door and then pointed down the hall to his right.

The guy nodded. "Right down there," he said.

"Thanks."

Ramón kept the smile plastered to his face as he sauntered along. Fifty feet ahead the bright lights of the nurses' station washed across the dim corridor. He checked back over his shoulder. The nosy Jap doctor man was back at the corner checking up on him. He could hear voices ahead.

The red-sweater nurse looked up. "Can I help you?"

"Loooking por maternity," Ramón said, with a thick Cuban accent.

The nurse straightened up and came rustling out from behind the desk. "You're lost," she said. "Maternity's on the ninth floor. Come with me."

As she took Ramón by the elbow, the writer man looked up and made a flicker of eye contact. Ramón didn't like what he saw. Something hard. Something sure. Not the usual tourist bravado. The guy was a player.

Unnerved, he stumbled slightly as he walked up the hall toward the pair of elevators along the left wall. She pushed the UP button, and immediately the silver door on the left slid open with a *bing*. Ramón kept smiling as she shepherded him inside and then reached in and pushed 9. "There you go," Nursie said.

Ramón resisted the urge to stop the elevator. To get off and hurry back to the street. No. Just be cool. Nursie seemed like the kind of bitch gonna stand there and make sure the car went to 9. Ramón did not wish to be remembered.

Hospital elevators are built for comfort, not for speed. A full five minutes passed before Ramón stepped back out onto Ninth Avenue. A thick icy drizzle hissed on the awning above his head. Gerardo and the car were nowhere in sight. To the north, the lights of a red-and-white fire department aid car tore circles in the darkness, as the crew rushed a gurney into the emergency room. Ramón jammed his hands into his pants pockets, nodded at the security guard, and hustled north, toward the puddles of darkness beneath skeletal oak trees.

He was half a block past the oaks when Gerardo swung the Mercedes around the corner of Ninth and Madison and began coming his way. He heard the door locks pop as the car slid to a stop in front of him and then heard the noise again as he slid into the seat.

"What now?" Gerardo asked.

The radio was on the Spanish-language channel, Música del Mundo. A soft samba spilled from the speakers. "I don't know," Ramón said.

For a moment, Gerardo stopped breathing. He squinted at Ramón in the darkness. Turned the radio off. Something was bad wrong. Ramón always knew what to do next. Gerardo swallowed some air and waited.

"We got problems," Ramón said.

"Like?"

"Like that girl who crashed her car is still alive. In the hospital. That's who he's visiting in there."

"What's the writer guy got to do with her?"

"I haven't got a fuckin' clue," Ramón said. "It's like he's got the eye on us or something."

Gerardo scowled. Lifted his hands from the wheel. "You said you seen her head come clean off."

"I did," Ramón said with a shrug. "Musta not been bad as it looked."

"That's not good. She seen us both."

"No shit," said Ramón. He slipped into his seat belt. "Let's get outa here."

"What about the writer guy?"

"Fuck him," said Ramón. "We gotta decide what to do, man. Things are gettin' outa hand here."

15

Thursday, October 19   9:29 a.m.

His name was Crispin, Edward J. Or at least that's what the name tag said. HARBORVIEW MEDICAL CENTER, PATIENT SERVICES REPRESENTATIVE. "I'm telling you, Mr.—"

"Corso."

"We quite literally don't have a room for her."

"Find one."

"You don't understand," he huffed. "We've already pushed her surgery back to Saturday morning in hopes that a room would free up." He shrugged. "As we speak, I still don't have a single post-op room available. Not one." He got to his feet and put a chubby hand on Corso's shoulder. "Providence can operate this afternoon. They've got plenty of space. She'll be quite happy with the service there."

Corso's eyes were cast to the side, staring down at the dimpled knuckles gripping his shoulder. Edward J. Crispin got the message and retrieved his hand. Thus chastened, he pulled his collection of chins down onto his chest and went all official.

"The space issue notwithstanding, Mr. Corso, and as much as it pains me to be forced to deal with such pedestrian issues as finances at a time like this"—he reached down and thumbed open a bright green folder; his overworked cardiovascular system had painted a bright red spot on each of his cheeks—"as of this morning, not including today"—he peeked down at his desk—"the charges for ser-vices total seventy-one thousand three hundred sixty-five dollars and thirty-three cents." He flicked the folder shut. "Plus tax."

Corso dropped a Visa card onto the folder. "Pay the bill," he said. "Start a tab for further charges."

Crispin made a rude noise with his lips. "If you do the math, sir, you'll find that liability possibilities could run"—he pursed his lips—"halfway to seven figures." He gave the figure a moment to sink in. "With all due respect, Mr. Corso, credit limits don't go that high."

"Why don't you run the card and see," Corso suggested.

Edward J. compressed his lips and jabbed a finger at the phone. "Alice, come in here for a moment, please." Almost immediately, the white louvered door behind him opened. She was maybe twenty. A mouth breather, wearing a white blouse under a blue denim jumper. Her black wiry hair was held at bay by a pair of tor-toiseshell hair clips. "Yes, Mr. Crispin."

He passed her the folder and the credit card and then leaned over and whispered in her ear. He waited until the door clicked closed before turning his attention back to Corso.

"You don't have to do this, you know. It's not like we're going to put her out in the street. Anyone and

everyone who comes to us gets the very best we have
to offer, regardless of their ability to pay, but we do try,
in cases such as this, to spread the liability around a
bit, if you catch my drift. Providence is a fully accred-
ited hospital. It's—"

"I want her to stay here."

He was about to start back on his spiel when his
phone buzzed. He picked up the receiver and listened.
"If you'll excuse me for a moment," he said, before
disappearing through the door. Corso could hear the
hiss of whispers but couldn't pick up the words.

Another minute and Crispin reappeared. He leaned
over and set the card and an invoice in front of Corso.
With a flourish, he pulled a pen from his coat pocket.
"If you'd just sign at the X, Mr. Corso."

Corso signed his name. "You'll keep her where she
is until you have a room for her."

Crispin did something midway between a shrug and
a nod. "We'll put something together," he said tentatively. He busied himself with tearing off the perfo-
rated strips and handing Corso a copy of the bill.
"We'll make it work," he said.

"That's the spirit," Corso said, as he left the room.

Corso took the stairs. He jogged one flight up to
ground level, then wormed his way through the lobby
congestion and out the main exit onto Ninth Avenue. A
gray sky swirled overhead as he stretched his long legs
out, crossing Ninth diagonally, swiveling through the
traffic until he eased up onto the opposite sidewalk and
began moving steadily north.

Three blocks up, at Madison, he turned left down
the steep hill. The breeze from the sound carried smells
of salt and seaweed. Half a block down, the Madison

Renaissance Hotel slid into view, its colorful flags stiff in the breeze. Another block and the federal courthouse slipped out from behind the Sorrento Hotel, its bleak plebeian facade black against the roiling gray sky.

The media horde had fallen into its feeding rhythm. This morning, Warren Klein held court at the back door. A knot of reporters jockeyed for position along the police barriers, as Corso crossed the freeway and approached the melee from the rear.

As Klein stepped up to the microphones, the clouds suddenly split, bathing the back of the courthouse in soft fall sunshine. Renee Rogers and Raymond Butler stood leaning against the building, squinting into the glare.

Corso could hear questions being shouted as he showed his ID to the nearest cop and ducked under the barrier. Klein's face was scrunched into a knot, and he was shading his eyes with his hand.

"Provided we're not faced with any undue delays—and I must say that, thus far in the trial, Judge Howell is moving the proceeding along with great dispatch—I'd hazard a guess that we'll have the case in the hands of the jury by the middle of next week."

Corso slid along the wall until he was rubbing shoulders with Renee Rogers.

"Warren's gonna look like a mole on TV," Rogers whispered.

"Not real media savvy, is he?" Corso said.

"He's hired a media consultant," Butler said. "To help polish his image, he says."

Corso couldn't hear the question, but whatever it was it got Klein started on his daily spiel about how it was an open-and-shut case. He was going to set up a foundation of extortion and negligence. He was going to prove Nicholas Balagula's connection to a maze of companies responsible for the construction of Fairmont Hospital, and, most important, he would tie Nicholas Balagula directly to the plan to fake core sample results and other test data.

Renee Rogers leaned over and whispered in Corso's ear, "You may be getting some company in the courtroom." Corso raised an eyebrow. "Both Seattle newspapers are suing for the right to be present at the trial. The Second Circuit Court is going to take it up this afternoon."

"And?"

"And recent decisions have been coming down on the side of the media."

"Klein doesn't seem worried."

"Warren thinks the sunshine was arranged," Butler said.

They shared a quiet laugh. Corso closed his eyes and languished, the warmth of the sun melting on his cheeks.

"You find out anything about what happened to your friend?" Rogers asked. When he opened his eyes, she was studying his face as if it were a road map.

"Nothing that makes any sense," Corso replied. "I made some calls. The guy in the truck was a janitor for a local school district. Lived in a ratty little apartment down in the south end. The guy was so amorphous nobody even reported him missing."

"Really?"

"And that's not the good part."

"Oh?"

"Before somebody went to all the trouble of burying him and the truck, they shot him nine times." Corso looked over at Rogers and their eyes met. "With three different guns. Five of the shots postmortem."

Rogers whistled softly. "Curiouser and curiouser."

"Lotta anger there," Butler offered. "It's usually a family member who gets that pissed off."

"I've got a line on an ex-wife," Corso said. "I'm going to follow up on it this afternoon."

Klein was separating himself from the crowd. "I hope to God this thing is as cut and dried as Klein thinks it is," Corso said.

Rogers and Butler made faces at each other. "Next couple days will tell the tale," Butler said. "We've got our expert witnesses. Elkins has got his own expert witnesses." He shrugged. "A lot's going to depend on what shakes out in there. Balagula's done a great job of insulating himself from his business enterprises." He waggled a hand. "It's touch and go." He looked over at Renee Rogers as if seeking agreement.

She picked her briefcase up from the sidewalk. "Much as it pains me to say it, Raymond, if I had to bet I'd bet Warren is probably going to luck out."

Corso broke out in a grin.

"What's so funny?" Rogers demanded.

"I was thinking how somebody once said that we have to believe in luck, or else there's no way to explain the success of people we don't like," he said.

She laughed and followed Ray Butler up the short length of sidewalk toward Warren Klein and the thick pair of brass doors. Corso stood and watched them file inside. Above the buzz of the crowd, a voice called his name and then another. Absentmindedly, he turned toward the crowd and found himself staring into the lens of a TV camera. He only said one word. One was all it took to stay off the evening news.

Thursday, October 19   1:51 p.m.

"Dr. Goldman, would you please provide the court with a brief description of your present academic position?"

Dr. Hiram Goldman was perfect: just this side of sixty, aging but not elderly, with a big shock of white hair combed back from a billboard forehead. He coughed into his hand and said, "I currently hold the position of executive director of the National Information Service for Earthquake Engineering."

"And your offices are located where?" Klein asked.

"At the University of California at Berkeley."

"And how far is that from the site of the Fairmont Hospital?"

"Approximately thirty miles."

Elkins was on his feet, wearing his bored face. "Your Honor, the defense will stipulate as to the witness's expertise in the area of seismology and earthquake engineering."

Judge Howell gave a cursory bang of the gavel. "So stipulated," he said.

Warren Klein shuffled through his notes for a moment before continuing. "Dr. Goldman, for the sake of the jury could you give us a brief"—he looked over his shoulder at the jury box—"layman's description of the San Andreas Fault system."

"Certainly," he said. "What is commonly referred to

as the San Andreas Fault is quite simply an eight-hundred-mile crack in the earth's crust."

"Eight hundred miles?"

"It runs northwesterly from the Gulf of California all the way to Cape Mendocino, just north of San Francisco."

"Would it be safe to say, Dr. Goldman—"

Before he could finish the question, Bruce Elkins was on his feet again. "The defense will also stipulate as to the existence of—"

Klein raised his voice. "If Your Honor please, I would like to be permitted to present my case in the manner I see fit."

Now Elkins looked like his feelings were hurt. "I was merely trying to comply with the bench's repeated admonitions regarding undue delays," he said. "Mr. Klein is reinventing the wheel here."

"I don't require his forbearance, Your Honor," Klein complained.

Fulton Howell glared at the lawyers as if they were a pair of unruly schoolboys before waving them up toward the bench. "Approach," was all he said.

Renee Rogers leaned toward Ray Butler, her forehead pleated.

"Since when does Elkins stipulate anything?" she asked.

"Been bothering me all day," Butler said. "I've never seen him this agreeable before."

Renee Rogers turned the other way. On the far side of the courtroom, Nicholas Balagula sat, staring absently off into space, like a snake sunning itself on a rock.

Klein built a case the way a castaway builds a fire:

urgently, but with great care, adding one tiny twig at a time and letting it burn until ready for something bigger, then adding another.

Elkins had, on five separate occasions, offered to stipulate for the record the very avenue of inquiry upon which Klein was at that moment driving. On each occasion, the judge had admonished him for undue delay, reminded him to stop referring to Klein's case as "Earthquake 101," and invited him to sit down.

Klein had been pecking at Dr. Goldman for nearly three hours when he hurried over to the prosecution table and retrieved a document. Renee Rogers got to her feet and took him by the elbow. She leaned over and spoke directly into his ear. "You need to pick up the pace, Warren. They're going to sleep in there," she said, tilting her head toward the jury box. Klein looked over at Butler, who nodded his solemn agreement. Klein heaved a sigh, dropped the document on the desk, and he turned back toward his witness.

"Dr. Goldman . . . how many earthquakes occur in California every year?"

"Certainly thousands. An exact number would be extremely difficult to compute."

"How so?"

"A great many of the shocks are sufficiently small as to escape notice."

"What's the smallest earthquake noticed by humans?"

"Something like a two on the Richter scale."

"For the sake of our jury, Dr. Goldman, could you give us a layman's explanation of the Richter scale?"

"The Richter scale measures the magnitude of an earthquake. The jury needs to know"—he indicated the jury box—"that the Richter scale is logarithmic."

"Which means?"

"A recording of seven, for instance, signifies a disturbance ten times greater than a disturbance of six." Goldman began talking directly to the darkened black panel. "What you on the jury must also understand is the amount of energy released in a seven is *thirty* times greater than that released by a six." Klein opened his mouth to ask another question, but the doctor, unsure as to whether he'd made his point, kept talking. "If you push those figures up one more notch, you get a better idea of how the scale operates. A recording of eight, would be"—he drew in the air with his finger—"thirty times thirty, or *nine hundred times* more powerful than our original reading of six."

Klein gave the jury a minute to do the math, before asking, "So, if anything under a two on the Richter scale is at the lower end of the spectrum, what is the upper end of the spectrum like?"

Hiram Goldman thought it over. "The two largest earthquakes ever recorded happened in 1906 off the coast of Ecuador and Colombia and in 1933 off the east coast of Honshu, Japan. Both were recorded at eight point nine on the Richter scale."

"And in California?"

"The 1906 quake was listed at a magnitude of eight point three."

Klein spoke directly to the jury. "Ladies and gentlemen of the jury, in order to give you some sense of the magnitude of an eight-point-three disturbance, Dr. Goldman has been kind enough to bring along an exhibit from the Library of the University of California at Berkeley."

He turned on his heel and headed for the easel. He

put one hand on the white material that covered the exhibit and whipped it off like a magician producing a rabbit.

Black-and-white photograph. A crowd of people stood along the jagged edge of a road that had been torn in two. To the right of the spectators, risen up to head level, was the continuation of the road, as if the earth had been ripped asunder by some unruly child.

"Dr. Goldman, would you tell the court what it is looking at here?"

"That's a photo from the 1906 earthquake. You're looking at a road that ran across the head of Tomales Bay. The road was offset nearly twenty-one feet."

"Can you explain the forces that caused this to happen?"

"Certainly. In this case, the Pacific plate moved nearly twenty-one feet north of its original position along the North American plate. The scraping together of these two plates is what causes the seismic activity in this region."

"And this was caused by an earthquake of a magnitude of eight point three?"

"Yes."

"How large was the earthquake that destroyed the north wall of Fairmont Hospital?"

"Two point one," he said immediately.

Klein made himself look surprised. "I thought you said anything under two was not noticeable by human beings."

"I did," the doctor said. "It was a murmur, a belch." He waved a hand. "It was hardly noticed at all."

"Other than to the hospital, what was the extent of damage to other surrounding property?"

"None."

Klein did his astonished routine. "How can you be sure of that?"

"Insurance companies run their claims by my department for documentation of the disturbance. As of this date, not a single insurance claim—other than those related to Fairmont Hospital, of course—not a single claim has been filed."

"No further questions," Klein said.

The judge checked his watch. "Cross, Mr. Elkins."

Elkins got to his feet. "I have no questions of this witness," he said.

Bang. "Court's adjourned until nine o'clock tomorrow morning." *Bang.*

16

"How'd you find me anyway?" Marie Hall demanded.

Corso reached into his jacket pocket and came out with the wedding invitation. He slipped the rubber band off, unrolled the picture, and turned it her way. "I went to the church. They sent me to your parents." He shrugged. "The rest is history."

She lived in the top half of a duplex at the south end of Phinney Ridge: a nicely furnished one-bedroom, overlooking an elementary school playground. Everything had color-coordinated ruffles and shams, right out of some decorating book.

She shook her head disgustedly. "I thought it was so romantic to have the invitation picture taken in the Japanese Garden," she said. "Never occurred to me for a minute that Donald picked it because it was free."

She poured herself a cup of coffee, and offered one to Corso, who turned it down.

"Like I told you on the phone, I don't see how I can

help you. I haven't seen or spoken to Donald since the day I walked out."

"When was that?"

"Fourteen months ago."

"Mind telling me why you walked out?"

"The question's not why I left Donald, it's how I managed to live with the guy for seven years. That's the mystery."

"Lotta people feel that way when it's over."

She stared off into space for a moment. "I just couldn't see myself without a man. The idea that I might be something above and beyond my role in a relationship was totally beyond me." She shrugged. "That's why I put up with it for so long. Why I lived like that."

She'd been pretty once: Kewpie-doll lips, nice even features, and a pair of big blue eyes. Somewhere in her mid-thirties and getting thick in the hips. Her shaggy blond hair had grown out brown at the roots and looked like she'd cut it herself.

"Was your former husband abusive?" Corso asked.

She sighed and stirred her coffee. "There's abusive, and there's abusive," she said. "If you mean did he physically assault me, the answer is no." For the first time, she made eye contact with Corso. "But if you're asking me whether or not I'm sorry he's gone, the answer is also no." She waved a hand. "I know how that sounds, and I don't much like it." She kept her gaze locked on Corso. "But there it is."

"If it's any consolation, seems like you have a lot of company who felt that way."

"Why do you say that?"

"Because Donald Barth dropped out of sight for the

better part of three months and nobody even reported him missing."

"Donald wasn't the type to inspire much of anything."

"Why's that?"

"Because he didn't have a life."

"Everybody has a life."

"He went to work; he ate; he slept; he'd screw me twice a week if I let him." She waved a hand. "That was it. If he really wanted to push the envelope, Donald would stop at a convenience store on the way home and buy himself a pint of buttermilk. Buttermilk was Donald's idea of a big time." She read Corso's face. "You think I'm making it up."

Corso held up a hand. "I'm keeping an open mind."

Her expression became almost wistful. "He could be very charming, when he wanted to be. He was better looking than that picture you got." She crossed the bookcase and eased an unframed photograph out from between a tall pair of art books.

He was thinner than in the wedding-invitation picture, with the craggy face of a mountain climber. A thick head of black hair was combed straight back from his forehead. He was smiling with his mouth, while his eyes said they wished they were somewhere else. "Quite the handsome guy," she said, in a practiced tone. "I was twenty-seven when I met Donald. I'd just run away from my first marriage. I was on my own for the first time in my life." She shook her head sadly. "I didn't realize it at the time, but I didn't really have an identity of my own. I was just part of whoever I was connected to."

"We all make mistakes."

"In the beginning, I thought he was saving money . . . so we could buy a house or something like that. So for the first four years or so, I shut up about only owning three dresses. I told myself you had to suffer a little to get what you wanted. Then, when he started giving it away—"

"Giving it to who?"

"Prep schools and then colleges."

She read Corso's confusion and continued. "He's got a son from his first marriage: Robert Downs. He uses his mother's name."

"How many . . . ?"

"I was his third."

"Uh-huh."

"He had this . . . this . . . thing . . . about how Robert had to have it better than he did. Robert had to go to the finest schools and get the best education so he could become a doctor."

"Lotta people feel that way about their kids."

"Yeah, but not like Donald. With him it was like a religion. It didn't matter that we lived in subsidized housing. It didn't matter that he never in seven years went out to lunch with the other guys or that the people where I worked were whispering behind my back about my ragged clothes. Nothing—none of that mattered as long as he could keep the damn tuition paid."

"You worked."

"Same job I've got now—except back then I came home and gave my check to Donald, who promptly sent it off to Harvard or someplace, while we didn't have a television. While we didn't turn on the lights until it was too dark to see." She jabbed at her palm with her index finger. "While we never once in seven years went out to a movie!" She heard the stridency in her voice and looked away. "I know I sound like a bitch, but it's true." She ran a hand through her hair. "I walked out of seven years of slavery with just over fifteen hundred bucks."

"What happened to community property?"

"What property?" she scoffed. "We didn't own anything but a pile of cheap furniture and that beat-up old truck he drove. I took the bus to work." She waved her hand around the room. "This might not be the Ritz, Mr. Corso, but it's way better than anything Donald Barth ever provided for me."

She was right. Her apartment and its carefully chosen contents were far newer and far grander than the rubble Donald Barth had left behind. She thrust her chin at Corso. "I'm halfway to my accounting degree. I've been going nights to Seattle Central. Unlike my ex-husband, I've got plans for the future," she said.

Corso leaned back in the chair and folded his arms across his chest. "So I guess you can't think of any reason why somebody would want to murder your ex-husband."

"The only person with a reason to murder Donald Barth was me."

Corso gave her a small smile. "What finally gave you the courage to leave?"

She turned away. "No one thing. It just sort of happened. I got so I couldn't stand being in the same room with him. About six months before we separated, I cut him off. " She fixed Corso in her gaze, as if defying him to take issue with her. "That's the only time I ever thought he might get violent. He told me I was his wife and had an obligation to take care of his needs." She laughed a bitter laugh. "Can you imagine that? Like we had a contract or something." She sighed. "Next thing I know he's not coming home after work. I start getting these phone calls that hang up." She got to her feet and crossed the room. "I moved into a women's shelter." When she turned back toward Corso, her eyes were wet. "You know what?" she asked.

"What?"

"He never even came looking for me. Never tried to talk me into coming back. Not once. He just went on with his life."

"You think he had a girlfriend while you were still married?"

"I'm sure of it. Donald wasn't about to go without his Monday and Thursday screw."

"If he had a regular girlfriend, you'd think she'd have noticed his absence."

She laughed. "I said Donald liked sex; I didn't say he was any good at it."

A smile from Corso seemed to encourage her.

"What Donald liked best about sex was that it was free."

17

Thursday, October 19   6:36 p.m.

"**H**e ain't got a clue," Gerardo said.
"Why's that?"

" 'Cause he's back here again. He had a clue, he wouldn't be comin' to the same place twice."

"Hmm," was all Ramón said.

They were parked a half mile north of the Briarwood Garden Apartments, backed out onto the dike that defined the north end of the marsh.

"He's spinnin' his wheels," Gerardo insisted.

"How'd he put the girl and the truck guy together?"

Gerardo shrugged. "What's it matter?"

"It matters because we're not clean on this thing until we figure it out. There's something . . . some connection he's following here we don't understand, and as long as he's following some trail we can't see, we got big problems."

"We never shoulda lied about the guy in the truck," Gerardo said.

Ramón could feel the anger burning in his cheeks. They'd been through it fifty times. He spoke through clenched teeth. "What fucking difference did it make? We shot him; some other asshole shot him. Makes no goddamn difference. Either way, him and the truck end up in the hill and then come sliding out on their own, and we gotta pop the Ball guy. Don't matter a rat's ass who done the work. All that other shit happens anyway."

"Nothin' been right since we done it," Gerardo said. "It's like the whole damn world's out of balance or something."

"Then we better spend our time figuring out what trail he's following, huh?" He looked over at Gerardo, who was slouched down behind the wheel with his lips pressed tight.

"Or maybe we just cut his trail and be done with it," Gerardo offered. "I'm startin' to think maybe that's the way to make things right again."

Ramón gave the smallest of nods. "Could be," he said. "Could be."

"I'm tellin' you."

"I'm listening."

"So?"

"So tonight we don't lose him. Tonight, we find out where he lives."

Thursday, October 19   7:16 p.m.

The Briarwood consisted of eight one-story four-plexes, built in the form of a square: two buildings to a side, facing outward, away from one another, with the parking lot in the middle. Only the bedroom and bathroom windows looked out over the lot.

Figuring Barth and the truck had to have been abducted from somewhere and that the Briarwood parking lot was as good a bet as any, Corso had decided to knock on doors, hoping maybe somebody had seen or heard something useful. No such luck.

Third or fourth door, the Somali family had invited him in and let him take a look around. That's when he knew he was screwed. The way the apartments were laid out, there was absolutely no reason to be looking out at the parking lot. Matter of fact, if you wanted to look out the bedroom window, you had to stand on the bed; if you wanted to look out the bathroom window, you had to stand on the toilet—which was where his hopes rested as he approached 2D, the apartment where Donald Barth had lived.

Probably a dozen residents hadn't answered their doors. Some of the apartments were dark and empty. In others, the sounds of shuffling feet or labored breathing had told him someone was there but was not opening the door. On several occasions he'd been told to go away . The only real speed bump was a guy on the ground floor of F building, who'd opened the door wearing a ripped T-shirt with spaghetti stains all over the front, a pair of plaid boxer shorts, and black socks. "What?" he growled from around the unlit cigar butt wedged in the corner of his mouth. "You got business with me, pretty boy?"

Corso started to answer, but the guy cut him off.

" 'Cause if you don't, and if you're trying to sell me some shit I don't want, I just might have to kick your ass."

He was about forty, almost as wide as he was tall, his cheeks sporting three days' worth of stubble. His arms and shoulders were covered with a carpet of curly black hair, thick enough to hide the skin below.

Behind him, the TV was blaring what had to be a porno movie. Bad jazz and a lot of oooing and aahing. "Oh, yeah, baby; don't stop; don't stop . . . that's it. . . ." Corso was at an angle to the screen. From where he stood the picture looked a lot like a bilge pump operating at high speed.

"I'm not selling anything," Corso said.

"What then?" the guy demanded.

Corso told him. The shrill TV voice was now demanding it harder and deeper.

"The guy over there?" The guy nodded toward D building.

"Yeah," Corso said.

"Before my time," he said. "He was gone by the time I got here. Once in a while, I talk to the old bat who lives in One-D, next door to him. I seen her yesterday. She told me all about how the cops was by and all. You talk to her yet?"

The frenzy on the TV had reached a peak. Either the room had spontaneously ignited or everybody involved was about to get their jollies at the same time.

"Talk to her. She's got nothing to do but mind everybody's business." He looked back over his shoulder. "Getting to the good part now," he said with a leer. For the first time he smiled, exhibiting a row of thick yellow teeth. "Unless maybe you want to come in for a while, pretty boy." He hefted and then dropped the package beneath his boxers.

Corso declined, turned quickly, and began striding away.

"Don't be shy," the guy rasped at his back. "Ya gotta

find your inner self." Gruff laughter followed Corso up the sidewalk and around the corner, like a pack of dogs.

A plywood ramp and a low metal hand rail had been built over the stairs to 1D, rendering the apartment wheelchair-accessible. He tried the bell but didn't hear anything, so he knocked. A little brass plate screwed to the door read KILBURN. Corso knocked again. From inside the apartment came the shuffle of feet and the clink of metal.

A bright white halogen light above the stairs tore a hole in the darkness and reduced Corso to squinting and shading his eyes with one hand. The door opened a crack.

"Whadda you want?" a voice said from the darkness. "We don't allow solicitors here."

"I'm not selling anything."

"Does Mr. Pov know you're here?"

"I know Mr. Pov," Corso hedged.

"What's his first name?"

"Nhim," Corso answered. "Mr. Nhim Pov."

The door closed and then, after a moment, opened all the way. She had to be ninety. Coke-bottle glasses. Thick silver hair in an old-fashioned pageboy cut. She held the doorknob in one hand and a golf club in the other.

"What do you want?"

"I'm looking into the death of Donald Barth. The man who lived in the apartment next door, up until a few months back."

She eyed him closely. "You another cop?"

"I'm a writer."

She peered up at Corso for a minute. "You're the one writes those crime books."

"Yes, ma'am. Frank Corso."

"Seen you on the tube a couple of times."

"That's me," Corso said.

She stepped aside. "Well, don't be standing out there like an idiot, come in."

She ushered Corso onto a threadbare green sofa. The floor was covered with twice as much furniture as the room called for, leaving nothing but plastic-covered trails winding among the furnishings. Wasn't the decor, however, that caught Corso's eye. It was the walls, nearly every inch of them was covered with framed photographs.

She used the golf club as a cane as she sat down in the brown recliner opposite the couch. "I lived too damn long," she said.

"Excuse me?"

"I said I lived too damn long. Had six children and outlived every damn one of them. Had sixteen grand-children and outlived five of them too."

Corso considered saying he was sorry to hear it but rejected the idea.

"It's not right to outlive everybody who cares about you. It's unnatural." She waved the golf club in the air. "You ever see those commercials on the TV? About how one a these days everybody gonna be able to live to a hundred?"

"Yes, ma'am, I have."

"Well you tell 'em you met Delores Kilburn and she says the whole idea's not all it's cracked up to be."

"I will," he assured her.

"Cops was here the other day."

"So I hear."

"I'll tell you the same thing I told them. I lived next

to that pair for five years and never said more that ten words to either of them." The club waved again. "Some of the most unfriendliest people I ever met. So if you're looking for some kind of inside dirt, I'm here to tell you, you come to the wrong place."

She looked at her hand and realized she was still brandishing the golf club. She groaned slightly as she turned around in the chair and leaned it against the wall.

"Poor Mr. Pov's had enough trouble for three lifetimes."

"You mean like being in a refugee camp and all?"

"That and everything else." She leaned forward in the chair. "Lost almost his entire family over there in Cambodia, you know." She drew a finger across her throat. "Slaughtered by that Pol Pot guy and the Khmer Rouge. Just killed 'em all. His wife and kids, his parents, all of 'em. Just like that."

"A terrible tragedy," Corso offered.

"And then his sister's death." She waved a hand. "It's a wonder to me the man could find the strength to go on."

"Going on is what people do best. It's why there's so many of us running around the planet."

"After all those years. After all the struggle. And to have it end like that."

"What happened?"

"You haven't heard?"

"No, ma'am."

She checked the room, as if looking for eavesdroppers. "Took poor Mr. Pov nearly ten years to get his sister Lily over here from Cambodia. All kinda red tape about how they wouldn't let her go and then how

America wouldn't let her in . . . and all the money he had to spend and all."

"And?"

"And he had everything set up. Had her a husband and everything. Nice Cambodian man from Seward Park. Owns a grocery. Drives a nice new Lincoln."

"I take it the wedding didn't come off."

Her eyes narrowed. "She killed herself. Hanged herself in the laundry room."

"Any idea why?"

She thought it over. "Lily was much younger than Mr. Pov. More Americanized." She shrugged. "Who knows why those people do things? Live in a whole other world than the rest of us. Got their own idea of right and wrong that don't make a stick of sense to folks like you and me. They come over here to live, but they're not like us." A light flickered in her eyes. She stopped. "Don't mean to come off as prejudiced or anything. I was right down there with the rest of them at the Cambodian church or whatever they call it, right there on Rainier Avenue, for the funeral." She looked up at Corso. "Had a hell of a turnout. Mr. Pov's a bigwig in the local Cambodian community, you know. Musta been five hundred people there." She shook a finger at Corso. "And I'll tell you one thing, Mr. Writer. Those Asians treat an old woman like me a lot better that Americans do. Found me a seat right in the front row. Treated me like I was gold, they did."

Corso stifled a sigh. "About Mr. and Mrs. Barth."

"He had her buffaloed. You could see it in her face. Like a deer in the headlights. Afraid of every damn thing she saw. I'd say hello, and she'd just stammer something and turn away, like she was ashamed or something."

Corso got to his feet. "Thanks for your trouble," he said.

She held out a hand. Corso stepped over, took her hand, and pulled her up from the chair. "You tell 'em Delores Kilburn says old age is overrated."

"I will," Corso assured her.

Corso stood on the front steps and listened to the locks snap behind him. Overhead, the moon floated high in the sky, ducking in and out of a jigsaw of thick black clouds. Corso warmed his hands in his coat pockets as he walked the length of the sidewalk and turned left, back into the center of the complex.

He rang the bell. "Coming," the voice said from inside.

A moment later, the door opened and Nhim Pov stood in his doorway.

"Ah," he said. "Mr. Corso."

Corso fished Donald Barth's wedding invitation from his pants pocket.

"I wanted to return this," he said.

"Thank you," the little man said. "But perhaps you would like to return it yourself." His eyes crinkled at Corso's momentary confusion. "His son is here. He's down at the shed right now."

18

Thursday, October 19   7:07 p.m.

Corso leaned against the wall and watched as Robert Downs sorted through the remnants of his father's life. He was a tall thin young man, with a full head of lank brown hair that was going to be gone before he saw forty. The single overhead bulb sent his shadow lurching over the walls and ceiling as he pawed through the dozen cardboard boxes.

Ten minutes later, Downs sat on the patched plastic couch with his head bent forward and his hands hanging down between his knees. "It's not much, is it?"

"I guess he had all he needed," Corso offered.

"Not a scrap of paper—" he began.

"Cops probably took all the paperwork."

Downs tapped his temple. "Of course. I'm not thinking very clearly," he said.

"You've had quite a shock."

Downs looked around, as if seeing the place for the first time. "The manager, Mr. . . . ."

"Pov," Corso said.

"Yes. Mr. Pov showed me the apartment he lived in.

There's an old woman living in there now, but she said it was okay."

"Nice of her."

"It was . . . it wasn't what I expected."

"Your father led a simple life."

"I had no idea. His letters always said he was in building maintenance."

"He was."

Robert Downs ran a well-manicured hand through his lank hair. "But I always assumed it was . . . somehow . . ." He searched for a phrase, didn't find anything suitable, and gave up.

"Something a bit more grandiose," Corso suggested.

Downs nodded. "Like he had his own firm or something."

"When was the last time you saw your father?"

"You mean like in person?" He read Corso's expression. "A couple of times he sent a videotape for Christmas, and I saw him that way."

"In the flesh."

"When I was eleven. He lived in southern California then. I went out to LA for two weeks. He took me to Disneyland. He had a nice apartment in Santa Monica, just a few blocks off the beach."

"What year was that?"

"Nineteen eighty-one."

"Long time."

Downs agreed. "My mother was bitter," he said. "She'd have preferred I never saw him again."

"What was she bitter about?"

"She always claimed he fooled around on her."

"I take it they didn't correspond?"

"Oh, no," he said. "I was six or seven before she

even admitted I had a father and that he was alive on the West Coast somewhere." He rolled his eyes. "It took me three years to get her to send me to California." He looked around again and jammed his hands into his pockets. "How could he live in a place like this?"

"His ex-wife says it's because he was sending all his money away to keep you in college and medical school."

His face was the color of ashes. "I had no idea he was living this way," he complained to the ceiling. "Those apartments . . . they're hovels." He stepped over to the storage unit and pawed at an open box of housewares. "I mean, look at the man's dishes." He gestured with the back of his hand. "This is it?" he demanded, of nobody in particular. "*This* is the total of a man's life, some broken-down furniture and a few cardboard boxes?"

Something in his tone annoyed Corso. "So then, if you'd known he was living in poverty, you'd have sent him his money back and enrolled in the state university?"

Downs's eyes narrowed. He opened his mouth to defend himself and then changed his mind. The muscles along his jawline rippled like snakes. He cupped his face in his long fingers and stayed that way for quite a while.

"You're right," he said finally. "I was being a first-class asshole, wasn't I? I mean, who the hell am I to be judging him? After everything he did for me . . . everything he gave up . . . and here I am, standing around judging the quality of the guy's life like I'm Martha Stewart or something."

Downs turned away from Corso and leaned his forehead against the chain link. He took several deep breaths and then began to cry. Corso watched until the shaking of his shoulders stopped; then he stepped into the storage area, found a roll of paper towels, and tore off a couple.

It took Robert Downs a few minutes to put himself back together. He honked three times into a towel and dropped it onto the floor.

"Why would anybody want to kill my father?" he asked.

"I was hoping you could tell me."

"The police called me yesterday morning."

"Where were you?"

"Boston. I live in Boston." He retrieved the other paper towel from his pants pocket and wiped his nose. "They asked me what I wanted done with the body." He looked to Corso, as if for forgiveness. "They had to say his name twice before I realized who it was they were talking about. That it was my father who was dead. And that I was . . . that nobody else had come forward for his remains."

"You know the details?" Corso asked.

"They said he was found in his truck. Buried in a hillside."

"Shot."

"That's what they said."

"My source says the medical examiner's office is going to report nine bullet wounds from three different weapons."

"That doesn't make any sense."

"No, it doesn't," Corso agreed. "None of this makes any sense."

They stood in silence. Somewhere out in the parking lot a car engine shuddered to a stop. A car door closed. They listened as the sound of footsteps faded to black.

"You going back to Boston?" Corso asked.

Downs wandered around in a circle, as if confused. "I'm . . . I mean, I was. . . ." He looked at his watch. "I'm getting married in three weeks," he said absently, then reached inside his sport jacket and came out with an airline ticket. "I've got a flight back in the morning, but I think . . . I think I'm going to stay for a while."

"Might not be a good idea for you to be mucking about in this," Corso said.

"Why's that?"

Corso told Downs about Dougherty.

"And you think what happened to your friend was a result of her looking into my father's death?"

"Yeah, I do."

"How could—"

"I have no idea," Corso interrupted. "But I'm going to keep turning over rocks until something crawls out."

"I can't just leave," Downs said. "I don't know why, but I can't. It's like I found something and lost it all at the same time." He looked to Corso for agreement. "You know what I mean?"

Corso said he did. He remembered his own father's army trunk with the big brass padlock, how his father kept it stored under a tarp in the garage rafters. In the years after he returned from the war, he'd opened it only once, when a friend from his army days had stopped by one hot August afternoon. They sat together all day, stripped down to their undershirts, sweating together in that stifling oven of a garage, talking quietly and looking at pictures. Together they drank a whole bottle of whiskey and then, late in the afternoon, they'd put their heads together and cried.

He could still hear the dry crack of the wood when, the day after his father's death, he'd torn the hasp off with a crowbar and rolled back the lid. He could still feel the stinging of his cheeks as he tried to ignore his guilt—the terrible guilt—about the sense of relief he'd felt when the VA doctor told them his father had passed away. About how his first thought hadn't been about the loss of a father or its effect on those he loved but had, instead, been about the trunk in the rafters and how now, in death, he might solve the riddle of his father in some fashion that had not been possible in life.

"It's a high-profile case. The cops are giving it the full treatment."

"That's what they said." Downs waved a hand. "There's nothing I can do, I know that. But . . . somehow . . . for some reason I don't understand, I can't go back to Boston until I try to sort things out here. Does that sound crazy?"

"Yeah, it does," Corso said. "But sometimes life's like that."

Robert Downs ran his hands through his hair. "I don't know where to begin."

"Maybe I can help you there."

"What do you mean?"

"You have a car?"

"Sure. A rental Chevy."

"Then start with the cops," Corso said. "Contrary to rumor, they're real good at what they do. Go see them first thing in the morning. See what they've come up with so far. While you're there, get a copy of your father's financial records."

Downs started to ask a question, but Corso cut him off. "If it's not about sex, it's probably about money."

"But my father didn't have a—"

"Let's eliminate the obvious, and then we can work from there."

"Okay." Downs sighed. "First the police."

"Get an official death certificate," Corso said. "Somewhere down the line you're going to need it."

"Then?"

Corso reached into his pants pocket and pulled out a business card.

"When you get that done, call me and we'll go down to the school district where he worked."

"Oh, listen, you don't have to. . . . I didn't mean to—"

Corso held up a moderating hand. "Mr. Downs," he said, "if you knew me at all, you'd know my offer's got nothing to do with charity. With you or without you, I'm going to find out what happened to my friend and why." He turned the hand palm up. "If, somewhere in the process, I can help you to come to grips with a father you never knew, all the better. What's true is that I think you can be of use to me."

"How so?"

"You've got the bona fides. You're his son and heir. The cops are going to give and tell you things they wouldn't tell anybody else. School districts are the most clamped-down, tight-mouthed organizations in the world. Other than admitting that somebody did indeed work for them, they generally won't divulge a thing."

"What makes you think they might know something worthwhile?"

"Your father spent a third of his life at work. As far as I'm concerned, that makes it a one-in-three chance that whatever your father got mixed up in was work-related."

"But what about . . . I mean, I saw it on TV. You're covering that gangster trial, aren't you?"

"Tomorrow's the day they try to tie Balagula to his businesses. Eight hours of charts and graphs, all of which I've seen before. If I'm going to miss a morning, tomorrow's the one."

"I don't know what to say."

"Good."

Thursday, October 19   8:21 p.m.

Lake Union lay flat and still, its surface gleaming like black oil beneath the full moon. Corso felt the unseen eyes the minute he got out of the car. He slowed down, allowing his vision to adjust to the darkness as he scoured the shadows for movement, looking for that slight vibration of line that separates blood from blackness. He whistled softly as he walked back up the line of cars toward the street. A Metro bus hissed by on Fairview Avenue, its bold advertising placards inviting folks to visit the Experience Music Project. Nobody between the cars. Nobody out on the sidewalk. He walked over and checked along the fenceline. Nothing.

He gave an exaggerated shrug, lengthened his stride, and began walking quickly back toward the dock. And then stopped dead, held his breath, listened. No doubt about it: He heard the click of heels. He was still working on what to do next when the sound of voices snapped his head around.

They were coming up from C dock. In the dim purple light, they seemed almost to emerge from the asphalt as they climbed the ramp to ground level. It was the couple from *Grisswold*, a Hans Christian forty-seven, about a quarter of the way down the dock. Marla and Steve Something-or-other from Gig Harbor. They used the boat maybe twice a year. When he'd left this morning, they been standing on the dock with Marty Kroll. Looked like Marty'd been giving them an estimate on refinishing the brightwork.

Marla tried to work up a smile and failed. "Hi, Frank," she said. She was pushing fifty. Tall and dark, she moved with a girlish grace that belied her years.

"Hey, how's it going?" Corso said.

"It's *going* to cost the better part of fifteen grand," Steve growled.

Steve was a big beefy specimen, red-faced and loud. Prone to sandals and Hawaiian shirts regardless of the weather. He sold something.

"Without new sails," Marla added.

"Which is *at least* another ten." Steve said.

Sympathizing about the cost of boat repairs with other owners was de rigueur. Especially on those fateful days when day-trippers find out why you can't let sailboats sit around for years.

"Those kinda boat units will kill you," Corso said.

"I'm gonna put her up for sale," Steve announced. Over Steve's shoulder, Corso thought he saw movement among the dark pillars that supported the marina office.

"We'll still have to do the work," Marla said. "And we won't have the boat."

Steve looked to Corso. "Whoever buys it's gonna want a survey," Corso said. "She's right. Nobody's going to give them a loan unless everything's in order."

"Shit," Steve spit out into the night air.

Marla tugged at his elbow. "Come on, honey. We'll get a bite and you'll feel better."

"Better be Burger King or something cheap," Steve grumbled as she moved him along. "I just wanted a place we could stay in the city," he groused. "Hell, we coulda flown over. Stayed at the Four Seasons. We coulda . . ."

Corso had seen it before, but it was always a little sad to see a grown man finally come to understand the folly of boat ownership. He wondered if Steve had ever uttered the much used line about how a boat is a hole into which you throw money. Now he knew what all real boaters know. Every minute of every day, your boat is rotting away beneath you, and all you can hope to accomplish, with all the sandpaper and Cetol, the brass polish and bottom paint, is an uneasy stalemate with the elements.

He watched as they got into a gray Cadillac Seville, backed out into the lot, and drove off. He stood still for another moment, waiting until the Cadillac's taillights were nothing but a red smear at the end of Fairview Avenue, before he turned and started down the ramp.

He used his key on the lock and then let the spring swing it shut with a dull *clank*. The line of boats sat silent and slack in the water as he hurried toward *Salt-*

heart, moored at the far end. He was halfway there when his hands, as if acting on their own, reached to raise his collar, and he realized that once again he could feel unknown eyes on his back.

19

She'd become the body electric. A flesh-and-blood software application. An extension cord for millennial medicine. Her heart reduced to a series of green electronic waves, her brain functions to a skittering red line on a bright white screen, her lungs to the rise and fall of a small black bellows. Tubes going in, tubes coming out, everything stimulating, and simulating, and yet she lay as still as death, her fingers relaxed, her eyes motionless beneath the lids.

Corso found himself thinking funeral thoughts. About the nature of life and how precious little what we call *the body* has to do with the person we are. How the body is little more than a container for the spark that makes us alive, that makes us unique, that makes us divine, and is ultimately no more meaningful or permanent than the red velvet box that delivers the diamond ring.

The soft *whoosh* of the door diverted his attention: the day nurse, a tall no-name-tag no-nonsense African-American woman of maybe thirty-five.

"There's a young man upstairs," she began.

"The boyfriend?"

She nodded. "He seems to feel—"

"Yeah," Corso said. "I know. I'll be going."

"He objects to you being here."

"We got off to a bad start," Corso said. "He'll get over it." He fetched his coat from the foot of the bed and shouldered his way into it. "You've got my number?"

"Yes, sir. Both Ms. Taylor and Mr. Crispin were very explicit. Any change in Ms. Dougherty's condition, you're to be notified immediately."

The look in her eyes said she was vaguely annoyed by the extra instructions and wanted to know what the hoopla was about.

"Thanks," Corso said. "I appreciate it."

She headed for the bed, Corso for the door. In the hall, he turned right and made for the elevators at the far end of the corridor. At the moment he pushed the UP button his cellular phone rang softly in his pocket. He pulled it out, raised the antenna.

"Corso."

"Mr. Corso, it's Robert Downs."

"Where are you?"

Downs told him.

"You're finished with the cops?"

Downs said he was.

Corso gave him directions to the hospital. "I'll meet you out front," he said.

Friday, October 20   10:53 a.m.

C orso shuffled through the pile of papers in his lap.
Pulled out a 1040 form.

"Last year, your father made thirty-seven thousand dollars." He pointed out over the dashboard. "Take the next exit. Stay left."

Downs put on his turn signal and moved to the right lane, running up the steep exit ramp onto Martin Luther King Way South. Doubling back over the freeway, running south alongside the northbound freeway.

"Thirty-seven thousand dollars netted him just over two thousand dollars a month." Corso shuffled some more papers. "From what I can see, he lived on eight hundred and spent the other twelve on your education."

Downs swallowed hard but kept his eyes on the road. Corso found a bank statement. "At the time of his death, he had a hundred thirty-nine dollars in his savings account." Corso scanned the bottom of the form. "His average savings account balance for the past two years is one hundred fifty-three dollars and twelve cents."

"I don't understand," Robert Downs said.

"Don't understand what?"

"How his average balance wasn't higher."

"Why's that?"

"Early last year, maybe a year and a half ago, my last year of med school, he missed a bunch of payments. I started getting letters from Harvard saying I better make other arrangements for payment or I was going to be dropped."

"And?"

"I called him. He was never there, so I kept leaving him messages."

"How long did this go on?"

"Three or four months. I'd already been to my bank. Signed the papers for a loan." Robert Downs looked over at Corso. "I was going to tell him it was all right. I had a loan. It was no problem."

"And?"

"He paid it off. Out of the blue. All of it. Not just what he was behind but the whole rest of the year."

"How much was that?

"Forty-something thousand."

Corso sat back in the seat. "Really?"

"Not only that, but the last time we spoke—"

"When was that?"

"A couple of months back."

"And?"

"I was telling him how I was probably going to have to go to work for an HMO. How private practice was so expensive I was going to have to spend a few years saving my pennies before I could even think about going out on my own."

"And?"

"And he told me to hang in there. Not to commit to anything. He said he might be able to help set me up on my own." He lifted one hand from the wheel and waved it around. "How could a guy with a hundred-fifty-dollar average balance be thinking about helping me get into private practice?"

"Beats me," Corso said. "Turn right at the bottom of the hill."

Downs did as he was told, making a sharp right, rolling the rented Malibu along an access road between a Fred Meyer store and an apartment complex.

"How much would it take to get yourself into private practice?"

"A hundred thousand, minimum." He threw a pleading glance at Corso. "That's why I always assumed he was . . . I assumed he had . . ."

"Means," Corso said.

"He made it sound like it was no problem. Like he just had to move some money around and it would be okay."

Corso ruffled the stack of papers. "If he had a portfolio he'd have been paying taxes on it." Corso turned the tax form over. "He claimed nothing but his salary and twelve dollars in interest income."

The haunted look on Robert Downs's face said he was as confused as Corso was.

"Take a right at the light. That's Renton Avenue. The school district building should be somewhere up the road on the right."

Half a mile up Renton Avenue, the Meridian School District was housed in a sleek modern building across from South Sound Ford. Robert Downs eased into a leaf-strewn parking space marked VISITOR and turned off the engine. He sighed and looked over at Corso. "What now?"

"Same deal," Corso said. "We're following the money. Did he cash in his retirement fund last year? Did he have an insurance policy he could borrow on? Was he into his credit union big-time? We're looking for any explanation of how a man with an average balance of less than two hundred bucks could come up with better than forty thousand dollars in a pinch."

Downs grabbed the door handle. "You coming?" he asked.

"They'll just make me wait outside," Corso said. "You better handle this one on your own." Downs heaved a sigh and got out of the car. As he stood for a moment with the door open, Corso could hear the rush of traffic and the car lot's colorful pennants snapping in the breeze.

Robert Downs was gone for thirty-three minutes. By the time he returned, carrying a thick manila folder, Corso had been through Donald Barth's financial records twice.

"Anything?" Corso asked as the younger man settled into the driver's seat.

Downs dropped the folder on the seat between them. "Nothing," he said. "He's got thirty-three thousand dollars in his retirement fund and a ten-thousand-dollar insurance policy, neither of which have been touched."

"You the beneficiary?"

"Yeah," Downs muttered, looking away.

"Nothing to be sad about, kid. It's how he would have wanted it. And you're damn near halfway to private practice."

Downs leaned his head against the window. "It doesn't seem right."

"What's that?"

"That I could occupy such a huge part in his life, when . . . you know."

Corso remained silent. Downs rubbed the side of his face.

"It's like he aimed his whole existence at me, and— you know—to me he was just an afterthought. This distant creep my mother talked about. And all the while he was toiling away so I could—"

He stopped talking and looked over at Corso.

"Listen to me," he said. "I sound like something off a soap opera."

"Fathers are tough," Corso said. "There's a lot of built-in baggage."

Downs silently agreed, turned the key, and started the engine. "The school district has a maintenance shop. He had a locker." He reached down, opened the manila folder, and came out with a small piece of yellow lined paper. "I got directions," he said.

Corso took the paper from his hand, studied it for a moment, and then pointed toward the opposite end of the parking lot. "Take the far exit. Turn right out of the lot."

"You find anything?" Downs asked.

"It's what I *didn't* find."

"Like what?"

"Like any records pertaining to medical school payments."

"Really?"

"He's got everything from your four years at Harvard. Every bill, every letter, every invoice." Corso spread his hands. "Then, for the past two years, nothing."

"You suppose the police . . . ?" Downs pointed the Chevy up a steep hill, into a seedy suburban neighborhood.

"Soon as we get back to town, you're going to check with them again. Make sure they didn't miss something."

"Maybe they're holding out on us."

"Maybe," Corso said, without believing it. "And then you need to call Harvard. Get a complete copy of your payment records. College, med school, the whole thing. Have them overnight it to you."

20

"I'll tell you the same thing I told the cops. Donald Barth's been with us fifteen months. A model employee. Never missed a day."

Dennis—call me Denny—Ryder was foreman of the West Hill Maintenance Shop. Age was turning his thick blond hair the color of dirty brass, but it hadn't stopped him from plastering it back into a duck-tailed pompadour that would have made Elvis proud. A black Harley Davidson Road King Classic rested lovingly along the rear wall. Corso was betting it was Denny Ryder's.

Ryder wiped the corners of his mouth with his thumb and forefinger and then flicked a glance over at Robert Downs, who was holding his father's uniform shirt up in front of his face, studying the fabric as if it were the Turin Shroud.

"Nice quiet fella. Did his job. Kept his mouth shut."

"Where'd he work before?" Corso asked.

Ryder's eyes took on a furtive cast. "Before what?"

"Before fifteen months ago."

"Musta been somewhere else in the district."

"You don't know for sure?"

"He transferred in with his seniority intact, so he must have worked somewhere else in the district."

"Must have?"

"I don't do the hiring and firing," he said disgustedly. "The eggheads up in Human Resources do that. I just keep 'em busy when they get here."

Again, he flashed a quick look over at Robert Downs, who had folded the two uniform shirts over his arm and now stood, staring dejectedly off into space.

"Like I said. I really didn't know the guy very well."

Corso turned to Downs. "You ready?"

Downs looked startled by the question. 'Oh . . . yes, sure." he seemed to shudder slightly as he started across the floor. He stuck out his hand. "Thanks for your help, Mr. Ryder," he said. Denny Ryder mumbled the obligatory condolences and then followed Corso over to the door, where he once again managed a furtive smile and a clumsy testimonial on the subject of Donald Barth. Hell-of-a-guy, good-bye.

Outside, the weather had gone to hell. A steady rain slanted in from the south. What an hour ago had been a bright blue sky was now a black blanket hanging twenty feet above the treetops like cannon smoke.

Robert Downs had raised his foot, as if to jog to the car, when Corso put a hand on his shoulder. "I'll meet you in the car," Corso shouted over the rush of the wind.

"I . . ." Downs began to stammer.

"I'll be right there," Corso assured him.

Downs nodded blankly and began jogging toward the car. Corso waited until the car door closed before turning and walking up the three stairs into the maintenance office.

Dennis Ryder's expression said he had half expected Corso to come back and wasn't happy about it. "Lose something?" he asked.

"Yeah," Corso said. "But I'm not quite sure what it is."

"What's that mean?" His tone held a challenge.

"It means I hear you talking, but I don't hear you saying anything. You sound like Jeffrey Dahmer's neighbors, talking about what a nice quiet boy he was."

Ryder swallowed a denial, scratched the back of his neck, and sighed. "I mean, what am I gonna say? With his kid here and all."

"I understand."

Ryder checked the room. "Barth was a first-class asshole," he said. "A complete loser loner. Thought he was better than everybody else." He waved a hand. "Cheapest sonofabitch I ever met." He threw a thumb back over his shoulder at the pop machine. "Never saw him so much as buy a pop. Never saw him buy a bag of chips or a candy bar. Two sandwiches and a bottle of tap water." He cut the air with the side of his hand. "That was it. Five days a week."

"So how come you don't know where Barth transferred in from?"

Ryder's eyes narrowed. "I didn't say that. I said Human Resources didn't provide me with that information."

"But you asked around."

"Wouldn't you? You come in one Monday morning." He waved a hand around. "I remember it was the fifteenth, because it was payday. And all of a sudden here's this guy who the district says is going to work full-time. They say he's got seven and a half years' seniority, which is more than anybody here but me." He shook his head, sending a single yellow lock down onto his forehead. "So naturally, I want to know where this guy came from. And you know what they say?" He waited for the question to sink in. "They say it's none of my damn business. Just put him to work. That's it."

"So?"

"I called the union."

"And the union said?"

"The union said, If they want to give us an extra position, we're sure as hell gonna take it."

"But you asked around anyway."

"Damn right I did."

"So?"

"So I find out he'd been working over in the North Hill shop. I call Sammy Harris—he's the lead over there—and I ask Sammy what the deal is, and he tells me pretty much the same thing I just told you. The guy's a loner. It's like he thinks he's better than everybody else or something. Eats lunch out in his truck by himself. Listens to classical music. Don't attend any of the social things. Just comes in, does his job, and goes home." Ryder stopped talking and squinted out the window. A white pickup with a Meridian School District logo on the door drove along the side of the building. Then another. And a third. "Crew's coming back for lunch," Ryder said.

"So how come they transfer Barth over here?" Corso asked.

"Well, that's the sixty-four-thousand-dollar question, now, isn't it?" Again he checked the room.

"Seems our friend Mr. Barth took a four-month leave of absence. By the time he got around to coming back, they didn't need him over on North Hill anymore, so they sent him here."

"Four months?"

"Yeah . . . from a job where if you're out more than three days in a row, you gotta bring a note from a doctor to keep from getting docked."

"Weird," Corso said. "When was this?"

"About this time last year is when he showed up. So he must have been out since early June sometime."

"Anybody tell you why he was gone?"

He shook his head. "Nope. District said I didn't need to know. Just put him back to work. Said it was confidential."

"What did Sammy have to say?" Corso asked.

Ryder chuckled. "Sammy said he don't have any idea either. Just gets a call from Human Resources one morning. They say Barth won't be in for a while. Period. That's it. Just won't be in for a while. But don't take him off the union rolls."

Corso pulled his notebook from his coat pocket. "Let me see if I've got this straight. Sometime last summer, Barth walks off his job and doesn't come back for over four months."

Ryder nodded. "Fourth of June to the eleventh of October. I looked it up for the cops yesterday."

Another pair of district pickup trucks rolled by the window.

"Then he shows up over here one morning, four months later, and you're supposed to just put him to work and not ask questions."

"That's it."

"Then what?"

"Then—what?—a couple of months ago, he stops coming in. I wait a few days—you know, HR already told me it was none of my business—so I wait a few days and call. They tell me to hang loose. Don't take him off the payroll. Don't do nothing. Just hang loose."

"And?"

Dennis Ryder's nostrils fluttered, as if the air were suddenly rank. "I'm still hanging when the cops come waltzing here Tuesday afternoon. Start showing me all these pictures of what's left of Barth and his truck." He eyed Corso closely. "I been straight with you, mister," he said. "How about a little comp time? You know what's going on here? Ain't often some guy we work with is found buried in the side of a hill like Jimmy Hoffa or something."

"Not a clue," Corso said. "I'm getting the same picture you laid out for me: a loner, kept away from everybody else, cheap." Corso shrugged. "If he had a vice it might have been that he liked the ladies a bit too much."

"Who told you that?"

"His ex."

Ryder took a deep breath, held it, looked around again. "You won't quote me." His eyes narrowed. "This kind of thing'd get me fired."

"No problem."

He pushed the breath out through his nose. "There *were* a couple of complaints."

"What kind?"

"Sexual harassment."

"Do tell."

"One over on North Hill and another one here."

"For doing what?"

Ryder made a rude noise with his lips and put on a disgusted face. "Who the hell knows, these days? You sneeze and somebody takes it wrong. You hang up a girlie calendar, and somebody feels like their constitutional rights are being shit on."

"You've got no idea what the beef was?"

Ryder shook his head. "District's real tight-assed about that kind of thing." He scratched a pair of quotation marks in the air. "Confidentiality," he said. "I'm not even allowed to ask."

Corso thought it over. "The person he was supposed to have harassed while he was here . . ."

Ryder was already shaking his head. "I can't tell you that. They'd have my ass in a New York minute."

"She—I'm assuming it was a she."

Ryder nodded vigorously. "Yeah."

"She still here?"

"Why?"

"I was thinking maybe you could ask her—you know, confidentially—if she might be willing to talk to me about it?"

Ryder chewed his lower lip.

"She says no, I'll take a hike," Corso added.

Ryder thought about it, made a what-the-hell gesture and turned and walked toward a door marked EMPLOYEES ONLY. "Stay here," he said, over his shoulder.

Corso watched the second hand sweep around four times before the door opened and a woman stepped into the room. She was younger than he'd expected: thirty or so, with a lot of city miles etched around her eyes and mouth, slim-hipped and flat-chested, with shoulder-length brown hair framing a pale oval face.

The patch on her uniform read KATE. She carried half a sandwich in one hand and a can of Diet Pepsi in the other.

"Cops were here yesterday," she said.

"I'm not a policeman," Corso said. "I'm a writer."

She recoiled slightly. "I don't want my name in the paper."

"No problem," he assured her. "I write books."

"Don't want my name in a book neither."

"Still not a problem," Corso assured her. "I'm just trying to figure out how a guy like Donald Barth ended up buried in the side of a hill."

She shook her head. "Weird, huh? Nothing like this ever happened anywhere around me before." She took a bite of her sandwich. While chewing, she took Corso in from head to toe. After washing the sandwich down with a big swig of Pepsi, she asked, "So what is it you want from me?" Her tone suggested she might be willing to entertain suggestions above and beyond mere information.

"You filed a complaint against Mr. Barth."

She rolled a piece of plastic wrap into a ball and threw it in the garbage can, then took another big pull on the Pepsi.

"He was a jerk," she said.

"Did he harass you?"

"What he did was piss me off," she said.

Corso kept his mouth shut, figuring she wouldn't have agreed to talk to him unless she wanted to tell her story.

"We had a thing going for a while," she said. "Nothing too serious, but you know . . . it was passable."

"Everybody says he was a loner. Did everything by

himself. How'd you manage to get involved with him?"

Her expression suggested she'd never considered the matter before. "I guess that was part of it," she said tentatively. "He had like this mystique about him. All secret and silent and withdrawn. He was different. He just sorta sat back and waited, like a spider." She skittered across the room as if she were on wheels. "Looking back on it, I guess that was his technique. He made it so's you had to chase after him."

"So what happened?"

She walked over to the window, spread the blinds with her fingers, and looked out. "It's like it was more exciting that way." She turned back toward the room and gestured toward the shop. "You know, what with the rest of the guys always coming on with the 'oooh babay baby' routine." She made a suggestive move with her hands and hips. "It's kinda refreshing to be on the other side of it once in a while."

"So?"

"So he's tellin' me how it's been years for him. How he hasn't been involved with a woman since his divorce and all that." She gave Corso a sideways smile. "You know; and that's got its appeal too. It's like you're in charge or something."

"Uh-huh."

She brought one hand up to her throat. "I know I'm clean. I get myself tested every time I—you know—strike up a new friendship, so to speak. And he's supposedly been living like a monk for years, so we can do it au natural, so to speak, which is a joy all to itself, if you know what I mean."

Corso's confirmation seemed to encourage her. "So

almost right away—soon as we get past the sweaty palms part in the beginning—I can tell something's wrong. Never back to his place. Always gotta be mine. We never go anywhere in public, 'cause—you know— we work together, and people might be thinkin' it's bad to mix business with pleasure." She made a rueful face. "At least that's what he said at the time."

She rested a hip on the desk and folded her arms. "So right away I'm thinking he's gotta be married or something." She held up a hand. "I got a rule. No married guys. Period. That's it."

"So?"

"So, I've got a friend in payroll, who tells me that, lo and behold, he's single. Got him a son who he doesn't have on the health plan, which means the son's either too old or has coverage someplace else."

"Either of which is okay with you."

"Sure," she says. "I'm not looking for anything permanent. I just want to make sure I'm not tearing up some other girl's world."

"Then?"

"Then it all goes to hell," she said. "We been together maybe two weeks, and all of a sudden he's not showing up at my place after work anymore. Doesn't say a word, just stops coming over." She bumped herself off the desk and put a hand on her hip. "So I see him at work and say, 'Hey, what's the deal? Haven't seen you lately.' And you know what he tells me?"

"What?"

"He tells me to get over it. Says he's moved on and I should move on too." Her free hand joined its mate at her waist. "Like I'm some snot-nosed kid or something."

"Ah," Corso said. "The woman scorned."

She laughed. "No, no," she said, "I was okay with it. I'm still thinking I woke this guy up after a long hibernation, and now he's running amok." She shrugged. "It figures. You know how guys are."

"Uh-huh."

"Until I tell my friend Susie about it—Susie's the one in payroll—anyway, a coupla days after I tell her about it, she calls me one night and tells me she went through his personnel file and guess what?"

"He's already had a sexual harassment complaint filed against him."

"Bingo." She began to smile. "Now I'm starting to get pissed. So I get the name and find an excuse to go over to the North Hill Shop, and, lo and behold, he ran the same number on her he ran on me." She raised her voice and added a singsong quality. "*I haven't been with a woman in years. I'm not sure I still know what to do.* Oh my, oh my." She shook her head disgustedly. "He gives her the same damn song and dance." She cut the air with her hand. "Unbelievable."

"And then he dumps her too."

"He doesn't even bother to tell *her*. She has to find out on her own." Corso waited. "Yeah. She comes back to the shop one night for something she forgot, and there he is sitting there in the parking lot in his truck mauling some little Asian honey."

"Not good."

"Damn right it's not good. Turns out this jerk is risking our lives. We're having unprotected sex with a guy who's screwing the known world."

"Ah."

"I hadn't even thought about a complaint until she—

the other girl—told me that's why she filed one." She nodded slightly, as if once again confirming her deci sion. "I decided she was right. This guy was putting our lives at risk. Any trouble I could make for that jerk was okay with me."

A buzzer sounded out in the shop.

"I gotta go," she said and headed for the door. She stopped and looked back over her shoulder. "As far as I'm concerned, Donald Barth got exactly what he deserved."

"Thanks for your time," Corso said.

She gave him a wicked smile. "Come back sometime."

"It's been years," Corso said with a grin.

She burst out laughing. "Yeah, sure."

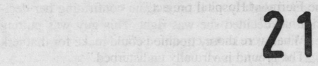

21

Friday, October 20   5:05 p.m.

Warren Klein paced back and forth in front of the jury like a lion in a cage. Ray Butler stood ready at the easel, which held a picture of the collapsed back wall of Fairmont Hospital, taken from a slightly different angle, so as to exclude the tiny foot. Renee Rogers sorted through a mountain of paperwork on the prosecution table, handing Klein folders whenever he strutted her way.

"Mr. Rozan," Klein said, "can you tell the jury the magnitude of an earthquake that could be expected to cause damage of this nature?"

Sam Rozan looked like your local greengrocer: bald little guy with a big mustache and thick wrists. Turned out he was chief earthquake engineer for the State of California and an expert of world renown. A man whose consulting résumé included every major planetary shake in the past fifteen years.

"That would depend almost entirely upon soil conditions."

"Have you had occasion to inspect the soil around the Fairmont Hospital project?"

"I have."

"What were those conditions?"

"The ground is virtually undisturbed."

"Virtually?"

"None of the signs of ground failure are present at the scene."

"What signs would those be?"

He counted on his fingers. "Ground cracking, lateral transposition, landslides, differential settlement." He stopped with four fingers in the air. "And at the extreme end of the spectrum, the liquefaction of the soil beneath the structure."

"So you're saying that—"

"Objection." Elkins was on his feet. "Mr. Klein is leading his own witness, Your Honor. If Mr. Klein wishes to testify—"

"Sustained," Fulton Howell said.

"I'll rephrase the question," Klein said.

Turned out he didn't need to. Rozan spoke up. "None of the ground conditions consistent with damage of that nature were present."

"None?"

"Not in the slightest."

"Having satisfied yourself that ground failure was not to blame, did you and your colleagues make a subsequent examination of the site in order to ascertain other possible causes for the collapse?"

"Yes. My staff and I conducted a full-scale on-site investigation."

"Were you able to come to a conclusion as to the cause of the tragedy?"

"Absolutely."

Klein looked at the jury box like a kindly uncle. "For the sake of clarity, Mr. Rozan, are you saying that you were absolutely able to reach a conclusion, or that you believe the conclusion you reached to be absolutely true?"

"Both," Sam Rozan said, without hesitation. "The reasons for the structural failure were staring us in the face. It was a no-brainer."

The room caught its collective breath, waiting for Elkins to get to his feet and fight for his client, but Bruce Elkins remained seated and impassive.

"How so?"

"The building didn't meet any of the established specifications for seismic-resistant design."

"Which are?"

Rozan waved a hand. "There is, of course, no ideal configuration for any particular type of building." Klein opened his mouth to ask another question, but Rozan went on. "There are, however, a number of basic guidelines."

"Could you enumerate those guidelines for us, please?"

Rozan went back to his fingers. "One: the building should be light and avoid unnecessary masses. Two: the building and its superstructure should be simple, symmetric, and regular in plan." He looked over at the jury box. "You don't want the building to be too much taller than it is wide. Three: the structure needs to have considerably more lateral stiffness than structures in nonseismic regions."

"Why is that?"

"Because the stiffer and lighter the building, the less sensitive it will be to the effects of shaking."

"How is it possible to build a structure that is both stronger and lighter at the same time?"

"That's accomplished by the quality of the materials in conjunction with the quality of the workmanship."

"And you say that the Fairmont Hospital was built without any of these qualities?" Klein looked to the jury and aimed his palms at the ceiling. "How can it be, Mr. Rozan, that a publicly funded structure in the most seismically active area of the country would be allowed to be erected without these safeguards?"

"It was not constructed according to specifications."

Klein looked astonished. "Surely there must have been some system of checks and balances in place to assure that seismic guidelines were being adhered to?"

"On a project of that size, you'd normally have a pair of state building inspectors working full-time on the site."

"Was that the case?"

"Yes, it was."

"That would be Joshua Harmon and Brian Swanson."

"Yes, it would."

"Have you or any member of your staff spoken to either of these gentlemen?"

For the first time, Sam Rozan looked confused. "That wasn't possible," he said tentatively. "As you know, they . . . both of them were—"

Suddenly Elkins was on his feet. "Objection," he said in a weary voice. "It's obvious where Mr. Klein is heading with this, Your Honor."

"I'm merely asking an expert witness about the standard procedure for an investigation of this nature."

Elkins made a rude noise. "Mr. Klein seeks to inflame the jury with facts not entered in evidence. He seeks—"

Fulton Howell had heard enough. "Approach the bench," he said.

As Elkins and Klein shuffled toward the front of the courtroom, Renee Rogers rocked her chair back onto two legs and whispered to Corso, "Maybe Warren does have a trick or two up his sleeve. This is very slick."

Corso arched an eyebrow. Rogers checked the bench, where the muted discussion continued. "Ordinarily, we couldn't include anything about crimes other than those with which the defendant is charged." She flicked another glance at the front of the room. "Hell, we can't even bring up crimes the defendant's been convicted of. Except, in this case, where he's asking an expert witness about his method of investigation. . . ."

The sound of shoes snapped her head around. Klein wore victory on his face. "Mr. Rozan, allow me to rephrase my previous question," he began. "When assigned an investigation of the scope of Fairmont Hospital, where do you and your staff generally begin?"

"With the on-site inspectors."

"Always?"

"It's the professional protocol." He shrugged. "A courtesy."

"But in this case you were not able to do so."

"That's correct."

"Why was that?"

"Once again, Your Honor—"

The judge waved Elkins off. "Allow the witness to answer."

"I must take exception—"

"Exception noted, Mr. Elkins."

Klein stepped in close to the witness. "Once again, Mr. Rozan, could you please tell us why you were unable to question the on-site inspection staff?"

"They were dead."

"Move for a mistrial on the grounds that—"

"Motion denied," the judge snapped. He waved his gavel at Bruce Elkins. "As I explained to you during our sidebar, Mr. Elkins, so long as Mr. Klein's questions regarding Messrs. Harmon and Swanson are solely directed toward establishing Mr. Rozan's method of investigation, the information may be entered into evidence."

Klein's right shoe squeaked as he hustled toward the prosecution table. "The Alameda County file," he said in a stage whisper.

Rogers handed him a bright yellow folder. Klein strode past the jury, headed for the front of the room.

"The People would like to introduce into evidence two autopsy reports provided by Mr. Eugene Berry, who was, at the time, medical examiner for Alameda County."

"This is an outrage!" Elkins stormed.

"I am merely attempting to corroborate Mr. Rozan's testimony as to why he was unable to conduct his investigation according to his established pattern of inquiry."

"Continue."

He waved his fistful of reports at the judge. "We can

either have the reports read into the record in their entirety or we can stipulate that the circumstances of death surrounding Mr. Harmon and Mr. Swanson fall under the umbrella of common knowledge."

"So stipulated," Howell said. "But you will limit your stipulation to the barest facts of their disposition."

Klein turned to face the jury box. "Seven weeks after the collapse of Fairmont Hospital, Mr. Joshua Harmon and Mr. Brian Swanson were found floating in San Pablo Bay. Each man had been shot twice in the back of the head. The medical examiner lists these wounds as the cause of death."

Klein dropped the reports on the desk of the court clerk and walked back over to his witness. "You said earlier, Mr. Rozan, that you believed the causes for the collapse of Fairmont Hospital were"—he hesitated, putting a finger to his temple—"I believe your phrase was that it was a *no-brainer*. Is that correct?"

"Yes. It was."

"Could you give us an example of what you meant?"

Sam Rozan looked over at Ray Butler, standing by the easel. Ray pulled the collapse picture off and leaned it against the legs. The next photo was of a splintered square of concrete. A yellow ruler had been placed along the base, for scale, seventeen inches a side.

"Mr. Rozan, could you give us some idea of what it is we're looking at in this exhibit?"

"The picture is of one of the pillars that supported the rear wall of Fairmont Hospital." He started to get to his feet, stopped, looked at the judge. "May I?"

Judge Howell nodded his assent. Rozan walked to the oversized photo and pointed with a stubby finger.

"Here—where the outer layer of concrete has fallen off—you can see the honeycombing." His voice began to rise. "This is a main structural support. It's supposed to be solid." He brushed the back of his hand across the picture. "This is unconscionable."

"Was this defect present in other back wall columns?"

"It was consistent with virtually every other pillar and column in the entire structure."

"To what do you attribute this lack of solidarity?"

"Everything," Rozan said quickly. "The concrete mixing, the placement, the consolidation, the curing— all of it was cheap, quick, and dirty." He pointed at the picture again. "You could peel away the outer layer of concrete with the kick of a boot."

Klein walked him through four more photos without Elkins so much as clearing his throat. By the time Klein thanked his witness and returned to his chair next to Rogers, the jury could be heard twisting around in their seats.

"Cross," the judge intoned.

Elkins stayed seated. "Not at this time, Your Honor. I would, however, like to retain the right to question this witness at another time."

Klein got to his feet. "As would I, Your Honor."

"So noted." *Bang*. The judge sat back in his chair and sighed. "We've run considerably past the customary adjournment hour. And as Mr. Elkins does not wish to cross-examine the witness at this time, this seems to be a suitable place to quit for the weekend." He looked from lawyer to lawyer. "If neither of you gentlemen objects."

Friday, October 20   5:28 p.m.

Bruce Elkins sat down at the defense table and looked over at his client, Nicholas Balagula. "You pay me for my best legal advice," he said.

Balagula nodded in agreement. "Handsomely," he said.

Elkins's gaze was stony. "I've changed my mind about our strategy. I have an obligation to give you the opportunity to find new counsel, should you disagree with what I now consider to be your best legal option."

"What strategy would that be?" Balagula asked.

Elkins leaned in close to his client. "I don't think we should put on a defense," he said in a low voice.

Balagula and Ivanov exchanged glances. "Really?" Ivanov said.

"At this stage of the proceedings, that's my best legal advice."

"And if I disagree?"

"Then it is my advice that we seek a plea."

Balagula waved a hand, as if shooing a fly. "Not an option," he said.

Elkins ran a hand over his head. "I don't like it either," he said. "You heard the testimony. If the state can connect you in any way to the construction conspiracy, prison could turn out to be the least of your worries." He held Nicholas Balagula in an unwavering gaze. "You could very well find yourself looking at a lethal injection."

"Why no defense?" Balagula asked.

"Because that way—even if this Lebow person connects you to the conspiracy—that way you'll have grounds for appeal on the basis of having been provided an incompetent and insufficient defense."

"Mr. Lebow can connect me to nothing," Balagula said.

"That's not what my sources are telling me. I'm being told he's going to testify that he was in the room when you ordered the falsification of the core-sample test results." Balagula started to speak, but Elkins cut him off. "If that happens, the party's over. Not me or anybody else can get you out of this."

Nicholas Balagula got to his feet. "You do what you think is best," he said.

22

S he was right where he expected to find her. Leaning back in a booth at Vito's, a half-empty martini
glass on the table in front of her. On the jukebox, Otis
Redding was working his way through "I've Been
Loving You Too Long."

Corso stood in the doorway until his eyes adjusted to
the deep-space dark. Half a dozen regulars held down
the bar stools. Renee Rogers had the booths to herself.

He got all the way to the table before she looked up
and made eye contact.

"Well, well," she said. "I guess I'm going to have to
work on being less predictable." She gestured with her
hand for Corso to take a seat.

"Good thing Elkins didn't want to cross-examine,"
he said.

"Mercifully." She raised her glass in a toast, took a
sip of the clear liquid.

"Klein's on a roll in there."

Her eyes were suddenly serious. "It's too damn
easy," she said.

"How's that?"

She thought it over. "It's hard to describe," she said finally. "You do this for as long as I have and you get a feel for the pace of a trial. The ebb and flow. A trial falls into a rhythm, like a song."

"And?"

She waved a hand and looked at the ceiling. "Something's not right. Raymond can feel it too. It's hard to describe. The timing is off. It's like we're rolling downhill with no brakes." She looked over at Corso and made a face. "It's a lawyer thing."

"You shared this with Klein?"

She snorted. "Both Ray and I tried, but Warren doesn't want to hear about it. He's convinced his case is so airtight that Elkins's finally giving up the ghost and facing the inevitable."

"Last time I saw the evidence connecting Balagula to the construction companies, it seemed pretty thin to me."

"It still is. It's the weak link in the case. Balagula did a great job of insulating himself from their businesses. No matter how you look at it, the construction trail always leads back to Harmon and Swanson."

"The two guys they found floating in San Pablo Bay."

"And the only two people on earth who could tie Balagula directly to the contractors." She took another small sip from her drink. "You were at the second trial. Elkins objected to every chart, every graph, and every witness I put up there. He had citations for every instance and objection."

"I remember."

"Today, he's Mr. Rogers. He gets up just often

enough to look like he's doing something. Last time out, it took us two weeks to get through what we got through today in two hours. He's going through the motions. I don't get it."

"Maybe Klein's right. Maybe he has got Balagula by the balls."

She gave a grudging nod. "Maybe," she said. "If we can prove that Balagula and Ivanov arranged for the fake inspections and the fabricated core tests, then by extension we prove they must have had some interest in the companies involved; otherwise there'd be no reason for them to be going to all that trouble and taking all that risk."

"And this Lebow guy is gonna make the connection?"

"He says he was present when it was discussed. That both Ivanov and Balagula were in the room at the time and that Balagula gave the order."

"That ought to do it," Corso said.

Renee Rogers massaged the bridge of her nose several times and then waved her hand disgustedly. "Enough already," she said. "I don't know why I'm obsessing over it. Either way, I'm out of here when the trial's over."

The bartender wandered over. Corso asked for ice water. Rogers covered her glass with her hand and shook her head. "What about you?" she asked. "How's your friend doing?"

"The same."

"You making any progress?" She ran her finger around the rim of the martini glass, as he told her about what he'd learned. "Sex and money," she said, when he'd finished. "The deadly duo."

"None of it gets me any closer to finding out what came down."

"You sound like I feel," she said.

They sat in silence for a moment. The ice water appeared. Corso downed half of it.

"Where's that market where they throw the fish around?" she asked. "The one they always show on TV."

"First and Pike. Four blocks west and six blocks north. Why?"

"Since I'm off for the weekend, I thought I might do a little sightseeing. I spent four months here last summer and never saw anything except the hotel, the bar, and the courthouse."

She watched as Corso took another sip of water and then sat back in his chair. Her eyes sparkled.

"You're not very quick on the uptake, Mr. Corso."

His face was blank. "How's that?"

"This is the point in the conversation where you're supposed to go all gallant and offer to show me around town."

"I know," he said, with a chuckle.

"If you're not careful, you're going to have me worrying that I've lost my charm. I could get a complex or something."

He laughed again. "Your charms are intact."

"Well, then?"

"I'm not much on the tourist traps."

"Then show me something else. Something only the locals get to see. Something known only to one of the city's true chroniclers such as yourself."

Corso thought it over. "You bring a pair of jeans and some real shoes?"

She looked down at her feet and then back up at Corso. "Yes, why?"

Corso threw a five-dollar bill on the table and stood up . "Come on," he said.

"I'll need an hour," she said, as she gathered her things.

He looked as if she were standing on his foot.

"You don't spend a lot of time with women, do you?"

Friday, October 20   7:32 p.m.

Corso poked his head out the pilothouse window. "Okay, now the stern line!" he shouted. Renee Rogers freed the line from the cleat and looked up at Corso through a cloud of diesel fumes. "Just bring it with you," he said, not wanting to risk her throwing the line on deck. If she missed, it would end up in the water, uncomfortably close to the props.

She came down the dock and then up the stainless-steel stairs to the deck. Corso opened the starboard door and pulled her inside as he backed the boat out of the slip. A fender groaned as the big boat rolled it along the dock. Corso dropped the engines to idle, reversed the transmissions, gave the starboard engine a little diesel, and swung the bow out into the channel.

Renee Rogers climbed the three steps into the pilothouse. "This was not *quite* what I had in mind," she said.

"You said you wanted to see something only the locals get to see." Corso held the wheel straight and let the bow thruster push the nose out into Lake Union. "Hold the wheel," he said.

"But I've nev—"

He hooked her with an arm and moved her behind the wheel. Instinctively, she grabbed the big teak wheel with both hands.

"Just aim at the other side of the lake and don't hit anything," he said.

It took him less than five minutes to stow the stairs, clean up the lines, and get the fenders back aboard. He swung the hinged section of rail back into place and stepped into the galley. Renee Rogers looked down from the pilothouse. "This is really something," she said. "I had no idea this huge lake was right in the middle of the city."

Corso stowed his coat in the forward shower. He climbed into the pilothouse, slipped behind Renee Rogers, and settled into the mate's chair.

The lake was a choppy green field, foamy and frantic, falling all over itself from a dozen directions. *Saltheart* bobbed slightly in the chop. Without warning, a deepening roar began to fill the cabin. A Lake Union Air Service seaplane buzzed over, not more than forty feet above the deck. "Wow," Rogers said softly, as she watched the yellow-and-white De Havilland Beaver descend. Five hundred feet ahead, the pontoons cut silver slices in the dark water. They watched as the water pulled the plane to a halt and the pilot swung the plane on its axis, until the whirling propeller was pointed back their way.

Above the taxiing plane, the city stood tall and twinkling, the buildings shadowed by a black sky, glowing purple at the edges.

Corso closed his eyes and allowed the water to pull the weight from his shoulders, let the movement of the boat and the deep rumble of the diesels loosen the grime of the day. And then he seemed to swim downward in the thick green water, with the hum of the engines in his ears and the taste of the water on his lips.

"Hey," Rogers said. He opened his eyes. They were coming up to the south end of the lake. The Wooden Boat Museum loomed ahead.

"What now?" she wanted to know.

"Go around the red buoy," he said, pointing.

She gave the buoy a wide berth as she brought the boat about. Corso reached over and eased the throttle forward. Eight hundred rpms. About five knots across the surface.

"My father had a boat," she said, "when I was a kid."

"What kind?"

"A ChrisCraft." She waved a hand around. "Not a palace like this. Just a little boat he and my Uncle George used to go fishing in. Maybe twenty feet."

"What'd your father do?"

"He was a county sheriff."

"Where?"

"Anderson County, Virginia."

"Where's that?"

"Way down in the southern part of the state. Almost in North Carolina."

"Still alive?"

"Oh, no," she said. "He died back in 'ninety-one." She flicked a glance in his direction. "Yours?"

He offered a wan smile. "Mine was a regular guest of the county sheriff."

"Still alive?"

He shook his head. "His liver gave out at forty."

"A pity."

"We didn't think so," he said.

To starboard, the shoreline was awash with houseboats. Once cozy weekend retreats, they were now gussied up into million-dollar barges for the army of cellular-software-dot-com millionaires who swarmed the city like portfolioed roaches.

"Where are we going?" she asked.

"I told you: to see something only seen by the locals."

"You're not going to tell me, are you?"

"No."

"That's very childish."

"I know."

She feigned annoyance, frowning and looking out the windows into the bright moonlight, swiveling her head in an arc to take it all in, until the frown disappeared and she said, "Look at all these boats. Does everybody in this city own a boat?"

"Sometimes you'd think so," Corso said. "They say we've got more boats per capita than any other place in the country."

Corso played tour guide as they motored under the freeway bridge into the west end of Portage Bay, past the University of Washington and the Seattle Yacht Club and into the Montlake Cut, past the massive steel chevrons of Husky Stadium and out into Union Bay, where Corso reached over and pushed the throttles forward to fifteen hundred rpms and a stately twelve knots. "Moon's gonna be just right," he said.

For five minutes, they ran parallel to the 520 bridge, where the headlights of the traffic formed a solid line of amber that seemed to slide around the floating bridge's elegant curves like an android snake.

At the far end of the bridge, Corso finally took the helm, motoring *Saltheart* under the east high-rise and into the south end of Lake Washington. Ahead in the gloom, Mercer Island floated low on the shimmering water.

Corso cut back on the throttles and angled closer to shore. He checked his course and then set the autopilot. "Come on. Let's go down on deck. We can see it better from there."

The eastern shoreline was littered with million-dollar mansions: sterile steel and glass monoliths, neo-antebellum Greek Revival Taras, fifties Ramblers, and Tudor reproductions all huddled cheek-by-jowl along the narrow bank. Corso pulled open the port door and followed Renee Rogers out on deck. He pointed to a break in lights that lined the shore. "There," he said. "You can only see it from the lake, and only this time of year, when the leaves are off the trees."

Renee Rogers leaned on the rail and squinted out through the gloom. At first it looked like a park. Then maybe a trendy waterfront shopping center. Very Northwest. Lots of environmentally conscious exposed rock and wood, meandering its way up and down the cliff and along the bank for the better part of an eighth of a mile.

She traced the outline with her finger. "Is that all one—"

"Yeah, it's all one house," Corso answered.

"Who—"

"Bill Gates," Corso said. "Forty-five thousand square feet. Somewhere in the vicinity of a hundred and ten million dollars."

"No kidding."

"You get a little preprogrammed electronic badge. As you walk around the house, it adjusts everything to your liking. The temperature, the lights, even the electronic art on the walls."

"Wonder what it's like to live in something like that."

"When he married Melinda, she said it was like living in a convention center. She hired a team of decorators to make parts of it into something more livable."

"Funny how it's all relative," she said. "An hour ago, I thought your boat was decadent. Now"—she gestured toward the shore—"it seems like a rowboat."

"You think owning a house like that would change your life?"

She looked at him like he was crazy. "What do you mean?"

"Sometimes I cruise by here and wonder whether having all that would really make any long-term difference in my life."

"About a hundred-million-dollar difference," she scoffed.

"Over and above the money."

"There's no such thing as over and above the money."

"Would you be happier?"

She searched his eyes for a sign of irony. "You're serious, aren't you?"

"I wouldn't," he said. "If Bill gave me the place tomorrow, lock, stock, and barrel, paid for, tax-free."

"Yeah?"

"Once the buzz wore off, once I'd had everybody I know over for dinner and got used to the idea of owning the most expensive piece of residential property in

America . . . ?" He hesitated. "A week later I wouldn't be any happier than I was when I got up this morning."

As the house slid slowly to stern, she seemed to consider and discard a number of responses. The moon was directly overhead. The surface of the lake glowed like molten glass. "Me neither," she said finally.

"You hungry?" Corso asked.

"What I am is thirsty."

"What would you like?"

"What do you drink?"

"Bourbon."

"Then let there be bourbon." She toasted with an imaginary glass. "And come to think of it, I'm starved."

Corso pulled open the liquor cabinet and pulled out a half gallon of Jack Daniel's. In the cabinet above the stove, he found a pair of thick tumblers, filled each with ice, and added four fingers of bourbon. He handed Renee Rogers her drink and lifted his own. "Here's to putting Nicholas Balagula behind bars."

They clicked glasses. Corso took a sip. Rogers swallowed half the drink. Corso set the bourbon bottle on the drainboard next to the sink. "Bottle's here," he said. "From now on, it's self-service."

"Just the way I like it."

"We could probably rustle up a couple of steaks and a salad on the way back, if you want."

"I'm not very handy."

"Look in the bottom of the refrigerator. I think there's a new bag of salad greens in there."

She crossed the galley, pulled open the refrigerator door, and extracted a plastic bag full of greens. Corso put the transmissions into neutral, throttled all the way back, and switched off the engines. For a moment, the big boat floated in silence. Then Corso pushed the chrome button on the console and the generator sprang to life.

"You actually cook for yourself?" she asked.

"All the time."

"I eat out. Or do takeout or call room service or whatever."

"There was a time when I couldn't go out without attracting a crowd and having cameras shoved in my face. I kinda got in the habit of eating in."

She watched the memory wash across his dark face. "You actually hate it, don't you?"

"Hate what?"

"The celebrity."

"Doesn't everybody?"

"A lot of them say they do, but I don't think so. I think it's chic and humble to pretend you don't like being famous, but I think most people, once they've had their moment in the sun, would rather have it than not, no matter what they say in public."

"Celebrity as the opiate of the people."

She laughed. "Something like that."

She bounced the bag of salad greens in the palm of her hand. "What are we gonna put on this?"

"Look on the refrigerator door. There's a bunch of different things in there. Pick something you like."

She rummaged around in the door for a minute and came out with an unopened bottle of honey mustard dressing. "This okay?" she asked.

"Works for me," Corso said.

She downed the rest of her drink and poured herself another and then downed half of that. Corso sprinkled salt and pepper on a pair of T-bone steaks.

"I'm going to the stern and fire up the barbecue," he said. He reached over and flipped up the teak lid above the sink. Plates, glasses, silverware. "Why don't you set the table and then dump some of that stuff on the salad and mix it up. You think you can handle that?"

She took a pull from her glass. "Are you making fun of me?"

"Just a little," he said. "I'll be right back."

23

Gerardo knew the drill. He'd been watching all day. The shift was about to change. For the next ten minutes, the hospital corridors would be virtually empty, as one shift of doctors, nurses, and orderlies left the floor and another came on duty.

He pushed his burnished aluminum cleaning cart to the side of the corridor and pretended to rearrange his cleaning supplies. Sixty feet down the hall, a pair of white-clad nurses came out of Room One-oh-nine and hurried up the hall toward the nurses' station.

He'd talked it over with Ramón, talked more than the whole fifteen years they'd together. Nothing was going right lately. The way things had been going, it might be time to clean up their messes. Might be best if Gerardo was ready to run backup too, just to be sure. Lotta stuff going on in that part of the hospital. Might be best to have another gun, just in case somebody walked in or something. You never knew.

* * *

Ramón Javier looked like he belonged at a board meeting. He wore a somber gray suit, a blue tie, and a pair of tasseled loafers that gleamed from a recent shine. The .22-caliber automatic with the noise suppressor was tucked into the back of his pants, leaving the lines of the suit undisturbed as he stepped off the elevator and started down the hall.

He saw Gerardo standing behind a cart full of towels, wearing rubber gloves and a pair of baby-blue scrubs. Not his color at all. Made him look like a troll. Ramón pretended not to notice him, instead striding by, heading for One-oh-nine down at the corner. Probably could have just walked in and popped her on his own, but things were a little bit loosey-goosey lately, so they were playing it safe. The whole damn thing shouldn't take more than a minute. A minute, and they'd be halfway back to the kind of programmed normality upon which Ramón thrived.

At the corner, he stopped, checked the corridor to his left, and looked back at Gerardo, who offered a small nod that said the room was empty. Gerardo busied himself with a clear plastic spray bottle. Ramón took a deep breath, pulled open the door, and stepped into the room.

* * *

As the door closed behind Ramón, Gerardo began a silent count in his head. If he got to a hundred, it meant trouble and he was going in. His mother told him trouble came in threes. Sixteen, seventeen, eighteen. They'd already had three: the dead guy, the truck coming unburied, and the girl walking in on them. Twenty-three, twenty-four. Didn't need no more damn disasters. Just a nice clean kill and out the door. He checked the hallway. Nothing but a big-ass nurse, standing with her hands on her hips way down at the opposite end of the building. Thirty-seven, thirty-eight.

* * *

The room was lit only by the machines surrounding the bed. Ramón pulled the .22 from the back of his pants, thumbed off the safety, and placed the end of the suppressor against the side of the bandaged head. He listened for the sound of feet in the hall, heard nothing, and pulled the trigger. The pile of bandages rocked violently to the right and then snapped back into place. The electronic images went wild, dancing over their monitors like insects on fire. The small symmetrical hole began to leak blood, as Ramón placed the suppressor against the top of the head and fired again. Just to be sure.

* * *

He was at fifty-one when he heard the voice. "Hey, you," she called from the opposite end of the hall. Nigger bitch. Big enough to plow a field. Gerardo pretended not to hear. "You speak English? ¿Habla inglés?"

Gerardo whistled softly and sorted through a pile of small towels until his hand came to rest upon the taped grip of the automatic. A warm feeling spread through his body, even as he listened to the sound of her shoes squeaking down the long corridor in his direction.

"You hear me down there?" she demanded. "We got a mess up in One-sixty-four."

She kept coming his way and then, suddenly, from

the direction of the nurses' station, a guy appeared, thirty-something, hair and brown beard in need of a trim. He carried a newspaper under his left arm. As he reached the corner, he hesitated for a moment and then grabbed the handle of One-oh-nine, pulled it open, and stepped inside.

"You got an earwax problem or what?" she demanded. No more than thirty feet away now. Beneath the pile of linen, Gerardo thumbed the safety off and turned her way, grinning maniacally. Pointing at his ear, as if to say he could not hear. When he peeked back over his shoulder, the hall was empty.

* * *

Ramón was halfway back to the door when it began to open. He stepped quickly into the shadow behind the door, which kept opening and opening until it had him pressed flat against the wall. The figure stepped into the room and stood for a second as the door hissed shut, letting his eyes adjust to the gloom. Ramón was already moving his way when the figure emitted a low moan and ran to the bedside. The bright white screen had gone black. The green hillocks of her heartbeat crawled over the screen like flatworms. The visitor reached out and touched her head, brought the hand up to his face, stared for a brief second at the stain, and turned, wide-eyed, toward the door. From a distance of two feet, Ramón shot him between the eyes.

* * *

A buzzer was going off. Her hand was on his elbow, pushing him up the hall. Gerardo's hand rested on the butt of his automatic. Eighty-three, eighty-four. He'd already decided: one hundred and the bitch dies. Then, a second later, Ramón was standing in the hall. He gave Gerardo a small nod that meant the job was done and then began following along in their wake.

"Come on." The bitch pulled harder on his arm. Gerardo snuck another peek, just as Ramón turned left at the exit sign and started for the stairs. At the far end of the hall, a trio of nurses hurried into Room One-oh-nine. He heard a scream and then another. The nurse loosened her grip and then let him go altogether. The door to One-oh-nine burst open. The front of the nurse's uniform was a glistening smear of blood. Her mouth was a frozen circle. Gerardo wrapped the automatic in a fresh towel and stuck it under his arm. For seventy feet, he shuffled along behind his captor as she hurried back toward the shouts and confusion. At the overhead exit sign, he straight-armed the door, stepped into the stairwell, and began jogging up the stairs. At the first landing, he threw his hip into the emergency exit door and stepped outside into the cool night air. "One down, one to go," he whispered to himself, as he started up the sidewalk.

24

Friday, October 20   **10:57 p.m.**

Along the north shore of Lake Union, the derelict ferry *Kalakala* lay beached like some moldering gray carcass washed ashore by the tide. Once the pride of the Seattle fleet, the Art Deco *Kalakala* had been rescued by a local businessman, whose sense of nostalgia had been offended by the notion that the ferry of his childhood seemed destined to live out its final days as an Alaskan fish-packing plant.

At considerable expense, he'd had her towed down from Alaska and berthed at her current location, only to find that his fellow Seattleites did not share his fondness for the old vessel. Not only were they unwilling to participate in her proposed multimillion-dollar renovation but most considered her little more than an eyesore and demanded that she be removed from sight forthwith. Under intense pressure from the city, her owner now sought a suitable buyer who might be willing to take her off his hands.

As the rusted hull slid to starboard, Renee Rogers

stepped over to the refrigerator and filled her glass with ice cubes, which she then drowned in bourbon.

"Warren would hate this," she said.

"Hate what?"

"Hate us bobbing around out here on the lake together. He gave me a little lecture the other day about what he called *commiserating* with you."

"Have we been doing that? And here I thought we were just trying to pick each other's brains over dinner."

She laughed and looked around. "We're almost back, aren't we?" she said.

"Up ahead on the left."

The purple had faded from the horizon, leaving a charcoal sky. The air had begun to thicken with mist, turning the full moon to a hazy nickel.

She took another pull from her drink. "So how come you never got married?" she asked, out of the blue.

Corso pulled his gaze from the lake and looked her way. Her eyes looked tired, and her words carried just the hint of a slur.

"How do you know I've never been married?"

She laughed. "I've read your file, of course. You don't think we let you in the courtroom without doing our homework, do you?"

"What about you?" Corso asked. "You've never managed it either."

She made a *tsk-tsk* sound. "You've got a file on me too, don't you?"

"Of course."

She laughed again. "You ever notice how small talk suffers when you're talking to somebody you've got a dossier on?"

Corso's shoulders shook with laughter. It took him a moment before he was able to speak. "Especially when they don't know."

Renee Rogers threw her head back and laughed. Corso kept on.

"You already know everything you'd normally ask them at a time like that, so you're five minutes into a conversation with a stranger, and if you're not careful you're asking them about that mole they had removed last year, a story that they can't, for the life of them, remember having shared with you."

"And they spend the rest of the night looking at you out of the corner of their eyes."

They shared another laugh, before Corso asked. "So? How come you never managed it either?"

"I asked you first."

He thought it over. "I was engaged once, but things didn't work out," he said, after a moment. "It's not like I planned it that way or anything. Always seemed to me like I might be ready to settle down after the next assignment or after the next big story." He shrugged. "It just kept getting pushed somewhere down the road until I was so used to being like I was"—he took one hand off the wheel—"that it stopped being an issue."

She folded her arms and turned her eyes inward.

"You like living alone?" she said, after a short silence.

"I'm used to it. The longer I do it, the more it suits me."

"You don't get lonely?"

"You can be married with five kids and still be lonely."

She gestured with her glass. "Your Honor. The witness is being unresponsive. Please direct him to answer the question."

He chuckled. "Yeah . . . Sometimes, I guess—you know—sometimes it would be nice to have somebody to do things with."

"I hate eating out alone," Renee Rogers offered.

"Me too. That's another reason why I cook."

She finished her drink. "When I get home, I'm going to dust off all the cookbooks I've gotten as presents over the years and give it a try." She held up two fingers, Boy Scout–style. "I hereby resolve to be more domestic." The slur was stronger now. She seemed to notice and turned her face toward the windows.

Corso pulled back on the throttles, allowing the wind and the water to slow the boat's momentum and ease *Saltheart* to a stop alongside the floating dock.

Renee Rogers pushed herself from the seat. "I'll help," she announced.

"No need," Corso said. "I've got it. Docking's easier," he lied.

He moved quickly down the stairs and out onto the deck. First he went forward and threw the bowline down onto the dock, then grabbed a trio of fenders and spaced them along the rail as he made his way to the stern. By the time he'd finished getting the stairs in place, the wind had moved the boat six feet from the dock and he had to step inside and readjust the bow thruster. Renee Rogers was leaning back against the sink, rolling her icy glass across her forehead. Corso stepped back outside, climbed to the bottom step, and hopped down onto the dock.

Took him five minutes to moor the boat to his satisfaction and reconnect the electrical power and the phone line. When he stepped back into the galley, Renee Rogers was leaning over the counter, taking deep breaths through her open mouth.

"You okay?" he asked.

She gave a silent shake of the head and continued staring down into the sink as Corso stepped around her and turned off the engines.

"Anything I can do?" he asked.

She stood up straight and brought a hand to her throat. "I don't know, I think maybe it's the rocking of the boat. I feel dizzy."

"Come on," he said, offering a hand. She took it, and he led her down into the salon and sat her on the couch. "Relax."

She leaned back on the couch, brought a hand up to her forehead, closed her eyes, and took several deep breaths.

"This is so embarrassing," she said.

"The water affects people differently."

She massaged the back of her neck and nodded slightly.

"Relax," Corso said. "I'm going to do a few chores. I'll be right back."

It took him the better part of ten minutes to round up all the plates and glasses, rinse everything, and get it into the dishwasher. When he returned to the salon, Renee Rogers hadn't moved. He sat down next to her on the sofa and jostled her arm. She tried three times before her eyes blinked open. "How ya doin'?" he asked.

"Not very well, I'm afraid. One minute I was feeling fine. . . ."

"Listen," Corso said. "I've got an idea. I've got a

real nice forward berth with its own head. Why don't you lie down there until you're feeling better."

She started to protest, but Corso kept talking.

"You wake up and feel better, we'll call you a cab. You sleep till morning, and I'll make you breakfast. Whatta you say?"

She tried to get to her feet. "I couldn't, really." Her hand slipped on the arm of the sofa, and she fell back onto the couch.

Corso held out his hand. "Come on," he said.

He left his hand extended until finally she reached out and took it. Slowly, he pulled her to her feet and led her back through the galley to the four stairs leading down to the forward berth and the chain locker. She slipped slightly on the second step, but Corso was there to take her by the shoulders and ease her to the lower deck.

He slid open the door to the berth. "Here it is," he said. "Take it easy for a while. See how you feel."

"This is terrible," she said. "I'm so embarrassed."

"Nothing to be embarrassed about," he said as he steered her into the room until the backs of her legs were against the bed. "Just make yourself comfortable."

She pulled the coverlet back, sat, and swung her feet up onto the bed, then noticed her shoes. She used her right foot to pry off the opposite sneaker, then reversed the process. Corso grabbed the Nikes and set them on the floor next to the bed.

"Just till I'm feeling better," she said.

"I'll button things up for the night and then come back and see how you're doing. We'll figure out where to go from there."

"Okay," she said, closing her eyes.

She was snoring before he got the door closed. He reached over, drew the coverlet over her shoulder, and made his way up and forward. Turned off the dock lights and the heat and finally, almost as an afterthought, flipped on the carpet alarm. He started outside to pull up the stairs but stopped himself. Figured he better wait and see what was going on with Rogers. On his way through the salon, he cracked a couple of windows.

25

The cornstalks stood dry and broken among the furrows, their shattered shafts pale against the frozen brown earth. Here and there, snow had gathered along the windward edges of the rows, like lace along the neck of a dress.

The preacher had to ask the operator to shut down the backhoe so he could be heard above the wind. Then he started on about other lives in other times, as the mourners stood hand in hand, waiting for him to speak his piece, so they could put the box in the ground and finally be free of everything but the memory. Or so they hoped.

As he read from the book, the sky darkened and the air was filled with the rush of wings. A flock of blackbirds filled the sky, soaring together, veering off at angles, and then, as if by signal, landing in the cornfield, where they began to pick among the stubble like refugees. And above the droning voice, above the whine of the wind and the rustle of the birds, the hollow metal sound began, metric and mechanical: bong . . . bong . . . bong . . .

Corso sat up in bed. The muted gong of the alarm system beat a rhythm in his ears. He checked the digital clock by his bedside. One thirty-five. Probably a dog, he thought. That big ugly shepherd they take out on the Catalina thirty-six.

He lay back and waited for the dog to wander off and the alarm to go silent. The wind had died. *Saltheart* floated lightly in the slip. The moment he felt the boat move, his heart began to pound in his chest. Somebody was coming up the stairs he had left in place. Nobody in the marina would come on board without permission. It just wasn't done. You hailed from the dock. You hammered on the hull. You did whatever you had to, but you didn't come aboard without permission. He sat back up and flipped the switch, turning off the alarm. Then the boat rocked again as a second person climbed the ladder to the deck, and he felt his mouth go dry.

He bumped himself down off the berth. Wearing only a pair of Kelly-green basketball trunks, he climbed the three stairs and poked his head up into the galley. Maybe Rogers was up and wandering around. It took a single glance to stop the breath in his chest and make his blood feel cold.

Shadows, two of them: one tall, one short. Short had come on board first. He was halfway to the stern when he stuck his fingers into the window crack and slid the window all the way open. Then the curtains were eased back. The cops maybe?

Tall came in head first. With the grace of a gymnast, he used his hands to cushion his roll down onto the couch, came up lightly on his feet, then reached back out the window. When the hand reappeared, it held a silenced automatic. Corso felt his insides contract. So much for the cops. Tall set the automatic off to the side on the settee and put both hands out the window. The sight of a pump shotgun in his hands got Corso moving.

He swallowed a mouthful of air and backed down the stairs. Once at the bottom, he quietly closed and locked the companionway door. He knew the puny barrel bolt wouldn't stop a determined child; he just hoped to slow them down. A movement beneath his feet announced the second man's arrival in the salon. Corso crawled down under the stairs.

His fingers trembled as he unlatched the brass dogs holding the engine-room hatch, but his brain was starting to work again. He knew what he had to do. They were only expecting one person on board. If they went forward, they'd find Rogers in the bunk, kill her, and then come looking for him. He had to draw them toward himself and then make his way through the engine room to Rogers in the bow, hoping like hell they didn't know anything about boats, didn't immediately realize that all they had to do was go up to the main deck and they could stroll wherever they wanted.

He pulled open the three storage drawers that were built into the bulkhead. Open, they prevented the door from swinging inward. He banged his hand hard on the door and ducked down under the stairs. They came his way. He heard the door handle rattle and the wood groan. Somebody walked back to the salon and then returned.

An instant later a deep muffled boom shattered the air, and the companionway door was reduced to splinters. The air was filled with floating pieces of fabric and fiber. They'd used a couch cushion to muffle the shotgun's roar. A second smothered blast, and the opened drawers were history. The splintered remains were still in the air, as Corso crawled into the engine room and snapped the four inside dogs closed.

He reached to his right, switched on the light, and moved as quickly and quietly as possible toward the bow. He duckwalked his way between the twin Lehman diesels, picked his way carefully over the exhaust manifolds and electrical lines. Through the forward storage area to the forward watertight door, where he sat on his haunches and took a deep breath. If they'd figured it out and were waiting, he was dead.

The first dog took him three tries. After that, he was cool. He pulled the door toward himself. He winced as he stuck his head out and peered up at the bottom of the stairs. Nothing, so he crawled out into the hall and stood up. Ran the same door-locking strategy with the barrel bolt and the open doors and then slid open the berth door.

Renee Rogers was sitting up in bed. She wore an expensive-looking gray bra-and-panty set and a serious frown. He clamped a hand over her mouth. She grabbed his wrist and tried to pull the hand away. "Shhhhh," Corso hissed. She began to struggle, digging her nails into his wrist. Corso reached for her free hand but missed. Her fingers were hooked into a claw, on their way to remove his eyes, when the shotgun roared out in the hall and the air was suddenly full of gunsmoke and debris. Her nails stopped an inch from his face. When he removed his hand, her mouth hung open.

Corso got to his knees and opened the overhead

hatch. He fought his fingers as he twisted the knob on the restraining arm, until it finally came off in his hand, allowing the hatch to flop all the way open. The shotgun roared again. Corso could hear them kicking out the remaining splinters of the door. He pointed up at the hatch.

Didn't have to tell her twice; she scrambled up and out in an instant. Corso wiggled his shoulders through the narrow opening and then used his arms to lever himself on deck. He took her by the hand. To port was the dock, to starboard, Lake Union. He pulled her toward the lake.

"Over the side," he whispered. "It's our only chance."

She nodded and put one leg over the rail.

"Stay close to me," he said.

"I can't swim," she said. Her lower lip quivered.

"I'll take care of you," he said.

They stepped off together. Her eyes were wide. Her instincts pulled her knees to her chest, as they hovered for a moment before plummeting down into the black water.

The icy water raked his skin like nails, froze the air in his lungs, and gave him an instant headache. He surfaced, shaking the water from his eyes. To his left, Rogers was making gasping sounds and thrashing the water to foam, in a frenzied attempt to stay afloat. He reached over, grabbed her wrist, and pulled her to him. Her face was white with terror. She locked her arms and legs around him in a death grip, sending them both below the surface. Corso held his breath and pried her loose, spun her in the water, and threw his arm around her chest in the classic lifeguard manner.

She came up gasping, whimpering. Her body shuddered uncontrollably as Corso began to stroke his way toward the stern. His "Shhhh" failed to stop her gasps. The effort made his legs ache. A cramp tore at his right calf.

From inside the boat, two more muffled shotgun blasts. They'd be on deck in a minute. At the stern, Corso grabbed the swim step with one hand. With the other, he spun Renee Rogers in the water. He slipped his knee between her legs and used it to keep her afloat. "Listen to me." Her lips were turning blue, but she nodded slightly. "You and I are going down under the swim step. There's room under there to breathe. Ready?"

He didn't wait for an answer, just put his arm around her waist and pulled her underwater. He managed a pair of scissor kicks before she struggled loose from his grasp and shot to the surface, banging her head on the underside of the swim step.

Corso came up facing her. The space between the underside of the swim step and the surface water was just big enough to keep their heads out of the water. Corso brought his finger to his lips. She was shaking so violently, he couldn't tell if she'd understood. Her face was the color of oatmeal. She was gasping for air.

The swim step was a lattice of teak, designed to keep water from collecting on its surface. She had her hands thrust up through a couple of the spaces, holding on for dear life. Unfortunately, anyone looking down from the stern would surely see her fingers and then they'd both be dead.

Corso pointed to her hands and shook his head. "Let go."

"No," she breathed.

Corso swam to the rear of the step, put his back against the hull, and grabbed hold of the support bracket. He gestured for her to come. She refused to move. "Theeey're gonnnnna seeee your fiiiiingers," he stuttered out. She looked up at her hands, over at Corso, and began to cry. He extended a hand. His legs were going numb from the cold. He could barely keep them moving. "Come on," he said.

She came his way hand over hand, exchanging one grip for another until she was locked against his side. "Hang on to me," he whispered. She tried to speak but couldn't get her jaw muscles to cooperate. She was shivering and clinging to him like a barnacle when he began to feel movement in the hull. They were coming toward the stern. He brought a finger to his lips, but she was too far gone to notice.

He heard the hinged section of rail swing up and the gate swing open. Ten seconds passed before the visitor stepped down onto the swim step. All Corso could see were parts of the bottoms of his shoes as he moved tentatively around the platform. Someone whispered in Spanish and the feet disappeared. Half a minute later, a slight roll of the hull told him at least one of them was on the dock.

He couldn't be sure, but above the gentle lapping of the waves and the chattering of his own teeth he thought maybe he heard the sounds of shoes on the dock.

He waited. What if it was a decoy? What if one of them was still on board? She was sobbing silently now. He held her tight and waited. Seemed like he waited for an hour. Until finally he knew that if he waited any longer, he'd die there in the water. Drown six feet from safety because his muscles wouldn't carry him the distance.

He pushed off the hull with his aching legs, propelling them out from under the step. His left arm was wrapped around Rogers. He threw his right arm up onto the wood and pressed her back against the edge. "You gotta help out here," he whispered in her ear. "We're almost there." She shivered harder but opened her eyes. "Just roll up onto the step." In slow motion, she loosened her left arm and grabbed a piece of the step. Her teeth chattered like castanets. He felt her grip loosen, lowered his body in the water, and grabbed her around the hips. "Ready? One . . . two . . . three!" He managed to force one leg and one hip up onto the surface. Then he got his shoulder under her and kept pushing until the rest of her torso and the other leg followed suit. She flopped over onto her stomach and began to vomit. Corso gathered his strength and forced a knee over the edge but couldn't muster the power to pull himself aboard. Then he felt her hands, pulling at him, and he tried again, finally flopping up next to her on his belly, breathing like a locomotive.

He lay there for a moment and then rose to his knees. He crawled to the port side of the step, hooked a frozen hand into one of the indented footholds, and pulled himself upright, where he could grab the handrails. He stood leaning against the transom. He couldn't feel his legs or his feet. And then the boat rocked . . . twice. His heart threatened to tear his chest. They must have been nearby . . . watching . . . waiting.

Rogers felt it too. She looked up, read the expression of helplessness on Corso's face, and began to sob.

They were on the stern now, just above his head. When he looked up, he was staring down the barrel of a gun. He closed his eyes and waited to die.

"Frank Corso," a voice boomed, "you're under arrest for the murders of David Rosewall and Margaret Dougherty. Anything you say can and will be used against you. You have a right to an attorney. If you cannot afford an attorney . . ."

Another voice was muttering in the background. "This is Sorenstam. Get me an Aid Car," it was saying. "Forty-seven-ninety Fairview. Send two if you've got 'em."

26

Wasn't till one of the uniforms came up with Rogers's wallet that Detectives First Class Troy Hamer and Roger Sorenstam begin to take what Corso was telling them seriously. They didn't give a damn about the damage to the boat. They were stuck on crimes of passion. All they knew was they had a witness to Corso's fight with the boyfriend, a nurse who said he'd objected to Corso's presence in Dougherty's room, and an LPN who saw a tall man with a black ponytail exiting the ground-floor side door of the hospital at the time of the murders. Dead to rights. Hold the sirens.

Corso sat on the couch wrapped in a wool blanket. The last of the EMTs were up front with Rogers when the uniform handed the wallet to Hamer. "She's telling the same story he is," he whispered, and shot a glance at Corso.

Hamer made a sour face. "We better get a crime-scene team down here," he said to Sorenstam.

Corso got to his feet. "I'm leaving," he said.

"We're still conducting an investigation here," Hamer snapped.

"I'm going to the hospital," Corso announced. "You need anything from me, I'll be there." He felt like the Tin Man as he shuffled across the carpet.

His exit stalled at the top of the stairs. The stairway and the hall were littered with exploded wood. Fresh splinters poked up like teeth. Corso used a foot to roll a pair of boat shoes out from under his writing table and then slipped them on.

The refuse snapped and popped beneath his feet as he made his way to his berth. His body ached as if he'd been beaten all over, and his fingers felt thick and clumsy as he struggled into a shirt and a pair of jeans.

The EMTs had immediately thrown them in the showers, Rogers up in the guest head and Corso in his own. Left them sitting under warm water until the water heater couldn't handle it anymore.

"There's nothing you can do up there," Sorenstam said.

"I'm going anyway."

"Don't be such an asshole," Hamer said. "The more I look around, the more I'm feeling like you don't want to burn any bridges here." He swept an arm around the boat. "Whoever wanted your ass, wanted it real bad." He left a little silence for Corso. "Looks to me like the kind of people who just might try, try again, if you know what I'm sayin'."

"Maybe you guys better get to protecting and serving."

"Maybe it's time you got straight with us," Sorenstam said.

"How's that?"

Hamer made an elaborate move to scratch the back of his head. "Let me see here. We got your girl-friend"—Corso opened his mouth to argue the point, but the cop waved him off—"taking her little pictures, until a pair of skels in a black Mercedes chase her down and damn near kill her. Somehow or other they find out she's still among the living and hustle their bustles down to Harborview Medical Center, where they off both her and her boyfriend and then"—he paused again—"they come down here and make a very determined effort to pop your scrawny ass."

"You want to give us a hint here?" Sorenstam asked. "Sounds like you may have rattled somebody's cage."

Corso looked from one to the other. Despite his best efforts, a sneer crept onto his lips. "You don't have shit, do you?"

"We've got you," Hamer said.

"You've been on this for four days, and you haven't got a goddamn thing." He tried to keep the disgust out of his voice. Tried to say something neutral. What came out was, "What the fuck have you been doing with your time, anyway?"

"We've been looking at you and the boyfriend," Sorenstam snapped.

Sure. That was the protocol. Eliminate those closest to the victim before widening the investigation. For the first time since he'd been given the news, he could feel the loss burning like a cold flame. Inside his head, a fa-miliar voice said that another pair of cops was already looking into Donald Barth. Said there was no reason to put it together for these two bozos—except. And then the voice changed. Except that Dougherty was dead, and the way things were shaking out he might have inadvertently been a player. The new voice asked him what might have happened if he'd shared what he knew with the cops.

"It's got something to do with the guy they found buried in his truck," he said.

Sorenstam pulled out a notebook and a pencil.

"His name's Donald Barth." It took Corso a full five minutes to lay it out for them. "Now you know everything I do," he said as he finished. "I suggest you talk to whoever caught the truck squeal and whoever they've got looking for this Joe Ball character. Maybe one of them has come up with something useful."

Sorenstam checked his notes. "So you're saying the missing person, this Joe Ball guy, the dead guy in the truck, the assault here, and the murders at the hospital are all tied together somehow."

"That's what it looks like to me."

"Any idea about the connection?"

"None."

"So how does any of that help us?" Hamer asked.

"It doesn't," Corso said.

"Where'd he get the forty thousand?"

"No idea."

"You think any of these women was pissed off enough—"

Corso was already shaking his head. "No."

Corso stepped around the cops and pulled a black leather jacket from the closet. He stuck one arm into the coat. "Find these guys," Corso said. "Find 'em before I do."

"What you're going to do"—Hamer jabbed a finger at him—"is keep the hell out of an ongoing investigation." Corso settled the jacket on his shoulders and started toward the bow. "Do you hear me?" Hamer bellowed after him.

Hamer was angry. Corso didn't blame him. They'd wasted a lot of manpower going around in circles. Last thing they wanted was to hear from some jive-ass writer about how they'd fucked up.

The forward passage was still clogged with cops and EMTs. Corso shouldered his way to the front. Renee Rogers sat on the bed, wearing the outfit she'd come aboard in. She looked small inside the clothes, as if the outfit belonged to an older sister.

"How you feeling?" Corso asked.

She had to think it over. "Like I'll never really be warm again."

"I'm going up to the hospital."

She reached out and touched his cheek. "Oh—your friend. I'm so sorry."

Corso nodded. "You walking okay?" he asked, after a moment.

"My legs feel like rubber bands, but they work."

"Let's get out of here. They've got a forensics team on the way. The place is about to be crawling with cops."

She put her hand on his. "You saved my life."

"We got lucky," he said.

Her eyes said she didn't believe a word of it but was too tired to argue.

"I'll drop you at the hotel."

She searched his eyes. "You sure you want to go up there?"

"It'll never be real to me if I don't," he said.

She said she understood and got to her feet. "Let's go," she said.

The walk started off shaky; she nearly fell off the stairs. Leaning on each other, they got steadier as they made their way up the dock to the gate. Corso's legs would barely push him up the steep ramp. When he looked back, Renee Rogers was having the same problem. She stood at the bottom shaking her head. He took her hand and pulled her to his side. Then walked to the top and repeated the process.

They were still holding hands when the flashbulbs began to pop and the reporters stepped from behind the cars, firing questions from the darkness. They'd had word of a shooting. Could he elaborate? Was he involved? If there was a shooting, did the police have a suspect? "That's the Rogers woman," he heard somebody say. "You know, the U.S. Attorney from the Balagula case." Her name joined his in the air as they pushed their way through the crowd toward the car.

Ten yards from sanctuary, Rogers was jostled by the crowd and dropped her purse, which burst open on impact, spilling some of the contents out on the ground.

Corso straight-armed the nearest photographer, setting off a stumbling chain reaction as she bent to retrieve her bag. Flashbulbs rendered him nearly blind as he led her to the car, let her in, and threw himself into the driver's seat.

Saturday, October 21   2:40 a.m.

"I'm sorry, sir, but you can't. . . ."
Corso ducked under the yellow police tape and started down the stairs. They'd fixed the elevators so they wouldn't go to the basement and strung enough

plastic police tape across the stairwells to circle the globe.

She couldn't have been more than twenty. "Please, sir," she whined at his back as he held on to the handrail and walked deliberately down the stairs. At the first landing, he looked up and saw her still standing at the top. "The police—" she began.

At the bottom, he pulled the door open, poked his head out into the hall, looked one way and then the other. In both directions, the corridor was full of people. To the left, it was mostly hospital employees, people the police would want to interview before allowing them to go home. To the right was One-oh-nine, where a pair of medical examiners, in bright yellow jackets, sipped coffee from plastic cups while they stood talking with a couple of county mounties.

His eyes stopped on a pair of metal gurneys, end to end along the wall. Resting, larvaelike, on top of each cart was a black rubber body bag, red straps around the chests and ankles. He felt like he always felt in the face of death, light and disconnected. Like he was coming unglued from the earth.

His legs ached as he started down the hall. A voice behind him called, "Hey!" He kept going. The door to One-oh-nine popped open. Rachel Taylor stepped out into the hall. As the door eased shut, Corso could hear the sound of angry voices coming from inside. She caught sight of Corso and stopped. "Oh," she said. "Miss Dougherty—"

The door opened again. Crispin, Edward J.: red-faced, disheveled, looking like he'd been rousted from his bed. Followed by what had to be a couple of cops.

He went slack-jawed at the sight of Corso coming his way.

"She's not here," he said. Corso stopped. "Your friend," Crispin tried. "She's not here anymore."

Corso's eyes moved to the body bags.

"No," Crispin said. "That's . . ." He looked to Nurse Taylor for help.

"Mrs. Guillen," Taylor said. "Ruth Guillen."

"I found her a room," Crispin blurted.

Rachel Taylor walked to Corso's side and took hold of his arm. She cast a baleful stare at Crispin. "Mr. Crispin circumvented the normal room-scheduling procedures." Another stare. "Second shift saw the room was empty and put Mrs. Guillen in it."

"She'd been in a head on-collision," Crispin added, as if her condition somehow mitigated whatever the problem was.

"Mr. Rosewall didn't know either," Taylor said. "He just walked in at the wrong time."

"I don't understand," Corso said, feeling himself beginning to sway.

"Miss Dougherty is upstairs in surgery," Rachel Taylor said.

27

They cut a hole in her head. "Not very big," the post-op nurse said with a smile. She held her fingers about an inch apart. "About the size of a stamp."

She busied herself changing an IV bag and straightening the covers. "Her vital signs are better this morning," she announced. "I think doctor is going to be pleased." Not *the* doctor or Dr. Something-or-other. Just *doctor*. Corso grunted.

He was holed up in a brown leatherette chair under the window, sipping lukewarm coffee through an articulated straw, trying not to wonder if things could get worse.

The door opened and another nurse marched in and dropped both morning papers in his lap. She stood with hands on half-acre hips, waiting for him to have a peek. Without looking down, Corso thanked her, folded the papers in two, and stuffed them between the cushion and the armrest. She huffed once, looked at the post-op nurse as if to say *Some people*, and left. Post-op was still chuckling when she completed her tasks and squeaked out of the room.

Corso waited a minute and then crossed to the bedside. Her rest was more troubled now. Her extremities twitched and, just after the last doctor had left, she groaned once, as if to say enough was enough, and tossed her head back and forth. He had the urge to pull the covers up over the spiraled words and images that encircled her bare arms, but she seemed so fragile, and her hold on life so tenuous, he couldn't bring himself to touch a thing.

He returned to the chair and looked down at the papers. He used two fingers to pry the top paper off and turn it face up on the seat. The *Seattle Times*. Lunar-landing-sized picture. He and Rogers, hand in hand at the top of the dock ramp, looking like they'd been rode hard and put up wet. Banner headline: EASTLAKE GUN BATTLE. He winced. Turned it over and grabbed the other paper. After the *Times*, how bad could it be?

Bad. MARINA SHOOT-OUT. The *Post Intelligencer* photographer had caught them by the car: Corso snarling at a cameraman, Renee Rogers, down on one knee, gathering her things back into her purse. You could see it plain as day, the strap and one cup of her brassiere hanging out on the asphalt. And the little wet bundle still nestled inside the bag that you knew just hadda be the panties. Warren's really gonna hate this, he thought.

Corso deposited both papers in the bathroom wastebasket and was on his way back to the chair when Detective Sorenstam poked his hat in the door and gestured for Corso to come out in the hall.

Hamer leaned against the wall, picking his teeth with a blue twist tie. Sorenstam had his notebook out. "We talked with Jonesy and his partner," he said.

"They caught the Barth squeal." Corso waited for him to get to the point. "The number crunchers read it like you do. Guy's living like a mouse for years. Sending all his cash back east so's his kid can get an education."

"Then, last year, he gets behind," Hamer offered.

"Med school's a bitch."

Hamer chewed the piece of plastic like a cigar. "He tries to borrow thirty grand from his credit union, but they turn him down. Back in Boston, the kid's trying to finagle a loan for himself."

"And then, *bingo!*" Sorenstam snapped his fingers. "All of a sudden he pays off the whole damn thing. All the way to the end of the year."

Hamer dropped the twist tie to the floor. "And while that's going on, this Barth guy is leaving the house every day, kissing the little woman good-bye and going where?" He didn't wait for a reply. " 'Cause he sure as hell wasn't going to his job at the school district. He's on leave June through September of 'ninety-nine."

"Neighbors say everything was status quo. His truck came and went as usual." Sorenstam shrugged. "Wife swears it was same-old same-old."

"So where did he go?" Corso asked.

"Someplace you could get forty grand," Hamer said.

"What about this Joe Ball guy?" Corso asked.

"Still missing," Hamer said.

"Missing Persons has a guy says your friend Miss Dougherty was the last person to see Mr. Ball before he turned up lost."

Corso held up a hand. "So let's assume our friend Mr. Ball was responsible for burying Donald Barth and his truck."

"Why would he want to do that?" Hamer asked.

"Probably because somebody paid him to."

"Okay."

"And whoever paid him is unhappy when the truck turns up."

Hamer bumped himself off the wall and wandered over. "And you're thinking your girlfriend here walked in on them expressing their displeasure."

"Could be," Corso said.

"There's a chase," Sorenstam prompted.

"She crashes."

"One of them gets out to finish the deal, but civilians show up."

"How'd they know she was still alive?" Corso asked. "How'd they know which hospital to find her in?"

"Maybe they followed the ambulance," Hamer said.

"Maybe," Corso muttered, without believing it for a minute.

"Doesn't explain their beef with you, though," Hamer said.

"Assuming they're the same people, of course," his partner added.

They stood in silence for a moment, before Corso asked, "You gonna put somebody on the door?"

Hamer looked puzzled. "What door?"

"This one."

"What for?"

"In case you haven't noticed, somebody's trying to kill her."

"She's safe up here. Nobody knows where she is," Hamer said.

"She's unlisted," Sorenstam assured him.

"*You* found her," Corso said.

"What's that supposed to mean?" Hamer demanded.

Corso leaned down and put his face in Hamer's. "You'll excuse me, won't you, if I'm not exactly dazzled by your investigative footwork?"

Hamer dropped his hands to his sides and leaned on Corso with his chest. "I was you, I'd worry about my own ass."

"You was me, you'd probably have detected something by now."

Sorenstam was using his forearms to push them apart. "Hey, now . . . hey, now . . . take it easy. We're all on the same side here." He looked from one to the other but came away empty.

"She needs protection," Corso insisted.

Hamer used his finger to pry something out from between his teeth and then spit it to the floor. "You think she needs protection, you do it," he said with a grin. "According to the papers, you seem to be on a roll when it comes to saving damsels in distress."

28

J oe Bocco just *happened* to be Italian. When you've got a name like that, a scar on your cheek, and you break legs for a living, a number of stereotypes come immediately to mind, not the least of which would be the assumption that, with his ancestry and occupation, he must be part of some wider, more well-known criminal conspiracy, involving others whose names likewise end in vowels.

Not so, though. Joe was an equal opportunity thug. Billed himself as private security. For the right piece of change, he'd dance the tarantella on somebody's spinal column for you or, if he was sure you were a pro, maybe even follow you through the front door of a rock house.

They'd met five years ago, when Corso had been working a story about the longshoremen's union. Lotta pension money turned out to be missing. Lotta people thought union president Tony Trujillo was responsible. Some of those same folks wanted him dead. Corso had interviewed Trujillo on a sweltering hot August day, down on Pier 18, while Joe Bocco sat in the corner wearing a turtleneck and a full-length raincoat. Never broke a sweat. Never even blinked. Two days later, a pair of cowboys tried to force Trujillo's limo off the Fourth Avenue Bridge. Bocco killed the driver and left the passenger paralyzed from the waist down. Front-page news.

Bocco checked the room, then looked over at Dougherty. "This the one from the paper?"

"Yeah."

He stroked his chin. "Which ain't the same one you was on the front page with?"

"No."

He marinated the thought for a moment and then turned his gaze back toward Meg. "So somebody tried to cap her and offed a couple of civilians instead."

Corso frowned. "Where'd you get that from? That wasn't in the papers."

"It's all over the radio."

"Shit," Corso said.

"Be better off the hitters didn't know, wouldn't it? They any kind of pros, they're gonna be pissed as hell." He pulled open the bathroom door and peered inside. "Obviously, you think they're coming back."

"Could be."

"And you want me to make sure she doesn't get any unwanted visitors."

"That's what I had in mind."

"I quoted you a rate on the phone. That gonna work for you?"

"Yeah."

"Sooner or later I gotta sleep."

"You got any brave friends?"

He shook his head. "Know a couple of fools, maybe."

"Have one of them relieve you."

"Be another seven-fifty."

"And Greenspan said there was no inflation."

Joe Bocco sneered. Did the insurance company commercial. "How can you put a price on peace of mind?" he asked.

Saturday, October 21   1:13 p.m.

Not a word in six hours. Not since this morning, when they seen the TV news about the bitch still being alive. Just sitting there on the bed, cleaning his piece over and over again, staring out the window at the water. When Ramón finally spoke, Gerardo nearly choked on his room-service burrito.

"Comes a time you gotta listen," Ramón said suddenly. "Somethin' in the world is talkin' to you, tryin' to take care of you, and all you gotta do is open up your ears and listen to what it's got to say."

"That what you been doing?" Gerardo asked around a mouthful of bun. "You been listening to the world?"

Ramón felt his anger rise. "I meant like, you know, metaphorically."

Gerardo dredged a pair of french fries in ketchup and stuffed them into his mouth. "What's that mean?" he asked. "Meta . . ."—he waved a pair of red fingers— "whatever you said. What's that mean?"

"It means I'm thinkin' we ought to maybe lay low for a while," he said, as much to himself as to Gerardo. "Maybe take a little time off." He looked at Gerardo. "You could visit your sister in Florida."

Gerardo washed the burrito down with Coke. "Kids must be getting big by now," he mused. He flicked a glance at Ramón. "You could maybe see your mom."

Ramón sighed. "We got nothing to say to each other."

"She's your mother, man."

"I'm telling you. It's not me, it's her. She don't want nothing to do with me. Got this new husband. Plays fucking golf. Don't want none of the old-time shit coming back at her. She don't talk to my sister neither."

Gerardo stopped chewing. Frowned. "We gonna tell the Russians?"

"Fuck, no. They'll cap us for sure."

Gerardo started to argue, but Ramón cut him off. "We'll get replaced just like we replaced those Colombian dudes." He held up two fingers. Two in the head. "They ain't gonna want us walkin' around. We know where the bodies are buried."

Gerardo waved the burrito around. "That's another one of those meta things, huh?"

Ramón wanted to explain that it was and it wasn't, but instead he kept things simple. "Yeah," he said.

"When we gonna go?"

"Soon as we take care of business."

Saturday, October 21   1:13 p.m.

"I told you he was in her pants," Nicholas Balagula said in Russian. It came out with a bit of reverberation because of the way the hotel's Swedish masseuse was pummeling his vertebrae as he spoke. She was a large red-faced woman with thinning blond

hair and a pair of big red hands strong enough to stran-
gle a heifer.

She grabbed a double handful of his smooth rubbery
flesh and began to knead it like bread. Balagula put on
his glasses and read the text beneath the picture of
Renee Rogers stuffing her underwear into her purse.
He looked up at Mikhail Ivanov, who was holding the
paper in front of his face. "You didn't—"

Ivanov raised an eyebrow. "Of course not."

"Not the Cubans?" Balagula asked.

"I did what you told me," Ivanov said. "They followed him home to the boat and then reported in. That
was it."

Balagula nodded. "When this is over," he began.

"I'll see to it personally," Ivanov said. They'd agreed.
When the trial was over, they disappeared into retirement. No need for the likes of Ramón and Gerardo.

She was using the sides of her hands like cleavers,
working her way up and down his spine. The thick skin
of his torso vibrated from the blows.

"The timing is interesting."

"I thought so too."

"Or perhaps Mr. Corso merely has a knack for making enemies."

"I wouldn't be surprised," Ivanov said.

Balagula reached back and grabbed the woman's
wrist. "Enough," he said in English. The woman
stepped back, offered a curt bow, and crossed the suite
to a black athletic bag she'd left on the side bar. She
pulled a white hand towel from the bag and wiped her
hands. "Charge to the room?" she asked.

"Please," Ivanov said, and she was out the door and
gone.

Nicholas Balagula pulled the towel from his buttocks and sat up. "Some company for tonight." Ivanov looked away. "Something fresh. Something not so long on the vine this time."

"You think this is easy?" Ivanov snapped. "In a strange city?"

Nicholas Balagula shuffled across the floor. As he walked, his privates swung to and fro beneath his belly. He put a hand on Ivanov's shoulder. "Soon, Mikhail," he said, "this farce will be over, and you can run to that house of yours in France. Find yourself a cow to service you." Ivanov stepped out from under the hand. "In the meantime . . ."

"I'll do the best I can," said Ivanov.

29

Saturday, October 21   4:54 p.m.

His mother, his brothers, and his sister were inside with the relatives, huddled around casseroles and coffee, the air filled with hushed talk about moving on to a better place and how maybe it was all for the best or was part of some grand plan not apparent to humble folk such as themselves.

He stood on the dirt floor of the garage, looking up at the trunk in the rafters, half expecting some specter to appear and demand to know why he wasn't inside with his mother and what in hell he thought he was doing. He shivered.

He pushed the rusted wheelbarrow over to the center of the room, stepped up into the bucket and grabbed the trunk with both hands. Somehow, he'd always imagined the trunk to be of great weight and so was momentarily taken aback when it turned out to be a mere fraction of what he'd expected.

The metal strapping was cold to the touch as he slid the trunk into his arms and then stepped down onto the

*floor and started across toward the ancient GMC
pickup truck backed halfway into the garage.*

*He wasted no time. Just set the trunk on the tailgate,
hurried over to the workbench, and grabbed a claw
hammer. The brass key that opened the lock was probably around somewhere, but he wasn't inclined to look.*

*With a single snap, the hammer pulled the hasp free
of the trunk. He took a deep breath and pushed open
the lid. The top layer was a shallow tray, divided into
compartments. Closest, a pair of rusty dog tags and
three dull brass shell casings. To the right, an American flag folded into a tight triangle. A stack of letters,
written in his mother's childish hand. Got as far as*
Dear Wayne *before his eyes refused. Bunches of army
insignia, campaign ribbons. A small porcelain figure
of a smiling hula dancer with* HAWAII *painted across the
base.*

*He grabbed the brass rings and lifted the tray from
the trunk. On top was a neatly folded dress uniform
and hat. He carefully pulled the hat and uniform out
and set them on the tray. Beneath the folded pants was
a brown paper sack from Baxter's Market.*

*He peeked inside. His breath caught in his throat. A
leaner, younger version of his father stared back at
him. He stood knee-deep in snow, leaning on an M1
rifle, looking like he'd rather be any other damn place
on earth. When he pulled the picture out, the headline
hit him in the face:* LOCAL POW COMES HOME TUESDAY.
*His hands shook as he picked the yellowed newspaper
article from the bag and carefully unfolded it. The* Bu-
ford County News, *November 10, 1954: Longtime
Tiree resident Wayne D. Corso returned to his wife and
family after nearly three years in a North Korean pris-*

oner-of-war camp. Captured early in the Korean con-
flict, Mr. Corso . . .

As he stood peering down into that broken vault,
he'd felt his childish sense of certainty float off and
disappear into the winter sky, until he was left with
only the disquieting suspicion that, from that moment
forward, the world would always be something other
than what it first seemed to be, a thought that left him
shivering in that dank garage, feeling more alone than
he'd ever felt in his life.

And then an iron hand gripped his shoulder, and he
knew it was him, come back to . . .

Corso opened his eyes. Joe Bocco stood next to his chair.

"I think she's waking up," he said.

Corso blinked twice, ran his hands over his face, and got to his feet.

Something certainly had changed. She was restless, trying to move her hands, which were secured to the metal bed rails by elastic bandages, designed to keep her from disrupting the IV tubes sprouting from her body like vines.

Corso walked to the side of the bed and put his hand on her arm. Her body jumped as if she were startled by the intrusion.

"Should I get somebody?" Bocco asked.

Corso said yes. Joe Bocco buttoned his coat and left the room at the exact moment when her eyes popped open. Her eyes squeezed down in pain when she tried to move her head and survey the room. She groaned and then tried to speak. Nothing.

Corso poured a glass of ice water from the chrome

pitcher by the bedside, stuck one of the hinged hospital straws in, and held it to her mouth. Took her lips three tries to master the sucking thing. She closed her eyes and made noises like a puppy having a bad dream as she slowly but surely emptied the glass. When her lips released the straw, he refilled the glass and repeated the process.

She was halfway through the second glass when Joe Bocco returned with a nurse. She was maybe thirty, a big woman but nicely shaped. Apple cheeks and sparkling blue eyes, hair a little too red to be real. Had a name tag with rhinestones around the edge that read TURNER. "Easy now," she said to Dougherty as she took the cup from Corso's hand. "There's no rush."

Dougherty's eyes opened and found the new voice.

"Nice to have you back," the nurse said, as she began to unwind the elastic. "You don't have to answer me; just listen," she said. "I'm going to free your hands now. I'm going to need you to keep your hands away from the top of your head."

Dougherty tried to nod and immediately regretted the action, as even a slight movement squeezed her eyes closed in pain. As the nurse made her way to the other side of the bed, Dougherty took her freed hand and rested it on her stomach. She looked over at Corso. "Hey," she croaked.

"Hey yourself," he said.

She swallowed twice and asked, "How long?"

"Since the crash?"

She blinked what Corso took to be a yes. He counted backward in his head.

"Four days," he said.

"What day?"

"It's Saturday the twenty-first."

"David?"

Corso looked over at the nurse, who gave him a somber shake of the head.

"He's been in a lot," Corso assured her, and then abruptly changed the subject. "Just blink if I'm right, okay?" *Blink.* "You walked in on something going on at Evergreen Construction." *Blink.* "A killing?" *Blink.* "You saw the killers?" *No blink.* "You didn't see the killers." *Blink.* "They chased you." *Blink.* "You crashed your car into a moving van." *Blink.* "That's all you know." *Blink.*

She looked over Corso's shoulder and noticed Joe Bocco for the first time. She frowned and mouthed the word *who*.

"His name is Joe," Corso said. "He'll be over there in the chair in case you need anything." On cue, Bocco crossed the room and settled himself into one of the chairs, facing the door.

Nurse Turner came back around the bed. "The young lady's had about all she can handle at a time like this," she said. "Why don't you come back tomorrow? She may be feeling better then." Corso started to protest, but when he looked over at Dougherty her eyes were closed and her mouth hung open in a manner she wouldn't have permitted if she had been awake.

He looked over at Joe Bocco. "You got everything you need?"

"Marvin gonna do ten to six," he said. "I'll be back after that."

Corso let the nurse lead him by the elbow toward the door. She looked back over her shoulder at Bocco. "You too. Come on."

Corso shook his elbow free. "Mr. Bocco will be staying," he said.

She wanted to argue, but something in Corso's flat gaze brought her brain around. "Oh, you mean from like before . . . downstairs."

Corso pulled open the door and followed her out into the hall.

30

C orso held his breath as the straps began to tighten. Somewhere beneath his feet a timber groaned and then the sound of falling water began, as the engine whined and the Travel Lift started to raise *Saltheart* from the water, pulling the big boat higher and deeper into its belly until the keel came clear of the dock and swung gently between the massive tires of the machine.

Paul's son Eric fed diesel to the engine, and the Travel Lift began to ease *Saltheart* forward, down the ramp, into the boatyard.

"You said you called Dave Williams."

Paul Hansen was third generation. His family had owned the Seaview Boatyard for over seventy years. "Yeah," Corso said, as he watched *Saltheart* roll off across the asphalt. "He said he'd start on the wood-work first thing Tuesday morning."

"So what that means is Thursday or Friday." Hansen waggled the clipboard. "You know how he is. He'll be shacked up with some Betty and I'll have to send one of the boys to roust him."

"He does good work."

"The best," Hansen agreed. "Long as you're not in a hurry."

"So how long you figure?" Corso asked.

Hansen checked his list. "Ten days minimum. You any got unauthorized through holes, maybe two weeks."

"All I'm sure of is that I've got a forward bilge pump that won't quit running, so either something clipped a waterline somewhere in the boat or I've got a bullet hole somewhere in the hull."

"Heard you had a little excitement the other night."

Across the yard, an old man with a white beard was sanding the window casings on an ancient tug, whose chipped and peeling transom announced her to be the *Cheryl Anne IV*. He was humming as he worked. Not a whole song, just some little part that he kept recycling over and over.

"Let's do the bottom the same color it is now," Corso said.

Hansen chuckled and scribbled on his clipboard. "She was due for bottom work in the spring, anyway," he said.

"Tell the crew I'm grateful for them coming down on a Sunday."

He shrugged. "Christmas is coming. They can use the extra cash."

A burst of static hit his radio. He pulled it from his back pocket, pushed it against his lips, and spoke. Another longer burst of gibberish crackled from the speaker.

"Bernie says your cab is at the gate."

"Have him let it in, will you? I've got more crap than

I want to carry that far." He gestured toward the dock, where a suitcase, a garment bag, a backpack, and an Igloo cooler lay in a heap.

Hansen relayed the message and returned the radio to his pocket. "Got a number where you're staying?"

"I'll call *you*," Corso said.

Hansen permitted himself a small smile. "Can't be too careful, I guess," he mused. "Be sure you keep in touch. You know how it is. There's always something we didn't count on in the estimate."

"That's what insurance is for."

"You call them yet?"

"Said they'll have somebody out tomorrow."

"What's your deductible?"

"Fifteen hundred."

Paul Hansen snorted. "So you're out what? Maybe five percent of the tag?"

Corso shrugged. "I'd rather have the boat."

The sound of tires pulled Corso's head around. Yellow cab. He crossed to the pile on the dock, threw the backpack over one shoulder, handed the garment bag and the cooler to Paul Hansen, and grabbed the suitcase.

Satisfied that any hard work was past tense, the cabdriver got out and opened the trunk. Hanson and Corso threw his stuff inside and closed the lid. Corso sighed and gazed blankly out over the forest of grounded boats.

Paul Hansen smiled and bopped him on the arm. "You getting that hard-core boaty look, Frank."

"What look is that?" Corso asked.

Hansen inclined his head toward the old man on the *Cheryl Anne*. "You're gonna end up like Ole there. I can see it coming."

"How's that?"

"Got him a nice snug little apartment over in Fremont. His kids pay for everything, utilities and all."

"Nice kids."

"He only goes there to shower and do his laundry."

"Why's that?"

"Because he can't sleep anywhere but onboard anymore. Don't matter whether she's afloat or on the hard. Either way, it's the only place he can get a wink."

"I'll call you," Corso said, as he got into the cab. "The Marriott on Fairview," he said to the driver.

Corso kept his eyes straight ahead. Something about the sight of *Saltheart* up on jacks always bothered him. Like somehow being on land took her one step closer to joining the legion of derelict vessels who were pulled from the water for repairs and then, for one reason or another, never made it back afloat and now languish in backyards, along waterways, or in forgotten corners of boatyards, hoping for a last-minute pardon, as the brass turns green and the paint curls to the ground.

The driver bounced out into the street and turned right down Leary Way, running along the ship canal, where the last of Seattle's commercial boatyards, dry docks, and parts suppliers still held out against the yuppie condo tribe, whose insatiable appetite for waterfront has reduced what was once the very soul of the city to something like an outnumbered cavalry troop, holed up in the fort, brave and defiant but knowing it's just a matter of time before it gets dark and the Apaches come and kill them all.

An electronic beep pulled Corso's attention to his

jacket pocket. He extracted his cell phone and looked at the caller ID number. Nothing he recognized, so he figured it must be Robert Downs. "Corso," he said into the receiver.

A woman's voice. "I hope you're having a better morning than I am," Renee Rogers said. "I just got off the phone with the AG herself."

"Trading recipes?"

"Getting canned."

"Really?"

He heard her sigh. "They're never quite that direct. If you read between the lines, I'm being offered the opportunity to resign. Nice letter of recommendation and out the door."

"I take it Warren was much displeased."

"Actually—to tell you the truth—the little jerk was happy about it."

"That figures."

"Tomorrow's my last day in court. They're sending a replacement to take over on Tuesday morning."

"I'm sorry to hear it . . . assuming you are."

"Tell you the truth, Corso, I'm feeling ambivalent as hell. Part of me says, Good, let's get on with whatever comes next in life and be done with it."

"Yeah."

"And another part of me feels like I've failed at something. Like I'm being sent home in disgrace with a brand on my cheek."

"Know the feeling well," Corso said.

She sighed again. "Yeah. I'll bet you do."

After a moment of silence, she asked, "How's your friend doing?"

Corso told her. The news seemed to buoy her slightly. "Well, at least there's *some* good news," she said.

"Except she doesn't know her boyfriend's dead."

"Jesus."

Corso cleared his throat. "I didn't mean for my life to slop over on yours," he said.

"Oh, hell, Corso. I was already on the skids." He heard her laugh. "It was as much my doing as yours. I'm the one wangled the invite from you."

His first instinct was to argue about who was more to blame, but he stifled it.

"You coming to court tomorrow?" she asked.

"Wouldn't miss it for the world."

"Should get Lebow on the stand sometime tomorrow afternoon."

"I'll be there."

"See you tomorrow," she said.

"Yeah."

Corso pointed at the Fremont Bridge and the western shore of Lake Union. "Go that way," he said to the cabdriver. "Let's take a slow drive around the lake." He scooted over to the water side of the seat, rolled down the window, and stuck his nose into the salty breeze.

He closed his eyes and let the wind take him out onto the water, out past the channel buoys and then dead north, to where the tall-tale monsters lurked beneath the hull, until, suddenly, he was among the islands. In his mind's eye, he saw Dougherty leaning over the bow, directing him this way and that, as they rode the flood tide through Thatcher Pass, *Saltheart* so close to the rocks they could smell the barnacles as they eased through the crack into the nearly landlocked body of water, smooth and black as oil in the lifting morning mists. And how, just as they'd put the rocks to stern, she'd pointed to the north shore of Blakey Island, at a family of deer as they emerged onto the shore like a smudged pencil drawing.

31

Sunday, October 22   10:59 a.m.

Joe Bocco leaned back against the wall. He had his feet crossed in front of him and wore an expression of extreme boredom. Sergeant Sorenstam popped the clip from a serious-looking Glock .40-caliber and worked the slide, sending a single round down onto the floor, where he accidentally kicked it once before picking it up and dropping it into his pocket. Sergeant Hamer had a pair of black-framed half-glasses resting on the end of his nose as he read the document in his hands.

"What's this?" Corso demanded.

"National asshole week," Bocco offered.

Hamer stepped over and waved a finger under Bocco's nose. "I'm not telling you again. You watch your mouth, you hear me?"

Sorenstam pocketed the piece. "This"—he looked over at Bocco in disgust—"Mr. Bocco here says he's in your employ."

"Yeah. He is."

"In what capacity?"

"As a private security consultant."

"Doing what?"

"Doing what you guys ought to be doing. Guarding Miss Dougherty."

The cops exchanged looks. Bocco looked over at Corso, then nodded at Hamer.

"Asshole here told her about the boyfriend," he said.

Hamer started for him. Sorenstam stepped between them, using his palms to keep his partner at bay. "Take it easy, take it easy," he said.

Hamer stepped back, adjusted his coat, and shrugged. "How the hell was I supposed to know?"

"Musta been sick for the sensitivity workshop," Bocco said.

This time it was Corso who stepped between the men. "Something wrong with his carry permit?" he asked Hamer.

"I'll let you know when I'm finished with it," Hamer snapped.

Corso turned his attention now to Sorenstam. "His license in order?"

"Seems to be."

"Then what's the problem?"

"The problem," Hamer said, "is we don't like cop wannabes."

Bocco burst out laughing. "Cop? Wannabe? Are you shitting me? I'd rather be Judge Judy's toilet slave," he said.

Hamer was red-faced and pointing again. "Watch your damn mouth."

Sorenstam sighed and took his time as he pulled the clip from his pocket and thumbed the loose round in on top of the others. From his other pocket he produced the Glock. He kept the business end pointed at the floor while he inserted the clip and snapped on the safety, then turned it handle first and handed it back to Bocco.

"Try not to hurt yourself," he said.

Bocco rocked himself off the wall, slid the gun into the holster on his hip, and then stepped around Sorenstam and held out his hand.

"Whadda you want?" Hamer demanded.

"My paperwork."

"I'm gonna call it in," Hamer said.

"Let's go," Sorenstam said.

They stood for a moment like statues. Bocco with his arm extended. Hamer with the paperwork held back, out of reach.

Sorenstam started up the hall. "Let's go, Troy. He's not worth the trouble."

Hamer opened his fingers, allowing the papers to float to the floor, turned, and followed his partner up the hall.

Bocco waited until they were out of sight before retrieving his PI license and gun permit from the floor. "Is it just me," he wanted to know, "or didn't cops used to be more competent?"

"Don't get me started," Corso said.

Joe Bocco stuffed the paperwork back into his wallet. "I didn't get a chance to see how she took the news. Minute I started ragging on them, they rousted me out into the hall. That's where you came in."

"Why don't you go downstairs and get yourself a cup of coffee or something," Corso said. "I'll see how she's doing."

Corso stood in the hall for a moment, composing

himself, and then pulled open the door and stepped inside. She was up on her right side facing the wall. As he crossed the room to her bedside, a slight movement of her shoulders told him she was aware of his presence.

He stood there with his hands on the top rail. She slid deeper into the covers and sniffed up a runny nose. He waited for what seemed like an hour before she carefully rolled over onto her back and looked his way. He could see the long-ago little girl in her tear-streaked face. Lost her kitten Buster and wasn't believing a word about this kitty heaven stuff. "Sorry you found out that way," Corso said.

She started to cry. "He was so sweet to me . . ." she began, before sliding into a series of racking sobs. Something about crying women brought out the worst in Corso. He felt compelled to *do* something. To right whatever wrong had brought forth the sorrow. To turn back time, if necessary. To do whatever it took to make it stop, not so much for the sufferer as for himself, because, for reasons he'd never understood, it was the suffering of others that connected him most readily to the well of sorrow he carried around in his own heart and forced him to wonder, once again, why his own pain was so much easier to ignore than that of others.

He clamped his jaw, as if to lock the homilies in his mouth, the preacher talk of better days in better places. Of lives cut short as part of the grand plan. Of divine justice, the power of acceptance, and how time heals all wounds. Instead, he reached down and put a hand on her shoulder.

"I'm going back to Boston on Tuesday," Robert Downs said. "I'm not accomplishing a damn thing here." He ran his hand through his hair and looked around the hotel suite.

It had been nearly seven o'clock when, after devouring a room-service cheeseburger and downing a pair of Heinekens, Corso had finally gotten around to checking his messages: six, all from Robert Downs.

"All I'm doing here is beating myself up for not knowing my father, and I can do that from home." He pulled a handful of papers from his back pocket and dropped them on the coffee table. "My Harvard financial records," he said. "Undergrad, grad, and med school. The whole thing."

"You're getting married pretty soon, aren't you?"

"Seventeen days," Downs said.

"Probably a lot of details to be attended to back in Boston."

He blew air out through his lips. "Pamela—my fiancée—she's obsessing. She calls every fifteen minutes. It's like I'm supposed to—" He stopped himself. "Listen to me." He wandered over and sat down in the chair on Corso's right. "I want to thank you for the help," Downs said.

Corso waved him off. "I told you before, Robert. I'm pursuing my own ends here. The school district would have stonewalled me. I'd never have gotten a peek at those," Corso said, gesturing at the folded pile of papers on the table. "We're even."

"I've been reading *Backwater*," Downs said, naming Corso's first book, "and I'm amazed at the way you take these people you didn't even know and imbue them with life." He waved a hand in the air. "It's like what I've been trying to do with my father: take all this disparate information and somehow shape it into the picture of a man who makes sense to me. I just can't do it."

"It's easier when you don't know them at all," Corso said. "That way you can start from scratch without any preconceptions."

"But how can you be sure you get it right?"

"You can't. All you can do is look at what a person leaves behind. Look at his art. Look at his children. Look at the feelings he's left behind in others. Then look at the little things in his life. Ask people about how he kept his car. Find out if he returned things on time. Did he remember birthdays? Send Christmas cards? Show up at graduations? You do enough of that, and you start to get a picture of the character who does things for reasons that make sense to other people."

"That's exactly it," Downs said. "I can't, for the life of me, understand this fixation the man had on me and my education. We hardly knew each other. I hadn't seen him in nearly twenty years, and then I find out that his every waking effort went toward me, while—I mean, I've gone years at a time without even *thinking* about him."

"Reasons is where you have to be most careful," Corso said. "That's where the self-serving bullshit and the psychobabble rear their ugly heads."

"Why is that?"

"Because, first off, when you start ascribing reasons for people's behavior, you're kind of assuming *they* were aware of why they were doing whatever it was, aren't you?" Corso didn't give him a chance to answer. "And that doesn't square with my experience at all. Seems to me a great deal of human behavior is every bit as mysterious to the person doing it as it is to those watching." Corso shrugged. "Let's say we knew your father had an impoverished childhood. We knew he always wanted to get an education but had been thwarted by circumstance. The natural leap would be to assume that his desire to see you become a doctor was just him living out his own desires vicariously through you."

"I don't know anything about his childhood," Downs said sadly.

"Doesn't matter," Corso said. "Because whatever we say after the fact, even if it seems to fit, is just conjecture. All we can be sure of is that your father did the things he did because, in his mind at least, that was what worked out best for him. Somehow or other, he got more pleasure sending his money off to schools than he would have gotten spending it himself."

Downs got to his feet. Jammed his hands deep into his pockets. "That doesn't leave much room for things like altruism or heroism."

"No, it doesn't," Corso said. "Mother Teresa did what she did because that's what felt best to her. Maybe she had a longer worldview than the rest of us. Maybe compassion made her all gooey inside. All I know for sure is that there was something in it for her."

"That's pretty cynical."

"Ask war heroes and they'll all tell you the same thing. It was over and done with before they ever thought about it. They were so scared or so mad or so outraged they acted on impulse. And you know why?"

"Why?"

"Because, for them, being heroes was the line of least resistance."

"How can that be?"

"It *can* be, because something inside was telling them they wouldn't be able to live with themselves if they didn't take action."

A silence settled over the room. Corso got to his feet, walked into the kitchen, and poured himself a glass of water. It was one of those businessman's suites: living room, kitchen, and a little office area downstairs; bedroom and bathroom upstairs. Extended Stay, they called it. "What are you doing tomorrow?" Corso asked.

Downs was pacing the living room. "I've got to sign the insurance paperwork and the pension fund paperwork. Stuff like that."

"What are you doing with his stuff?"

"Mr. Pov. He's going to take care of it for me."

"He'll probably find a home for a lot of it."

"Hard to believe."

Downs stopped pacing, took a deep breath. "You'll let me know if anything develops? If you ever figure out what this is all about?"

"Hell, I ever figure this one out I'll write a book about it."

Downs walked into the kitchen and offered a hand. "Thanks," he said. The men shook hands, and then Downs turned and walked to the door. He didn't sneak a last look, just pulled open the door and left.

And it was as if the whisper of the door and the clicking of the lock were the sounds of Corso himself hissing to a halt and coming to rest. Suddenly he felt bruised and tired and old. His throat was dry and seemed to be getting sore. His eyes felt scratchy, as if they were packed with fine sand.

He sipped at his water as he wandered into the living room and sat back down on the couch. He set the water on the glass top of the coffee table and picked up the packet of financial records. He unfolded papers and used his hands to iron out the wrinkles.

Later, when he recalled the moment, he knew he'd have to spice it up a bit in the book. Add a little drama. Like how he'd studied the records for hours and was just about to give up when suddenly, in a flash of insight, it came to him. Readers didn't want to hear he'd been using the heels of his hands to straighten Robert Downs's financial records when the back page became separated from the others and he glanced down and read the last item, the list of those who had previously requested these records. Mr. Donald Barth, thirteen times. Mr. Robert Downs, four times. South Puget Sound Public Employees Credit Union, once. Fresno Guarantee Trust, once. Boston Hanover Bank, one time.

32

Monday, October 23   11:23 a.m.

Sam Rozan, chief earthquake engineer for the State of California, twirled an end of his mustache as he thought it over. "That's hard to say," he said finally. "At least thirty million dollars."

Warren Klein leaned on the witness box. "So the perpetrators of this fraud, in your opinion, profited to the sum of what you estimate to be thirty million dollars."

"At a conservative estimate," Sam Rozan said.

"Thank you, Mr. Rozan. That will be all."

The judge pointed to Bruce Elkins. "Cross."

Elkins got slowly to his feet. "Not at this time, Your Honor."

Fulton Howell was scowling now. He opened his mouth to rebuke Elkins but instead turned his attention to Klein. "Mr. Klein, am I to understand that the government's next witness will be its last?"

"Yes, Your Honor." Klein had his Boy Scout face on.

The judge shuffled though a stack of papers on the bench. Unable to find what he was looking for, he leaned over and whispered to the court clerk, who picked her way through several files before handing one to the judge.

"Mr. Elkins," the judge began. "In your pretrial brief you indicated the defense's intention to call nine witnesses. Could you please indicate to the court how long, in terms of days, you believe the defense will require to complete its case?"

"It is the defense's intention to rest, Your Honor."

"Without calling witnesses?"

"Yes, Your Honor."

He crooked a finger at both lawyers. "Approach the bench." Neither Elkins nor Klein had gotten a full step closer to the judge, when suddenly Fulton Howell bellowed, "No! Stay where you are. I want this on the record."

For the first time, Howell was visibly upset. Wagging a finger like a parent to a child, he directed his ire toward Bruce Elkins.

"Mr. Elkins, if you think for one minute that you are going to subvert the justice system by laying the grounds for an incompetent-representation defense, you've got another think coming. Do you hear me?"

"Your Honor—"

"Shut up, sir. Because, Mr. Elkins, if that is indeed your intention, I will personally take you before the ethics board and see to it that, in addition to never practicing law again, you are punished to the fullest extent possible under the law. Am I making myself clear?"

"Yes, Your Honor."

A moment passed. "Well?" the judge demanded.

"It is my considered legal opinion that it is in my client's best interest not to offer a defense."

Fulton Howell's hands were shaking. A deep, ruddy glow had consumed his throat. "Perhaps you would be so kind as to explain to the court how it is you have reached that conclusion."

"Certainly, Your Honor," Elkins said. "It's quite simple. We do not believe the state has proved its case within a reasonable doubt. We don't believe they have provided this jury with a single strand of connective tissue that attaches my client, Nicholas Balagula, to any of the sundry enterprises responsible for the tragedy at Fairmont Hospital. Not one witness. Not a single piece of paper with my client's name scribbled on it." His voice was rising now. "The state's case is nothing but inference and innuendo." He pounded the table. "I believe resting the defense best expresses our utter contempt for the pile of unsubstantiated rumors the prosecution calls a case. And I believe that tactic will best enable this jury to experience our complete faith that they can be trusted to see through the lies."

Fulton Howell was unimpressed. "That's quite a risk, Mr. Elkins."

"I have discussed the matter with my client and offered him the opportunity to obtain different counsel, should he so desire."

Howell looked over at Nicholas Balagula. "Is that so, Mr. Balagula?"

"Yes, it is."

"And you understand that Mr. Elkins is risking your life on the single throw of a dice, so to speak."

"I understand. I am innocent," he said. "I have nothing to fear."

Howell searched Balagula's face for irony, and finding none, sat back in his chair.

"I am informed by the U.S. Marshal's Service that for security reasons they will require fifteen minutes and an empty courtroom in order to safely deliver the prosecution's final witness to these proceedings." He checked his watch. "Normally, with the approach of the noon hour, we would adjourn until after lunch. However, owing to the unusually stringent security required in this case, we will adjourn for twenty minutes only." *Bang*. "Court will reconvene at eleven-fifty sharp," *Bang*. "Bailiffs, clear the courtroom."

Warren Klein was having a discussion with the court clerk. Ray Butler and Renee Rogers gathered the piles of papers and folders together in the center of the table. At the far end of the room, Balagula, Ivanov, and Elkins formed a tight muttering knot as they moved leisurely up the long aisle together behind a phalanx of bailiffs.

"Hey."

The sound pulled Corso's head around. Renee Rogers. Black leather purse slung over one shoulder, big pile of files in her arms. "You were late this morning."

"I slept in," Corso said. He'd had twelve hours of dreamless sleep. If the maid hadn't come to the door, he'd probably still be in bed.

"I slept all day Sunday," she said. "I just couldn't seem to get enough."

Corso pulled open the gate. Renee Rogers stepped through, and they started up the aisle together. "I'd offer to help with the files," Corso said, "but I'm afraid it'd look like I was carrying your books."

She laughed. "The whole world already thinks we're sleeping together. We were on CNN last night. Did you see it?"

"I don't watch much television."

"Neither do I, but Warren called and insisted I turn it on."

"Thoughtful."

"In living color. Looking like we just got out of the shower."

Corso pulled open the arched door and allowed Renee Rogers to precede him into the lobby. Two of the street doors were open. The breeze rushed in with the noise of the crowd on its back, swirling around the marble canyon like a squall.

"My mother called this morning," Rogers said. "She allowed as how you were a good-looking specimen and, according to the news, quite well off, but she wanted to know if maybe we couldn't keep it a bit lower-key. She said the postman had looked at her oddly today."

Corso laughed as they angled over toward the nearest corner. "So what do you think of the no-defense defense?" Corso asked.

Rogers shrugged. "Risky," she said. "It's going to come down to whether or not the jury believes what Victor Lebow has to say."

"Any reason they shouldn't?"

"Juries tend not to like witnesses who've been granted immunity."

"Must be what Elkins is counting on."

"He's done his homework. He's hoping he can discredit Lebow in front of the jury. If he manages that, we've got us a horse race."

"What kind of witness is Lebow?"

She waggled her free hand. "I've seen better. He didn't immediately come forward—which Elkins is going to be all over—and he's got a criminal record."

"I came upon something last night," Corso said.

"What kind of something?"

"Something that could tell us how Balagula compromised your jury."

"Really?"

"Rogers," a voice called.

Her gaze remained riveted to Corso. "You're sure?"

"Not quite."

"We've got work to do, Rogers," Warren Klein bawled. "Courtroom C. Two minutes." He wiggled a pair of fingers and then clicked off across the floor, with Ray Butler trotting along behind like a pack mule.

For a moment, Corso thought she was going to launch the files, shot-put style, at his back. Sanity prevailed, however. She hitched her purse strap higher on her shoulder, took a better purchase on her folders, and turned to Corso.

"I shall be professional to the end," she said, with exaggerated solemnity.

"To the end," Corso said.

"Or until I kill him," she said, and marched off.

Corso wandered over to the open door. For security reasons, the entire media swarm had been moved to the area adjacent to the back door of the courthouse. Bruce Elkins was outside, addressing the assembled multitude.

". . . whose entire case is about to hang on the word of a convicted felon: a man who has been convicted of federal perjury charges. A man who was granted immunity on a variety of federal charges in return for testifying against my client, and whose only function will be to obliquely connect my client to a conspiracy in which they have otherwise found it impossible to demonstrate my client's involvement."

At eleven forty-five, the courtroom doors were re-opened. When Corso strolled back inside a minute later, Elkins, Balagula, and Ivanov were already ensconced at the defense table. At the front of the room, a dozen U.S. marshals stood shoulder to shoulder, gazing impassively out at the empty seats.

A minute later, the prosecution team arrived. Renee Rogers cast a wish-us-luck gaze Corso's way as she walked by. Corso got to his feet and slipped out of his coat. By the time he folded it over the seat and sat back down, Judge Howell had resumed his place behind the bench and located the gavel. *Bang.*

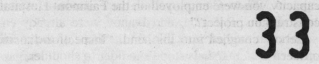

33

Monday, October 23   11:53 a.m.

"Would you tell us your name, please."

"Victor Lebow."

Unlike those of the previous witnesses, Victor Lebow's physical presence did little to inspire confidence. He was a thin man in his late fifties, with greasy hair and a twitchy left eye that flickered like a candle every time Klein asked him a question. He sat in the witness box, sweating into a gray wool suit that looked like it belonged to somebody else.

Predictably, Warren Klein wasn't taking any chances. He seemed determined to take his witness from childhood up until the minute he entered into a criminal conspiracy with Nicholas Balagula. Equally predictably, Bruce Elkins objected to every word Victor Lebow uttered.

Two minutes into Lebow's testimony, however, Judge Howell lost patience with Elkins's repeated objections and threatened to have him removed from the room if he didn't sit down and keep quiet, an attitude Elkins now adopted with an air of stoic martyrdom.

"Could you please, Mr. Lebow, explain to us in what capacity you were employed on the Fairmont Hospital construction project?"

Lebow coughed into his hand. "Inspection liaison officer."

"And could you explain to the jury, Mr. Lebow, precisely what an"—Klein made quotation marks in the air with his fingers—"inspection liaison officer does?"

Lebow thought it over. "I worked in between the testing lab and the state inspectors."

"What exactly were your responsibilities, Mr. Lebow?"

"Mostly I took the concrete core samples from the job site and delivered them to the lab for testing."

"Testing for what?"

"Strength and rigidity."

"Could you tell us something about how such tests are conducted?"

Lebow crossed and uncrossed a leg. "Sure," he said. "They put them in a hydraulic press and stress them to the breaking point."

"What laboratory conducted the tests?"

"Phillips Engineering Technology of Oakland."

"How often were these tests conducted?"

"Once a week."

"So once a week you took concrete core samples from the Fairmont Hospital job site to the laboratory for testing."

"Objection, Your Honor. Asked and answered."

"Sustained."

Klein walked quickly over to the defense table, where Ray Butler handed him a piece of paper. "Mr.

Lebow, can you tell us what amount of stress the core samples were expected to endure before failing?"

"The specifications called for a minimum of fifty thousand pounds per square inch," Lebow said. He craned his neck around the courtroom as if searching for someone who might disagree. "Theoretically," he added.

Klein walked to the side of the witness box, handed the piece of paper to Victor Lebow, and looked up at the judge. "Your Honor, I have handed Mr. Lebow a copy of People's Exhibit Thirty-eight, already offered in evidence."

"So noted," the judge said.

Klein now stepped in closer to Lebow. "Can you tell me, Mr. Lebow, whether or not you recognize the document you are presently holding?"

Lebow's eye was flickering like a signal flare. "Yes, I do."

"Would you tell us what it is, please?"

Again Victor Lebow nervously checked the room. "It's the week-to-week test results of the core samples."

"Is that your signature at the bottom of each week, attesting to the validity of the results?" Lebow nodded silently. "Please answer out loud for the record, Mr. Lebow?"

"Yes," he stammered. "That's my signature."

"Your signature attests to exactly what, Mr. Lebow?"

He looked confused. "I don't understand," he said.

"Well, Mr. Lebow, as you didn't conduct the stress tests yourself"—Klein reached into the jury box and turned the page over—"you can see here that the tests themselves were attested to by several employees of Phillips Engineering. I'm assuming that those signatures attest to the testing validity, and I was asking you specifically what *your* signature attested to."

Lebow thought it over. "I guess it says that the samples I gave them for testing were the same ones I got from the inspectors on the job site."

"Were they?"

"Excuse me?"

"Were the samples you delivered to Phillips Engineering for testing the same samples you took from the job site?"

Lebow looked up at the judge, as if asking for relief. Fulton Howell glowered down at the little man like the Old Testament Jehovah. "Answer the question."

"No," Lebow said in a low voice.

Klein cupped a hand around his ear. "Could you speak up, please?"

"No," Lebow said again, angry now. "They weren't the same samples I got from the job site."

Klein took his time now, milking the moment for all it was worth, casting his eyes from the judge to the jury and finally to Bruce Elkins, as if daring him to object.

"Mr. Lebow, if the samples you delivered for testing, and whose validity you attested to with your signature, did not come from the job site, where *did* they come from?"

"They were made up special."

"So the samples you delivered to Phillips Engineering—"

Elkins was on his feet. "Your Honor!"

Judge Howell waved him back down. "Move along, Mr. Klein, once again, the question has already been asked and answered."

"Who made up the samples you took to Phillips?"

"I don't know." He threw his hands up. "I mean, I didn't see 'em get made or anything."

For the first time in days, Warren Klein frowned. "Who did *you* get them from, Mr. Lebow?"

"I got them from the on-site inspectors."

"You're referring to Joshua Harmon and Brian Swanson."

"Yeah."

Klein paced in front of the jury box. "If you don't mind my asking, Mr. Lebow, what induced you to take part in a fraud such as this?"

Victor Lebow hesitated and then looked down into his lap. "I needed the money."

"Excuse me?" Klein taunted.

"I said I needed the money," Lebow answered angrily. "I had a consulting business, went tits up. . . ." He looked up at the judge. "Sorry. I went bankrupt. I was under a lot of pressure."

"And how much were you paid to perpetrate this fraud?"

"Two thousand dollars a week."

"For how long?"

"The whole project."

"Sixty-some weeks."

"Yes."

Lebow was squirming around in the seat like he was on a griddle.

"Would you tell us please, Mr. Lebow, how it came to pass that you were drawn into this conspiracy?"

"They knew about my money problems." He looked up at the judge again, pulled at his collar, and continued. "Said I could get myself out of debt if I played along."

"Played along how?"

"You know, if I dumped the real samples and delivered the ones they made up special."

"Dumped?"

"Yeah," Lebow said. "In the bay. I've got me a little boat. For striper fishing, you know." He looked around for other anglers but found the cupboard bare.

"I'd take 'em out on Saturday mornings with me and dump 'em while I was fishing."

"Tell me, Mr. Lebow, was anyone in this courtroom today present when you were offered the two thousand dollars a week to switch samples?"

Victor Lebow pulled a pair of black-framed glasses from the inside pocket of his suit jacket. He put them on and slowly surveyed the room. Satisfied, he returned the glasses to his pocket.

"Well?" Warren Klein prodded.

Lebow looked up at the judge.

"Answer the question, Mr. Lebow."

Lebow looked around the room again. "No," he said, in a low voice.

"Excuse me?" Klein managed.

"I said no."

Nicholas Balagula never blinked. Neither did Ivanov. They sat there like they were at the movies. Bruce Elkins flicked a confused glance at his client and then tentatively began to rise.

"Perhaps you didn't understand my question, Mr. Lebow," Klein began.

"Your Honor," Elkins said.

"Yes, Mr. Elkins," the judge replied.

Elkins brought a hand to his brow, then shook his head. "Never mind, Your Honor. Please excuse the interruption," he said, as he sat back down.

Warren Klein wore his most conspiratorial smile as he wandered over to the witness box and leaned on the rail. "I think you may have misunderstood me, Mr. Lebow, so let's start from the beginning, okay?"

"Whatever you say," Lebow said.

"I asked you whether or not the parties responsible for drawing you into this conspiracy were present in this courtroom today."

"And I said *no*," Lebow said.

Before Klein could collect his wits, Fulton Howell leaned out over the bench and shook his gavel at the witness. His voice shook as he spoke. "Mr. Lebow," he began. "Unless I'm mistaken, you have signed a deposition stating that the defendant Nicholas Balagula and his associate Mr. Ivanov were present in the room when the falsification scheme was hatched. That's true, is it not, Mr. Lebow?"

Victor Lebow sat staring down into his lap.

"Mr. Lebow," the judge prompted. "I direct you to answer my question. Did you or did you not sign a deposition in which you swore that the defendant Nicholas Balagula was present at the time of the conspiracy?"

"I did, yeah," Lebow answered, without looking up.

"Are you now contradicting that sworn statement?"

"Yeah. I guess I am."

"There'll be no guessing here, Mr. Lebow. Was Mr.

Balagula or Mr. Ivanov or both present when the conspiracy was proposed?"

Lebow pulled the glasses from his pocket, put them on, and peered over at the defense table. "I never seen either of those guys before in my life," he said.

34

The air seemed to have been sucked from the room. In disbelief, Bruce Elkins looked back over his shoulder at his client, only to find Nicholas Balagula sitting quietly in his chair, whispering to Mikhail Ivanov from behind his hand. Elkins felt cold and unable to draw breath, almost the way he'd always imagined the onset of a heart attack would feel. Then, without willing it so, he found himself on his feet.

"Call for an immediate dismissal of charges," he said.

Fulton Howell's face had already moved through the deep-red stage and was now something more akin to blue.

"Your motion is noted, Mr. Elkins. Now sit back down." He squeezed the words out from between his teeth like putty.

"Your Honor—" Klein began.

The judge waved him off. "Sit," was all he said. He leaned out over the bench again. "Would you tell this court, Mr. Lebow, why it was you saw fit to give false witness in a matter of such seriousness?"

Victor Lebow had an answer ready. "They threatened me."

"Who threatened you, Mr. Lebow?"

He pointed at the prosecution table. "Over there," he said. "Them."

"Are you referring to Mr. Klein, Mr. Butler, and Ms. Rogers?"

"Not her. The other two."

"How did they threaten you, Mr. Lebow?"

"With jail. I mean, they kept saying I was going to prison for a long time." His face was a knot. "And, you know, all the bad things that were going to happen to me in jail. How I was gonna get fucked up the ass and all. They kept telling me I was gonna be the only one who took the rap. And that the real bad guys would go free, and it was just gonna be me in the jailhouse."

"And so you decided to implicate Mr. Balagula."

Lebow shook his head. "I never heard of the guy before"—he pointed at the prosecution table—"until that Klein guy kept saying his name."

"What else did he say?"

"He said Harmon and Swanson were on the pad and that it was this Balagula guy who was paying the freight."

"And you merely took their word for the fact that Mr. Balagula was the guilty party?"

Lebow shrugged. "Tell you the truth, I didn't much care," he said. "By the time they started talking about how I could maybe not go to jail if this guy Balagula was convicted, I woulda signed just about anything."

"Your Honor," Klein protested, "we have both transcripts and tape recordings of our conversations with Mr. Lebow, and I assure you—"

Fulton Howell ignored Klein. "You are aware, Mr. Lebow, that your testimony here today forfeits any immunity agreement you may have been granted in return for your testimony against Mr. Balagula."

Lebow's lower lip was beginning to quiver. "I know."

"And that you are, in all probability, facing a sizable term in a federal prison."

"Yeah, I know."

"And with that in mind, you still insist that Mr. Balagula was not present when you entered into this conspiracy and that your original statements were false?"

"I do."

The judge sat back for a moment, taking the witness in. "Could you perhaps tell the court why it is that you have chosen to change your story at this late stage in the proceedings?"

"I hadda to do the right thing," Lebow stuttered. "If I kept on with this Balagula story, they were gonna send the wrong guy to jail and the real bums responsible for all those dead babies was going to be walking around the streets."

"So you've changed your story in the interest of justice."

"Yeah, that's it."

"Why did you wait until now?" The judge's voice was rising. "For pity sake, why did you allow the expenditure of so much time and money before you told the truth? You could have come forward months ago."

"I was scared," Lebow said. "People said they were gonna kill me. I didn't know what to do. I . . . wanted . . . to . . ." He hiccuped once and began to sob. The judge watched for a disbelieving moment, then dropped his hands to the bench with a slap and shook his head in disgust.

"I want to see Mr. Klein and Mr. Elkins in my chambers. Mr. Lebow is to be remanded to custody." He pointed at the defense table. "I want to see the transcripts of your conversations with Mr. Lebow and the recordings thereof, ASAP."

"I'll need a little time, Your Honor," Warren Klein protested.

Howell ignored him, turning his attention to Elkins instead. "I want you to consider your position as an officer of the court, Mr. Elkins, as well as the ramifications of suborning perjury."

Elkins puffed his chest. "I take exception to that remark, Your Honor."

"Exception noted. Court is adjourned until nine o'clock Wednesday morning, when I will rule on Mr. Elkins's call for a dismissal of charges."

Fulton Howell jerked a thumb back over his shoulder. "Chambers," he growled.

Klein walked over to Ray Butler. They stood together whispering before Klein disengaged and made his way to the front of the room.

* * *

Bruce Elkins lingered at the defense table. The jury could be heard rustling out the side door, and the spectators disappeared through the door at the front of the room. Elkins leaned in close and swept his eyes from Balagula to Ivanov and back. "You set this up, didn't you?"

Neither man answered.

"You arranged the whole thing," Elkins persisted.

"I think they're waiting for you," Nicholas Balagula said.

"I won't be party to it," Elkins hissed. "I will not sit idly by and allow you to subvert the criminal justice system." He pounded the desk, caught himself, and looked around. "I'll resign before I'll be part of this"— he searched for a word—"this abomination."

Balagula looked at him like he was a schoolchild. "We have been miraculously spared the wrath of an *unjust* and *spiteful* prosecution," he said, using Elkins's own words. "Just do your job, Mr. Elkins. As I keep telling you, I'm innocent, so the rest will take care of itself."

"Mr. Elkins." It was one of the bailiffs. "The judge is waiting."

Elkins reluctantly got to his feet. Balagula smiled up at him. "Have you no faith that truth and justice will prevail, Mr. Elkins?"

The lawyer was talking to himself as he made his way out of the courtroom.

* * *

Renee Rogers scratched her chair back along the floor and stood up. She stretched and then wandered over to Corso's side.

"Can you believe this?"

Corso shook his head in disgust. "It was a setup, all the way. Balagula took one look at Klein and knew all he had to do was give him a shiny new witness and Warren would be just the asshole to run with it."

"But Victor Lebow is going to prison. How in hell do you induce a guy into going to prison for you?"

"For how long?"

"Eight to fifteen."

"So he serves what?"

"Fifty months minimum."

"A million bucks."

"Huh?"

"You're broke. You're facing felony charges from the hospital disaster. You're getting death threats from the victim's families. You've just declared bankruptcy. Balagula comes to you with an offer you can't refuse. Go to the cops. Claim it was Balagula who gave you the phony core samples. Claim you were there. That you can put the smoking gun in his hand. After what happened to Harmon and Swanson, they're gonna lock you up like Fort Knox. Then, when the time comes to testify, you change your tune. Take the rap. You let the heat die down, let everybody forget about you, and walk away four years later with a million bucks. A quarter million a year. Twenty thousand a month. Tax-free."

She thought it over. "Assuming you're right, you think Elkins knew?"

"Unless he's the greatest actor I've ever seen," Corso said, "he was just as blown away as the rest of us." She nodded solemnly. Corso continued. "There'd be no reason to tell Elkins. He's too fond of appearing on talk shows to agree to suborn perjury. All Balagula had to do was put things in place, let Elkins do his job, and wait."

"I don't believe this," Rogers said. "That sonofabitch has screwed us again. He's gonna walk."

"The judge said he wanted to see the transcripts."

She laughed. "Which are going to show that Lebow is telling the truth. That's exactly how it's done. You scare the crap out of them and then offer them a way out. It's standard operating procedure."

"You never know with juries."

"No way," she scoffed. "Howell's not going to send it to any jury. He's going to come down with a directed not-guilty verdict, and Balagula's going to waltz out of here a free man."

A door opened at the top of the aisle. A green-jacketed U.S. marshal started down the aisle. As the door stood open, the noise of the media horde outside rushed into the courtroom, more of a snarl than a roar—and then, as the door snapped shut, silence again.

"Sounds like the grapevine has delivered the news," Corso said.

"Amazing how that works," she said disgustedly.

They went silent as the cop walked past them, lifted the rail, and made his way over to the nearest bailiff. They leaned together in animated conversation.

"Question," Corso said.

"What?"

"Last trial. Here in Seattle."

"Yeah?"

"You had the jury in a hotel for the duration of the trial."

"Uh-huh."

"Which hotel?"

"The Carlisle Tower."

"And you fed them three meals a day, right?"

"At least."

"Who paid the bill?"

"Initially or ultimately?"

"Both."

"Initially, it was King County, who then bled the General Accounting Office for reimbursement."

"How detailed do you figure the bill was?"

She pursed her lips. "Knowing the GAO, I'd say they probably wanted it itemized down to the last Q-Tip. Why?"

"Which department do you figure would handle that for King County?"

"I'd start with the county auditor."

The door to the judge's chambers burst open and banged against the wall. Warren Klein came storming out into the courtroom. He strode quickly across the floor, threw his coat over one arm, and grabbed his briefcase before turning his attention to Renee Rogers. Three words into his speech, and you knew two things: one, he'd rehearsed it; two, it needed more work. "If your busy social schedule will permit, Ms. Rogers, we'll be working at the hotel this afternoon. Two o'clock." Showed two fingers. "Despite your unfortunate lame-duck status, we're hoping you'll contribute some final advice about how to avoid this impending disaster you and the other incompetents have foisted upon us."

"I'll see if I can't pencil you in," she said.

They stood for a moment, their gazes locked, before Warren Klein barged through the gate and up the aisle. "Professional to the end," Corso whispered.

Halfway between the bench and the defense table, Ray Butler stood with his cell phone pressed to the side of his head. Occasionally his lips moved, but mostly he listened.

The movement of his hand caught Renee Rogers's attention. He was pointing at the phone and rolling his eyes. He began to move her way, talking now. "Yes . . . yes, I understand. I'll see to it. . . . Yes." He rested one cheek on the table and listened for a full minute before having a sigh and pocketing the phone. His expression made it clear he hadn't been chortling with his wife about the new house.

He looked up at Renee Rogers. "You want to guess?" he asked.

"We'll be having breakfast with the AG tomorrow morning."

"She's coming here?"

"As we speak."

Her lips were nearly invisible. "She's going to make sure the shit rolls downhill."

"We're gonna need wheelbarrows," Butler said.

"Dump trucks," she amended.

35

Monday, October 23   4:21 p.m.

"**T**ry the county auditor," she suggested.

"Already been there," Corso said. "And the accounting office. And county records." Before she could respond, he said, "And I have been assured that hard copies of the material I'm looking for are to be found somewhere in your files."

Wearily, she checked the clock. "It's closing time. You come back tomorrow and maybe we can—"

"I really need it tonight," he interrupted. He gave her his best smile.

The woman shrugged. "Then you're out of luck, buddy," she said. "If Marcy were here, it might be a different story."

"Marcy?"

"On vacation with her sister. Maui. Two weeks." She checked the clock again. "I'm from accounts payable. I'm just holding down the fort until she gets back."

Corso waited. The woman leaned over the counter and, in a stage whisper, said, "Not to speak ill of the sun-tanned, but King County better hope she comes home in one piece."

"Why's that?"

"Because otherwise she might take her filing system to the grave with her, in which case nobody is ever going to find anything in here again."

She turned her back on Corso and began to straighten up. Pushing things around on the desk, sliding the chair in. When she walked to the long line of gray file cabinets and began to push the lock buttons, Corso piped up. "I've got an idea," he said.

She stopped and looked dubiously over in his direction. "Such as?"

"Such as, the bill I'm looking for went out sometime in the last half of last year. Can you find the paperwork from that time frame?"

"Yeah, " she said. "But she doesn't file the material by date or category. Or by any other method I've ever heard of." She waved a disgusted hand. "We'd literally have to start at the front and work our way back to find what you're looking for."

"Maybe not," Corso said.

She raised an eyebrow and went back to pushing buttons.

"Which one has the accounts payable for the last half of last year?"

She stopped and walked eight feet down the row of identical cabinets. She patted the next-to-last one. "Someplace in here."

"Open it up," Corso suggested.

This time, she gave him the other eyebrow.

"Please," he said.

With a sigh, she thumbed open the latch and jerked the drawer out.

"Just open the drawers in that cabinet and pull out whatever appears to be the biggest file. If that's not the one I'm looking for, I'll go away and leave you alone."

"The biggest?"

"Thickest. The one with the most pages."

She looked at Corso and then the clock. She bent at the waist and pulled open the bottom drawer. Then the next and the next and finally the top one again. She slid the top two closed and reached into the third drawer down. "No contest," she announced. "This one's way bigger than anything else in there."

She used her foot to close the remaining drawers as she perused the file. "Hmmmm," she said. She looked Corso over again.

"What is it?" Corso asked.

"Jury expenses."

"That's the one."

She hefted the file in her hand. "Biggest one I've ever seen."

"Could you make me a copy?"

"You're kidding, right?"

"Do I look like a guy who's kidding?" he asked.

Corso pointed to the sign on the wall. COPIES, $1.00 PER PAGE.

"I hear it's gone up to two bucks a page," he said.

"Three," she deadpanned.

"Damn Republicans."

Monday, October 23   7:45 p.m.

Forced onto a jury, torn from their friends and families, sequestered in a downtown hotel for months, the jurors tended to take it out on the menu. Surf and turf. The thirty-six-ounce porterhouse. Don't forget the cheese sauce for the asparagus. Once the revenge factor burned off, most seemed to settle into a routine. Some ended up eating hardly anything at all. By the time it was over, juror number 3 was living on cereal and dry toast. Juror number 5, on the other hand, never met a cheesecake he didn't like. Corso figured he'd either spent his out-of-court hours on a treadmill or he'd gained fifty pounds.

That's how they had them listed: Jurors 1 through 12 and then 13A and 14A, alternates. The expenses incurred by each were itemized on separate documents. He'd started at juror number 1 and was working his way toward the back. He'd been at it for nearly two hours, and was only halfway through, when the waitress came out from behind the counter again with the coffeepot. Without looking up, Corso said, "No, thanks."

"We close at eight," she said.

"Okay," he said, without looking up.

"Maybe a little earlier so's I can make the ten bus."

Corso began to laugh. "No shit," he said.

"Hey, now, mister—" she began.

He pointed to the page with his finger. "Big as life." He turned the page and then the next. "Every night. Same damn thing."

"You okay?" she asked.

He looked up and smiled. "Depends on who you ask," he said. He sorted through the pile of pages and selected half a dozen, which he folded into fourths and stuck in his inside jacket pocket. He threw a twenty on the table and slid out of the booth.

"You got anything smaller?" she asked.

Corso threw his arm around her. She drew the steaming pot back as if to defend herself. Corso kissed her on the cheek. "Tell you what. You throw away the rest of those papers for me and keep the change. How's that?"

"Works for me," she said, without hesitation.

Corso patted her shoulder once and headed for the door.

The sky was black on black. A flash of lightning skittered above Elliott Bay. A cold winter rain angled in from the south. Corso cursed silently, wishing he hadn't left the Subaru up at the hospital this morning before court. Especially since Dougherty had never stirred, and he'd been forced to spend an hour and a half talking with Joe Bocco's leg-breaker buddy, Marvin, whose entire stock of misinformation seemed to be garnered from ESPN.

Corso turned his collar up and began to lope uphill. Despite the effort, he couldn't keep from smiling. Wait until he told Dougherty. Give her something else to think about, other than David.

By the time he reached Ninth Avenue he was beginning to pant, so he slowed to a walk. Rain or no rain, he didn't want to be winded when he told her the story. Ahead in the distance, Harborview Hospital peeked out from a curtain of rain, its edges wavering and uncertain against the sky. He stopped under the canvas awning of a print shop and shook the rain from his clothes and hair.

Standing there, brushing at himself, facing away from the street, with the rain snapping and popping against the awning, Corso never heard it coming. He was still muttering to himself, practicing his delivery to Dougherty, when the steel wire slipped around his neck and dragged him to his knees.

His first instinct was to get his fingers between the wire and his neck. He clawed at his throat until the warm wetness whispered it was too late. His head felt as it might burst. He tried to throw himself onto his back, but his assailant could not be moved. His eyes burned, his vision was beginning to blur. The next-to-last thing he saw was another set of legs in front of him on the sidewalk. And then the shoe starting at his face. He jerked his head to the left and, in that instant before the shoe connected, he saw the black Mercedes sitting at the curb with the doors open.

36

Monday, October 23   7:51 p.m.

Monday, October 23   7:51 p.m.

A s the four men slipped the ropes through their gloved hands, lowering the casket into the frozen earth, the birds went silent, the sky went white. . . .

Suddenly Corso was awake, his ears pricking at the sound of the voices.

"We'll put him where we put that Ball motherfucker. He like goin' down there so bad, we let his ass stay there till kingdom come."

Another voice, farther away. "He come around yet?"

"Startin' to."

"We want him awake. I don't want to be carrying that shit."

"We gonna do that again? Make 'im carry his own weight?"

"You want to do it?"

Close voice chuckled. "You know what I been thinkin', man?"

"What's that?"

"I been thinkin' this whole fuckin' mess started with

that asshole in the truck that we was supposed to pop but what was dead when we got there."

"Yeah."

"And how that was like a hit we got paid for but didn't do."

"You got a point here?"

"And now we end up doin' a hit we *ain't* gettin' paid for. All kinda evens out in the end. It's like one of those 'meta' things of yours."

Corso was wedged along the floor in the backseat of a moving car. His hands were tied behind his back. A foot suddenly pressed hard against his neck, driving his face down into the rubber floor mat. "You stay real still, hombre," a voice said. "We just about there."

Seemed like an hour, but it couldn't have been more than three minutes until the car began to slow, and then it turned and they weren't on paved road anymore. He could hear the whisk of grass and brush on the under-carriage as the car eased along.

"We'll put him down with the other one," the voice from the front seat said.

The car glided smoothly over a series of bumps and then swung in a slow circle and eased to a stop. The shoe on the back of his neck was replaced by the feel of cold metal. "Easy now," the voice behind him whis-pered. Above the sound of rain beating on the car, he heard the click of the door and the shift of weight as the driver got out and opened the rear door. "Ready?" the driver asked.

The guy in the backseat grabbed Corso by the belt. Another pair of hands gripped his shoulders, and in a single heave he was dragged from the car. He landed on his chest in the wet grass. He heard a pair of doors close. "Look," he heard Backseat say. "Fuckhead's feet are starting to float. We need to add some more weight."

"Better put two on nosy man here," Front Seat said.

And then they had him by the elbows and were jerking him to his feet.

"Gotta get up and walk now, nosy man. Not like we gonna carry your ass or nothin'."

When they began pulling on his arms, Corso realized he couldn't feel his hands. His knees nearly buckled from his own weight. He staggered slightly, regained his balance, looked around. Two of them: one nearly as tall as he was, long black hair worn in a ponytail. The other was a troll, a short dark specimen with a pockmarked face and one ear noticeably higher than the other.

"Get movin'," the troll said. "That way, down the end."

Corso looked around. Something was familiar, but he couldn't quite fathom what it was. "We figure you like it here so much," Ponytail said, "we'll let you stay."

And then Corso saw the bright light reflected in the water on his left. He looked to the south and saw the marsh and, beyond, the Briarwood Garden Apartments. They were parked on the levee that defined the northern extreme of the Black River marsh. Beneath the low sky, the water was stippled by the falling rain, its wavering surface broken here and there by grassy hillocks and broken-tooth stumps protruding above the surface. Along the edges, reeds and clumps of bulrushes waved in the wind like signal flags.

The only light came from the Speedy Auto Parts sign up the road. As he followed the reflection back across the marsh, he saw a pair of feet sticking up from the water. The shoelaces had burst, the bloated ankles were three times their normal size, pumped floating full by the expanding gases of death, forcing the feet up and out of the water as if the owner had dived into the muck and stuck.

They'd driven as far as they could. Three concrete pylons blocked the grassed-over road that ran along the top of the levee. Ponytail walked around and stood directly in front of Corso. In his right hand he carried a silver automatic with a gray silencer screwed onto the front. "Open your mouth," he said. When Corso failed to comply, he dug the barrel hard into Corso's solar plexus. Corso grunted and leaned forward. Next thing he knew his mouth was filled with metal and the pressure of the suppressor clicked on his teeth, forcing him up straight. "You just stand real still, nosy man," Ponytail said, pushing Corso's head back as his partner began to untie Corso's hands.

The steady rain beat down onto his face, wetting his cheeks, forcing his eyelids to flutter from the aerial assault. With the final strand removed, his arms flapped around to his sides. His wrists burned, and he could feel the cold blood struggling to move in his fingers. Slowly, the silencer slid from his mouth.

Ponytail motioned with the automatic. "That way," he said.

Corso hesitated, only to be propelled forward by a blow to the kidneys.

"Move your ass," the troll growled.

Corso rubbed at his wrists as he lurched forward; his hands were beginning to tingle as he stepped between the pylons into knee-deep grass.

Ahead in the darkness, the road was blocked by a pile of rubble. The troll passed by on Corso's left, hurrying up to the pile. He pointed at a spot about halfway up the pile. "This one," he said. "This one first."

As Corso approached, he could see that what had appeared to be a pile of light-colored rock was, in reality, a pile of broken concrete. Somebody's driveway, jackhammered to pieces, loaded into a truck, and surreptitiously dumped along the top of the levee. "Here," the troll said again.

The shards varied between six and eight inches in thickness, smooth on the top, wavy and rough with aggregate on the bottom. The troll slapped the pile with his hand.

"Come on, asshole. Hurry up."

The chunk of concrete was shaped like a triangle. Three feet in length. Nearly that long at the base, tapering to a point at the apex. "Let's go," Ponytail said, prodding Corso forward with the silenced automatic.

Corso bent his knees, got his left forearm beneath the jagged piece of stone, and straightened his legs. Must have weighed a hundred and fifty pounds. Corso lurched under the weight, adjusted his grip for balance, and turned back the way they'd come.

Ponytail held his gun by his side as he backed up, beckoning Corso forward with his free hand. "Come on," he said.

Corso moved carefully. His head roared and throbbed from the strain. Mindful of his footing, he shuffled along beneath the burden, until he was parallel with the submerged body, where Ponytail held up his hand.

"Dump it over the side," he said.

Corso staggered to the edge of the levee. The marsh was six feet below. It wasn't until he noticed the wavering, stippled surface of the black water that Corso remembered it was raining. He bent at the waist and let the chunk of concrete fall from his arms. It thumped onto the steep slope, rolled end over end, and stuck, point down, in the shallows.

"Go get it," the troll said.

Corso did as he was told, sliding down the muddy bank into the cold ankle-deep water. Unable to get under the piece, he was forced to lift it with his arms. He staggered and went to one knee, then righted himself and straightened up.

The troll was in the water with him now. Water up to Corso's shin was over the troll's knees. He waved Corso toward the half-submerged corpse, a dozen feet from shore. "Put it over the legs," he ordered. "Right behind the knees."

By the time Corso was in place, the frigid marsh water covered his knees. Three feet beneath the surface, the remains of Joe Ball lay festering and bloated, his torso held beneath the shimmering surface by another piece of concrete.

For some odd reason, Corso was overcome with the urge to be gentle. As if to spare the dead further indignity, he carefully placed the stone across the backs of the knees and let it go. When he straightened up, the protruding feet were gone. In another month, the gases would dissipate and the weight would push the corpse into the bottom of the marsh, where the body would begin to come apart. Small pieces of flesh would float to the surface, where, one by one, they'd be discovered by the birds and eaten, until finally nothing remained of Joe Ball save metal and bone.

"Let's go," the troll said.

Corso had to pull his feet from the gurgling muck one at a time as he labored back to the levee. His throat was constricted, but his mind was racing, trying to find a way out. Stifling an overpowering urge to run, he clawed his way back to the top of the levee and got to his feet. He knew he wouldn't get thirty feet before they shot him down and dragged him back to join Joe Ball, facedown in the muck.

"Let's go. Do it again," the troll said.

Corso steadied himself and retraced his footsteps back to the pile of broken concrete. They walked on either side of him, out of each other's line of fire, guns at the ready. The second chunk of concrete was nearly square and harder to carry. Corso had to keep adjusting his grip as he shuffled along the berm and finally let it fall from his arms and roll, end over end, down into the water.

"One more," Ponytail said.

Corso was beginning to shake. From fear, from the cold rain— he couldn't tell. Music was playing in his head now, voices and organs, getting louder and louder, something he'd never heard before. As if, all his life, he'd carried the sound track of his death inside himself, waiting, all this time, for the credits to roll and the end to be at hand. His legs wobbled as he started back. The troll prodded him in the side with his gun. "You get this one, nosy man," he leered. "You make us carry it, I'm gonna put a couple in your balls. Let you lay around a bit before I cap you."

He moved forward as if he were sleepwalking. The

music was blaring now. Morose and multivoiced, it filled his ears. "This one." Ponytail pointed to a jagged piece of concrete slightly smaller than the others. As Corso grabbed it and began to lift, the side of the pile collapsed, sending a dozen pieces of concrete bouncing down into the grass at the troll's feet. "Goddammit," the little man screamed, rubbing at his ankle with his free hand. He growled and grabbed the offending piece of stone from the grass and hurled it out into the marsh, where it landed with a splash. "Son of a—"

He didn't get all the words out before a movement in the marsh jerked his eyes from Corso. The snap of six-foot wings cut the air as a great blue heron took flight. Corso shifted his burden, getting his hand and elbow beneath it, and then, with every bit of strength left in his body, shot-putted the concrete at the troll.

It landed on his ankles. The troll howled like an animal and fell over onto his back, screaming at the sky. He had one foot jerked free when Corso landed on him, driving the breath from the small body. Corso had both hands on the gun when the flat report of Ponytail's silenced automatic split the air. Corso saw the back of his left hand explode in a mist of blood and bone but hung on with his right, allowing his momentum to pull the gun from the little man's grasp, as he slid down the side of the levee on his stomach. He fought for traction with his knees and then brought the gun to bear, he felt the tug of a bullet at the collar of his coat, before he heard the sound of the gun.

Ponytail had covered half the ground when Corso squeezed off his first round. It took Ponytail high in the right shoulder, spinning him nearly around in a circle, sending his gun off into space. He fell to one knee, then quickly jumped up, looking desperately around his feet for his weapon.

Corso crawled to the top of the bank. "Don't" was all he said.

Ponytail clutched his damaged shoulder and stood still. A scraping sound pulled Corso's vision toward the pile. The troll had extricated his other foot and was now kneeling in the grass. "Over here," Corso said, but the little man merely curled his lips and spat down onto the ground. Corso pointed the gun in his direction and let fly. The slug hit a chunk of concrete about two feet from the side of his head, sending a geyser of stone and dust into the air. The troll ducked behind his hands.

"Over here," Corso said again. This time the little man struggled to his feet and hobbled across the levee to his partner's side.

"Keys are in the car," Ponytail said.

Corso started for the car.

"You better drive far away," said the troll. " 'Cause this ain't over, motherfucker." He jabbed a finger at Corso. "We gonna find you. Maybe not today. Maybe not tomorrow. But you can make the rent on it."

"Find that fat cunt in the hospital too," said Ponytail with a smile. "Take care of her big ass, once and for all."

And then his lips moved again, but Corso couldn't hear the words because the music was deafening now, rolling out of every pore of his body. As he raised the gun, the music reached a crescendo and stayed there, pounding in his head like hell's hammers.

From a distance of eight feet, Corso shot the troll between the eyes. The man's face was a mask of astonishment as he sank to his knees and then fell backward onto the ground, twitching.

Ponytail's mouth was agape as he knelt by his partner's side. "Gerardo," he said quietly, shaking the little man's shoulder as if to rouse him from sleep. "Oh, Gerardo!" The muscles along his jaw moved like knotted rope, but by the time he turned his fury toward Corso it was too late. The silencer was no more than a foot from his temple when Corso pulled the trigger, sending the man's brains spewing out over his partner's body. He toppled onto his back and lay motionless. A small trickle of blood ran from the corner of his mouth. And suddenly the night was silent.

Corso stood for a moment, breathing deeply and listening to the hiss of the rain. Only then did the burning red pain in his left hand float to the level of consciousness. Clutching the hand to his chest and moaning, Corso walked over to the men. He stood there rocking on unsteady legs for a moment, and then he pointed the gun and again shot each man in the head. Then again and again, until nothing was happening because the gun was empty.

He dropped to one knee. Set the gun in the grass and used his good hand to pat each man down. Extracted a wallet from each man's pocket and used his foot to roll one and then the other down the levee, into the water. He then retrieved the gun and, with all his might, heaved the automatic out into the marsh, before he started stumbling toward the car.

37

The desk clerk didn't like what he saw, not a bit. Guy standing there with one hand jammed in his coat pocket, like he had a gun or something, looking like he'd spent the last week holed up under a bridge. As the man approached the registration desk, the clerk's index finger hovered over the button marked SECURITY. He pushed it.

"Robert Downs, please," the guy croaked.

Wasn't till he got close that the clerk noticed he was leaving wet tracks on the carpet. That he wasn't wearing socks. That his pants were soaked from the knees down and that, despite having his coat buttoned all the way up, his throat appeared to be circled by an angry purple welt. He fingered the button again. Twice.

"Room number?" the clerk said.

"I don't know the room number," the guy said in his rough voice.

"I can't connect you, sir, unless you know the room number."

"You call him," the guy rasped. "Tell him Frank

Corso is downstairs and needs to have a word with him."

Over the guy's left shoulder, a pair of hotel security guards emerged from the luggage room. The desk clerk breathed a sigh of relief as they advanced toward the desk.

The guy picked up something in his eyes and looked back over his shoulder. The movement brought a grunt from somewhere deep inside. "Please," the guy said. "I know I look like hell. Just call Mr. Downs for me."

The clerk held up a hand. Security stopped about six feet away. He dialed the phone and waited for a moment. "Mr. Downs," he said. "This is Dennis at the desk. Yes, sir. Sorry to bother you, sir, but there's a gentleman down here in the lobby asking for you." He listened and then looked up at Corso.

"Frank Corso," the guy said.

"Frank Corso," the clerk repeated. He pressed the phone tighter to his ear.

"Ah, yes. . . . Mr. Downs, I was wondering if instead of sending the gentleman up—I was wondering if it might be possible for you to come down to the lobby instead." He nodded. "Yes, sir. Thank you, sir." He hung up. "Mr. Downs will be down in a moment."

It was more like five minutes before Robert Downs appeared, wearing a black turtleneck over a pair of rumpled gray slacks. His hair was tousled and his face puffy. He crossed the lobby to Corso's side. "I was—I have an early . . ." He stammered as he took Corso in. He stepped in closer and studied Corso's throat. "What—?" he began.

Corso touched him on the shoulder and pulled him closer. "We need to go upstairs," he whispered.

Robert Downs hesitated for a moment and then nodded his head. He took Corso by the elbow and, under the baleful gaze of the security guards, led him back across the lobby to the elevator, where they waited no more than thirty seconds before a muted *ding* announced the arrival of the car. Downs put his arm around Corso's waist and drew him into the elevator.

They didn't speak on the ride up to the third floor or on the walk down the long hall. Corso leaned against the wall as Downs took three tries at swiping his card before he got the door open. He stepped to one side and ushered Corso into the room. Downs gestured toward the desk. "Sit down," he said. Corso shook his head and walked slowly into the bathroom. Downs followed. Corso's face twisted into a knot as he slowly, incrementally, pulled his left hand from his coat pocket and set it gently in the sink.

The black sock covering his hand was completely soaked with blood. He'd used the other sock for his right hand as he drove the Mercedes, so as not to leave fingerprints.

"Jesus," Downs muttered, his hands beginning to peel the sock from Corso's hand. The sink's drain was closed. Blood was beginning to collect. Corso groaned as Downs lifted his hand and inched off the last of the sock. "Steady now," Downs said, as he turned on the water and then tested it with his finger.

Satisfied, he gently moved Corso's palm beneath the warm trickle. Again Corso groaned. Downs scowled as he turned the hand over and washed off the back.

"This is a—" he began. "You've been shot."

"Nice to see a Harvard education paying dividends," Corso said through gritted teeth.

Despite himself, Downs managed a weak smile.

"Fix it," Corso said.

"We've got to get you to a hospital," Downs declared.

Corso shook his head. "I can't go to a hospital. They'll report it as a gunshot wound. You're going to have to fix it for me."

"The hand is a maze of nerves," Downs said. "There's no way I can possibly—" He looked around. "In a setting like this—"

Corso got nose to nose with him. "You're going to have to do the best you can."

"Your hand will never function properly again."

"That's a chance I'll have to take."

Downs broke the stare-down, stepped out into the hall, and ran a hand through his hair. "Did this . . . is this about my father's death?"

"Yes," Corso said.

"Do you know who—"

"I've got an idea," Corso said.

Downs thought it over for a moment. Corso imagined him weighing his obligations against his medical license. Then, without a word, he took Corso's hand again and ran it beneath the warm stream of water until it was free of blood, took a washcloth, doubled it over the exit wound in the palm, and then did the same for the back.

"Stay still," he said to Corso. "This is going to hurt for a minute." He took a hand towel and twirled it into a tightrope, then slipped the middle beneath Corso's hand. "Hang on," he whispered, as he tied the towel around the hand as tightly as he was able. Corso's vision went white for a moment. When his knees buckled, he braced himself against the sink.

Downs put an arm around Corso's waist and led him over to the small sofa by the window. "Take off your coat," he said, and helped Corso remove the jacket. He gently pushed Corso's head back and inspected the oozing line of purple flesh encircling his neck. "Nasty," he muttered to himself.

Corso didn't seem to hear.

"Is there an all-night drugstore in the city?"

"Bartell's on Broadway," Corso croaked.

"How do I get there?"

Corso gave him directions. "I'll be back," Downs said.

Corso waited until he was sure Robert Downs was gone and then retrieved his jacket from the floor. He put the two wallets on the bed and went through them. Pair of Florida driver's licenses: Gerardo Limón and Ramón Javier. Cubans, Corso guessed: Limón with a Miami address, Javier from Boca Raton. He dropped the licenses onto the couch and sat for a moment with his head thrown back, trying to muster his strength.

He felt nauseated and unsteady on his feet as he made his way to the closet and pulled open the door. On the shelf above the ironing board, he found what he was looking for, the extra pillow. He carried it back to the couch, where, using his good hand and his feet, he managed to remove the cover.

He rested again and then fished the keys to the Mercedes from his pants pocket and dropped them into the pillowcase, followed by the wallets and the licenses. He crossed to the desk, hefted a large glass ashtray, and returned to the couch, where he added the prize to the pile in the sack.

He tied a knot in the pillowcase and carried it over

to the curtain covering the west wall. He found the
cord and pulled until the sliding glass door was exposed. It was one of those fake balconies; little more
than a railing to keep guests from falling into Puget
Sound. As he leaned against the wall, gathering himself, he remembered the famous picture of the Beatles,
fishing out of a window in this very hotel, back in the
sixties. During the last remodel, they'd added the faux
balconies and banned angling.

When his stomach settled down, he popped the lock
and slid the door open. He could hear the lap of waves
under the hotel and the shrill cries of gulls. His nostrils
caught the smells of creosote and salt water. His mouth
hung open as he leaned against the rail, twirled the
bundle in the air, and let fly. The pillowcase hit the
water, floated for a moment, and then quickly disappeared beneath the waves.

The strain sent his senses ajar again. He reeled
across the room and threw himself on the couch. Next
thing he knew, he was dreaming of flying. Just holding
his arms out and being borne above the branches by a
spring wind. Of soaring and gamboling in the sky, beneath a bright yellow sun.

* * *

When he opened his eyes again, Robert Downs was
kneeling by his side, opening a blue-and-white box of
gauze. "You passed out," Downs said.

"Yeah," was all Corso could manage.

"Probably for the best. It let me stitch you up without you twitching on me."

Corso looked down at his hand. The jagged hole in

his palm had been drawn together by half a dozen black stitches. Same thing on the back.

"In about a week, take a pair of nail scissors to the knots and then pull out all the pieces," Downs said. He looked into Corso's eyes, trying to get a read on him. "Okay?" he said.

"Yeah."

Downs took Corso's hand in his and began to wrap it with gauze. By the time the gauze ran out, the hand looked like that of a boxer, ready for the ring. Downs secured the end with a piece of tape and looked up at Corso.

"I'm going to call the airlines and change my flight," he said.

Corso swallowed several times. "Go back to Boston," he said finally.

"There must be something I can do. . . ."

Corso reached out and grabbed the young man by the shoulder, squeezing hard.

"Go home. Go back to your girlfriend. Get married. There's nothing you can do here except get in the way."

"Are you—?"

"I'm sure."

Robert Downs searched Corso's face and then reached into the white plastic bag that lay on the floor by his side. He pulled out a plastic prescription bottle and placed it on the table next to Corso; then he got to his feet and walked into the bathroom.

Corso heard the water running. In a minute Downs reappeared, carrying a glass of water, which he set down next to the prescription. "You take two of these, three times a day," he said, shaking a trio of orange capsules out into his palm. "For infection. Make sure you take them until they're gone."

The plastic pills stuck in Corso's mouth like stones; it took the whole glass of water to wash them down. Corso lifted his bandaged hand toward his throat, winced, and returned it to his lap.

"I cleaned the throat laceration," Downs said. "There might be a little permanent scarring, I can't tell. It'll be all right, but there's nothing I can do about the short-term cosmetics."

Corso whispered his thanks and got to his feet, at which moment he realized he wasn't wearing trousers. He looked around the room and found them hanging over the heater, crossed the room gingerly, making no sudden moves. Took him about twice as long as usual to get his pants on, and he probably would never have gotten the belt hitched if Downs hadn't taken pity on him and lent a hand. Corso sat on the edge of the bed. "Could you spare a pair of socks?" he said.

Downs furrowed his brow and said, "Sure." After maybe thirty seconds of messing with his suitcase, he came up with a rolled pair of athletic socks. "Clean," he announced, pulling the socks apart and dropping them in Corso's lap.

The socks were easier than the pants, his shoes easier still. Corso looked down over the front of himself. The once forest-green polo shirt was streaked with blood and littered with bits of wood and straw. Corso eased it over his head and dropped it on the floor. He smirked at Robert Downs. "Sooner or later, it was bound to happen," he said.

Downs looked confused. "What's that, Mr. Corso?"

"Somebody was gonna want the shirt off your back."

The younger man looked down at himself. "You mean this?" He fingered the turtleneck. "My shirt?"

"The very same," Corso said.

"It's not clean. I've worn it a couple of—"

"Doesn't matter."

Downs shrugged and pulled the shirt over his head. He started to hand it to Corso, changed his mind, and took it back. Pulling the sleeves right side out, he rolled the neck down and put it over Corso's head. Getting his left hand the length of the sleeve left Corso panting. The sleeves were a couple of inches short, but otherwise the shirt fit fine.

Robert Downs adjusted the turtleneck and then stepped back to admire his handiwork. "For a guy who's been shot and strangled in the same night, you don't look half bad," he announced.

"I'll take that as a compliment," Corso said.

Downs helped Corso into his jacket, then went around brushing and picking the coat free of debris. "You're going home, right?"

"I'd hate to have to lie to my doctor," Corso said, patting himself down. He found his other sock in the outside pocket and dropped it to the floor on top of his shirt. In one inside pocket, he found the pages from Accounts Payable, soaked nearly through, but readable. From the other inside pocket he pulled his phone. He wiped the damp plastic on the side of the coat and pushed the power button with his thumb. It worked. He started to switch hands, thought better of it, and set the phone on the bed before he dialed.

"Send a cab to the Edgewater Hotel," he said. He turned to Robert Downs. "Thanks for taking care of me."

Downs shrugged. "Makes us even, I guess."

Corso grudgingly nodded.

"You should get some rest," Downs said.

Corso almost smiled. "Thank you, doctor."

"I'm serious."

"Gotta see a lady about some buttermilk," Corso said.

38

Monday, October 23   **11:23 p.m.**

O ne blue eye. Three brass chains. "It's late," she whispered through the crack in the door. "I've got a midterm tomorrow. I can't—"

"I'll just be a minute," Corso said.

"Is this about Donald?"

"Yes."

She heaved an audible sigh. "That's my past. I don't want to—"

"It's about you too," Corso said. "I think you better open the door."

Instead, the door closed. He waited a silent moment, wondering whether she'd gone back to bed before the first chain rattled.

Marie Hall wore one of those billowing flannel nightgowns favored by single women on cold nights— the white a little off from the washing machine, little shriveled roses around the edges—that and a pair of bright blue Road Runner socks. She closed the door behind Corso and stood with her hands on her hips.

"This may be the middle of the afternoon to you famous writer types, Mr. Corso, but I work for a living, so if you don't mind let's get to whatever it is you think is so important as to show up here at this time of night."

"I want you to tell me the truth."

Her foot began to tap. "You're starting to piss me off, you know that? I shared my private life with you. I answered your questions. And now you see fit to invade my privacy in the middle of the night and insult me!" She pulled the door open. "So—if you'll excuse me." She gestured toward the opening. Corso wandered farther into the apartment.

"I don't think you'll want your neighbors to hear this," he said.

"Get out."

"I need to know about the money," Corso said.

"Do I have to call the police?"

"I'm betting the police would find the scenario real interesting."

She pushed the door closed and started for the phone on the kitchen wall. Corso kept talking. "About how your husband, Donald, was a member of the second Balagula jury." She stood with the phone poised in the air, a foot from her ear. "About how he sold his ass to Nicholas Balagula for something like a hundred thousand bucks and about how you somehow managed to screw him out of half the money."

"Money? There was no money," she scoffed, pushing a button on the phone. She looked over as if to give Corso one last chance to leave.

"If you push that second one, Marie, the cops are coming. No matter what. There's no calling it off." Her finger wavered.

"You know what I'm betting?" Corso said. She didn't answer. "I'm betting if I were to run a serious financial check on you, I'd find you've got a little nest egg tucked away somewhere. A little something you can draw on for college tuition or"—he swept his hand around the room—"for a coupla nice pieces of furniture maybe." She started to protest, but Corso waved her off. "Probably got it squirreled away in some nice safe mutual fund or something like that."

"Don't be—"

"I'm betting that if I were to go down to where you work and ask around, I'd find out that for most of last summer you didn't take the bus to work like you usually did. I'm betting you drove a yellow pickup truck."

"You're crazy, you know that?" The tone was right, the gaze stony. Her lower lip, however, was not cooperating.

"Donald didn't need the truck. He was locked up in a downtown hotel." Corso reached into his inside coat pocket. Pulled out the list of jury expenses and threw it on the coffee table. "Ordering T-bone steaks and drinking buttermilk every night with his dinner."

"Get out," she said.

Corso turned on his heel and started for the door. Stopped with his hand on the knob. "I'll leave," he said. "I'm not in the business of terrifying people. But we need to get something straight here." She seemed to be paying attention, so he went on. "A couple of innocent people are dead because you sold your silence." He waved a finger at the woman. "So I'm putting you on notice, Marie Hall. As of tomorrow morning, I'm aiming every information source I own at you. In a week, I'm going to know things about you and your life even *you* probably don't remember. I'm going to be more intimate with you than your parents or your lovers." He waggled the finger again. "And if I find out you had anything to do, directly or indirectly, with letting Nicholas Balagula go free? I'm not only going to go public with it, I'm also going directly to the authorities with whatever I have."

He made a good show of it, closing the door with a bang and stomping down the stairs. He'd just arrived at the lower landing when the upstairs door opened.

"Please," she said, in a strangled voice. "I have so little."

She began to hiccup and then to sob. Before Corso could process the data, she disappeared into the apartment, leaving the door wide open.

Corso stood at the bottom of the stairs. He recognized the feeling, the odd mixture of triumph and revulsion he always felt at moments like this, when he'd managed to poke a hole in the nest of truths, half-truths, and outright lies that we all, over time, come to swear is the story of our lives.

He took his time walking back up. Stepped into the apartment and looked around.

She hadn't gotten the bathroom door closed. At the far end, she knelt in front of the toilet. The sound of her retching scratched the air like sandpaper.

Corso wandered into the living room, moving over by the stereo, where she was no longer visible. The sound followed him like a stray dog. He picked among her CDs. Heart. Barry Manilow. Barbra Streisand. All kinds of easy listening. Ricky Martin was in the player, Sarah McLachlan nearby.

When he looked up, she was standing in the hall with a towel pressed to her mouth.

"Tell me what happened," Corso said.

"It wasn't me!" she blubbered.

"I know. Just tell me what happened."

"They came one night. Maybe two days into the trial."

Corso stopped her. "You sure it was that early?"

"Positive," she said. "It was the first Wednesday night."

"Who came?"

"Three men."

"What did they look like?"

She described all three men. An older guy with a European accent and a couple of Hispanic guys. One tall, one short. Older European guy giving the orders. From the descriptions, Corso figured it had to be Mikhail Ivanov, accompanied by the dear departed Gerardo Limón and Ramón Javier.

"So what happened?"

"They pushed their way in." She was starting to blubber again.

"Take it easy," Corso said. "Just tell me the story."

She stuck her face into the towel and wept for several moments.

"They made me call Donald at the hotel," she said, when she'd recovered.

"You could call your husband?"

"Every night between seven-thirty and eight-thirty."

"Directly?"

"Oh, no. You had to go through a policeman first, who made sure who was calling. They had caller ID, and after a while—you know—you kind of got to know them and they kind of got to know you."

"So you called your husband. What happened then?"

She looked like she was going to cry again. "I don't know," she said, her lip trembling. "They put a gun to my head. They took me in the bedroom while the older guy talked to Donald."

"Then what?"

"After a while, the guy came in and said Donald wanted to talk to me." She wiped her mouth with the towel and then threw it over the back of a chair. "Donald said I shouldn't tell anybody that the men had come. Said it was super important. Said our whole lives depended on it."

"And you went along for the ride?"

She nodded miserably.

"It was probably for the best," Corso said.

Big tears ran down her cheeks. "I should have—"

"If either you or Donald had refused, they'd have killed you right there and then. Donald had never seen them. You were the only eyewitness. They had nothing to lose. If Donald goes to the cops, they get a mistrial and somebody finds your body."

"I don't understand," she said.

"If you're right about the date, they had the list of potential jurors from the very beginning. They went looking for a weak link, and Donald was it. He was a fanatic about his son's education. He was behind in his payments to Harvard. They were making noises about asking the kid to leave. He'd applied for a loan and been turned down. Donald was exactly what they were looking for."

"About a month later, I found the receipt in the mail."

"From?"

"Harvard." She looked sheepish. "I steamed it open."

"He'd paid it all."

"Forty-two thousand dollars."

"And you put two and two together."

She squared her shoulders. "No matter what you might think, Mr. Corso, I'm not stupid. Of course I figured it out." She stared at Corso as if daring him to disagree. "You know what he tried to tell me?" She didn't wait for a reply. "He tried to tell me the money he sent to Harvard was all of it. That he was broke again."

"And you said?"

"I said the bill to Harvard was for forty-two thousand and the bill for my silence was going to be the same."

"And he ponied up?"

"I should have asked for more."

"You ever find out exactly how much he got?"

She shook her head and began to cry again. "What's going to happen to me?" she said between sniffles. "I'm going to go to jail, aren't I?"

"You're an accessory before and after the fact in both bribery and jury tampering. They want to get nasty, they can charge you with interfering with a murder investigation and filing a false statement."

"It's not fair!" she cried. "I earned every dime of that money! Living with him all those years, doing without. I had a right. . . . I only took what was mine."

"You'll get off a lot lighter than Donald did."

She looked up from her self-pity party. "I don't understand. It was all over. Why did they kill Donald after everything was all done?"

"I think he was killed because he tried to go to the well again."

"What do you mean?"

"His son needed money to go into private practice. I'll probably never be able to prove it, but I think Donald Barth looked up one day and saw that Balagula was coming back to Seattle for another trial and decided to put the bite on him again." Corso shook his head sadly. "Which with a guy like Balagula was a very, very bad idea."

She steeled herself. "I won't testify," she said, in a voice that made Corso a believer. "I'm not going to spend the rest of my life in fear, looking back over my shoulder, waiting for something to strike. I couldn't stand that. I'll go to jail first."

It took everything Corso had not to smile. It was like Renee Rogers said. First you scare the shit out of them and then you offer them a way out.

"What if I told you there was a way you could avoid testifying against Balagula and maybe stay out of jail at the same time?"

Hope flickered on and off in her eyes. "Oh, please," she sobbed.

"You'll have to do what I tell you."

"I will."

"You'll have to be a good actress."

She sat up straight like she was in school. Straightened her nightgown. "What do I have to do? Just tell me. I can do it."

"All you have to do is make one phone call," Corso said with a smile.

39

The pages fluttered slightly as the book arched across the room and hit Corso in the chest. "Who told you to pay my bill?" Dougherty demanded. She was sitting up in bed wearing scrubs, makeup, and a frown. Joe Bocco slid down in the chair, hiding a smile behind his hand.

"Goddammit, Corso, if I want your help I'll ask for it." She looked around for something else to throw but couldn't find anything that wasn't connected to the bed.

Corso bent and picked up the book. "Any good?" he inquired.

"Dark," she said, then pointed a long manicured finger. "Don't change the subject."

Bocco got to his feet. "You kids don't mind," he said with a smirk, "I'll wait out in the hall while you work this out."

He crossed to the door, pulled it open, and allowed himself a final shake of the head before disappearing from view.

Corso walked over to the bed and dropped the book in her lap. "You seem to be feeling quite a bit better."

"I was doing just fine until I inquired about the state of my hospital bill, and next thing I know they send in this Crispy character who gives me a smarmy little smile and tells me everything is taken care of."

"Edward Crispin," Corso corrected.

"Whatever." She reached for the book again.

Corso took a step back. "I didn't want to lose you," Corso said.

"What did you say?"

"I said I didn't want to lose you."

"I don't need a goddamn sugar daddy. I'm a functioning, self-supporting adult. If I want—" She stopped. The frown disappeared. "Oh, Jesus, Corso, don't get soupy on me here. You'll ruin your image."

"It's only money," he said.

"You've got no respect for money, Corso."

"Money's not important unless you don't have any."

"That's easy for you to say."

"I felt the same way when I was broke. Nothing was ever about the money." He waved a hand. "Way I see it, I'm just a conduit through which money passes."

The movement of his right hand in the air pulled her eyes to his left hand, which was pushed deep into his pants pocket. "What's with the hand in the pocket?" she asked.

"What? A guy can't stand with his hand in his pocket?"

"That's not Frank Corso body language at all," she said. "What's the deal?" Corso didn't answer. "And that fruity shirt. You look like a bad foreign film."

With great care, Corso slid the bandaged hand from his pocket. "I had a little cooking accident," he said.

"A cooking accident," she repeated.

"Yeah."

"Come here," she ordered. Corso stood still. "Come on," she prodded.

This time, Corso wandered over to the bedside. She looked him over, then reached up and pulled the turtleneck aside. She winced. "Damn, Corso. That's nasty. Looks like whatever you were cooking tried to cook you back."

"I'm taking Joe with me when I go," he said.

She eased the material back over the welt. "Looks like you need him more than I do."

"Yeah."

"So you're going to stop over in finance and tell Crispy Critters the bill is on me, right?"

"Sure."

She looked him over. "You liar. You've got no intention of doing any such thing, do you?"

"Nope."

"Get out of here, then," she said. "If you're not going to show me any respect, you can leave."

Corso eased his damaged hand into his jacket pocket and silently left the room. Joe Bocco leaned against the wall in the corridor. "You kids get your spat worked out?"

Corso ignored him. "I don't need you here anymore," he said.

"So our friends . . ."

"Won't be back," Corso finished.

Corso watched the wheels turning in Bocco's head. "Then, way I figure it, I owe you a refund of—"

"I'm going to need you tonight. Marvin too."

"What's the gig?"

Corso laid it out for him.

"You're saying this guy's a pro?"

"For sure."

"Sounds to me like we could use an extra pair of hands."

"You got a pair in mind?"

"Got a woman I worked with a few times. She'll make good cover."

"Get her."

"What time?"

"I'm thinking we'll schedule the drop for eleven."

"If this guy's careful, we're going to need to be in place early."

"This guy's very careful," Corso said. "And very dangerous."

"This is gonna cost ya," Joe Bocco said.

"What else is new?"

Tuesday, October 24   9:22 a.m.

Mikhail Ivanov took a deep breath and coughed into his hand. His voice must not betray him. He knew it would be a mistake to underestimate Ramón and Gerardo. They complemented one another well. The strengths of one masked the weaknesses of the other. Ramón was smart but a bit too introspective for a man in his line of work. Whatever Gerardo lacked in intelligence and sophistication, he made up for with the kind of animal instinct that senses earthquakes days in advance.

He'd thought it over earlier and decided that the final disposition of Gerardo and Ramón would take place after they returned to the Bay Area, making today's contact a mere holding action, ostensibly paying them for services rendered while he worked out a suitable scenario for their permanent removal.

He dialed. The phone began to ring. And ring. Ivanov stood with the phone pressed to his head for a full two minutes, before using his thumb to break the connection. He couldn't recall a time when they hadn't answered their phone. Thinking he must have misdialed, he tried again and got the same result.

Mikhail Ivanov was troubled as he pulled open the door and stepped out into the hall. The sight that greeted him did little to lift the pall.

The guy was there in the hallway, the sex peddler. Sixty feet away, knocking on Nico's door. "May I help you?" Ivanov asked the man evenly, as he started up the corridor toward him.

"Goddamn right," the man blurted.

Ivanov's practiced eye noticed how his right arm was tense, as if holding a great weight. Ivanov moved that way, approaching the man obliquely. "What can I do for you?"

The craggy, creased face was more haggard than usual. He looked as if he hadn't slept for a couple of days. "He messed the boy up."

"You've been paid for your services," Ivanov offered.

"Inside," the guy said. "He's all screwed up."

"You better go," Ivanov said.

The guy's face flushed. "Didn't you hear me, motherfucker? The docs are telling me—"

When he began to pull his hand from his pocket, Mikhail Ivanov was ready. He clamped an iron grip onto the wrist and used the man's own momentum to lift the arm high into the air. A silver stiletto flashed beneath the lights. When the man looked up at his weapon, Ivanov kneed him once in the balls and then, when he bent in agony, again in the face. In an instant, the flesh peddler was on his back in the hotel corridor while Ivanov stood above him, patting his suit back into place and inspecting the knife.

Between gasps, the flesh peddler tried to speak. "I'll get you . . . I'll . . ."

Ivanov dropped one knee onto the man's chest, driving the air from his body. As the man watched in horror, he slipped the blade of the knife between the man's lips, into his mouth. "What you are going to do, my friend, is ride that elevator back to the lobby and then run, just as fast as your little legs will carry you, back to whatever rat-infested sty a piece of shit like you lives in, and when you get there"—he rattled the knife blade around the guy's teeth—"you will give thanks that I let you leave here alive."

Ivanov's wrist twitched twice. The man emitted a piteous howl. Ivanov got to his feet. The guy sounded like he was gargling as he brought his hands to his mouth. He stared at his bloody palms for a disbelieving moment and then clamped them back over his ruined mouth. As he struggled to his feet, droplets of blood from the sliced corners of his mouth fell onto the thick wine-red carpet and disappeared.

Blood seeped between his fingers, as he waited for an elevator to arrive. He was rocking on his feet now, emitting a low keening wail and moving back and forth, as if dancing to a rhythm unheard.

Ivanov carefully wiped the knife clean on the carpet and stuck it in his pocket. When he looked down the hall toward the elevator, the flesh peddler was gone.

Tuesday, October 24   10:02 a.m.

The sky was layered gray: lighter to the west out over Elliott Bay, where Bainbridge Island was little more than a smudge on the mist; darker and more menacing to the east as it tightened its coils around the buildings on Beacon Hill.

Corso stood on the corner of Second Avenue and Royal Brougham Way. He'd chosen the spot because it was directly in between Safeco Field and the new football palace that Microsoft billionaire Paul Allen was building out of pocket, two blocks to the north. In this neighborhood, limos were commonplace, twenty-four/seven.

When the gleaming Cadillac slid soundlessly to a stop a foot from his shins, the door seemed to open on its own. Renee Rogers sat in the jump seat, facing the rear, her briefcase clutched in her lap, her expression bland and ultraprofessional.

Corso got in and closed the door. At the other end of the opulent brocade seat sat the Attorney General of the United States. She looked more like a kindly aunt or a small-town librarian than the chief law enforcement officer for the most powerful nation in the world. The car started up Royal Brougham Way.

She looked Corso over. "I saw you once on *Good Morning America*. I didn't realize you were so tall."

Corso didn't know what to say, so he merely nodded. She lifted her chin.

"We never had this conversation. Do you understand?"

"Yes."

She glanced at Rogers. "Ms. Rogers tells me you think you have a scenario by which we might be able to salvage our present untenable position."

"I believe so, yes," Corso said.

"Let's hear it."

"It goes back to the second trial," Corso began.

The Attorney General raised an eyebrow. "If Ms. Rogers can stand the mention of it, I guess I can too."

"It starts with a man named Donald Barth. He was a juror at the second trial."

She looked at him over her glasses. "And how would you come to that conclusion, Mr. Corso? The identities of those jurors have been destroyed."

He told her about Balagula having the master list of jurors from the beginning. About Berkley Marketing, Allied Investigations, and Henderson, Bates & May. And finally about Marie Hall's admissions. "I'll be damned," she said. "Go on."

As he talked, she took a lens-cleaning kit from the storage area in the door and began to clean her glasses. She looked older without the thick lenses magnifying her eyes. She didn't speak again until he'd finished and had settled back in the seat.

She adjusted the glasses on her nose and sighed. "When I told your publisher, Noel Crossman, that I'd allow you to sit in on the trial, I was hoping for a sense of closure to this whole thing."

She allowed silence to settle in the car's interior.

"There can be only one answer, of course." She shot a glance at Renee Rogers and then back at Corso. "This scenario that you envision—were it to come off as planned"—she shrugged—"then it most certainly would have to be part of an overall strategy by my office to finally bring Mr. Nicholas Balagula to bay."

"Of course," Corso said.

"And if something were to go awry?" She flattened her generous lips. "Then—" She looked over at Corso with a flat, emotionless expression.

"Then the secretary will disavow any knowledge of our actions," Corso finished for her.

She cocked her head at him and smiled. "Where's that line from?" she asked.

"The original *Mission Impossible*. The voice on the tape recording always said that right before it caught fire."

The smile disappeared. "That is precisely what the secretary will do," she said.

"Ms. Rogers is going to need the authority to make a deal. She's going to have to be able to offer—"

The Attorney General held up a hand. "If the matter reaches a successful conclusion, Ms. Rogers's actions will be regarded as part of the overall plan and her authority to make legal concessions will have been granted directly through me."

"And if it doesn't?" Corso asked.

"Then she will have substantially exceeded her authority and any agreement into which she may have entered will necessarily be null and void." She waved a hand. "At best . . ." She hesitated for effect. "Even if it works out exactly as you envision, Mr. Corso, major elements of the constituency are going to have their noses bent out of shape." Corso began to speak, but the Attorney General cut him off. "They prefer their justice simple: good guys win, bad guys lose. This one is going to raise some hackles." She sat for a time having a discussion with herself. "We never had this conversation," she said, after a moment. She resettled herself in the seat and stared out the window.

They rode without speaking. "Understood?" she asked, finally.

They said it was. She must have had a signal arranged with the driver or a hidden button that she pushed. Ten seconds later, the car slid to a stop at the curb, directly across Royal Brougham Way from where they'd picked him up, twenty minutes earlier. The car door opened. "If you two will excuse me," the Attorney General said. "I have a press conference at eleven-thirty."

Corso stepped out into the rain, leaned down, and offered Rogers a hand. She took hold and joined him on the sidewalk. They stood side by side in the steady drizzle and watched the big black car disappear into the mist.

Tuesday, October 24   2:51 p.m.

Marie Hall read through the script again. "I don't know if I can do this." She brought a hand to her throat. "I'm so nervous."

"That's good," Corso said. "You ought to be nervous. You'll sound authentic."

"What if he—"

"Just follow the script."

Corso attached the microphone to the telephone and checked the tape recorder volume. "Ready when you are," he said.

She took a deep breath and began to dial. After a moment, a cheerful voice said, "Weston Hotel."

"Room Twenty-three fifty," she said.

"Thank you," the voice said.

The phone rang twice. "Yes."

"Mr. Ivanov?"

Silence.

"I saw your picture in the paper today."

"Who is this?"

"You came to my house."

"I'm hanging up now."

"You put a gun to my head."

"I don't know what you're talking about."

"You and those other two men. Last year. You made me call my husband at the hotel." She waited a minute. "You remember. I know you do."

"What do you want?"

"The paper says you and that baby killer are gonna get off."

"What do you want," Mikhail Ivanov said again.

"I want a hundred thousand dollars," she said, "and I want it tonight."

"You must be crazy."

"Crazy," she said, nearly in a whisper. "I'll show you crazy when I tell the goddamn cops. You hear me? I'll go right now. Don't you think I won't."

Ten seconds of silence ensued before Ivanov said, "Perhaps we can reach an area of accommodation."

"We better," she said.

Tuesday, October 24   3:09 p.m.

Mikhail Ivanov dropped a ten-dollar bill onto the room-service cart as the waiter rolled it toward the door. "Thank you, sir," the man muttered. Ivanov walked over and held the door open. The waiter thanked him again and disappeared.

Nicholas Balagula generally napped right after lunch, so Ivanov's presence in his room at this time of day was unusual. Balagula wiped the corners of his mouth with a linen napkin. "So?"

"We have a serious problem."

"Oh?"

"The woman whose husband—the one who became unburied."

"His wife."

"Yes."

"What about her?"

"She called. She says she saw my picture in the newspaper. Says she recognized me from when the Cubans and I went to her house."

"And?"

"She's demanding one hundred thousand dollars for her silence. She wants it today or she says she'll go to the authorities."

"The timing is awkward," Balagula said.

"Couldn't be worse."

Balagula shook his head. "What makes these people think they can hold me up?"

"Greed seems to run in this woman's family."

"She takes no lesson from the Barth fellow?"

"Apparently not."

"She cannot be allowed to interfere," Balagula said.

"This farce ends tomorrow." He looked up at Ivanov and shrugged. "Set something up. Send our Cuban friends."

"That's also a problem."

"What problem is that?"

"I can't reach our Cuban friends. They don't answer their phone."

"Since when?"

"This morning. An hour ago, I had the maid at their hotel check the room. They didn't sleep in their beds last night. I also had the bellman check the parking lot for the car."

"Not there."

"No."

Balagula rose from the chair and paced around the room. "The problem must be handled," he said, after a minute. "We've come too far to allow anything to interfere."

"I know."

Nicholas Balagula stopped pacing and shrugged. "It appears, Mikhail, that you're going to be forced out of retirement."

"Yes . . . it does."

"She'll be alone," Balagula said.

"You think?"

"If she's foolish enough to try to hold me up, she's foolish enough to want to keep the money for herself. If she brings anyone, she'll have to split the money. No, she'll be alone."

"She said she'd call back tonight with where she wants to meet."

Nicholas Balagula thought it over. "Get the money. If the situation allows, kill her. If not, pay her and we'll send the Cubans for her later."

40

Tuesday, October 24   11:03 p.m.

Mikhail Ivanov recognized her from half a block away. She'd gained a bit of weight, but even under the streetlights she still had those narrow blue eyes like his mother's. He recalled the look of terror in those eyes when Gerardo put the gun to her head and led her into the bedroom, and how she couldn't stop crying as she listened to her husband's voice on the phone. He'd never have guessed she had the nerve for this.

She'd chosen her ground poorly: some sort of open-air church monument, three fluted stone columns standing at the edge of a bum-infested park. He'd been nearby for an hour and a half and, while the car traffic was unrelenting, the foot traffic was spotty. Those who did walk down Pine Street favored the opposite side of the street, where they did not have to cross freeway on-ramps. He was confident his task could be accomplished.

The bum was the only problem. Curled up asleep on the bench closest to Pine Street, he'd be no more than thirty feet from where Mikhail Ivanov envisioned making his move. During the past hour and a half, the tramp had risen three times: twice, early on, to stumble down into the park and relieve himself, and finally, half an hour back, to cross the street to the market and buy three tall cans of what appeared to be malt liquor. Since downing the contents of the cans, he had been snoring contentedly away. Perhaps if all went according to plan, he would awaken to find a bloody knife in his hand.

She wandered into the far corner of the park and looked around. Silhouetted against the black sky, she appeared to stand in some ancient ruin, left to rot amid the urban squalor. Mikhail Ivanov shifted the black athletic bag to his left hand and started forward, only to have a baby stroller nearly run over his feet. "Sorry," he mumbled to the thickset woman who acknowledged his apology with a smile and a nod. Watching her swinging her hips for a moment as she moved downhill, he breathed deeply and collected his wits. Satisfied with his state of composure, he waited for a lull in the traffic and then started across the street.

She was walking in small circles, staying just where he wanted her, on the Pine Street side, where it was dark and the traffic sparse. The half dozen cars, trucks, and vans along the curb had all been in place when he'd arrived and were probably parked for the night. Even better, Nico was right. She'd come alone. His right hand fondled the flesh peddler's stiletto in his overcoat pocket.

As he stepped up onto the sidewalk he began to visualize the move, the embrace of death he'd learned so long ago in the prison yard, so smooth and easy that, under the proper conditions, the victim could be leaned against a wall or a fence, standing up, stone dead.

As he passed the sleeping bum, he hesitated, leaned over, and looked down into the filthy face. A tiny piece of pink tongue hung from the side of the mouth. He was snoring quietly. Satisfied, Mikhail Ivanov strode across the uneven stones toward the woman moving among the columns at the far side.

He saw her eyes widen as she recognized him in the darkness. Saw her search her soul for courage as he came close. A final peek over his shoulder revealed the bum still unconscious on the bench. Across Pine Street, the woman had stopped walking and was making adjustments to the baby. On the Boren Avenue side, the sidewalks were bare.

He lengthened his stride, walked right up in front of her and set the bag on the bench. As he'd hoped, so much money, so close, was too much for her to ignore. She reached down and grabbed the bag's handle, at which point he slipped his arm under hers and drew her tight against his chest. His left hand was now on the back of her head, forcing her face hard against his coat, muffling her cries, as he brought the stiletto forward and up in a motion designed to eviscerate. She grunted from the force of the knife's impact. Had he not been holding her, she would have dropped to her knees. And yet . . . something was wrong. He could feel it.

He felt the knife penetrate the coat, but that was all. The sudden lessening of tension when a knife penetrates the body's outside wall, when the hand can feel the blade, wet and at large in the innards . . . it wasn't there. The point had somehow been deflected.

He drew the knife back and plunged again with all his might. Again she grunted. Again her legs buckled. Again the knife was deflected by something beneath her coat. Then he heard the scrape of a shoe, followed by the sound of a door sliding open, and before his eyes the street came alive around him. With all his strength, he tried to pull the blade upward.

A hand grabbed his wrist: the bum. The bum's other hand grabbed him around the waist and began pulling him backward. From the corner of his eye, he could see the woman with the stroller sprinting his way with a gun in her hand. He released his victim and turned to face the tramp. He lashed out once with the blade, heard a wail, and dropped the knife on the stones. His hand was on the automatic in his pocket when he felt the kiss of cold steel on the side of his face.

"Don't move a fucking muscle," the voice said. Ivanov shifted his eyes toward the sound. The man had thinning black hair and a scar running the length of his left cheek. He also had a sawed-off shotgun pressed to the side of Ivanov's head.

"Fucker cut me," the bum wailed. Marie Hall's mouth hung open as she struggled to her feet. She walked unsteadily over to the bum, pulled the scarf from her head, and began to wind it around his damaged wrist.

"Goddman it. Goddman it," the bum chanted.

Another hand grabbed Ivanov's arm and began to pull it from his coat pocket.

"Better be clean when it comes out of that pocket, buddy," Shotgun said. Ivanov relaxed his hand and allowed it to be pulled from his pocket. He felt fingers slide into his pocket and remove his gun and then felt the steel bracelet snap around his wrist. The shotgun ground harder into his temple as his other hand was forced behind his back and cuffed. "Go over him good," Shotgun said.

The woman dropped to one knee and began to frisk her way up to his groin. Took her five seconds to find the Beretta strapped to his left ankle. She set it on the uneven stones and completed her search.

"I want to see an attorney," Ivanov said.

In the darkness, someone laughed. Ivanov turned toward the sound. Frank Corso stepped out from behind the nearest pillar. "He's clean," the woman pronounced.

"Let's go," Corso said, picking up the athletic bag.

The shotgun was pulled away. The woman grabbed his shackled wrists and pushed him forward, toward the red minivan sitting at the curb with its sliding door agape. Behind him, he heard Corso's voice.

"Mary Anne, you and Marie take Marvin to Harborview." When Ivanov tried to turn and look, Shotgun grabbed him by the arm and forced him forward, causing him to stumble on the rough stones and nearly fall.

Shotgun got in first, all the way back in the third row of seats. The woman helped Ivanov up onto the big bench seat and then rolled the door closed. Outside in the park, the tramp cradled his arm like an infant. Marie Hall had shed her coat and was in the process of removing a Kevlar vest. The yawning barrel of the shotgun rested icily on the back of Ivanov's neck as Corso climbed into the passenger seat. A capped figure at the wheel put the van in DRIVE.

41

The driver pulled the van to a halt.

"What's this?" Ivanov demanded.

The street was deserted. Corso swiveled the passenger seat around to face him. "This, Mr. Ivanov, is the proverbial offer you can't refuse." He gestured with his head. "That building across the street is the King County Jail." He held up a video camera. "I've got your attempt to murder Marie Hall on tape." The camera dropped from view and was replaced by a small gray tape recorder. Corso pushed the button. Marie Hall's voice said, *I'll show you crazy when I tell the goddamn cops. You hear me? I'll go right now. Don't you think I won't.*

Ten seconds of hissing silence, and then Ivanov's voice: *Perhaps we can reach an area of accommodation.*

We better.

It will be difficult to obtain that much money at this time of day.

Don't start with me. I'll go right to the damn cops.

I didn't say it couldn't be done, merely that it will be difficult. Perhaps if—

Corso snapped it off. "Sounds a lot like you, to me."

"What do you want?"

"Nicholas Balagula," Corso answered.

Were it not for the barrel pressing against the back of his neck, Mikhail Ivanov would have thrown his head back and laughed. "Be serious."

"You've taken the fall for him twice before. You gonna do it again?"

Corso turned to the driver, who until that moment had neither turned Ivanov's way nor spoken.

"He's looking at how much for jury tampering and attempted murder?" Corso asked.

The driver reached up and removed the blue baseball cap, sending a wave of brown hair cascading down onto her shoulders. She turned and looked directly into Mikhail Ivanov's eyes. "They'll call it twenty to life. He'll serve a minimum of sixteen years in a federal facility," Renee Rogers said. "Minimum."

"You'll be nearly eighty when you get out," Corso said. "That going to work for you, Mr. Ivanov? We combine what we've got on tape with Ms. Hall's testimony, and this is a slam dunk. You willing to spend the rest of the time you've got left behind bars to protect Nicholas Balagula?"

Ivanov was visibly shaken by the sight of Renee Rogers. "You can't," he stammered. "This isn't . . ."

"I can and I will, Mr. Ivanov," she snapped. "I'm not playing by the rules anymore. If this is what it takes to bring Nicholas Balagula to justice, that's the way it's gonna have to be."

"So make up your mind," Corso said. "You're either

going to help us nail your boss or we're going across the street right now and deliver you to the local authorities on charges of jury tampering and attempted murder."

"It's up to you, Mr. Ivanov," Rogers added.

Ivanov turned his head and looked out the side window for a moment. "Go to hell," he said finally.

"Okay," said Rogers. "Let's take him in."

Corso stepped out into the street and pulled open the sliding door. He took Ivanov by the elbow and started to pull him out onto the pavement. Suddenly Ivanov jerked his arm free and said, "Wait." He looked from Corso to Rogers and back. "And you—what—cut me some sort of deal? A plea bargain?"

"You disappear," said Rogers.

Ivanov's lips twisted into a sneer. "Into your silly Witness Protection Program?" He made a rude noise with his lips. "I think not."

"You walk," Rogers said. "On your own. You gather up whatever you have and you disappear."

Ivanov's eyes narrowed. "Just like that?"

"Just like that," Rogers repeated.

A garbage truck roared to a stop across the street. Amid the clatter of a pair of emptying Dumpsters, Ivanov said, "Since we were boys. . . ."

"What?" Rogers said.

"We've been together since we were boys," Ivanov said sadly.

"And in all that time," Corso said, "if there were risks to be taken, you took them. If somebody had to go to jail, you were the one."

"I was—"

"Has he ever, even once, stepped into the breach? Come forward and taken the beating for you? Ever?"

" 'Cause he's certainly not going to do it now," Rogers added. "He's going to walk out of that courtroom tomorrow a free man, and he's going to disappear before we think of anything else to charge him with, leaving you rotting in jail."

Ivanov took several deep breaths. "You want me to say what?"

"We want you to testify that you were present when the scheme to fake the concrete samples was implemented," Rogers said quickly. Before Ivanov could reply, she went on. "We also want you to confess to arranging the murders of Donald Barth, Joseph Ball, Brian Swanson, and Joshua Harmon."

Ivanov nearly smiled. "I clean up all your loose ends at once for you, eh?"

"One more thing," Corso said.

Ivanov turned his face away, shaking his head in disgust.

"You also confess to having personally killed Gerardo Limón and Ramón Javier, in an attempt to clean up your own loose ends."

"All at Mr. Balagula's behest, of course," Renee Rogers added.

Slowly, Ivanov swiveled his head around until he was staring Corso in the face.

A look of admiration swept over his features. "Really," he said. He nodded twice, as if agreeing with himself. "I told Nico you were a dangerous man. But I had no idea—"

"Well?" Rogers prodded. "What'll it be?"

"But I didn't—" Ivanov began.

"We don't care," Rogers said. "When you walk out

of that courtroom tomorrow morning, you have seven days to leave the country. We will keep your murder confessions confidential. But if you ever show up again on our radar screens, we'll prosecute you for three murders. Other than that, we will formally agree not to seek your extradition from whatever country you might choose to live in."

Ivanov shifted his gaze to Rogers. "You have the authority?"

"I do," Rogers lied.

"In writing?"

"Yes."

"Comes a time a man needs to look out for himself," Corso added.

Across the street, the garbage truck roared off, swirling diesel fumes and bits of airborne refuse in the night air. "You know what the joke is?" Ivanov asked.

"What's that?" said Corso.

"The hospital wasn't our fault. All we did was reduce the concrete by ten percent. We've done it a hundred times before." He shook his head sadly. "It was those two inspectors, Harmon and Swanson." He looked up at Corso. "They took out another ten percent of their own. Next thing you know they're driving sports cars and buying houses in Marin County."

"Greed's a terrible thing, isn't it, Mr. Ivanov?" Corso gibed.

Ivanov didn't answer, merely looked away.

"You agree to our terms?" Rogers said.

Ivanov dropped his chin to his chest. "Yes," he said.

Renee Rogers slid out of the driver's seat and stood in the street, pushing the buttons on her cell phone.

Then she spoke, first identifying herself and then demanding, "Two U.S. marshals to the corner of Fourth and Cherry. Pronto."

Joe Bocco pushed the jump seat forward, stepped out of the van, dropped to one knee, and jacked three rounds out onto the pavement. After pocketing the ammunition, he slid the sawed-off shotgun into a sleeve sewn into the lining of his raincoat and got to his feet. "If you guys don't mind, I think I'll pass on the marshals." He nodded toward the van. "He ain't going anywhere."

"I'll call you tomorrow," Corso said.

"Thank you, Mr. Bocco," Renee Rogers said.

He gave her a silent two-fingered salute and walked off. Corso and Rogers stood together in the street, watching until Joe Bocco rounded the corner on Spring Street and disappeared from view.

She put her hands on her hips and sighed. "This doesn't feel nearly as good as I imagined it would."

"How come?"

She looked toward the van and Ivanov. "I can't believe we're letting this slimeball go. He's every bit as responsible." She shook her head. "It's just not right."

"What's right got to do with it?"

"I like to think it has everything to do with it."

"You gotta stop confusing justice and the law."

"Oh, pleeeease—"

"Lawyers . . . the courts . . . you guys . . . you dispense the law. Justice is dispensed on the ends of piers and in back alleys."

Her eyes narrowed. "That's what the cliché says, isn't it?"

"It got to be a cliché by being true."

The muscles along the edge of her jaw rippled. She gave a grudging nod and jammed her hands into her pockets.

"I think this is where I came in," Corso said.

She swept her eyes over his face. "You're not coming to court tomorrow?"

"I'll catch it on the news."

They stood uneasily for a moment before Renee Rogers stepped forward and gave him a hug. He hesitated and then slowly wrapped his arms around her.

"Thank you again for saving my life," she said, and let him go.

"I told you—" he began.

She reached up and put two fingers over his lips. "I know, Mr. Hard Guy was just saving himself." She held his gaze. "I had my eye on you that night, you know."

"Things got a little out of hand," Corso said with a shrug.

Her eyes crinkled into a smile. "At least I was wearing my good underwear."

"Your mother would be proud," Corso said.

She managed a tight smile and turned toward the van and Ivanov.

"See ya," Corso said, and strode off up the street. He walked about twenty feet and then stopped and turned aroud.

"Hey."

She looked over her shoulder. "Hey what?"

"You know what Ivanov was saying about Harmon and Swanson buying themselves houses in Marin County?"

"Yeah."

"I had a guy say the same thing to me about the Joe Ball character. About how he and his wife just bought a house. Seems like every place we go people are buying real estate after they get involved with Balagula and Ivanov here."

Her spine stiffened. "So?"

"When you get Ivanov spilling his guts, ask him about how they got the jury list from the last trial. I'll bet you dollars to doughnuts the name Ray Butler gets bandied about."

She was silent for a long moment. "Sometimes I'm not sure I like you," she said.

"Join the club."

42

Wednesday, October 25   10:04 a.m.

Judge Fulton Howell took his time getting situated behind the bench. Satisfied that his chair was in exactly the right place and that the drape of his robe was correct, he turned his frowning visage toward the nearly empty courtroom. *Bang*.

"In light of the testimony of Victor Lebow—" he began.

Renee Rogers got to her feet. "Your Honor."

Out of habit, the judge looked over at Warren Klein, who sat stonefaced behind the prosecution table. When Klein failed to meet his gaze, he turned his attention back to Renee Rogers. "Ms. Rogers," he said.

"The prosecution would like to call a final witness."

The judge folded his arms over his chest and leaned back in the chair. "I was under the impression that Mr. Lebow was to be the state's final witness."

"Yes, Your Honor. As of Monday afternoon, it was our intention to have Mr. Lebow be the final witness for the prosecution."

"And?" the judge prompted.

"New developments in the case have provided the state with additional information that we believe, in the interests of justice, should be introduced in this court."

"In the interests of justice?"

"Yes, Your Honor."

"As I recall, Mr. Lebow's last-minute testimony was allowed on much the same supposed basis."

"Yes, Your Honor."

The judge looked over at the defense table. For the first time, Bruce Elkins sat with his hands steepled beneath his chin. Nicholas Balagula had abandoned his day-at-the-beach slouch and was now sitting bolt-upright in his chair.

"Mr. Elkins?"

"It was my impression that the state had rested its case."

"No, Your Honor, the state had not," Rogers said.

Fulton Howell deepened his scowl and called for the court reporter, who walked over, put her head together with the court clerk's, and returned to the bench with several pages of trial transcript. After a moment, the judge looked up and addressed himself to Bruce Elkins. "Apparently your impression was faulty, Mr. Elkins. The prosecution never rested its case prior to my call for an adjournment."

Elkins shrugged. "As previously stated, Your Honor, the defense does not wish to dignify these spurious proceedings. We remain confident that the jury will see through the web of innuendo which the state calls a case and will reach the judicious conclusion."

"I take it, then, you have no objection, Mr. Elkins."

"None," Elkins said, with a wave of the hand.

Fulton Howell's distaste for the tactic was evident

on his face. He swiveled his head back to face Renee Rogers. "Before I rule on this matter, Ms. Rogers, let me make it clear that any semblance of yesterday's travesty of justice will not be tolerated."

"Yes, Your Honor," she said.

His voice began to rise. "I will not permit this court to become any more of a laughingstock than it has already become. Whatever testimony this witness may offer had better be both verifiable and germane to this case. Am I making myself clear?"

Renee Rogers lifted her chin a notch. "The testimony is of sufficient magnitude and is sufficiently verifiable to have led to the investigation of one of our own staff members, Your Honor."

The judge looked from Klein to Rogers and back. "Would that explain the absence of Mr. Butler from today's proceedings?"

"Yes, it would, Your Honor."

He now turned his attention to the defense table. "And Mr. Ivanov?" he inquired.

Elkins spread his hands. "I have no knowledge as to the whereabouts of Mr. Ivanov."

"Mr. Balagula?"

"Mr. Ivanov is indisposed."

"Indisposed?"

"Yes."

"Indisposed in what manner?"

Renee Rogers broke in. "Your Honor."

"If you don't mind, counselor." His voice dripped acid.

"Your Honor," she said again, "with the court's forbearance, Mr. Ivanov will be the state's next and final witness."

Silence settled over the room like new-fallen snow. Judge Fulton Howell moved his gaze from table to table as if watching a tennis match replayed at half speed.

"Do something," Nicholas Balagula said to his attorney. He reached out and prodded Elkins in the back: once, twice. Hard. "Do something, goddammit!" he demanded. When he received no response, he jumped to his feet and started up the aisle. He made it about halfway to the door before a pair of U.S. marshals came out of the woodwork, blocked his path, and then, when he tried to force his way through, wrestled him to the floor, where he was handcuffed and subsequently pulled to his feet.

Most of those in the room at the time believed Bruce Elkins buried his face in his hands in a show of frustration. Truth was, the move was designed to hide his lips, which despite his best efforts seemed intent on arranging themselves into a smile.

43

While hope springs eternal and charity begins at home, faith apparently requires the assistance of iron bars. The Ming Ya Buddhist Foundation of Seattle sat on Martin Luther King Way South, wedged between a derelict steel yard and an Arco gas station. The red-rimmed windows of the bottom two floors were protected by wrought-iron security bars, whose decorative loops and whirls were more reminiscent of New Orleans than of New Delhi.

Corso parked on the side street. On this side, a set of wooden stairs led up to a porch. Above the narrow door, a dozen gold Chinese characters glittered. At each end of the landing, a red lantern waved its tassels in the breeze.

Corso walked down the slight incline to the front of the temple, where, high up under the eaves, a pair of golden dragons flanked a molten sun.

Corso knocked on the red metal door. Nothing. He knocked again, harder this time, and waited. Still nothing. He had turned and started back the way he'd come when he heard the scrape of the door.

The boy was somewhere between twelve and fourteen. Bald and barefoot, he took Corso in from head to toe. He held the door open with his back and inclined his head, as if to question. "I need to talk to someone," Corso said.

Without hesitation, the boy leaned back into the door and pushed it all the way open. Corso stepped inside. The boy's feet pattered on the bare floor as he hurried around Corso. He pointed at Corso's shoes and then at a reed mat to the right of the door, where a pair of Nike sandals rested.

Corso dropped to one knee and then the other as he removed his shoes and placed them beside the sandals. The kid was off down the hall like a rabbit. Halfway down he stopped short, slid back a screen, and disappeared from view. Corso stood still. He could heard muted voices. After a moment, the boy stepped back into the hall and stood with his hands at his sides, not moving. Corso walked toward him, bending low under the doorway. A Buddhist monk sat cross-legged on the floor. At the sight of Corso, he adjusted the saffron-colored robe on his shoulder and smiled. His broad brown hand gestured to his left. Corso heard the door slide shut behind him.

He padded across the room, sat on the floor, and forced his legs across one another. Rice-paper screens covered the windows. The air was filled with the pleasant odor of incense. The room was dominated by a life-sized Buddha. Gold and gleaming, it sat between a pair of low tables, draped with red silk. Candles flickered on the tables.

"How can I help you, Mr. . . ."

"Corso."

"Ah."

"I have a few questions."

"Ah," the monk said again.

"About a woman named Lily Pov."

"A tragedy."

"Yes."

"And you are seeking what?"

"Understanding."

"Of what?"

Corso told him.

* * *

"I could not expect you to understand, Mr. Corso," the monk said.

"Try me."

"You spoke of a funeral for Lily Pov. Here at the temple."

"Yes."

He shrugged his smooth brown shoulders. "In the Buddhist tradition, there is no such thing. What would usually happen would be that the family and friends would go to the Pov home. They would bring an envelope with money to help pay for the funeral expenses. There would be an *ahjar sar*."

"A what?"

"Perhaps, in the Christian tradition, a deacon."

"Sort of a middleman between the sacred and the secular."

"Yes. The *ahjar sar* would bless the gifts and the mourners. Food would be served. This would go on all day."

"So if this is something that usually happens at home, why was Lily Pov's"—Corso searched for a word—"*bereavement* held here at the temple?"

"Mr. Pov has many friends in the local Khmer community, far too many for his house. We offered the temple as a courtesy."

"You know that she killed herself."

"So I was told."

"Any idea why?"

"We are not like Catholic priests. We do not hear confessions."

"Surely there must have been talk."

"There is seldom a shortage of talk."

"Hypothetically . . ." Corso began.

"Hypothetically," the monk repeated.

"Why would a woman who had waited nearly ten years to come to this country, who was engaged to a Cambodian man—"

"Engaged?"

"Promised in marriage."

"Ah."

"A woman who had the support of her elder brother and, as you say, the entire Cambodian community— why would a woman such as this choose to kill herself?"

He gave a serene shrug. "Who can say? Perhaps it was her duty."

"Her duty?" Corso considered this comment. "What if the prospective husband changed his mind and decided he didn't want her for a wife?"

"For no reason?"

"Yes."

"Then it is more likely that Mr. Pov would have

killed the prospective husband. In the Cambodian tradition, he would be within his rights to do so."

"What if . . . before the wedding . . . she became involved with another man?"

The question seemed to startle the monk. "Then the man to whom she was promised might be well within his rights to kill her. As would her brother. It would then be her duty to save them the trouble and take matters into her own hands." He read Corso's expression. "I'm sure this all sounds rather quaint and bloodthirsty to your ears, Mr. Corso, but as I told you earlier, our customs are often seen as odd by outsiders."

"People change their minds all the time."

"In your tradition, Mr. Corso, not in ours."

"Till death do us part."

"Hmmm," was all the monk said.

44

Wednesday, October 25   11:01 a.m.

On the far side of the marsh, three white vans were parked along the top of the levee, doors open, orange lights pulsing. Corso watched as a pair of men in bright yellow jackets wheeled a gurney to the rear of one of the vans and lifted a slack, black bundle inside. He pulled his eyes back across the surface of the water, his gaze floating from the rushes, whose brown tops leaked white into the fall wind, to the matted grassy hillocks cowering a foot above the waterline, to the rotten stumps and the lace of lilies, spread here and there across the wavering surface. And finally to the near shore, where the little man stood, stiff and straight at the water's edge, his fingers laced behind his back, his elbows touching.

Corso crossed the grass and stood silently at his side.

"The birds have all gone," Nhim Pov said, after a moment. "They have no tolerance for the noise and the engines and the lights."

"They'll be back," Corso said.

Nhim Pov pointed at the vans with his chin. "They've been here all morning. Ever since it was light enough to see."

"Tomorrow they'll be somewhere else."

Nhim Pov inclined his head. "Certainly, there is no shortage of death and misery."

"No . . . there never is."

"The son of Mr. Barth. He called. Said he's going back to Boston. Asked me to distribute what was left of his father's things."

"It's time for him to get on with his life."

Nhim Pov nodded. "One must go forward. Time never looks back." He brought his hands out from behind his back and heaved a sigh. For the first time, he looked at Corso. "So, you are still working on your story?"

"The story's over," Corso said. "This morning, a man confessed to the murder of Donald Barth."

Nhim Pov averted his eyes. "What is that saying you Americans have? Confession is something for the soul."

"Tonic," Corso said. "Confession is tonic for the soul."

"Yes."

"He will go to trial?"

"No," Corso said. "The confession was part of a plea agreement. The matter is closed."

"For all time?"

"Yes."

"Do you imagine he feels better now that he has unburdened his soul?"

Corso watched the wind plow furrows in the marsh water as he thought it over.

"I think . . . like most of us, he just did what he felt he had to do."

"Sometimes that is all that remains."

"Or so it seems at the time."

Nhim Pov emitted a dry laugh. "There are no mistakes, Mr. Corso. In the final act, everything comes to the end for which it was intended. If this man killed Donald Barth, I'm sure he had a good reason."

"And if it was another man who actually killed Mr. Barth?"

"Why would the first man have confessed if he was not guilty?"

"Perhaps he was *induced* to do so."

Nhim Pov smiled. "Forced by outside influences."

"Yes."

"Then I must assume the real killer had an equally good reason for his deed. Everything is done for a reason."

"What would be a good enough reason to kill another man?"

"Honor," Nhim Pov said immediately.

"Whose honor, the killer or the killed?"

"Both," Nhim Pov snapped. "To live without honor is to be no more than a beast of the field. To die without honor—" He broke off, his eyes locked on Corso's. The two men stood in silent conversation for what seemed an eternity.

"What about fear?" Corso asked. "What of a man who kills from fear?"

Nhim Pov sighed. "What is more universal than fear? What would make him more human than fear? A man without fear is not a man at all."

Half a mile away, the three white vans were moving,

turning around one by one, and heading back toward the road, lights flashing like orange pinwheels.

The two men stood in the quiet, watching the procession bounce out into the road and head north toward the freeway. Corso turned to leave. Nhim Pov's hand on his elbow stopped him. Pov started to speak but stopped himself. Corso pointed.

Above the tree line a dozen canvasback ducks veered across the sky, wheeled once around the marsh, and then splashed into the water, where, amid impatient quacks and airborne feathers, they began to feed.

45

The Attorney General of the United States stood behind the bank of microphones, her short hair rippling in the breeze. "And I am pleased that the jury has so quickly and unequivocally brought this matter to an end, so that the long-suffering victims of Nicholas Balagula's criminal empire can finally find some sense of closure and some measure of peace in this tragedy," she concluded. The press began to fire questions but she ignored them. Smiling and waving like the queen, she turned and walked away from the podium.

"How long was the jury out?" Corso asked.

"Twenty-eight minutes. Guilty on all sixty-three counts."

Meg Dougherty pushed the button on the remote control. The screen went black.

"Am I crazy or did that woman just take credit for the whole thing?"

"Only the winning part," Corso said.

"So you've finally got an ending for your book."

Corso couldn't help himself. He laughed out loud.

"Guess what?" Dougherty said.

"I'll bite."

"The *Times*'s insurance company is picking up my hospital bill. Since I was working for them when it happened, they figured it was only fair."

"Not to mention good publicity."

"There's that."

Corso wandered over to the window and pushed the curtain aside. The morning sun poured itself onto the floor. As Corso stood looking down on Ninth Avenue, Meg Dougherty asked, "You okay?"

Without turning her way, he said, "I suppose."

"Want to tell me about it?"

He shook his head.

"It's that bad?"

"It's that something," he said. He released the curtain and ambled toward the bed, then stopped in the middle of the floor and shrugged. "One of my oldest movies up and changed its ending on me."

She tilted her head on the pillow. "What movie is that?"

"The Western. The one where the intrepid sheriff"—he patted his chest—"faces down the lawless gang." He waved a hand. "All alone." He read her puzzled expression. "You know," he said. "Sun directly overhead, lots of dust, guy with a star on his chest. That kind of thing."

"*High Noon*?"

"More or less."

"So?"

He hesitated, seeming to listen to some inner voice, and then said, "So maybe I didn't turn out to be as brave and intrepid as I'd always imagined."

"How so?"

He winced. "It was much more ambiguous than I figured. It was hard to tell the good guys from the bad guys. There didn't seem to be any moral high ground. More like we all just got down in the swamp together and rolled around in the muck."

"And you *do* love the moral high ground."

He nodded sadly but did not speak. The streaming sunlight highlighted flecks of airborne dust, filling the room with a glittering curtain of mist. Corso eased his right hand into the shimmering shaft of light, turning it this way and that until, satisfied that the sun had touched it all, he returned it to his pocket.

"When are they going to let you out of here?" he said finally.

"Two weeks," she said.

"Ought to take me about that long to put an ending on the Balagula book," he said. "After that I could use some help on—"

She waved him off. "Thanks," she said, "but I've still got a lot to process. A lot of healing to do."

She almost smiled as he tried to speak with boyish enthusiasm.

"Maybe we could . . . you know . . . after you've had time to—"

"We'll see," she said, turning her face away.

Corso hesitated and then wandered over to the bedside, where he stood looking down at her. He bent over the rail and kissed her once on the cheek, lingering a moment before straightening and making for the door.

"Corso."

He stopped and looked back over his shoulder. She had tears in her eyes.

"You're the best friend I ever had," she said.

She couldn't tell whether the movement of his head was a nod or a tremor. Either way, he grabbed the door handle, slid through the narrow crack, and disappeared.